Selected
Stories
of
H. G. WELLS

SELECTED
STORIES
OF
H. G. WELLS

*Edited and with an Introduction
by Ursula K. Le Guin*

THE MODERN LIBRARY

NEW YORK

2004 Modern Library Paperback Edition

LIBRARY OF CONGRESS CATALOGING-IN-PUBLICATION DATA

Wells, H. G. (Herbert George), 1866–1946.
[Short stories. Selections]
Selected stories of H. G. Wells/edited and with an introduction
by Ursula K. Le Guin.—Modern Library pbk. ed.
p.   cm.
ISBN 0-8129-7075-6
1. Science fiction, English.   I. Le Guin, Ursula K.   II. Title.

PR5772.L4 2004
823'.912 2—dc22   2003070628

Modern Library website address: www.modernlibrary.com

Printed in the United States of America

2   4   6   8   9   7   5   3   1

CONTENTS

SELECTED STORIES OF H. G. WELLS

PART ONE
VISIONARY SCIENCE FICTION

PART TWO
TECHNOLOGICAL AND PREDICTIVE
SCIENCE FICTION

PART THREE

HORROR STORIES

PART FOUR

FANTASIES

PART FIVE

FABLES

PART SIX

PSYCHO-SOCIAL SCIENCE FICTION

Introduction

Wells's Worlds

Ursula K. Le Guin

Herbert George Wells was born in 1866, in the heyday of Queen Victoria's reign, and died at nearly eighty, just after the end of the Second World War. Like most of us, he experienced what is often dismissed as a science fictional invention: existence in incompatibly different worlds, time-travel to an unknown planet.

For the last couple of centuries, people who live more than thirty years or so have been likely to realize, suddenly or gradually, that they are strangers in a changed, incomprehensible world: lands of exile for refugees, cities of ruin for those whose nation suffers war, a labyrinth of high technology in which the untrained mind strays bewildered, a world of huge wealth which the poor stare at through the impenetrable glass of a shop window or a TV set.... From the early nineteenth century on, the stable, single worlds of pre-industrial societies were broken down and drawn into a multiverse of constantly increasing variety and change.

Caught in those transformations, H. G. Wells wrote about them all his life.

He was no passive observer. He worked long and hard to change his world—in the first place, to get himself into a better situation in it. He was born into the servant class in a rigidly hierarchical society, his father a gardener, his mother a personal maid at Uppark, a country house of the gentry. The bright, ambitious boy got himself out of that (but always looked back with love at the lovely rural England of his childhood). He got himself out of apprenticeship to a cloth seller (where he learned a great deal about the lower middle class), and back into school—education, the road up. He won a scholarship to the Normal School of Science, where he studied biology under Thomas Huxley and others, and the new universe of science opened out to him along with the social and intellectual realms of professional status. Injury and illness led him from teaching to writing. By his mid-thirties he was an increasingly successful and respected author, building himself a fine new house—a world away from the servants' quarters at Uppark.

He was ambitious also to improve the world for other people. He became a socialist and briefly a member of the theoretical Socialist group, the Fabian Society, which wasn't activist enough for him; a utopian futurist; a feminist—up to a point; a critic of society, of injustice, of capitalist commercialism; an unsuccessful Labour candidate; a tireless prophet both of cataclysm and of social betterment. In his late seventies, writing *Mind at the End of Its Tether*, after all the struggles and both the wars, after sticking it out in London through the bombing, he was still looking for hope for mankind, though he could find it only in the idea of a new humanity, a changed, improved species: "Adapt or perish, now as ever, is Nature's inexorable imperative."

Trained as a biologist under a very great teacher, he never wavered in his acceptance of Darwin's dynamic view of existence: life understood not as a Social Darwinist struggle for mere domination, not as a Christian Darwinist ascent to humanity as a final goal, but life as evolution: necessary and unceasing change. What stays fixed, dies. What adapts, goes on. The more flexibly it adapts, the farther it goes. Openness is all. Change can be brainless and brutal or intelligent and constructive. Morality enters the system only with the thinking, choosing mind. Wells imagined both dark and bright futures because his creed allowed both while promising neither, and because the eighty years of his life were years of immense intellectual and technological accomplishment and appalling violence and destruction.

———

In his own eyes and those of his contemporaries, Wells's realistic novels established his importance as a writer. Idea-centered, observant of social class and stress, topical, provocative, often satirical, sometimes passionately indignant, books such as *Ann Veronica* and *Tono-Bungay* are comparable to Bernard Shaw's plays, though they haven't worn quite as well. Wells was a quirky, sometimes heavy-handed novelist, and most of his novels, though entertaining and in flashes brilliant, have dated. What has lasted, beyond any expectation of his own and in defiance of all the snobberies of academia, are his "scientific romances"—novellas and short stories of fantasy and science fiction.

They were written before the realistic works, most of them before he was forty. His early reputation was founded on them. Later on he was rather dismissive of them, partly no doubt because it galls an artist to hear people forever talk about work done decades ago, partly because he was a demanding self-critic and knew a good many of his early stories were potboilers. Moreover, the modern critical canon excluded all nonrealistic fiction as inherently inferior, and Wells was a self-made man, competitive, edgy about aspersions of inferiority. Possibly he convinced himself that imaginative fiction is less powerful or useful than the fiction of social observation. His training after all was in science, not in art, and scientists are taught to put observation first. But his calling was art, not science, and his nature was that of a visionary, a seer of the unseen, the unobservable. He could never be satisfied by the world as we see it, as it is. He had to change it, reinvent it, or dream a new one.

The Time Machine, The First Men in the Moon, The War of the Worlds, The Invisible Man, The Island of Dr. Moreau—these are what the name H. G. Wells means to most of us now. And rightly so. These short novels established whole genres. They left a set of indelibly vivid images, imageries, archetypes in the minds of generations of readers—and filmmakers, graphic artists, comic book devotees, TV sci-fi fans, pop cultists, and Po-Mo pundits. Introducing the recent Modern Library edition of *The Time Machine,* I wrote, "Nobody can write science fiction, or discuss science fiction as literature, without having read them; they are fundamental in a way even Verne is not, though Mary Shelley is. They established certain mythical tendencies in our fiction, which we have explored ever since."

Wells wrote science fiction long before it had a name. He called it "scientific romance," and later "fantasy of possibility"—better names, perhaps, than the one it's stuck with. His originality and inventiveness were astonishing. Whatever kind of science fiction you look at, you're likely to find an example of it—a first example of it—among his tales. He didn't distinguish between science fiction and fantasy because nobody did then or for years to come; but he invented a literature, because he was the first man to write fiction as a scientist. His imagination was formed and informed by the study of biology, a science in its bright dawn of discovery and expansion, and he brought that sense of limitless possibility, both playful and fearful, to his speculations and explorations of other worlds where the mind alone can go.

And then he turned to social commentary, political exhortation, and programmatic utopias, and stopped writing short stories. Almost all the stories in this volume were written and published in the last decade of the nineteenth century and the first of the twentieth, before the First World War—many of them before the death of Queen Victoria. Enough to make one reconsider the meaning of the word "Victorian."

———

Some students of science fiction insist that its particular quality depends on its ideas alone, so that attention to literary considerations apart from clarity and narrative drive, or to character as opposed to stereotype, merely weakens or dilutes it. There are memorable stories to support this view, and Wells wrote several of them. His interest in society and psychology and his high literary standards, however, led him away from such a narrow focus on idea-driven plot.

Introducing his own selection of his short stories (*The Country of the Blind and Other Stories,* 1913), he discusses the form and his relation to it. Citing the work of Kipling, Henry James, Conrad, and many others, he calls the 1890s the high point of the short story and speaks of "lyrical brevity and a vivid finish" as its virtues. Chekhov had not yet been translated, to show the limitless possibilities of the form. Maupassant's bleak, tight, neat tales were the accepted model. Wells could not be comfortable with that. "I am all for laxness and variety in this as in every field of art. Insistence upon rigid forms and austere unities seems to me the instinctive reaction of the sterile against the fecund," he wrote. "I refuse altogether to recognise any hard and fast type for the Short Story...." He was surely right to do so; but his own almost patronizing description of it as "this compact and amusing form" hardly includes Henry James's, or Kipling's, or his own best stories, though it describes the lesser ones very well.

He knew the difference, of course. In 1939, in his discussion of his revision of what is probably his finest story, "The Country of the Blind," he says he had lost his tolerance for the idea story, the gimmick, the trick ending—the potboiler he had written so many of. "You laid hands on almost anything that came handy, a droning dynamo, a fluttering bat, a bacteriologist's tube...ran a slight human reaction round it, put it in the oven, and there you were." He could have gone on doing it forever, he says, but for the feeling that "not only might the short story be a lovely, satisfying, significant thing, but that it ought to be so, that a short story that wasn't whole and complete like a living thing, but just something bought and cut off like half a yard of chintz on a footstool, was either an imposture or a lost opportunity." But "the vogue for appreciating the exceptional in short stories was passing," he says, and when he tried to write stories that didn't suit the market, editors rejected his submissions, and so he "drifted out of the industry."

He had quit selling cloth by the yard at seventeen when he broke his apprenticeship. Selling words by the yard got him going as a writer, but maybe it led him to underestimate the form itself. For it is certainly untrue that the short story flowered in the 1890s and then declined into triviality; it went on developing and flourishing right through the twentieth century. I wonder if what stopped him was not so much the editors' lack of appreciation for the exceptional as the critics' increasing restriction of literary fiction to social and psychological realism, all else being brushed aside as subliterary entertainment. No matter how good his stories, if they were fantastic in theme or drew on science or history or any intellectual discipline for their subject, they could be dismissed categorically as "genre fiction."

It is a risk every imaginative writer runs, even now; writers who crave literary respectability still hasten to deny that their science fiction is science fiction. At least Wells stood by his imaginary guns. But he stopped firing them.

Meanwhile, *The Time Machine* has never been out of print for a hundred and some years now. And though only a few of the short stories have come near that genuine literary permanence, the best of them remain vividly alive, amazingly pertinent, sometimes unnervingly prescient, as haunting as nightmares or as bright unrecallable dreams.

I chose twenty-six stories from the eighty-four collected in John Hammond's massive and invaluable *Complete Short Stories of H. G. Wells.*

I selected for excellence, of course, not as defined by the standards of realism, which have little use or application here, but generic excellence. Was the story outstanding in itself for intellectual urgency or moral passion, for some particular virtue or strangeness or beauty? Was the story outstanding of its kind, and was the kind an interesting one? Was it fruitful, vital, did it lead forward to other works of other writers? It makes no sense to me to define "great" art as inimitable, unique, a dead end, and to prize only such greatness. Seeing art as a community enterprise both in place and time, I think an art that leads to more art is more valuable than sterile excellence.

Certain stories I left out with regret; one is "A Story of the Days to Come," full of interesting stuff, but so long it would have taken up half the book. I would have liked to include some of the satirical, joking tales that Wells was good at, such as "Aepyornis Island" and "The Pearl of Love"—but being light, they got pushed out of the boat.

Because almost all Wells's stories are genre stories and because I value them as such, I arranged them, not chronologically, but in sections by kind. Each section has a brief introduction, discussing what kind of stories they are, where this kind of story came from and what it may have led to.

As for trying to sum up the stories as a whole, as a set, it's difficult. Wells is an elusive writer. Certainly one sees his distinctive style throughout the book. Many of the stories are told in a journalistic tone, easy and breezy, extremely self-confident but unpretentious, clear, moving forward at a good clip—it all seems quite simple, quite artless, which is exactly what the author wanted. He distrusted the high aesthetic manner (a charming note to his friendship with Henry James is that each man confessed he often longed to rewrite the other's stories). But he was a careful writer and tireless rewriter, keenly aware of what he was doing, sensitive and skilled in his craft. A modulation of his tone can be as effective as a key-change in music.

We are often told that, in stories written less to reveal individual experience or character than to entertain or inform or stimulate the imagination, plot is needed to provide structure, and action is all-important. Wells plotted cleverly, and his action scenes are vivid and suspenseful; but his true mastery, I think, was in that very difficult, underestimated, even maligned element of storytelling, visual description. Wells can make you see what he wants you to see. When this is something that does not in fact exist, a fantastic scene, a dream or prophecy, his power seems uncanny. He was—literally—a visionary. Perhaps the finest things he wrote are the wonderful description of a lunar morning in *The First Men in the Moon* and the glimpses of the dying world at the end of *The Time Machine.* In the short stories one comes again and again on a similarly vivid scene, a glimpse into another world, fearful or radiant or simply very strange. These visions have the authority, in memory, of something seen with one's own eyes. A squadron of airplanes over Naples (two years before Kitty Hawk)— two men laughing and making faces at people who stand frozen in time—a dreaming garden behind a door in a wall—the faces of the townsfolk in the Country of the Blind....

PUBLICATION HISTORY

Throughout his more than fifty-year career, H. G. Wells wrote over eighty short stories. Some stories were first published in periodicals, others in five short-story collections. Many of these stories appeared numerous times in Wells's collections, sometimes slightly revised, other times reworded or with new endings, as was the case with "The Country of the Blind." Numerous bibliographies detailing the publication history of Wells's fiction and nonfiction can be found online or in reference libraries.

The following list details where the stories included in this edition were first published and their subsequent republications in short-story collections.

"A Slip Under the Microscope": *Yellow Book*, January 1896; later in *The Plattner Story and Others* (1897) and *The Country of the Blind and Other Stories* (1913).

"The Remarkable Case of Davidson's Eyes": *Pall Mall Budget*, March 28, 1895; later in *The Stolen Bacillus and Other Incidents* (1895) and *The Country of the Blind and Other Stories* (1913).

"The Plattner Story": *New Review*, April 1896; later in *The Plattner Story and Others* (1897) and *The Country of the Blind and Other Stories* (1913).

"Under the Knife": *New Review,* January 1896; later in *The Plattner Story and Others* (1897) and *The Country of the Blind and Other Stories* (1913).

"The Crystal Egg": *New Review,* May 1897; later in *Tales of Space and Time* (1899) and *The Country of the Blind and Other Stories* (1913).

"The New Accelerator": *Strand Magazine,* December 1901; later in *Twelve Stories and a Dream* (1903) and *The Country of the Blind and Other Stories* (1913).

"The Stolen Body": *Strand Magazine,* November 1898; later in *Twelve Stories and a Dream* (1903).

"The Argonauts of the Air": *Phil May's Annual,* December 1895; later in *The Plattner Story and Others* (1897) and *Thirty Strange Stories* (1897).

"In the Abyss": *Pearson's Magazine,* August 1, 1896; later in *The Plattner Story and Others* (1897).

"The Star": *Graphic,* December 1897; later in *Tales of Space and Time* (1899) and *The Country of the Blind and Other Stories* (1913).

"The Land Ironclads": *Strand Magazine,* December 1903.

"A Dream of Armageddon": *Black and White Budget,* May–June 1901; later in *Twelve Stories and a Dream* (1903) and *The Country of the Blind and Other Stories* (1913).

"The Lord of the Dynamos": *Pall Mall Budget,* September 6, 1894; later in *The Stolen Bacillus, and Other Incidents* (1895), *Thirty Strange Stories* (1897), and *The Country of the Blind and Other Stories* (1913).

"The Valley of Spiders": *Strand Magazine,* March 1903; later in *Twelve Stories and a Dream* (1903) and *The Country of the Blind and Other Stories* (1913).

"The Story of the Late Mr. Elvesham": *Idler,* May 1896; later in *The Plattner Story and Others* (1897), *Thirty Strange Stories* (1897), and *The Country of the Blind and Other Stories* (1913).

"The Man Who Could Work Miracles": *Illustrated London News,* July 1898; later in *The Country of the Blind and Other Stories* (1913).

"The Magic Shop": *Strange Magazine,* June 1903; later in *Twelve Stories and a Dream* (1903) and *The Country of the Blind and Other Stories* (1913).

"Mr. Skelmersdale in Fairyland": *London Magazine,* July 1898; later in *Twelve Stories and a Dream* (1903).

"The Door in the Wall": *Daily Chronicle,* July 14, 1906; later in *The Country of the Blind and Other Stories* (1913).

"The Presence by the Fire": *Penny Illustrated Paper*, August 14, 1897.

"A Vision of Judgment": *Butterfly*, September 1899; later in *The Country of the Blind and Other Stories* (1913).

"The Story of the Last Trump": first published as chapter 10 of *Boon, the Mind of the Race, the Wild Asses of the Devil, and the Last Trump, Being a First Selection from the Literary Remains of George Boon, Appropriate to the Times* (1915).

"The Wild Asses of the Devil": first published as chapter 8 of *Boon.*

"Answer to Prayer": *New Statesman*, April 10, 1937.

"The Queer Story of Brownlow's Newspaper": *Strand Magazine*, February 1932.

"The Country of the Blind": the first version of this story appeared in *Strand Magazine*, April 1904, and later in *The Country of the Blind and Other Stories* (1913). The revised, expanded version appeared in *The Country of the Blind* (1939).

PART ONE

VISIONARY
SCIENCE FICTION

The first story in this book is the only one in it that obeys the rules of fictional realism. Nothing impossible happens, so it isn't fantasy. Nothing "futuristic" or "predictive" or "speculative" happens, so most people wouldn't call it science fiction. But it is about scientists. And about being young, and poor, and ambitious.

It certainly draws its setting from Wells's experience at the Normal School of Science (now the Imperial College of Science and Technology) as a scholarship student among mostly middle-class students and professors. The competition in science to be first, get the top mark, the hot job, was fierce enough to drive students to cheating, already in the 1880s—a sad note. But what the story really is about is, to alter C. P. Snow's title, "the conscience of the poor." An insecure, angry, striving boy, a cobbler's son among the sons (and daughters) of the professional classes, is tempted by pure chance to cheat. He knows all too well that lower social status is assumed to mean lower ethical standards. So what does he do? The moral question posed is complex; the outcome is subtle and disturbing.

It is significant that the crux of the story is what young Hill sees on a microscope slide: a field of vision. That's why I put the story in this section, though it is "scientist fiction" rather than science fiction. In one way or another all the stories in this section have to do with *what somebody sees.* "I saw it with my own eyes"—that's how we attest to the reality of the implausible. Imaginative literature takes us into other worlds, altered states of consciousness, alien perceptions, by making us see another reality or see through other eyes. H. G. Wells was singularly gifted at presenting such changed fields of vision with intense, vivid actuality.

"The Remarkable Case of Davidson's Eyes" is a what-if: what if a man could see only what he'd see if he were someplace else? The premise is perfectly fantastic, but the setting is a laboratory, and Wells works out the implications elegantly, with science-fictional accuracy and aplomb.

"The Plattner Story" and "The Stolen Body" are two quite different approaches to a similar subject: a man disappears—one in an explosion, one in an experiment—out of ordinary life, sees some very strange things, and reappears.... The tale is like that of the Time Traveler, but instead of the future these men visit other worlds coexistent with ours, ominous and weird. These are ghost stories, reveling in the uncanny, playing with the theme of alternate realities, of a world that shadows, that tries to break through, into what we call the real world.

"Under the Knife" is a story of altered states of mind: the psychology of a man just before a major operation; an out-of-body experience, in which the disembodied patient sees the surgeon make a fatal mistake; and then a tremendous, headlong, visionary voyage through time and space and spirit.... I think this is one of the most extraordinary stories in this book, and I can't imagine anyone but this author writing anything remotely like it. It is quintessential Wells.

In "The Crystal Egg," the medium of vision, the way of seeing the other world, is through a crystal. A familiar idea, with ages of wishful thinking behind it. And the tale with its curiosity-shop setting seems to be of a familiar fantasy type. But when we see what is to be seen through the stone, and realize where it is, we're reading classic science fiction. Yet, returning to the fantasy element, I cherish the notion that J. R. R. Tolkien may well have read this story, and that in the crystal egg lies the ancestor of the *palantir*.

"The New Accelerator" is a highly original time-travel story, with many descendants in fiction throughout the twentieth century. The idea of moving really, *really* fast, so fast nobody could even see you, so fast that time would seem to freeze—did we learn that notion from Wells, or is it something children have always imagined? Certainly Professor Gibberne is Superman's great-grandfather.... Again, Wells works out with wonderful vividness what the (as far as we know) impossible experience would feel like, look like, sound like—and how it would affect those experiencing it. There are some fine throwaway lines, too. My favorite is "We ceased to smoulder almost at once."

A Slip Under
the Microscope

Outside the laboratory windows was a watery-grey fog, and within a close warmth and the yellow light of the green-shaded gas lamps that stood two to each table down its narrow length. On each table stood a couple of glass jars containing the mangled vestiges of the crayfish, mussels, frogs, and guineapigs upon which the students had been working, and down the side of the room, facing the windows, were shelves bearing bleached dissections of spirits, surmounted by a row of beautifully executed anatomical drawings in whitewood frames and overhanging a row of cubical lockers. All the doors of the laboratory were panelled with blackboard, and on these were the half-erased diagrams of the previous day's work. The laboratory was empty, save for the demonstrator, who sat near the preparation-room door, and silent, save for a low, continuous murmur, and the clicking of the rocker microtome at which he was working. But scattered about the room were traces of numerous students: hand-bags, polished boxes of instruments, in one place a large drawing covered by newspaper, and in another a prettily bound copy of *News from Nowhere*, a book oddly at variance with its surroundings. These things had been put down hastily as the students had arrived and hurried at once to secure their seats in the adjacent lecture theatre. Deadened by the closed door, the measured accents of the professor sounded as a featureless muttering.

Presently, faint through the closed windows came the sound of the

Oratory clock striking the hour of eleven. The clicking of the microtome ceased, and the demonstrator looked at his watch, rose, thrust his
hands into his pockets, and walked slowly down the laboratory towards
the lecture theatre door. He stood listening for a moment, and then his
eye fell on the little volume by William Morris. He picked it up,
glanced at the title, smiled, opened it, looked at the name on the fly-
leaf, ran the leaves through with his hand, and put it down. Almost
immediately the even murmur of the lecturer ceased, there was a sudden burst of pencils rattling on the desks in the lecture theatre, stirring, a scraping of feet, and a number of voices speaking together.
Then a firm footfall approached the door, which began to open, and
stood ajar as some indistinctly heard question arrested the newcomer.

The demonstrator turned, walked slowly back past the microtome,
and left the laboratory by the preparation-room door. As he did so,
first one, and then several students carrying notebooks entered the
laboratory from the lecture theatre, and distributed themselves
among the little tables, or stood in a group about the doorway. They
were an exceptionally heterogeneous assembly, for while Oxford and
Cambridge still recoil from the blushing prospect of mixed classes,
the College of Science anticipated America in the matter years ago—
mixed socially too, for the prestige of the College is high, and its
scholarships, free of any age limit, dredge deeper even than do those
of the Scotch universities. The class numbered one-and-twenty, but
some remained in the theatre questioning the professor, copying the
blackboard diagrams before they were washed off, or examining the
special specimens he had produced to illustrate the day's teaching. Of
the nine who had come into the laboratory three were girls, one of
whom, a little fair woman wearing spectacles and dressed in greyish-
green, was peering out of the window at the fog, while the other two,
both wholesome-looking, plain-faced schoolgirls, unrolled and put on
the brown holland aprons they wore while dissecting. Of the men, two
went down the laboratory to their places, one a pallid, dark-bearded
man, who had once been a tailor; the other a pleasant-featured, ruddy
young man of twenty, dressed in a well-fitting brown suit; young Wedderburn, the son of Wedderburn the eye specialist. The others formed
a little knot near the theatre door. One of these, a dwarfed, spectacled
figure with a hunch back, sat on a bent wood stool; two others, one
a short, dark youngster and the other a flaxen-haired, reddish-

complexioned young man, stood leaning side by side against the slate sink, while the fourth stood facing them, and maintained the largest share of the conversation.

This last person was named Hill. He was a sturdily built young fellow, of the same age as Wedderburn; he had a white face, dark grey eyes, hair of an indeterminate colour, and prominent, irregular features. He talked rather louder than was needful, and thrust his hands deeply into his pockets. His collar was frayed and blue with the starch of a careless laundress, his clothes were evidently ready-made, and there was a patch on the side of his boot near the toe. And as he talked or listened to the others, he glanced now and again towards the lecture theatre door. They were discussing the depressing peroration of the lecture they had just heard, the last lecture it was in the introductory course in zoology. "From ovum to ovum is the goal of the higher vertebrata," the lecturer had said in his melancholy tones, and so had neatly rounded off the sketch of comparative anatomy he had been developing. The spectacled hunchback had repeated it with noisy appreciation, had tossed it towards the fair-haired student with an evident provocation, and had started one of those vague, rambling discussions on generalities so unaccountably dear to the student mind all the world over.

"That is our goal, perhaps—I admit it, as far as science goes," said the fair-haired student, rising to the challenge. "But there are things above science."

"Science," said Hill confidently, "is systematic knowledge. Ideas that don't come into the system—must anyhow—be loose ideas." He was not quite sure whether that was a clever saying or a fatuity until his hearers took it seriously.

"The thing I cannot understand," said the hunchback, at large, "is whether Hill is a materialist or not."

"There is one thing above matter," said Hill promptly, feeling he made a better point this time, aware, too, of someone in the doorway behind him, and raising his voice a trifle for her benefit, "and that is, the delusion that there is something above matter."

"So we have your gospel at last," said the fair student. "It's all a delusion, is it? All our aspirations to lead something more than dogs' lives, all our work for anything beyond ourselves. But see how inconsistent you are. Your socialism, for instance. Why do you trouble about the interests of the race? Why do you concern yourself about the beggar in the gutter? Why are you bothering yourself to lend that book"—he indicated William Morris by a movement of the head—"to everyone in the lab?"

"Girl," said the hunchback indistinctly, and glanced guiltily over his shoulder.

The girl in brown, with the brown eyes, had come into the laboratory, and stood on the other side of the table behind him, with her rolled-up apron in one hand, looking over her shoulder, listening to the discussion. She did not notice the hunchback, because she was glancing from Hill to his interlocutor. Hill's consciousness of her presence betrayed itself to her only in his studious ignoring of the fact; but she understood that, and it pleased her. "I see no reason," said he, "why a man should live like a brute because he knows of nothing beyond matter, and does not expect to exist a hundred years hence."

"Why shouldn't he?" said the fair-haired student.

"Why *should* he?" said Hill.

"What inducement has he?"

"That's the way with all you religious people. It's all a business of inducements. Cannot a man seek after righteousness for righteousness' sake?"

There was a pause. The fair man answered, with a kind of vocal padding, "But—you see—inducement—when I said inducement," to gain time. And then the hunchback came to his rescue and inserted a question. He was a terrible person in the debating society with his questions, and they invariably took one form—a demand for a definition. "What's your definition of righteousness?" said the hunchback at this stage.

Hill experienced a sudden loss of complacency at this question, but even as it was asked, relief came in the person of Brooks, the laboratory attendant, who entered by the preparation-room door, carrying a number of freshly killed guineapigs by their hind legs. "This is the last batch of material this session," said the youngster who had not previously spoken. Brooks advanced up the laboratory, smacking down a couple of guineapigs at each table. The rest of the class, scenting the prey from afar, came crowding in by the lecture theatre door, and the discussion perished abruptly as the students who were not already in their places hurried to them to secure the choice of a specimen. There was a noise of keys rattling on split rings as lockers were opened and dissecting instruments taken out. Hill was already standing by his table, and his box of scalpels was sticking out of his pocket. The girl in brown came a step towards him, and leaning over his table said softly, "Did you see that I returned your book, Mr. Hill?"

During the whole scene she and the book had been vividly present in his consciousness; but he made a clumsy pretence of looking at the book and seeing it for the first time. "Oh yes," he said, taking it up. "I see. Did you like it?"

"I want to ask you some questions about it—some time."

"Certainly," said Hill. "I shall be glad." He stopped awkwardly. "You liked it?" he said.

"It's a wonderful book. Only some things I don't understand."

Then suddenly the laboratory was hushed by a curious braying noise. It was the demonstrator. He was at the blackboard ready to begin the day's instruction, and it was his custom to demand silence by a sound midway between the "Er" of common intercourse and the blast of a trumpet. The girl in brown slipped back to her place: it was immediately in front of Hill's, and Hill, forgetting her forthwith, took a notebook out of the drawer of his table, turned over its leaves hastily, drew a stumpy pencil from his pocket, and prepared to make a copious note of the coming demonstration. For demonstrations and lectures are the sacred text of the College students. Books, saving only the professor's own, you may—it is even expedient to—ignore.

Hill was the son of a Landport cobbler, and had been hooked by a chance blue paper the authorities had thrown out to the Landport Technical College. He kept himself in London on his allowance of a guinea a week, and found that, with proper care, this also covered his clothing allowance, an occasional waterproof collar, that is; and ink and needles and cotton and such-like necessaries for a man about town. This was his first year and his first session, but the brown old man in Landport had already got himself detested in many public-houses by boasting of his son, "the Professor." Hill was a vigorous youngster, with a serene contempt for the clergy of all denominations, and a fine ambition to reconstruct the world. He regarded his scholarship as a brilliant opportunity. He had begun to read at seven, and had read steadily whatever came in his way, good or bad, since then. His worldly experience had been limited to the island of Portsea, and acquired chiefly in the wholesale boot factory in which he had worked by day, after passing the seventh standard of the Board school. He had a considerable gift of speech, as the College Debating Society, which met amidst the crushing machines and mine models in the metallurgical theatre downstairs, already recognised—recognised by a violent battering of desks whenever he rose. And he was just at that fine emotional age when life opens at the end of a narrow pass like a broad valley at one's feet, full of the promise of wonderful discoveries and tremendous achievements. And his own limitations, save that he knew that he knew neither Latin nor French, were all unknown to him.

At first his interest had been divided pretty equally between his biological work at the College and social and theological theorising, an employment which he took in deadly earnest. Of a night, when the big museum library was not open, he would sit on the bed of his room in Chelsea with his coat and a muffler on, and write out the lecture notes and revise his dissection memoranda until Thorpe called him out by a whistle—the landlady objected to open the door to attic visitors—and then the two would go prowling about the shadowy, shiny, gas-lit streets, talking, very much in the fashion of the sample just given, of the God Idea and Righteousness and Carlyle and the Reorganisation of Society. And in the midst of it all, Hill, arguing not only for Thorpe but for the casual passer-by, would lose the thread of his argument glancing at some pretty painted face that looked meaningly at him as he passed. Science and Righteousness! But once or twice lately there had been signs that a third interest was creeping into his life, and he had found his attention wandering from the fate of the mesoblastic somites or the probable meaning of the blastopore, to the thought of the girl with the brown eyes who sat at the table before him.

She was a paying student; she descended inconceivable social altitudes to speak to him. At the thought of the education she must have had, and the accomplishments she must possess, the soul of Hill became abject within him. She had spoken to him first over a difficulty about the alisphenoid of a rabbit's skull, and he had found that, in biology at least, he had no reason for self-abasement. And from that, after the manner of young people starting from any starting-point, they got to generalities, and while Hill attacked her upon the question of socialism—some instinct told him to spare her a direct assault upon her religion—she was gathering resolution to undertake what she told herself was his aesthetic education. She was a year or two older than he, though the thought never occurred to him. The loan of *News from Nowhere* was the beginning of a series of cross loans. Upon some absurd first principle of his, Hill had never "wasted time" upon poetry, and it seemed an appalling deficiency to her. One day in the lunch hour, when she chanced upon him alone in the little museum where the skeletons were arranged, shamefully eating the bun that constituted his midday meal, she retreated, and returned to lend him, with a slightly furtive air, a volume of Browning. He stood sideways towards her and took the book rather clumsily, because he was holding the bun in the other hand. And in the retrospect his voice lacked the cheerful clearness he could have wished.

That occurred after the examination in comparative anatomy, on the day before the College turned out its students and was carefully locked up by the officials for the Christmas holidays. The excitement of cramming for the first trial of strength had for a little while dominated Hill to the exclusion of his other interests. In the forecasts of the result in which every one indulged he was surprised to find that no one regarded him as a possible competitor for the Harvey Commemoration Medal, of which this and the two subsequent examinations disposed. It was about this time that Wedderburn, who so far had lived inconspicuously on the uttermost margin of Hill's perceptions, began to take on the appearance of an obstacle. By a mutual agreement, the nocturnal prowlings with Thorpe ceased for the three weeks before the examination, and his landlady pointed out that she really could not supply so much lamp oil at the price. He walked to and fro from the College with little slips of mnemonics in his hand, lists of crayfish appendages, rabbits' skull-bones, and vertebrate nerves, for example, and became a positive nuisance to foot passengers in the opposite direction.

But, by a natural reaction, Poetry and the girl with the brown eyes ruled the Christmas holiday. The pending results of the examination became such a secondary consideration that Hill marvelled at his father's excitement. Even had he wished it, there was no comparative anatomy to read in Landport, and he was too poor to buy books, but the stock of poets in the library was extensive, and Hill's attack was magnificently sustained. He saturated himself with the fluent numbers of Longfellow and Tennyson, and fortified himself with Shakespeare;

found a kindred soul in Pope and a master in Shelley, and heard and fled the siren voices of Eliza Cook and Mrs. Hemans. But he read no more Browning, because he hoped for the loan of other volumes from Miss Haysman when he returned to London.

He walked from the lodgings to the College with that volume of Browning in his shiny black bag, and his mind teeming with the finest general propositions about poetry. Indeed, he framed first this little speech and then that with which to grace the return. The morning was an exceptionally pleasant one for London; there was a clear hard frost and undeniable blue in the sky, a thin haze softened every outline, and warm shafts of sunlight struck between the house blocks and turned the sunny side of the street to amber and gold. In the hall of the College he pulled off his glove and signed his name with fingers so stiff with cold that the characteristic dash under the signature he cultivated became a quivering line. He imagined Miss Haysman about him everywhere. He turned at the staircase, and there, below, he saw a crowd struggling at the foot of the notice-board. This, possibly, was the biology list. He forgot Browning and Miss Haysman for the moment, and joined the scrimmage. And at last, with his cheek flattened against the sleeve of the man on the step above him, he read the list—

CLASS I
H. J. Somers Wedderburn
William Hill

and thereafter followed a second class that is outside our present sympathies. It was characteristic that he did not trouble to look for Thorpe on the physics list, but backed out of the struggle at once, and in a curious emotional state between pride over common second-class humanity and acute disappointment at Wedderburn's success, went on his way upstairs. At the top, as he was hanging up his coat in the passage, the zoological demonstrator, a young man from Oxford who secretly regarded him as a blatant "mugger" of the very worst type, offered his heartiest congratulations.

At the laboratory door Hill stopped for a second to get his breath, and then entered. He looked straight up the laboratory and saw all five girl students grouped in their places, and Wedderburn, the once retiring Wedderburn, leaning rather gracefully against the window, playing with the blind tassel and talking apparently to the five of them. Now, Hill could talk bravely enough and even overbearingly to one girl, and he could have made a speech to a roomful of girls, but this business of standing at ease and appreciating, fencing, and returning quick remarks round a group was, he knew, altogether beyond him. Coming up the staircase his feelings for Wedderburn had been generous, a certain admiration perhaps, a willingness to shake his hand conspicuously and heartily as one who had fought but the first round. But before Christmas Wedderburn had never gone up to the end of the room to talk. In a flash Hill's mist of vague excitement condensed abruptly to a vivid dislike of Wedderburn. Possibly his expression changed. As he came up to his place, Wedderburn nodded carelessly to him, and the others glanced round. Miss Haysman looked at him and away again, the faintest touch of her eyes. "I can't agree with you, Mr. Wedderburn," she said.

"I must congratulate you on your first class, Mr. Hill," said the spectacled girl in green, turning round and beaming at him.

"It's nothing," said Hill, staring at Wedderburn and Miss Haysman talking together, and eager to hear what they talked about.

"We poor folks in the second class don't think so," said the girl in spectacles.

What was it Wedderburn was saying? Something about William Morris! Hill did not answer the girl in spectacles, and the smile died out of his face. He could not hear, and failed to see how he could "cut in." Confound Wedderburn! He sat down, opened his bag, hesitated whether to return the volume of Browning forthwith, in the sight of all, and instead drew out his new notebooks for the short course in elementary botany that was now beginning, and which would terminate in February. As he did so, a fat heavy man with a white face and pale grey eyes—Bindon, the professor of botany, who came up from Kew for January and February—came in by the lecture theatre door, and passed, rubbing his hands together and smiling, in silent affability down the laboratory.

————

In the subsequent six weeks Hill experienced some very rapid and curiously complex emotional developments. For the most part he had Wedderburn in focus—a fact that Miss Haysman never suspected. She told Hill (for in the comparative privacy of the museum she talked a good deal to him of socialism and Browning and general propositions) that she had met Wedderburn at the house of some people she knew, and "he's inherited his cleverness; for his father, you know, is the great eye specialist."

"*My* father is a cobbler," said Hill, quite irrelevantly, and perceived the want of dignity even as he said it. But the gleam of jealousy did not offend her. She conceived herself the fundamental source of it. He suffered bitterly from a sense of Wedderburn's unfairness, and a realisation of his own handicap. Here was this Wedderburn who had picked up a prominent man for a father, and instead of his losing so many marks on the score of that advantage, it was counted to him for righteousness! And while Hill had to introduce himself and talk to Miss Haysman clumsily over mangled guineapigs in the laboratory, this Wedderburn, in some backstairs way, had access to her social altitudes, and could converse in a polished argot that Hill understood perhaps, but felt incapable of speaking. Not, of course, that he wanted to. Then it seemed to Hill that for Wedderburn to come there day after day with cuffs unfrayed, neatly tailored, precisely barbered, quietly perfect, was in itself an ill-bred, sneering sort of proceeding. Moreover, it was a stealthy thing for Wedderburn to behave insignificantly for a space, to mock modesty, to lead Hill to fancy that he himself was beyond dispute the man of the year, and then suddenly to dart in front of him, and incontinently to swell up in this fashion. In addition to these things, Wedderburn displayed an increasing disposition to join in any conversational grouping that included Miss Haysman; and would venture, and indeed seek occasion, to pass opinions derogatory to socialism and atheism. He goaded Hill to incivilities by neat, shallow, and exceedingly effective personalities about the socialist leaders, until Hill hated Bernard Shaw's graceful egotisms, William Morris's limited editions and luxurious wall-papers, and Walter Crane's charmingly absurd ideal working men, about as much as he hated Wedderburn. The dissertations in the laboratory, that had been his glory in the previous term, became a danger, degenerated into inglorious tussles with Wedderburn, and Hill kept to them only out of an obscure perception that his honour was involved. In the debating society Hill knew quite clearly that, to a thunderous accompaniment of banged desks, he could have pulverised Wedderburn. Only Wedderburn never attended the debating society to be pulverised, because—nauseous affectation!—he "dined late."

You must not imagine that these things presented themselves in quite such a crude form to Hill's perception. Hill was a born generaliser. Wedderburn to him was not so much an individual obstacle as a type, the salient angle of a class. The economic theories that, after infinite ferment, had shaped themselves in Hill's mind, became abruptly concrete at the contact. The world became full of easy-mannered, graceful, gracefully dressed, conversationally dexterous, finally shallow Wedderburns, Bishops Wedderburn, Wedderburn MPs, Professors Wedderburn, Wedderburn landlords, all with finger-bowl shibboleths and epigrammatic cities of refuge from a sturdy debater. And everyone ill-clothed or ill-dressed, from the cobbler to the cabrunner, was, to Hill's imagination, a man and a brother, a fellow-sufferer. So that he became, as it were, a champion of the fallen and oppressed, albeit to outward seeming only a self-assertive, ill-mannered young man, and an unsuccessful champion at that. Again and again a skirmish over the afternoon tea that the girl students had inaugurated left Hill with flushed cheeks and a tattered temper, and the debating society noticed a new quality of sarcastic bitterness in his speeches.

You will understand now how it was necessary, if only in the interests of humanity, that Hill should demolish Wedderburn in the forthcoming examination and outshine him in the eyes of Miss Haysman; and you will perceive, too, how Miss Haysman fell into some common feminine misconceptions. The Hill-Wedderburn quarrel, for in his unostentatious way Wedderburn reciprocated Hill's ill-veiled rivalry, became a tribute to her indefinable charm: she was the Queen of Beauty in a tournament of scalpels and stumpy pencils. To her confidential friend's secret annoyance, it even troubled her conscience, for she was a good girl, and painfully aware, through Ruskin and contemporary fiction, how entirely men's activities are determined by women's attitudes. And if Hill never by any chance mentioned the topic of love to her, she only credited him with the finer modesty for that omission.

So the time came on for the second examination, and Hill's increasing pallor confirmed the general rumour that he was working hard. In the aërated bread shop near South Kensington Station you would see him, breaking his bun and sipping his milk with his eyes intent upon a paper of closely written notes. In his bedroom there were propositions about buds and stems round his looking-glass, a diagram to catch his eye, if soap should chance to spare it, above his washing basin. He missed several meetings of the debating society, but he found the chance encounters with Miss Haysman in the spacious ways of the adjacent art museum or in the little museum at the top of the College, or in the College corridors, more frequently and very restful. In particular, they used to meet in a little gallery full of wrought-iron chests and gates near the art library, and there Hill used to talk, under the gentle stimulus of her fluttering attention, of Browning and his personal ambitions. A characteristic she found remarkable in him was his freedom from avarice. He contemplated quite calmly the prospect of living all his life on an income below a hundred pounds a year. But he was determined to be famous, to make, recognisably in his own proper person, the world a better place to live in. He took Bradlaugh and John Burns for his leaders and models, poor, even impecunious, great men. But Miss Haysman thought that such lives were deficient on the aesthetic side, by which, though she did not know it, she meant good wallpaper and upholstery, pretty books, tasteful clothes, concerts, and meals nicely cooked and respectfully served.

At last came the day of the second examination, and the professor of botany, a fussy, conscientious man, rearranged all the tables in a long narrow laboratory to prevent copying, and put his demonstrator on a chair on a table (where he felt, he said, like a Hindu god), to see all the cheating, and stuck a notice outside the door, "Door closed," for no earthly reason that any human being could discover. And all the morning from ten till one the quill of Wedderburn shrieked defiance at Hill's, and the quills of the others chased their leaders in a tireless pack, and so also it was in the afternoon. Wedderburn was a little quieter than usual, and Hill's face was hot all day, and his overcoat bulged with textbooks and notebooks against the last moment's revision. And the next day, in the morning and in the afternoon, was the practical examination, when sections had to be cut and slides identified. In the morning Hill was depressed because he knew he had cut a thick section, and in the afternoon came the mysterious slip.

It was just the kind of thing that the botanical professor was always doing. Like the income tax, it offered a premium to the cheat. It was a preparation under the microscope, a little glass slip, held in its place on the stage of the instrument by light steel clips, and the inscription set forth that the slip was not to be moved. Each student was to go in turn to it, sketch it, write in his book of answers what he considered it to be, and return to his place. Now, to move such a slip is a thing one can do by a chance movement of the finger, and in a fraction of a second. The professor's reason for decreeing that the slip should not be moved depended on the fact that the object he wanted identified was characteristic of a certain tree stem. In the position in which it was placed it was a difficult thing to recognise, but once the slip was moved so as to bring other parts of the preparation into view, its nature was obvious enough.

Hill came to this, flushed from a contest with staining re-agents, sat down on the little stool before the microscope, turned the mirror to get the best light, and then, out of sheer habit, shifted the slip. At once he remembered the prohibition, and, with an almost continuous motion of his hands, moved it back, and sat paralysed with astonishment at his action.

Then, slowly, he turned his head. The professor was out of the room; the demonstrator sat aloft on his impromptu rostrum, reading the *Q. Jour. Mi. Sci.;* the rest of the examinees were busy, and with their backs to him. Should he own up to the accident now? He knew quite clearly what the thing was. It was a lenticel, a characteristic preparation from the elder-tree. His eyes roved over his intent fellow-students and Wedderburn suddenly glanced over his shoulder at him with a queer expression in his eyes. The mental excitement that had kept Hill at an abnormal pitch of vigour these two days gave way to a curious nervous tension. His book of answers was beside him. He did not write down what the thing was, but with one eye at the microscope he began making a hasty sketch of it. His mind was full of this grotesque puzzle in ethics that had suddenly been sprung upon him. Should he identify it? or should he leave this question unanswered? In that case Wedderburn would probably come out first in the second result. How could he tell now whether he might not have identified the thing without shifting it? It was possible that Wedderburn had failed to recognise it, of course. Suppose Wedderburn too had shifted the slide? He looked up at the clock. There were fifteen minutes in which to make up his mind. He gathered up his book of answers and the coloured pencils he used in illustrating his replies and walked back to his seat.

He read through his manuscript, and then sat thinking and gnawing his knuckle. It would look queer now if he owned up. He *must* beat Wedderburn. He forgot the examples of those starry gentlemen, John Burns and Bradlaugh. Besides, he reflected, the glimpse of the rest of the slip he had had was after all quite accidental, forced upon him by chance, a kind of providential revelation rather than an unfair advantage. It was not nearly so dishonest to avail himself of that as it was of Broome, who believed in the efficacy of prayer, to pray daily for a first-class. "Five minutes more," said the demonstrator, folding up his paper and becoming observant. Hill watched the clock hands until two minutes remained; then he opened the book of answers, and, with hot ears and an affectation of ease, gave his drawing of the lenticel its name.

When the second pass list appeared, the previous positions of Wedderburn and Hill were reversed, and the spectacled girl in green, who knew the demonstrator in private life (where he was practically human), said that in the result of the two examinations taken together Hill had the advantage of a mark—167 to 166 out of a possible 200. Everyone admired Hill in a way, though the suspicion of "mugging" clung to him. But Hill was to find congratulations and Miss Haysman's enhanced opinion of him, and even the decided decline in the crest of Wedderburn, tainted by an unhappy memory. He felt a remarkable access of energy at first, and the note of a democracy marching to triumph returned to his debating society speeches; he worked at his comparative anatomy with tremendous zeal and effect, and he went on with his aesthetic education. But through it all, a vivid little picture was continually coming before his mind's eye—of a sneakish person manipulating a slide.

No human being had witnessed the act, and he was cocksure that no higher power existed to see it; but for all that it worried him. Memories are not dead things, but alive; they dwindle in disuse, but they harden and develop in all sorts of queer ways if they are being continually fretted. Curiously enough, though at the time he perceived clearly that the shifting was accidental, as the days wore on his memory became confused about it, until at last he was not sure—although he assured himself that he *was* sure—whether the movement had been absolutely involuntary. Then it is possible that Hill's dietary was conducive to morbid conscientiousness; a breakfast frequently eaten in a hurry, a midday bun, and, at such hours after five as chanced to be convenient, such meat as his means determined, usually in a chophouse in a back street off the Brompton Road. Occasionally he treated himself to threepenny or ninepenny classics, and they usually represented a suppression of potatoes or chops. It is indisputable that outbreaks of self-abasement and emotional revival have a distinct relation to periods of scarcity. But apart from this influence on the feelings, there was in Hill a distinct aversion to falsity that the blasphemous Landport cobbler had inculcated by strap and tongue from his earliest years. Of one fact about professed atheists I am convinced; they may be—they usually are—fools, void of subtlety, revilers of holy institutions, brutal speakers, and mischievous knaves, but they lie with difficulty. If it were not so, if they had the faintest grasp of the idea of compromise, they would simply be liberal churchmen. And, moreover, this memory poisoned his regard for Miss Haysman. For she now so evidently preferred him to Wedderburn that he felt sure he cared for her, and began reciprocating her attentions by timid marks of personal regard; at one time he even bought a bunch of violets, carried it about in his pocket, and produced it with a stumbling explanation, withered and dead, in the gallery of old iron. It poisoned, too, the denunciation of capitalist dishonesty that had been one of his life's pleasures. And, lastly, it poisoned his triumph in Wedderburn. Previously he had been Wedderburn's superior in his own eyes, and had raged simply at a want of recognition. Now he began to fret at the darker suspicion of positive inferiority. He fancied he found justifications for his positions in Browning, but they vanished on analysis. At last—moved, curiously enough, by exactly the same motive forces that had resulted in his dishonesty—he went to Professor Bindon, and made a clean breast of the whole affair. As Hill was a paid student, Professor Bindon did not ask him to sit down, and he stood before the professor's desk as he made his confession.

"It's a curious story," said Professor Bindon, slowly realising how the thing reflected on himself, and then letting his anger rise,—"A most remarkable story. I can't understand your doing it, and I can't understand this avowal. You're a type of student—Cambridge men would never dream—I suppose I ought to have thought—Why *did* you cheat?"

"I didn't cheat," said Hill.

"But you have just been telling me you did."

"I thought I explained—"

"Either you cheated or you did not cheat.—"

"I said my motion was involuntary."

"I am not a metaphysician, I am a servant of science—of fact. You were told not to move the slip. You did move the slip. If that is not cheating—"

"If I was a cheat," said Hill, with the note of hysterics in his voice, "should I come here and tell you?"

"Your repentance, of course, does you credit," said Professor Bindon, "but it does not alter the original facts."

"No, sir," said Hill, giving in in utter self-abasement.

"Even now you cause an enormous amount of trouble. The examination list will have to be revised."

"I suppose so, sir."

"Suppose so? Of course it must be revised. And I don't see how I can conscientiously pass you."

"Not pass me?" said Hill. "Fail me?"

"It's the rule of all examinations. Or where should we be? What else did you expect? You don't want to shirk the consequences of your own acts?"

"I thought, perhaps"—said Hill. And then, "Fail me? I thought, as I told you, you would simply deduct the marks given for that slip."

"Impossible!" said Bindon. "Besides, it would still leave you above Wedderburn. Deduct only the marks— Preposterous! The Departmental Regulations distinctly say—"

"But it's my own admission, sir."

"The Regulations say nothing whatever of the manner in which the matter comes to light. They simply provide—"

"It will ruin me. If I fail this examination, they won't renew my scholarship."

"You should have thought of that before."

"But, sir, consider all my circumstances—"

"I cannot consider anything. Professors in this College are machines. The Regulations will not even let us recommend our students for appointments. I am a machine, and you have worked me. I have to do—"

"It's very hard, sir."

"Possibly it is."

"If I am to be failed this examination, I might as well go home at once."

"That is as you think proper." Bindon's voice softened a little; he perceived he had been unjust, and, provided he did not contradict himself, he was disposed to amelioration. "As a private person," he said, "I think this confession of yours goes far to mitigate your offence. But you have set the machinery in motion, and now it must take its course. I—I am really sorry you gave way."

A wave of emotion prevented Hill from answering. Suddenly, very vividly, he saw the heavily lined face of the old Landport cobbler, his father. "Good God! What a fool I have been!" he said hotly and abruptly.

"I hope," said Bindon, "that it will be a lesson to you."

But, curiously enough, they were not thinking of quite the same indiscretion.

There was a pause.

"I would like a day to think, sir, and then I will let you know—about going home, I mean," said Hill, moving towards the door.

———

The next day Hill's place was vacant. The spectacled girl in green was, as usual, first with the news. Wedderburn and Miss Haysman were talking of a performance of *The Meistersingers* when she came up to them.

"Have you heard?" she said.

"Heard what?"

"There was cheating in the examination."

"Cheating!" said Wedderburn, with his face suddenly hot. "How?"

"That slide—"

"Moved? Never!"

"It was. That slide that we weren't to move—"

"Nonsense!" said Wedderburn. "Why! How could they find out? Who do they say—?"

"It was Mr. Hill."

"Hill!"

"Mr. Hill!"

"Not—surely not the immaculate Hill?" said Wedderburn, recovering.

"I don't believe it," said Miss Haysman. "How do you know?"

"I *didn't*," said the girl in spectacles. "But I know it now for a fact. Mr. Hill went and confessed to Professor Bindon himself."

"By Jove!" said Wedderburn. "Hill of all people. But I am always inclined to distrust these philanthropists-on-principle—"

"Are you quite sure?" said Miss Haysman, with a catch in her breath.

"Quite. It's dreadful, isn't it? But, you know, what can you expect? His father is a cobbler."

Then Miss Haysman astonished the girl in spectacles.

"I don't care. I will not believe it," she said, flushing darkly under her warm-tinted skin. "I will not believe it until he has told me so himself—face to face. I would scarcely believe it then," and abruptly she turned her back on the girl in spectacles, and walked to her own place.

"It's true, all the same," said the girl in spectacles, peering and smiling at Wedderburn.

But Wedderburn did not answer her. She was indeed one of those people who seem destined to make unanswered remarks.

THE REMARKABLE CASE
OF DAVIDSON'S EYES

The transitory mental aberration of Sidney Davidson, remarkable enough in itself, is still more remarkable if Wade's explanation is to be credited. It sets one dreaming of the oddest possibilities of intercommunication in the future, of spending an intercalary five minutes on the other side of the world, or being watched in our most secret operations by unsuspected eyes. It happened that I was the immediate witness of Davidson's seizure, and so it falls naturally to me to put the story upon paper.

When I say that I was the immediate witness of his seizure, I mean that I was the first on the scene. The thing happened at the Harlow Technical College, just beyond the Highgate Archway. He was alone in the larger laboratory when the thing happened. I was in a smaller room, where the balances are, writing up some notes. The thunderstorm had completely upset my work, of course. It was just after one of the louder peals that I thought I heard some glass smash in the other room. I stopped writing, and turned round to listen. For a moment I heard nothing; the hail was playing the devil's tattoo on the corrugated zinc of the roof. Then came another sound, a smash—no doubt of it this time. Something heavy had been knocked off the bench. I jumped up at once and went and opened the door leading into the big laboratory.

I was surprised to hear a queer sort of laugh, and saw Davidson standing unsteadily in the middle of the room, with a dazzled look on his face. My first impression was that he was drunk. He did not notice me. He was clawing out at something invisible a yard in front of his face. He put out his hand slowly, rather hesitatingly, and then clutched nothing. "What's come to it?" he said. He held up his hands to his face, fingers spread out. "Great Scott!" he said. The thing happened three or four years ago, when everyone swore by that personage. Then he began raising his feet clumsily, as though he had expected to find them glued to the floor.

"Davidson!" cried I. "What's the matter with you?" He turned round in my direction and looked about for me. He looked over me and at me and on either side of me, without the slightest sign of seeing me. "Waves," he said; "and a remarkably neat schooner. I'd swear that was Bellows' voice. *Hullo!*" He shouted suddenly at the top of his voice.

I thought he was up to some foolery. Then I saw littered about his feet the shattered remains of the best of our electrometers. "What's up, man?" said I. "You've smashed the electrometer!"

"Bellows again!" said he. "Friends left, if my hands are gone. Something about electrometers. Which way *are* you, Bellows?" He suddenly came staggering towards me. "The damned stuff cuts like butter," he said. He walked straight into the bench and recoiled. "None so buttery that!" he said, and stood swaying.

I felt scared. "Davidson," said I, "what on earth's come over you?"

He looked round him in every direction. "I could swear that was Bellows. Why don't you show yourself like a man, Bellows?"

It occurred to me that he must be suddenly struck blind. I walked round the table and laid my hand upon his arm. I never saw a man more startled in my life. He jumped away from me, and came round into an attitude of self-defence, his face fairly distorted with terror. "Good God!" he cried. "What was that?"

"It's I—Bellows. Confound it, Davidson!"

He jumped when I answered him and stared—how can I express it?—right through me. He began talking, not to me, but to himself. "Here in broad daylight on a clear beach. Not a place to hide in." He looked about him wildly. "Here! I'm *off*." He suddenly turned and ran headlong into the big electromagnet—so violently that, as we found afterwards, he bruised his shoulder and jawbone cruelly. At that he stepped back a pace, and cried out with almost a whimper: "What, in

Heaven's name, has come over me?" He stood, blanched with terror and trembling violently, with his right arm clutching his left, where that had collided with the magnet.

By that time I was excited and fairly scared. "Davidson," said I, "don't be afraid."

He was startled at my voice, but not so excessively as before. I repeated my words in a clear and as firm a tone as I could assume. "Bellows," he said, "is that you?"

"Can't you see it's me?"

He laughed. "I can't even see it's myself. Where the devil are we?"

"Here," said I, "in the laboratory."

"The laboratory!" he answered in a puzzled tone, and put his hand to his forehead. "I *was* in the laboratory—till that flash came, but I'm hanged if I'm there now. What ship is that?"

"There's no ship," said I. "Do be sensible, old chap."

"No ship!" he repeated, and seemed to forget my denial forthwith. "I suppose," said he slowly, "we're both dead. But the rummy part is I feel just as though I still had a body. Don't get used to it all at once, I suppose. The old ship was struck by lightning, I suppose. Jolly quick thing, Bellows—eigh?"

"Don't talk nonsense. You're very much alive. You are in the laboratory, blundering about. You've just smashed a new electrometer. I don't envy you when Boyce arrives."

He stared away from me towards the diagrams of cryohydrates. "I must be deaf," said he. "They've fired a gun, for there goes the puff of smoke, and I never heard a sound."

I put my hand on his arm again, and this time he was less alarmed. "We seem to have sort of invisible bodies," said he. "By Jove! there's a boat coming round the headland. It's very much like the old life after all—in a different climate."

I shook his arm. "Davidson," I cried, "wake up!"

It was just then that Boyce came in. So soon as he spoke Davidson exclaimed: "Old Boyce! Dead too! What a lark!" I hastened to explain that Davidson was in a kind of somnambulistic trance. Boyce was interested at once. We both did all we could to rouse the fellow out of his extraordinary state. He answered our questions, and asked us some of his own, but his attention seemed distracted by his hallucination about a beach and ship. He kept interpolating observations concerning some boat and the davits, and sails filling with the wind. It made one feel queer, in the dusky laboratory, to hear him saying such things.

He was blind and helpless. We had to walk him down the passage, one at each elbow, to Boyce's private room, and while Boyce talked to him there, and humoured him about this ship idea, I went along the corridor and asked old Wade to come and look at him. The voice of our Dean sobered him a little, but not very much. He asked where his hands were, and why he had to walk about up to his waist in the ground. Wade thought over him a long time—you know how he knits his brows—and then made him feel the couch, guiding his hands to it. "That's a couch," said Wade. "The couch in the private room of Prof. Boyce. Horsehair stuffing."

Davidson felt about, and puzzled over it, and answered presently that he could feel it all right, but he couldn't see it.

"What *do* you see?" asked Wade. Davidson said he could see nothing but a lot of sand and broken-up shells. Wade gave him some other things to feel, telling him what they were, and watching him keenly.

"The ship is almost hull down," said Davidson presently, apropos of nothing.

"Never mind the ship," said Wade. "Listen to me, Davidson. Do you know what 'hallucination' means?"

"Rather," said Davidson.

"Well, everything you see is hallucinatory."

"Bishop Berkeley," said Davidson.

"Don't mistake me," said Wade. "You are alive and in this room of Boyce's. But something has happened to your eyes. You cannot see; you can feel and hear, but not see. Do you follow me?"

"It seems to me that I see too much." Davidson rubbed his knuckles into his eyes. "Well?" he said.

"That's all. Don't let it perplex you. Bellows here and I will take you home in a cab."

"Wait a bit." Davidson thought. "Help me to sit down," said he presently; "and now—I'm sorry to trouble you—but will you tell me all that over again?"

Wade repeated it very patiently. Davidson shut his eyes, and pressed his hands upon his forehead. "Yes," said he. "It's quite right. Now my eyes are shut I know you're right. That's you, Bellows, sitting by me on the couch. I'm in England again. And we're in the dark."

Then he opened his eyes. "And there," said he, "is the sun just rising, and the yards of the ship, and a tumbled sea, and a couple of birds flying. I never saw anything so real. And I'm sitting up to my neck in a bank of sand."

He bent forward and covered his face with his hands. Then he opened his eyes again. "Dark sea and sunrise! And yet I'm sitting on a sofa in old Boyce's room!... God help me!"

That was the beginning. For three weeks this strange affection of Davidson's eyes continued unabated. It was far worse than being blind. He was absolutely helpless, and had to be fed like a newly hatched bird, and led about and undressed. If he attempted to move, he fell over things or struck himself against walls or doors. After a day or so he got used to hearing our voices without seeing us, and willingly admitted he was at home, and that Wade was right in what he told him. My sister, to whom he was engaged, insisted on coming to see him, and would sit for hours every day while he talked about this beach of his. Holding her hand seemed to comfort him immensely. He explained that when we left the College and drove home—he lived in Hampstead village—it appeared to him as if we drove right through a sandhill—it was perfectly black until he emerged again—and through rocks and trees and solid obstacles, and when he was taken to his own room it made him giddy and almost frantic with the fear of falling, because going upstairs seemed to lift him thirty or forty feet above the rocks of his imaginary island. He kept saying he should smash all the eggs. The end was that he had to be taken down into his father's consulting-room and laid upon a couch that stood there.

He described the island as being a bleak kind of place on the whole, with very little vegetation, except some peaty stuff, and a lot of bare rock. There were multitudes of penguins, and they made the rocks white and disagreeable to see. The sea was often rough, and once there was a thunderstorm, and he lay and shouted at the silent flashes. Once or twice seals pulled up on the beach, but only on the first two or three days. He said it was very funny the way in which the penguins used to waddle right through him, and how he seemed to lie among them without disturbing them.

I remember one odd thing, and that was when he wanted very badly to smoke. We put a pipe in his hands—he almost poked his eye out with it—and lit it. But he couldn't taste anything. I've since found it's the same with me—I don't know if it's the usual case—that I cannot enjoy tobacco at all unless I can see the smoke.

But the queerest part of his vision came when Wade sent him out in a Bath-chair to get fresh air. The Davidsons hired a chair, and got that deaf and obstinate dependant of theirs, Widgery, to attend to it. Widgery's ideas of healthy expeditions were peculiar. My sister, who had been to the Dogs' Home, met them in Camden Town, towards King's Cross, Widgery trotting along complacently, and Davidson, evidently most distressed, trying in his feeble, blind way to attract Widgery's attention.

He positively wept when my sister spoke to him. "Oh, get me out of this horrible darkness!" he said, feeling for her hand. "I must get out of it, or I shall die." He was quite incapable of explaining what was the matter, but my sister decided he must go home, and presently, as they went uphill towards Hampstead, the horror seemed to drop from him. He said it was good to see the stars again, though it was then about noon and a blazing day.

"It seemed," he told me afterwards, "as if I was being carried irresistibly towards the water. I was not very much alarmed at first. Of course it was night there—a lovely night."

"Of course?" I asked, for that struck me as odd.

"Of course," said he. "It's always night there when it is day here ... Well, we went right into the water, which was calm and shining under the moonlight—just a broad swell that seemed to grow broader and flatter as I came down into it. The surface glistened just like a skin—it might have been empty space underneath for all I could tell to the contrary. Very slowly, for I rode slanting into it, the water crept up to my eyes. Then I went under and the skin seemed to break and heal again about my eyes. The moon gave a jump up in the sky and grew green and dim, and fish, faintly glowing, came darting round me—and things that seemed made of luminous glass; and I passed through a tangle of seaweeds that shone with an oily lustre. And so I drove down into the sea, and the stars went out one by one, and the moon grew greener and darker, and the seaweed became a luminous purple-red. It was all very faint and mysterious, and everything seemed to quiver. And all the while I could hear the wheels of the Bath-chair creaking, and the footsteps of people going by, and a man in the distance selling the special *Pall Mall*.

"I kept sinking down deeper and deeper into the water. It became inky black about me, not a ray from above came down into that darkness, and the phosphorescent things grew brighter and brighter. The snaky branches of the deeper weeds flickered like the flames of spirit-lamps; but, after a time, there were no more weeds. The fishes came staring and gaping towards me, and into me and through me. I never imagined such fishes before. They had lines of fire along the sides of them as though they had been outlined with a luminous pencil. And there was a ghastly thing swimming backward with a lot of twining arms. And then I saw, coming very slowly towards me through the gloom, a hazy mass of light that resolved itself as it drew nearer into multitudes of fishes, struggling and darting round something that drifted. I drove on straight towards it, and presently I saw in the midst of the tumult, and by the light of the fish, a bit of splintered spar looming over me, and a dark hull tilting over, and some glowing phosphorescent forms that were shaken and writhed as the fish bit at them. Then it was I began to try to attract Widgery's attention. A horror came upon me. Ugh! I should have driven right into those half-eaten—things. If your sister had not come! They had great holes in them, Bellows, and . . . Never mind. But it was ghastly!"

For three weeks Davidson remained in this singular state, seeing what at the time we imagined was an altogether phantasmal world, and stone blind to the world around him. Then, one Tuesday, when I called I met old Davidson in the passage. "He can see his thumb!" the old gentleman said, in a perfect transport. He was struggling into his overcoat. "He can see his thumb, Bellows!" he said, with the tears in his eyes. "The lad will be all right yet."

I rushed in to Davidson. He was holding up a little book before his face, and looking at it and laughing in a weak kind of way.

"It's amazing," said he. "There's a kind of patch come there." He pointed with his finger. "I'm on the rocks as usual, and the penguins are staggering and flapping about as usual, and there's been a whale showing every now and then, but it's got too dark now to make him out. But put something *there*, and I see it—I do see it. It's very dim and broken in places, but I see it all the same, like a faint spectre of itself. I found it out this morning while they were dressing me. It's like a hole in this infernal phantom world. Just put your hand by mine. No—not there. Ah! Yes! I see it. The base of your thumb and a bit of cuff! It looks like the ghost of a bit of your hand sticking out of the darkling sky. Just by it there's a group of stars like a cross coming out."

From that time Davidson began to mend. His account of the change, like his account of the vision, was oddly convincing. Over patches of his field of vision, the phantom world grew fainter, grew transparent, as it were, and through these translucent gaps he began to see dimly the real world about him. The patches grew in size and number, ran together and spread until only here and there were blind spots left upon his eyes. He was able to get up and steer himself about, feed himself once more, read, smoke, and behave like an ordinary citizen again. At first it was very confusing to him to have these two pictures overlapping each other like the changing views of a lantern, but in a little while he began to distinguish the real from the illusory.

At first he was unfeignedly glad, and seemed only too anxious to complete his cure by taking exercise and tonics. But as that odd island of his began to fade away from him, he became queerly interested in it. He wanted particularly to go down into the deep sea again, and would spend half his time wandering about the low-lying parts of London, trying to find the water-logged wreck he had seen drifting. The glare of real daylight very soon impressed him so vividly as to blot out everything of his shadowy world, but of a night time, in a darkened room, he could still see the white-splashed rocks of the island, and the clumsy penguins staggering to and fro. But even these grew fainter and fainter, and, at last, soon after he married my sister, he saw them for the last time.

And now to tell of the queerest thing of all. About two years after his cure I dined with the Davidsons, and after dinner a man named Atkins called in. He is a lieutenant in the Royal Navy, and a pleasant, talkative man. He was on friendly terms with my brother-in-law, and was soon on friendly terms with me. It came out that he was engaged to Davidson's cousin, and incidentally he took out a kind of pocket photograph case to show us a new rendering of his *fiancée*. "And, by the bye," said he, "here's the old *Fulmar*."

Davidson looked at it casually. Then suddenly his face lit up. "Good heavens!" said he. "I could almost swear—"

"What?" said Atkins.

"That I had seen that ship before."

"Don't see how you can have. She hasn't been out of the South Seas for six years, and before then—"

"But," began Davidson, and then: "Yes—that's the ship I dreamt of; I'm sure that's the ship I dreamt of. She was standing off an island that swarmed with penguins, and she fired a gun."

"Good Lord!" said Atkins, who had now heard the particulars of the seizure. "How the deuce could you dream that?"

And then, bit by bit, it came out that on the very day Davidson was seized, HMS *Fulmar* had actually been off a little rock to the south of Antipodes Island. A boat had landed overnight to get penguins' eggs, had been delayed, and a thunderstorm drifting up, the boat's crew had waited until the morning before rejoining the ship. Atkins had been one of them, and he corroborated, word for word, the descriptions Davidson had given of the island and the boat. There is not the slightest doubt in any of our minds that Davidson has really seen the place. In some unaccountable way, while he moved hither and thither in London, his sight moved hither and thither in a manner that corresponded, about the distant island. *How* is absolutely a mystery.

That completes the remarkable story of Davidson's eyes. It's perhaps the best authenticated case in existence of real vision at a distance. Explanation there is none forthcoming, except what Prof. Wade has thrown out. But his explanation involves the Fourth Dimension, and a dissertation on theoretical kinds of space. To talk of there being "a kink in space" seems mere nonsense to me; it may be because I am no mathematician. When I said that nothing would alter the fact that the place is eight thousand miles away, he answered that two points might be a yard away on a sheet of paper, and yet be brought together by bending the paper round. The reader may grasp his argument, but I certainly do not. His idea seems to be that Davidson, stooping between the poles of the big electromagnet, had some extraordinary twist given to his retinal elements through the sudden change in the field of force due to the lightning.

He thinks, as a consequence of this, that it may be possible to live visually in one part of the world, while one lives bodily in another. He has even made some experiments in support of his views; but, so far, he has simply succeeded in blinding a few dogs. I believe that is the net result of his work, though I have not seen him for some weeks. Latterly

I have been so busy with my work in connection with the Saint Pancras installation that I have had little opportunity of calling to see him. But the whole of his theory seems fantastic to me. The facts concerning Davidson stand on an altogether different footing, and I can testify personally to the accuracy of every detail I have given.

THE PLATTNER STORY

Whether the story of Gottfried Plattner is to be credited or not, is a pretty question in the value of evidence. On the one hand, we have seven witnesses—to be perfectly exact, we have six and a half pairs of eyes, and one undeniable fact; and on the other we have—what is it?—prejudice, common sense, the inertia of opinion. Never were there seven more honest-seeming witnesses: never was there a more undeniable fact than the inversion of Gottfried Plattner's anatomical structure, and—never was there a more preposterous story than the one they have to tell! The most preposterous part of the story is the worthy Gottfried's contribution (for I count him as one of the seven). Heaven forbid that I should be led into giving countenance to superstition by a passion for impartiality, and so come to share the fate of Eusapia's patrons! Frankly, I believe there is something crooked about this business of Gottfried Plattner; but what that crooked factor is, I will admit as frankly, I do not know. I have been surprised at the credit accorded to the story in the most unexpected and authoritative quarters. The fairest way to the reader, however, will be for me to tell it without further comment.

Gottfried Plattner is, in spite of his name, a freeborn Englishman. His father was an Alsatian who came to England in the Sixties, married a respectable English girl of unexceptionable antecedents, and died, after a wholesome and uneventful life (devoted, I understand, chiefly to the laying of parquet flooring), in 1887. Gottfried's age is seven-and-twenty. He is, by virtue of his heritage of three languages, Modern Languages Master in a small private school in the South of England. To the casual observer he is singularly like any other Modern Languages Master in any other small private school. His costume is neither very costly nor very fashionable, but, on the other hand, it is not markedly cheap or shabby; his complexion, like his height and his bearing, is inconspicuous. You would notice perhaps that, like the majority of people, his face was not absolutely symmetrical, his right eye a little larger than the left, and his jaw a trifle heavier on the right side. If you, as an ordinary careless person, were to bare his chest and feel his heart beating, you would probably find it quite like the heart of anyone else. But here you and the trained observer would part company. If you found his heart quite ordinary, the trained observer would find it quite otherwise. And once the thing was pointed out to you, you too would perceive the peculiarity easily enough. It is that Gottfried's heart beats on the right side of his body.

Now that is not the only singularity of Gottfried's structure, although it is the only one that would appeal to the untrained mind. Careful sounding of Gottfried's internal arrangements, by a well-known surgeon, seems to point to the fact that all the other unsymmetrical parts of his body are similarly misplaced. The right lobe of his liver is on the left side, the left on his right; while his lungs, too, are similarly contraposed. What is still more singular, unless Gottfried is a consummate actor we must believe that his right hand has recently become his left. Since the occurrences we are about to consider (as impartially as possible), he has found the utmost difficulty in writing except from right to left across the paper with his left hand. He cannot throw with his right hand, he is perplexed at meal times between knife and fork, and his ideas of the rule of the road—he is a cyclist—are still a dangerous confusion. And there is not a scrap of evidence to show that before these occurrences Gottfried was at all left-handed.

There is yet another wonderful fact in this preposterous business. Gottfried produces three photographs of himself. You have him at the age of five or six, thrusting fat legs at you from under a plaid frock, and scowling. In that photograph his left eye is a little larger than his right, and his jaw is a trifle heavier on the left side. This is the reverse of his present living conditions. The photograph of Gottfried at fourteen seems to contradict these facts, but that is because it is one of those cheap "Gem" photographs that were then in vogue, taken direct upon metal, and therefore reversing things just as a looking-glass would. The third photograph represents him at one-and-twenty, and confirms the record of the others. There seems here evidence of the strangest confirmatory character that Gottfried has exchanged his left side for his right. Yet how a human being can be so changed, short of a fantastic and pointless miracle, it is exceedingly hard to suggest.

In one way, of course, these facts might be explicable on the supposition that Plattner has undertaken an elaborate mystification on the strength of his heart's displacement. Photographs may be fudged, and left-handedness imitated. But the character of the man does not lend itself to any such theory. He is quiet, practical, unobtrusive, and thoroughly sane from the Nordau standpoint. He likes beer and smokes moderately, takes walking exercise daily, and has a healthy high estimate of the value of his teaching. He has a good but untrained tenor voice, and takes a pleasure in singing airs of a popular and cheerful character. He is fond, but not morbidly fond, of reading—chiefly fiction pervaded with a vaguely pious optimism,—sleeps well, and rarely dreams. He is, in fact, the very last person to evolve a fantastic fable. Indeed, so far from forcing this story upon the world, he has been singularly reticent on the matter. He meets inquirers with a certain engaging—"bashfulness" is almost the word, that disarms the most suspicious. He seems genuinely ashamed that anything so unusual has occurred to him.

It is to be regretted that Plattner's aversion to the idea of post-mortem dissection may postpone, perhaps for ever, the positive proof that his entire body has had its left and right sides transposed. Upon that fact mainly the credibility of his story hangs. There is no way of taking a man and moving him about *in space*, as ordinary people understand space, that will result in our changing his sides. Whatever you do, his right is still his right, his left his left. You can do that with a perfectly thin and flat thing, of course. If you were to cut a figure out of paper, any figure with a right and left side, you could change its sides simply by lifting it up and turning it over. But with a solid it is different. Mathematical theorists tell us that the only way in which the right and left sides of a solid body can be changed is by taking that body clean out of space as we know it,—taking it out of ordinary existence, that is, and turning it somewhere outside space. This is a little abstruse, no doubt, but anyone with a slight knowledge of mathematical theory will assure the reader of its truth. To put the thing in technical language, the curious inversion of Plattner's right and left sides is proof that he has moved out of our space into what is called the Fourth Dimension, and that he has returned again to our world. Unless we choose to consider ourselves the victims of an elaborate and motiveless fabrication, we are almost bound to believe that this has occurred.

So much for the tangible facts. We come now to the account of the phenomena that attended his temporary disappearance from the world. It appears that in the Sussexville Proprietary School, Plattner not only discharged the duties of Modern Languages Master, but also taught chemistry, commercial geography, bookkeeping, shorthand, drawing, and any other additional subject to which the changing fancies of the boys' parents might direct attention. He knew little or nothing of these various subjects, but in secondary as distinguished from Board or elementary schools, knowledge in the teacher is, very properly, by no means so necessary as high moral character and gentlemanly tone. In chemistry he was particularly deficient, knowing, he says, nothing beyond the Three Gases (whatever the three gases may be). As, however, his pupils began by knowing nothing, and derived all their information from him, this caused him (or anyone) but little inconvenience for several terms. Then a little boy named Whibble joined the school, who had been educated, it seems, by some mischievous relative into an inquiring habit of mind. This little boy followed Plattner's lessons with marked and sustained interest, and in order to exhibit his zeal on the subject, brought at various times substances for Plattner to analyse. Plattner, flattered by this evidence of his power to awaken interest and trusting to the boy's ignorance, analysed these and even made general statements as to their composition. Indeed he was so far stimulated by this pupil as to obtain a work upon analytical chemistry, and study it during his supervision of the evening's preparation. He was surprised to find chemistry quite an interesting subject.

So far the story is absolutely commonplace. But now the greenish powder comes upon the scene. The source of the greenish powder seems, unfortunately, lost. Master Whibble tells a tortuous story of finding it done up in a packet in a disused limekiln near the Downs. It would have been an excellent thing for Plattner, and possibly for Master Whibble's family, if a match could have been applied to that powder there and then. The young gentleman certainly did not bring it to school in a packet, but in a common eight-ounce graduated medicine bottle, plugged with masticated newspaper. He gave it to Plattner at the end of the afternoon school. Four boys had been detained after school prayers in order to complete some neglected tasks, and Plattner was supervising these in the small classroom in which the chemical teaching was conducted. The appliances for the practical teaching of chemistry in the Sussexville Proprietary School, as in most private schools in this country, are characterised by a severe simplicity. They are kept in a cupboard standing in a recess and having about the same capacity as a common travelling trunk. Plattner, being bored with his passive superintendence, seems to have welcomed the intervention of Whibble with his green powder as an agreeable diversion, and, unlocking this cupboard, proceeded at once with his analytical experiments. Whibble sat, luckily for himself, at a safe distance, regarding him. The four malefactors, feigning a profound absorption in their work, watched him furtively with the keenest interest. For even within the limits of the Three Gases, Plattner's practical chemistry was, I understand, temerarious.

They are practically unanimous in their account of Plattner's proceedings. He poured a little of the green powder into a test-tube, and tried the substance with water, hydrochloric acid, nitric acid, and sulphuric acid in succession. Getting no result, he emptied out a little heap—nearly half the bottleful, in fact—upon a slate and tried a match. He held the medicine bottle in his left hand. The stuff began to smoke and melt, and then—exploded with deafening violence and a blinding flash.

The five boys, seeing the flash and being prepared for catastrophes, ducked below their desks, and were none of them seriously hurt. The window was blown out into the playground, and the blackboard on its easel was upset. The slate was smashed to atoms. Some plaster fell from the ceiling. No other damage was done to the school edifice or appliances, and the boys at first, seeing nothing of Plattner, fancied he was knocked down and lying out of their sight below the desks. They jumped out of their places to go to his assistance, and were amazed to find the space empty. Being still confused by the sudden violence of the report, they hurried to the open door, under the impression that he must have been hurt, and have rushed out of the room. But Carson, the foremost, nearly collided in the doorway with the principal, Mr. Lidgett.

Mr. Lidgett is a corpulent, excitable man with one eye. The boys describe him as stumbling into the room mouthing some of those tempered expletives irritable schoolmasters accustom themselves to use— lest worse befall. "Wretched mumchancer!" he said. "Where's Mr. Plattner?" The boys are agreed on the very words. ("Wobbler," "snivelling puppy," and "mumchancer" are, it seems, among the ordinary small change of Mr. Lidgett's scholastic commerce.)

Where's Mr. Plattner? That was a question that was to be repeated many times in the next few days. It really seemed as though the frantic hyperbole, "blown to atoms," had for once realised itself. There was not a visible particle of Plattner to be seen; not a drop of blood nor a stitch of clothing to be found. Apparently he had been blown clean out of existence and left not a wrack behind. Not so much as would cover a sixpenny piece, to quote a proverbial expression! The evidence of his absolute disappearance, as a consequence of the explosion, is indubitable.

It is not necessary to enlarge here upon the commotion excited in the Sussexville Proprietary School, and in Sussexville and elsewhere, by this event. It is quite possible, indeed, that some of the readers of these pages may recall the hearing of some remote and dying version of that excitement during the last summer holidays. Lidgett, it would seem, did everything in his power to suppress and minimise the story. He instituted a penalty of twenty-five lines for any mention of Plattner's name among the boys, and stated in the schoolroom that he was clearly aware of his assistant's whereabouts. He was afraid, he explains, that the possibility of an explosion happening, in spite of the elaborate precautions taken to minimise the practical teaching of chemistry, might injure the reputation of the school; and so might any mysterious quality in Plattner's departure. Indeed, he did everything in his power to make the occurrence seem as ordinary as possible. In particular, he cross-examined the five eye-witnesses of the occurrence so searchingly that they began to doubt the plain evidence of their senses. But, in spite of these efforts, the tale, in a magnified and distorted state, made a nine days' wander in the district, and several parents withdrew their sons on colourable pretexts. Not the least remarkable point in the matter is the fact that a large number of people in the neighbourhood dreamed singularly vivid dreams of Plattner during the period of excitement before the return, and that these dreams had a curious uniformity. In almost all of them Plattner was seen, sometimes singly, sometimes in company, wandering about through a coruscating iridescence. In all cases his face was pale and distressed, and in some he gesticulated towards the dreamer. One or two of the boys, evidently under the influence of nightmare, fancied that Plattner approached them with remarkable swiftness, and seemed to look closely into their very eyes. Others fled with Plattner from the pursuit of vague and extraordinary creatures of a globular shape. But all these fancies were forgotten in inquiries and speculations when, on the Wednesday next but one after the Monday of the explosion, Plattner returned.

The circumstances of his return were as singular as those of his departure. So far as Mr. Lidgett's somewhat choleric outline can be filled in from Plattner's hesitating statements, it would appear that on Wednesday evening, towards the hour of sunset, the former gentleman, having dismissed evening preparation, was engaged in his garden, picking and eating strawberries, a fruit of which he is inordinately fond. It is a large old-fashioned garden, secured from observation, fortunately, by a high and ivy-covered red-brick wall. Just as he was stooping over a particularly prolific plant, there was a flash in the air and a heavy thud, and before he could look round, some heavy body struck him violently from behind. He was pitched forward, crushing the strawberries he held in his hand, and with such force that his silk hat—Mr. Lidgett adheres to the older ideas of scholastic costume—was driven violently down upon his forehead, and almost over one eye. This heavy missile, which slid over him sideways and collapsed into a sitting posture among the strawberry plants, proved to be our long-lost Mr. Gottfried Plattner, in an extremely dishevelled condition. He was collarless and hatless, his linen was dirty, and there was blood upon his hands. Mr. Lidgett was so indignant and surprised that he remained on all-fours, and with his hat jammed down on his eye, while he expostulated vehemently with Plattner for his disrespectful and unaccountable conduct.

This scarcely idyllic scene completes what I may call the exterior version of the Plattner story—its exoteric aspect. It is quite unnecessary to enter here into all the details of his dismissal by Mr. Lidgett. Such details, with the full names and dates and references, will be found in the larger report of these occurrences that was laid before the

Society for the Investigation of Abnormal Phenomena. The singular transposition of Plattner's right and left sides was scarcely observed for the first day or so, and then first in connection with his disposition to write from right to left across the blackboard. He concealed rather than ostended this curious confirmatory circumstance, as he considered it would unfavourably affect his prospects in a new situation. The displacement of his heart was discovered some months after, when he was having a tooth extracted under anaesthetics. He then, very unwillingly, allowed a cursory surgical examination to be made of himself, with a view to a brief account in the *Journal of Anatomy*. That exhausts the statement of the material facts; and we may now go on to consider Plattner's account of the matter.

But first let us clearly differentiate between the preceding portion of this story and what is to follow. All I have told thus far is established by such evidence as even a criminal lawyer would approve. Every one of the witnesses is still alive; the reader, if he have the leisure, may hunt the lads out tomorrow, or even brave the terrors of the redoubtable Lidgett, and cross-examine and trap and test to his heart's content; Gottfried Plattner, himself, and his twisted heart and his three photographs are producible. It may be taken as proved that he did disappear for nine days as the consequence of an explosion; that he returned almost as violently, under circumstances in their nature annoying to Mr. Lidgett, whatever the details of those circumstances may be; and that he returned inverted, just as a reflection returns from a mirror. From the last fact, as I have already stated, it follows almost inevitably that Plattner, during those nine days, must have been in some state of existence altogether out of space. The evidence to these statements is, indeed, far stronger than that upon which most murderers are hanged. But for his own particular account of where he had been, with its confused explanations and well-nigh self-contradictory details, we have only Mr. Gottfried Plattner's word. I do not wish to discredit that, but I must point out—what so many writers upon obscure psychic phenomena fail to do—that we are passing here from the practically undeniable to that kind of matter which any reasonable man is entitled to believe or reject as he thinks proper. The previous statements render it plausible; its discordance with common experience tilts it towards the incredible. I would prefer not to sway the beam of the reader's judgment either way, but simply to tell the story as Plattner told it me.

He gave me his narrative, I may state, at my house at Chislehurst; and so soon as he had left me that evening, I went into my study and wrote down everything as I remembered it. Subsequently he was good enough to read over a type-written copy, so that its substantial correctness is undeniable.

He states that at the moment of the explosion he distinctly thought he was killed. He felt lifted off his feet and driven forcibly backward. It is a curious fact for psychologists that he thought clearly during his backward flight, and wondered whether he should hit the chemistry cupboard or the blackboard easel. His heels struck ground, and he staggered and fell heavily into a sitting position in something soft and firm. For a moment the concussion stunned him. He became aware at once of a vivid scent of singed hair, and he seemed to hear the voice of Lidgett asking for him. You will understand that for a time his mind was greatly confused.

At first he was distinctly under the impression that he was still in the classroom. He perceived quite distinctly the surprise of the boys and the entry of Mr. Lidgett. He is quite positive upon that score. He did not hear their remarks, but that he ascribed to the deafening effect of the experiment. Things about him seemed curiously dark and faint, but his mind explained that on the obvious but mistaken idea that the explosion had engendered a huge volume of dark smoke. Through the dimness the figures of Lidgett and the boys moved, as faint and silent as ghosts. Plattner's face still tingled with the stinging heat of the flash. He was, he says, "all muddled." His first definite thoughts seem to have been of his personal safety. He thought he was perhaps blinded and deafened. He felt his limbs and face in a gingerly manner. Then his perceptions grew clearer, and he was astonished to miss the old familiar desks and other schoolroom furniture about him. Only dim, uncertain, grey shapes stood in the place of these. Then came a thing that made him shout aloud, and awoke his stunned faculties to instant activity. *Two of the boys, gesticulating, walked one after the other clean through him.* Neither manifested the slightest consciousness of his presence. It is difficult to imagine the sensation he felt. They came against him, he says, with no more force than a wisp of mist.

Plattner's first thought after that was that he was dead. Having been brought up with thoroughly sound views in these matters, however, he was a little surprised to find his body still about him. His second conclusion was that he was not dead, but that the others were: that the explosion had destroyed the Sussexville Proprietary School and every soul in it except himself. But that, too, was scarcely satisfactory. He was thrown back upon astonished observation.

Everything about him was extraordinarily dark: at first it seemed to have an altogether ebony blackness. Overhead was a black firmament. The only touch of light in the scene was a faint greenish glow at the edge of the sky in one direction, which threw into prominence a horizon of undulating black hills. This, I say, was his impression at first. As his eye grew accustomed to the darkness, he began to distinguish a faint quality of differentiating greenish colour in the circumambient night. Against this background the furniture and occupants of the classroom, it seems, stood out like phosphorescent spectres, faint and impalpable. He extended his hand, and thrust it without an effort through the wall of the room by the fireplace.

He describes himself as making a strenuous effort to attract attention. He shouted to Lidgett, and tried to seize the boys as they went to and fro. He only desisted from these attempts when Mr. Lidgett, whom he as an Assistant Master naturally disliked, entered the room. He says the sensation of being in the world, and yet not a part of it, was an extraordinarily disagreeable one. He compared his feelings not inaptly to those of a cat watching a mouse through a window. Whenever he made a motion to communicate with the dim, familiar world about him, he found an invisible, incomprehensible barrier preventing intercourse.

He then turned his attention to his solid environment. He found the medicine bottle still unbroken in his hand, with the remainder of the green powder therein. He put this in his pocket, and began to feel about him. Apparently, he was sitting on a boulder of rock covered with a velvety moss. The dark country about him he was unable to see, the faint, misty picture of the schoolroom blotting it out, but he had a feeling (due perhaps to a cold wind) that he was near the crest of a hill, and that a steep valley fell away beneath his feet. The green glow along the edge of the sky seemed to be growing in extent and intensity. He stood up, rubbing his eyes.

It would seem that he made a few steps, going steeply downhill, and then stumbled, nearly fell, and sat down again upon a jagged mass of rock to watch the dawn. He became aware that the world about him was absolutely silent. It was as still as it was dark, and though there was a cold wind blowing up the hill-face, the rustle of grass, the soughing of the boughs that should have accompanied it, were absent. He could hear, therefore, if he could not see, that the hillside upon which he stood was rocky and desolate. The green grew brighter every moment, and as it did so a faint, transparent blood-red mingled with, but did not mitigate, the blackness of the sky overhead and the rocky desolations about him. Having regard to what follows, I am inclined to think that that redness may have been an optical effect due to contrast. Something black fluttered momentarily against the vivid yellow-green of the lower sky, and then the thin and penetrating voice of a bell rose out of the black gulf below him. An oppressive expectation grew with the growing light.

It is probable that an hour or more elapsed while he sat there, the strange green light growing brighter every moment, and spreading slowly, in flamboyant fingers, upward towards the zenith. As it grew, the spectral vision of *our* world became relatively or absolutely fainter. Probably both, for the time must have been about that of our earthly sunset. So far as his vision of our world went, Plattner by his few steps downhill, had passed through the floor of the classroom, and was now, it seemed, sitting in mid-air in the larger schoolroom downstairs. He saw the boarders distinctly, but much more faintly than he had seen Lidgett. They were preparing their evening tasks, and he noticed with interest that several were cheating with their Euclid riders by means of a crib, a compilation whose existence he had hitherto never suspected. As the time passed they faded steadily, as steadily as the light of the green dawn increased.

Looking down into the valley, he saw that the light had crept far down its rocky sides, and that the profound blackness of the abyss was now broken by a minute green glow, like the light of a glow-worm. And almost immediately the limb of a huge heavenly body of blazing green rose over the basaltic undulations of the distant hills, and the monstrous hill-masses about him came out gaunt and desolate, in green light and deep, ruddy black shadows. He became aware of a vast number of ball-shaped objects drifting as thistledown drifts over the high ground. There were none of these nearer to him than the opposite side of the gorge. The bell below twanged quicker and quicker, with something like impatient insistence, and several lights moved hither and thither. The boys at work at their desks were now almost imperceptibly faint.

This extinction of our world, when the green sun of this other universe rose, is a curious point upon which Plattner insists. During the Other-World night it is difficult to move about, on account of the vividness with which the things of this world are visible. It becomes a riddle to explain why, if this is the case, we in this world catch no glimpse of the Other-World. It is due, perhaps, to the comparatively vivid illumination of this world of ours. Plattner describes the midday of the Other-World, at its brightest, as not being nearly so bright as this world at full moon, while its night is profoundly black. Consequently, the amount of light, even in an ordinary dark room, is sufficient to render the things of the Other-World invisible, on the same principle that faint phosphorescence is only visible in the profoundest darkness. I have tried, since he told me his story, to see something of the Other-World by sitting for a long space in a photographer's dark room at night. I have certainly seen indistinctly the form of greenish slopes and rocks, but only, I must admit, very indistinctly indeed. The reader may possibly be more successful. Plattner tells me that since his return he has seen and recognised places in the Other-World in his dreams, but this is probably due to his memory of these scenes. It seems quite possible that people with unusually keen eyesight may occasionally catch a glimpse of this strange Other-World about us.

However, this is a digression. As the green sun rose, a long street of black buildings became perceptible, though only darkly and indistinctly, in the gorge, and, after some hesitation, Plattner began to clamber down the precipitous decent towards them. The descent was long and exceedingly tedious, being so not only by the extraordinary steepness, but also by reason of the looseness of the boulders with which the whole face of the hill was strewn. The noise of his descent—now and then his heels struck fire from the rocks—seemed now the only sound in the universe, for the beating of the bell had ceased. As he drew nearer he perceived that the various edifices had a singular resemblance to tombs and mausoleums and monuments, saving only that they were all uniformly black instead of being white as most sepulchres are. And then he saw, crowding out of the largest building very much as people disperse from church, a number of pallid, rounded, pale-green figures. These scattered in several directions about the broad street of the place, some going through side alleys and reappearing upon the steepness of the hill, others entering some of the small black buildings which lined the way.

At the sight of these things drifting up towards him, Plattner stopped, staring. They were not walking, they were indeed limbless; and they had the appearance of human heads beneath which a tadpole-like body swung. He was too astonished at their strangeness, too full indeed of strangeness, to be seriously alarmed by them. They drove towards him, in front of the chill wind that was blowing uphill, much as soap-bubbles drive before a draught. And as he looked at the nearest of those aproaching, he saw it was indeed a human head, albeit with singularly large eyes, and wearing such an expression of distress and anguish as he had never seen before upon mortal countenance. He was surprised to find that it did not turn to regard him, but seemed to be watching and following some unseen moving thing. For a moment he was puzzled, and then it occurred to him that this creature was watching with its enormous eyes something that was happening in the world he had just left. Nearer it came, and nearer, and he was too astonished to cry out. It made a very faint fretting sound as it came close to him. Then it struck his face with a gentle pat—its touch was very cold—and drove past him, and upward towards the crest of the hill.

An extraordinary conviction flashed across Plattner's mind that this head had a strong likeness to Lidgett. Then he turned his attention to the other heads that were now swarming thickly up the hillside. None made the slightest sign of recognition. One or two, indeed, came close to his head and almost followed the example of the first, but he dodged convulsively out of the way. Upon most of them he saw the same expression of unavailing regret he had seen upon the first, and heard the same faint sounds of wretchedness from them. One or two wept, and one rolling swiftly uphill wore an expression of diabolical rage. But others were cold, and several had a look of gratified interest in their eyes. One, at least, was almost in an ecstasy of happiness. Plattner does not remember that he recognised any more likenesses in those he saw at this time.

For several hours, perhaps, Plattner watched these strange things dispersing themselves over the hills, and not till long after they had ceased to issue from the clustering black buildings in the gorge did he resume his downward climb. The darkness about him increased so much that he had a difficulty in stepping true. Overhead the sky was now a bright pale green. He felt neither hunger nor thirst. Later, when he did, he found a chilly stream running down the centre of the gorge, and the rare moss upon the boulders, when he tried it at last in desperation, was good to eat.

He groped about among the tombs that ran down the gorge, seeking vaguely for some clue to these inexplicable things. After a long time he came to the entrance of the big mausoleum-like building from which the heads had issued. In this he found a group of green lights burning upon a kind of basaltic altar, and a bell-rope from a belfry overhead hanging down into the centre of the place. Round the wall ran a lettering of fire in a character unknown to him. While he was still wondering at the purport of these things, he heard the receding tramp of heavy feet echoing far down the street. He ran out into the darkness again, but he could see nothing. He had a mind to pull the bell-rope, and finally decided to follow the footsteps. But although he ran far, he never overtook them; and his shouting was of no avail. The gorge seemed to extend an interminable distance. It was as dark as earthly starlight throughout its length, while the ghastly green day lay along the upper edge of its precipices. There were none of the heads, now, below. They were all, it seemed, busily occupied along the upper slopes. Looking up, he saw them drifting hither and thither, some hovering stationary, some flying swiftly through the air. It reminded him, he said, of "big snowflakes"; only these were black and pale green.

In pursuing the firm, undeviating footsteps that he never overtook, in groping into new regions of this endless devil's dyke, in clambering up and down the pitiless heights, in wandering about the summits, and in watching the drifting faces, Plattner states that he spent the better part of seven or eight days. He did not keep count, he says. Though once or twice he found eyes watching him, he had word with no living soul. He slept among the rocks on the hillside. In the gorge things earthly were invisible, because, from the earthly standpoint, it was far underground. On the altitudes, so soon as the earthly day began, the world became visible to him. He found himself sometimes stumbling over the dark green rocks, or arresting himself on a precipitous brink, while all about him the green branches of the Sussexville lanes were swaying; or, again, he seemed to be walking through the Sussexville streets, or watching unseen the private business of some household.

And then it was he discovered, that to almost every human being in our world there pertained some of these drifting heads; that everyone in the world is watched intermittently by these helpless disembodiments.

What are they—these Watchers of the Living? Plattner never learned. But two that presently found and followed him, were like his childhood's memory of his father and mother. Now and then other faces turned their eyes upon him: eyes like those of dead people who had swayed him, or injured him, or helped him in his youth and manhood. Whenever they looked at him, Plattner was overcome with a strange sense of responsibility. To his mother he ventured to speak; but she made no answer. She looked sadly, steadfastly, and tenderly— a little reproachfully, too, it seemed—into his eyes.

He simply tells this story: he does not endeavour to explain. We are left to surmise who these Watchers of the Living may be, or if they are indeed the Dead, why they should so closely and passionately watch a world they have left for ever. It may be—indeed to my mind it seems just—that, when our life has closed, when evil or good is no longer a choice for us, we may still have to witness the working out of the train of consequences we have laid. If human souls continue after death, then surely human interests continue after death. But that is merely my own guess at the meaning of the things seen. Plattner offers no interpretation, for none was given him. It is well the reader should understand this clearly. Day after day, with his head reeling, he wandered about this green-lit world outside the world, weary and, towards the end, weak and hungry. By day—by our earthly day, that is—the ghostly vision of the old familiar scenery of Sussexville, all about him, irked and worried him. He could not see where to put his feet, and ever and again with a chilly touch one of these Watching Souls would come against his face. And after dark the multitude of these Watchers about him, and their intent distress, confused his mind beyond describing. A great longing to return to the earthly life that was so near and yet so remote consumed him. The unearthliness of things about him produced a positively painful mental distress. He was worried beyond describing by his own particular followers. He would shout at them to desist from staring at him, scold at them, hurry away from them. They were always mute and intent. Run as he might over the uneven ground, they followed his destinies.

On the ninth day, towards evening, Plattner heard the invisible footsteps approaching, far away down the gorge. He was then wandering over the broad crest of the same hill upon which he had fallen in his entry into this strange Other-World of his. He turned to hurry down into the gorge, feeling his way hastily, and was arrested by the sight of the thing that was happening in a room in a back street near the school. Both of the people in the room he knew by sight. The windows were open, and blinds up, and the setting sun shone clearly into it, so that it came out quite brightly at first, a vivid oblong of room, lying like a magic-lantern picture upon the black landscape and the livid green dawn. In addition to the sunlight, a candle had just been lit in the room.

On the bed lay a lank man, his ghastly white face terrible upon the tumbled pillow. His clenched hands were raised above his head. A little table beside the bed carried a few medicine bottles, some toast and water, and an empty glass. Every now and then the lank man's lips fell apart, to indicate a word he could not articulate. But the woman did not notice that he wanted anything, because she was busy turning out papers from an old-fashioned bureau in the opposite corner of the room. At first the picture was very vivid indeed, but as the green dawn behind it grew brighter and brighter, so it became fainter and more and more transparent.

As the echoing footsteps paced nearer and nearer, those footsteps that sound so loud in that Other-World and come so silently in this, Plattner perceived about him a great multitude of dim faces gathering together out of the darkness and watching the two people in the room. Never before had he seen so many of the Watchers of the Living. A multitude had eyes only for the sufferer in the room, another multitude, in infinite anguish, watched the woman as she hunted with greedy eyes for something she could not find. They crowded about Plattner, they came across his sight and buffeted his face, the noise of their unavailing regrets was all about him. He saw clearly only now and then. At other times the pictures quivered dimly, through the veil of green reflections upon their movements. In the room it must have been very still, and Plattner says the candle flame streamed up into a perfectly vertical line of smoke, but in his ears each footfall and its echoes beat like a clap of thunder. And the faces! Two more particularly, near the woman's: one a woman's also, white and clear-featured, a face which might have once been cold and hard but which was now softened by the touch of a wisdom strange to earth. The other might have been the woman's father. Both were evidently absorbed in the contemplation of some act of hateful meanness, so it seemed, which they could no longer guard against and prevent. Behind were others, teachers it may be who had taught ill, friends whose influence had failed. And over the man, too—a multitude, but none that seemed to be parents or teachers! Faces that might once have been coarse, now purged to strength by sorrow! And in the forefront one face, a girlish one, neither angry nor remorseful but merely patient and weary, and, as it seemed to Plattner, waiting for relief. His powers of description fail him at the memory of this multitude of ghastly countenances. They gathered on the stroke of the bell. He saw them all in the space of a second. It would seem that he was so worked upon by his excitement that quite involuntarily his restless fingers took the bottle of green powder out of his pocket and held it before him. But he does not remember that.

Abruptly the footsteps ceased. He waited for the next and there was silence, and then suddenly, cutting through the unexpected stillness like a keen, thin blade, came the first stroke of the bell. At that the multitudinous faces swayed to and fro, and a louder crying began all about him. The woman did not hear; she was burning something now in the candle flame. At the second stroke everything grew dim, and a breath of wind, icy cold, blew through the host of watchers. They swirled about him like an eddy of dead leaves in the spring, and at the third stroke something was extended through them to the bed. You have heard of a beam of light. This was like a beam of darkness, and looking again at it, Plattner saw that it was a shadowy arm and hand.

The green sun was now topping the black desolations of the horizon, and the vision of the room was very faint. Plattner could see that the white of the bed struggled, and was convulsed; and that the woman looked round over her shoulder at it, startled.

The cloud of watchers lifted high like a puff of green dust before the wind, and swept swiftly downward towards the temple in the gorge. Then suddenly Plattner understood the meaning of the shadowy black arm that stretched across his shoulder and clutched its prey. He did not dare turn his head to see the Shadow behind the arm. With a violent effort, and covering his eyes, he set himself to run, made perhaps twenty strides, then slipped on a boulder and fell. He fell forward on his hands; and the bottle smashed and exploded as he touched the ground.

In another moment he found himself, stunned and bleeding, sitting face to face with Lidgett in the old walled garden behind the school.

———

There the story of Plattner's experiences ends. I have resisted, I believe successfully, the natural disposition of a writer of fiction to dress up incidents of this sort. I have told the thing as far as possible in the order in which Platner told it to me. I have carefully avoided any attempt at style, effect, or construction. It would have been easy, for instance, to have worked the scene of the death-bed into a kind of plot in which Plattner might have been involved. But quite apart from the objectionableness of falsifying a most extraordinary true story, any such trite devices would spoil, to my mind, the peculiar effect of this dark world, and its livid green illumination and its drifting Watchers of the Living, which, unseen and unapproachable to us, is yet lying all about us.

It remains to add, that a death did actually occur in Vincent Terrace, just beyond the school garden, and, so far as can be proved, at the moment of Plattner's return. Deceased was a rate-collector and insurance agent. His widow, who was much younger than himself, married last month a Mr. Whymper, a veterinary surgeon of Allbeeding. As the portion of this story given here has in various forms circulated orally in Sussexville, she has consented to my use of her name, on condition that I make it distinctly known that she emphatically contradicts every detail of Plattner's account of her husband's last moments. She burnt no will, she says, although Plattner never accused her of doing so: her husband made but one will, and that just after their marriage. Certainly, from a man who had never seen it, Plattner's account of the furniture of the room was curiously accurate.

One other thing, even at the risk of an irksome repetition, I must insist upon lest I seem to favour the credulous superstitious view. Plattner's absence from the world for nine days is, I think, proved. But that does not prove his story. It is quite conceivable that even outside space hallucinations may be possible. That, at least, the reader must bear distinctly in mind.

Under the Knife

"What if I die under it?" The thought recurred again and again as I walked home from Haddon's. It was a purely personal question. I was spared the deep anxieties of a married man, and I knew there were few of my intimate friends but would find my death troublesome chiefly on account of their duty of regret. I was surprised indeed and perhaps a little humiliated, as I turned the matter over, to think how few could possibly exceed the conventional requirement. Things came before me stripped of glamour, in a clear dry light, during that walk from Haddon's house over Primrose Hill. There were the friends of my youth; I perceived now that our affection was a tradition which we foregathered rather laboriously to maintain. There were the rivals and helpers of my later career: I suppose I have been cold-blooded or un-demonstrative—one perhaps implies the other. It may be that even the capacity for friendship is a question of physique. There had been a time in my own life when I had grieved bitterly enough at the loss of a friend; but as I walked home that afternoon the emotional side of my imagination was dormant. I could not pity myself, nor feel sorry for my friends, nor conceive of them as grieving for me.

I was interested in this deadness of my emotional nature—no doubt a concomitant of my stagnating physiology; and my thoughts wandered off along the line it suggested. Once before, in my hot youth, I had suffered a sudden loss of blood and had been within an ace of death. I remembered now that my affections as well as my passions had drained out of me, leaving scarcely anything but a tranquil resignation, a dreg of self-pity. It had been weeks before the old ambitions, and tendernesses, and all the complex moral interplay of a man, had reasserted themselves. Now again I was bloodless; I had been feeling down for a week or more. I was not even hungry. It occurred to me that the real meaning of this numbness might be a gradual slipping away from the pleasure-pain guidance of the animal man. It has been proven, I take it, as thoroughly as anything can be proven in this world, that the higher emotions, the moral feelings, even the subtle tendernesses of love, are evolved from the elemental desires and fears of the simple animal: they are the harness in which man's mental freedom goes. And it may be that, as death overshadows us, as our possibility of acting diminishes, this complex growth of balanced impulse, propensity, and aversion whose interplay inspires our acts, goes with it. Leaving what?

I was suddenly brought back to reality by an imminent collision with a butcher-boy's tray. I found that I was crossing the bridge over the Regent's Park Canal which runs parallel with that in the Zoological Gardens. The boy in blue had been looking over his shoulder at a black barge advancing slowly, towed by a gaunt white horse. In the Gardens a nurse was leading three happy little children over the bridge. The trees were bright green; the spring hopefulness was still unstained by the dusts of summer; the sky in the water was bright and clear, but broken by long waves, by quivering bands of black, as the barge drove through. The breeze was stirring; but it did not stir me as the spring breeze used to do.

Was this dulness of feeling in itself an anticipation? It was curious that I could reason and follow out a network of suggestion as clearly as ever: so, at least, it seemed to me. It was calmness rather than dulness that was coming upon me. Was there any ground for the belief in the presentiment of death? Did a man near to death begin instinctively to withdraw himself from the meshes of matter and sense, even before the cold hand was laid upon his? I felt strangely isolated—isolated without regret—from the life and existence about me. The children playing in the sun and gathering strength and experience for the business of life, the park-keeper gossiping with a nursemaid, the nursing mother, the young couple intent upon each other as they passed me, the trees by the wayside spreading new pleading leaves to the sunlight, the stir in their branches—I had been part of it all, but I had nearly done with it now.

Some way down the Broad Walk I perceived that I was tired, and that my feet were heavy. It was hot that afternoon, and I turned aside and sat down on one of the green chairs that line the way. In a minute I had dozed into a dream, and the tide of my thoughts washed up a vision of the resurrection. I was still sitting in the chair, but I thought myself actually dead, withered, tattered, dried, one eye (I saw) pecked out by birds. "Awake!" cried a voice; and incontinently the dust of the path and the mould under the grass became insurgent. I had never before thought of Regent's Park as a cemetery, but now through the trees, stretching as far as eye could see, I beheld a flat plain of writhing graves and heeling tombstones. There seemed to be some trouble: the rising dead appeared to stifle as they struggled upward, they bled in their struggles, the red flesh was tattered away from the white bones. "Awake!" cried a voice; but I determined I would not rise to such horrors. "Awake!" They would not let me alone. "Wike up!" said an angry voice. A cockney angel! The man who sells the tickets was shaking me, demanding my penny.

I paid my penny, pocketed my ticket, yawned, stretched my legs, and, feeling now rather less torpid, got up and walked on towards Langham Place. I speedily lost myself again in a shifting maze of thoughts about death. Going across Marylebone Road into that crescent at the end of Langham Place, I had the narrowest escape from the shaft of a cab, and went on my way with a palpitating heart and a bruised shoulder. It struck me that it would have been curious if my meditations on my death on the morrow had led to my death that day.

But I will not weary you with more of my experiences that day and the next. I knew more and more certainly that I should die under the operation; at times I think I was inclined to pose to myself. At home I found everything prepared; my room cleared of needless objects and hung with white sheets; a nurse installed and already at loggerheads with my housekeeper. They wanted me to go to bed early, and after a little resistance I obeyed.

In the morning I was very indolent, and though I read my newspapers and the letters that came by the first post, I did not find them very interesting. There was a friendly note from Addison, my old school friend, calling my attention to two discrepancies and a printer's error in my new book, with one from Langridge venting some vexation over Minton. The rest were business communications. I had a cup of tea but nothing to eat. The glow of pain at my side seemed more massive. I knew it was pain, and yet, if you can understand, I did not find it very painful. I had been awake and hot and thirsty in the night, but in the morning bed felt comfortable. In the night-time I had lain thinking of things that were past; in the morning I dozed over the question of immortality. Haddon came, punctual to the minute, with a neat black bag; and Mowbray soon followed. Their arrival stirred me up a little. I began to take a more personal interest in the proceedings. Haddon moved the little octagonal table close to the bedside, and, with his broad black back to me, began taking things out of his bag. I heard the light click of steel upon steel. My imagination, I found, was not altogether stagnant. "Will you hurt me much?" I said in an off-hand tone.

"Not a bit," Haddon answered over his shoulder. "We shall chloroform you. Your heart's as sound as a bell." And as he spoke, I had a whiff of the pungent sweetness of the anaesthetic.

They stretched me out, with a convenient exposure of my side, and, almost before I realised what was happening, the chloroform was being administered. It stings the nostrils, and there is a suffocating sensation, at first. I knew I should die—that this was the end of consciousness for me. And suddenly I felt that I was not prepared for death: I had a vague sense of a duty overlooked—I knew not what. What was it I had not done? I could think of nothing more to do, nothing desirable left in life; and yet I had the strangest disinclination for death. And the physical sensation was painfully oppressive. Of course the doctors did not know they were going to kill me. Possibly I struggled. Then I fell motionless, and a great silence, a monstrous silence, and an impenetrable blackness came upon me.

There must have been an interval of absolute unconsciousness, seconds or minutes. Then, with a chilly, unemotional clearness, I perceived that I was not yet dead. I was still in my body; but all the multitudinous sensations that come sweeping from it to make up the background of consciousness had gone, leaving me free of it all. No, not free of it all; for as yet something still held me to the poor stark flesh upon the bed—held me, yet not so closely that I did not feel myself external to it, independent of it, straining away from it, I do not think I saw, I do not think I heard; but I perceived all that was going on, and it was as if I both heard and saw. Haddon was bending over me, Mowbray behind me; the scalpel—it was a large scalpel—was cutting my flesh at the side under the flying ribs. It was interesting to see myself cut like cheese, without a pang, without even a qualm. The interest was much of a quality with that one might feel in a game of chess between strangers. Haddon's face was firm and his hand steady; but I was surprised to perceive (*how* I know not) that he was feeling the gravest doubt as to his own wisdom in the conduct of the operation.

Mowbray's thoughts, too, I could see. He was thinking that Haddon's manner showed too much of the specialist. New suggestions came up like bubbles through a stream of frothing meditation, and burst one after another in the little bright spot of his consciousness. He could not help noticing and admiring Haddon's swift dexterity, in spite of his envious quality and his disposition to detract. I saw my liver exposed. I was puzzled at my own condition. I did not feel that I was dead, but I was different in some way from my living self. The grey depression that had weighed on me for a year or more and coloured all my thoughts, was gone. I perceived and thought without any emotional tint at all. I wondered if everyone perceived things in this way under chloroform, and forgot it again when he came out of it. It would be inconvenient to look into some heads, and not forget.

Although I did not think that I was dead, I still perceived quite clearly that I was soon to die. This brought me back to the consideration of Haddon's proceedings. I looked into his mind, and saw that he was afraid of cutting a branch of the portal vein. My attention was distracted from details by the curious changes going on in his mind. His consciousness was like the quivering little spot of light which is thrown by the mirror of a galvanometer. His thoughts ran under it like a stream, some through the focus bright and distinct, some shadowy in the half-light of the edge. Just now the little glow was steady; but the least movement on Mowbray's part, the slightest sound from outside, even a faint difference in the slow movement of the living flesh he was cutting, set the light-spot shivering and spinning. A new sense-impression came rushing up through the flow of thoughts, and lo! the light-spot jerked away towards it, swifter than a frightened fish. It was wonderful to think that upon that unstable, fitful thing depended all the complex motions of the man; that for the next five minutes, therefore, my life hung upon its movements. And he was growing more and more nervous in his work. It was as if a little picture of a cut vein grew brighter, and struggled to oust from his brain another picture of a cut falling short of the mark. He was afraid: his dread of cutting too little was battling with his dread of cutting too far.

Then, suddenly, like an escape of water, from under a lock-gate, a great uprush of horrible realisation set all his thoughts swirling, and simultaneously I perceived that the vein was cut. He started back with a hoarse exclamation, and I saw the brown-purple blood gather in a swift bead, and run trickling. He was horrified. He pitched the red-stained scalpel onto the octagonal table; and instantly both doctors flung themselves upon me, making hasty and ill-conceived efforts to remedy the disaster. "Ice!" said Mowbray, gasping. But I knew that I was killed, though my body still clung to me.

I will not describe their belated endeavours to save me, though I perceived every detail. My perceptions were sharper and swifter than they had ever been in life; my thoughts rushed through my mind with incredible swiftness, but with perfect definition. I can only compare their crowded clarity to the effects of a reasonable dose of opium. In a moment it would all be over, and I should be free. I knew I was immortal, but what would happen I did not know. Should I drift off presently, like a puff of smoke from a gun, in some kind of half-material body, an attenuated version of my material self? Should I find myself suddenly among the innumerable hosts of the dead, and know the world about me for the phantasmagoria it had always seemed? Should I drift to some spiritualistic *séance,* and there make foolish, incomprehensible attempts to affect a purblind medium? It was a state of unemotional curiosity, of colourless expectation. And then I realised a growing stress upon me, a feeling as though some huge human magnet was drawing me upward out of my body. The stress grew and grew. I seemed an atom for which monstrous forces were fighting. For one brief, terrible moment sensation came back to me. That feeling of falling headlong which comes in nightmares, that feeling a thousand times intensified, that and a black horror swept across my thoughts in a torrent. Then the two doctors, the naked body with its cut side, the little room, swept away from under me and vanished as a speck of foam vanishes down an eddy.

I was in mid-air. Far below was the West End of London, receding rapidly,—for I seemed to be flying swiftly upward,—and, as it receded, passing westward, like a panorama. I could see, through the faint haze of smoke, the innumerable roofs chimney-set, the narrow roadways stippled with people and conveyances, the little specks of squares, and the church steeples like thorns sticking out of the fabric. But it spun away as the earth rotated on its axis, and in a few seconds (as it seemed) I was over the scattered clumps of town about Ealing, the little Thames a thread of blue to the south, and the Chiltern Hills, and the North Downs coming up like the rim of a basin, far away and faint with haze. Up I rushed. And at first I had not the faintest conception what this headlong rush upward could mean.

Every moment the circle of scenery beneath me grew wider and wider, and the details of town and field, of hill and valley, got more and more hazy and pale and indistinct, a luminous grey was mingled more and more with the blue of the hills and the green of the open meadows; and a little patch of cloud, low and far to the west, shone ever more dazzlingly white. Above, as the veil of atmosphere between myself and outer space grew thinner, the sky, which had been a fair springtime blue at first, grew deeper and richer in colour, passing steadily through the intervening shades until presently it was as dark as the blue sky of midnight, and presently as black as the blackness of a frosty starlight, and at last as black as no blackness I had ever beheld. And first one star and then many, and at last an innumerable host broke out upon the sky: more stars than anyone has ever seen from the face of the earth. For the blueness of the sky is the light of the sun and stars sifted and spread abroad blindingly: there is diffused light even in the darkest skies of winter, and we do not see the stars by day only because of the dazzling irradiation of the sun. But now I saw things—I know not how; assuredly with no mortal eyes—and that defect of bedazzlement blinded me no longer. The sun was incredibly strange and wonderful. The body of it was a disc of blinding white light: not yellowish as it seems to those who live upon the earth, but livid white, all streaked with scarlet streaks and rimmed about with a fringe of writhing tongues of red fire. And, shooting half-way across the heavens from either side of it, and brighter than the Milky Way, were two pinions of silver-white, making it look more like those winged globes I have seen in Egyptian sculpture, than anything else I can remember upon earth. These I knew for the solar corona, though I had never seen anything of it but a picture during the days of my earthly life.

When my attention came back to the earth again, I saw that it had fallen very far away from me. Field and town were long since indistinguishable, and all the varied hues of the country were merging into a uniform bright grey, broken only by the brilliant white of the clouds that lay scattered in flocculent masses over Ireland and the west of England. For now I could see the outlines of the north of France and Ireland, and all this island of Britain save where Scotland passed over the horizon to the north, or where the coast was blurred or obliterated by cloud. The sea was a dull grey, and darker than the land; and the whole panorama was rotating slowly towards the east.

All this had happened so swiftly that, until I was some thousand miles or so from the earth, I had no thought for myself. But now I perceived I had neither hands nor feet, neither parts nor organs, and that I felt neither alarm or pain. All about me I perceived that the vacancy (for I had already left the air behind) was cold beyond the imagination of man; but it troubled me not. The sun's rays shot through the void powerless to light or heat until they should strike the matter in their course. I saw things with a serene self-forgetfulness, even as if I were God. And down below there, rushing away from me,—countless miles in a second,—where a little dark spot on the grey marked the position of London, two doctors were struggling to restore life to the poor hacked and outworn shell I had abandoned. I felt then such release, such serenity as I can compare to no mortal delight I have ever known.

It was only after I had perceived all these things that the meaning of that headlong rush of the earth grew into comprehension. Yet it was so simple, so obvious, that I was amazed at my never anticipating the thing that was happening to me. I had suddenly been cut adrift from matter: all that was material of me was there upon earth, whirling away through space, held to the earth by gravitation, partaking of the earth's inertia, moving in its wreath of epicycles round the sun, and with the sun and the planets on their vast march through space. But the immaterial has no inertia, feels nothing of the pull of matter for matter: where it parts from its garment of flesh, there it remains (so far as space concerns it any longer) immovable in space. *I* was not leaving the earth: the earth was leaving *me,* and not only the earth, but the whole solar system was streaming past. And about me in space, invisible to me, scattered in the wake of the earth upon its journey, there must be an innumerable multitude of souls, stripped like myself of the material, stripped like myself of the passions of the individual and the generous emotions of the gregarious brute, naked intelligences, things of newborn wonder and thought, marvelling at the strange release that had suddenly come on them!

As I receded faster and faster from the strange white sun in the black heavens, and from the broad and shining earth upon which my being had begun, I seemed to grow, in some incredible manner, vast: vast as regards this world I had left, vast as regards the moments and periods of a human life. Very soon I saw the full circle of the earth, slightly gibbous, like the moon when she nears her full, but very large; and the silver shape of America was now in the noonday blaze wherein (as it seemed) little England had been basking but a few minutes ago. At first the earth was large and shone in the heavens, filling a great part of them; but every moment she grew smaller and more distant. As she shrunk, the broad moon in its third quarter crept into view over the rim of her disc. I looked for the constellations. Only that part of Aries directly behind the sun, and the Lion, which the earth covered, were hidden. I recognised the tortuous, tattered band of the Milky Way, with Vega very bright between sun and earth; and Sirius and Orion shone splendid against the unfathomable blackness in the opposite quarter of the heavens. The Pole Star was overhead, and the Great Bear hung over the circle of the earth. And away beneath and beyond the shining corona of the sun were strange groupings of stars I had never seen in my life—notably, a dagger-shaped group that I knew for the Southern Cross. All these were no larger than when they had shone on earth; but the little stars that one scarcely sees shone now against the setting of black vacancy as brightly as the first-magnitudes had done, while the larger worlds were points of indescribable glory and colour. Aldebaran was a spot of blood-red fire, and Sirius condensed to one point the light of a world of sapphires. And they shone steadily: they did not scintillate, they were calmly glorious. My impressions had an adamantine hardness and brightness: there was no blurring softness, no atmosphere, nothing but infinite darkness set with the myriads of these acute and brilliant points and specks of light. Presently, when I looked again, the little earth seemed no bigger than the sun, and it dwindled and turned as I looked until, in a second's space (as it seemed to me), it was halved; and so it went on swiftly dwindling. Far away in the opposite direction, a little pinkish pin's head of light, shining steadily, was the planet Mars. I swam motionless in vacancy, and, without a trace of terror or astonishment, watched the speck of cosmic dust we call the world fall away from me.

Presently it dawned upon me that my sense of duration had changed: that my mind was moving not faster but infinitely slower, that between each separate impression there was a period of many days. The moon spun once round the earth as I noted this; and I perceived clearly the motion of Mars in his orbit. Moreover, it appeared as if the time between thought and thought grew steadily greater, until at last a thousand years was but a moment in my perception.

At first the constellations had shone motionless against the black background of infinite space; but presently it seemed as though the group of stars about Hercules and the Scorpion was contracting, while Orion and Aldebaran and their neighbours were scattering apart. Flashing suddenly out of the darkness there came a flying multitude of particles of rock, glittering like dust-specks in a sunbeam, and encompassed in a faintly luminous haze. They swirled all about me, and vanished again in a twinkling far behind. And then I saw that a bright spot of light, that shone a little to one side of my path, was growing very rapidly larger, and perceived that it was the planet Saturn rushing towards me. Larger and larger it grew, swallowing up the heavens behind it, and hiding every moment a fresh multitude of stars. I perceived its flattened, whirling body, its disc-like belt, and seven of its little satellites. It grew and grew, till it towered enormous; and then I plunged amid a streaming multitude of clashing stones and dancing dust-particles and gas-eddies, and saw for a moment the mighty triple belt like three concentric arches of moonlight above me, its shadow black on the boiling tumult below. These things happened in one-tenth of the time it takes to tell of them. The planet went by like a flash of lightning; for a few seconds it blotted out the sun, and there and then became a mere black, dwindling, winged patch against the light. The earth, the mother mote of my being, I could no longer see.

So with a stately swiftness, in the profoundest silence, the solar system fell from me, as if it had been a garment, until the sun was a mere star amid the multitude of stars, with its eddy of planet-specks, lost in the confused glittering of the remoter light. I was no longer a denizen of the solar system: I had come to the Outer Universe, I seemed to grasp and comprehend the whole world of matter. Ever more swiftly the stars closed in about the spot where Antares and Vega had vanished in a luminous haze, until that part of the sky had the semblance of a whirling mass of nebulae, and ever before me yawned vaster gaps of vacant blackness and the stars shone fewer and fewer. It seemed as if I moved towards a point between Orion's belt and sword; and the void about that region opened vaster and vaster every second, an incredible gulf of nothingness, in which I was falling. Faster and ever faster the universe rushed by, a hurry of whirling motes at last, speeding silently into the void. Stars glowing brighter and brighter, with their circling planets catching the light in a ghostly fashion as I neared them, shone out and vanished again into inexistence; faint comets, clusters of meteorites, winking specks of matter, eddying light-points, whizzed past, some perhaps a hundred millions of miles or so from me at most, few nearer, travelling with unimaginable rapidity, shooting constellations, momentary darts of fire, through that black, enormous night. More than anything else it was like a dusty draught, sunbeam-lit. Broader, and wider, and deeper grew the starless space, the vacant Beyond, into which I was being drawn. At last a quarter of the heavens was black and blank, and the whole headlong rush of stellar universe closed in behind me like a veil of light that is gathered together. It drove away from me like a monstrous jack-o'-lantern driven by the wind. I had come out into the wilderness of space. Ever the vacant blackness grew broader, until the hosts of the stars seemed only like a swarm of fiery specks hurrying away from me, inconceivably remote, and the darkness, the nothingness and emptiness, was about me on every side. Soon the little universe of matter, the cage of points in which I had begun to be, was dwindling, now to a whirling disc of luminous glittering, and now to one minute disc of hazy light. In a little while it would shrink to a point, and at last would vanish altogether.

Suddenly feeling came back to me—feeling in the shape of overwhelming terror: such a dread of those dark vastitudes as no words can describe, a passionate resurgence of sympathy and social desire. Were there other souls, invisible to me as I to them, about me in the blackness? or was I indeed, even as I felt, alone? Had I passed out of being into something that was neither being nor not-being? The covering of the body, and covering of matter, had been torn from me, and the hallucinations of companionship and security. Everything was black and silent. I had ceased to be. I was nothing. There was nothing, save only that infinitesimal dot of light that dwindled in the gulf. I strained myself to hear and see, and for a while there was naught but infinite silence, intolerable darkness, horror, and despair.

Then I saw that about the spot of light into which the whole world of matter had shrunk there was a faint glow. And in a band on either side of that the darkness was absolute. I watched it for ages, as it seemed to me, and through the long waiting the haze grew imperceptibly more distinct. And then about the band appeared an irregular cloud of the faintest, palest brown. I felt a passionate impatience; but the things grew brighter so slowly that they scarcely seemed to change. What was unfolding itself? What was this strange reddish dawn in the interminable night of space?

The cloud's shape was grotesque. It seemed to be looped along its lower side into four projecting masses, and, above, it ended in a straight line. What phantom was it? I felt assured I had seen that figure before; but I could not think what, nor where, nor when it was. Then the realisation rushed upon me. *It was a clenched Hand.* I was alone in space, alone with this huge, shadowy Hand, upon which the whole Universe of Matter lay like an unconsidered speck of dust. It seemed as though I watched it through vast periods of time. On the forefinger glittered a ring; and the universe from which I had come was but a spot of light upon the ring's curvature. And the thing that the hand gripped had the likeness of a black rod. Through a long eternity I watched this Hand, with the ring and the rod, marvelling and fearing and waiting helplessly on what might follow. It seemed as though nothing could follow: that I should watch for ever, seeing only the Hand and the thing it held, and understanding nothing of its import. Was the whole universe but a refracting speck upon some greater Being? Were our worlds but the atoms of another universe, and those again of another, and so on through an endless progression? And what was I? Was I indeed immaterial? A vague persuasion of a body gathering about me came into my suspense. The abysmal darkness about the Hand filled with impalpable suggestions, with uncertain, fluctuating shapes.

Came a sound, like the sound of a tolling bell; faint, as if infinitely far, muffled as though heard through thick swathings of darkness: a deep, vibrating resonance, with vast gulfs of silence between each stroke. And the Hand appeared to tighten on the rod. And I saw far above the Hand, towards the apex of the darkness, a circle of dim phosphorescence, a ghostly sphere whence these sounds came throbbing; and at the last stroke the Hand vanished, for the hour had come, and I heard a noise of many waters. But the black rod remained as a great band across the sky. And then a voice, which seemed to run to the uttermost parts of space, spoke, saying, "There will be no more pain."

At that an almost intolerable gladness and radiance rushed upon me, and I saw the circle shining white and bright, and the rod black and shining, and many things else distinct and clear. And the circle was the face of the clock, and the rod the rail of my bed, Haddon was standing at the foot, against the rail, with a small pair of scissors on his fingers; and the hands of my clock on the mantel over his shoulder were clasped together over the hour of twelve. Mowbray was washing something in a basin at the octagonal table, and at my side I felt a subdued feeling that could scarce be spoken of as pain.

The operation had not killed me. And I perceived, suddenly, that the dull melancholy of half a year was lifted from my mind.

THE CRYSTAL EGG

There was, until a year ago, a little and very grimy-looking shop near Seven Dials, over which, in weather-worn yellow lettering, the name of "C. Cave, Naturalist and Dealer in Antiquities" was inscribed. The contents of its window were curiously varied. They comprised some elephant tusks and an imperfect set of chessmen, beads and weapons, a box of eyes, two skulls of tigers and one human, several moth-eaten stuffed monkeys (one holding a lamp), an old-fashioned cabinet, a fly-blown ostrich egg or so, some fishing-tackle, and an extraordinarily dirty, empty glass fish-tank. There was also, at the moment the story begins, a mass of crystal, worked into the shape of an egg and brilliantly polished. And at that two people, who stood outside the window, were looking, one of them a tall, thin clergyman, the other a black-bearded young man of dusky complexion and unobtrusive costume. The dusky young man spoke with eager gesticulation, and seemed anxious for his companion to purchase the article.

While they were there, Mr. Cave came into his shop, his beard still wagging with the bread and butter of his tea. When he saw these men and the object of their regard, his countenance fell. He glanced guiltily over his shoulder, and softly shut the door. He was a little old man, with pale face and peculiar watery blue eyes; his hair was a dirty grey, and he wore a shabby blue frock-coat, an ancient silk hat, and carpet slippers very much down at heel. He remained watching the two men as they talked. The clergyman went deep into his trouser pocket, examined a handful of money, and showed his teeth in an agreeable smile. Mr. Cave seemed still more depressed when they came into the shop.

The clergyman, without any ceremony, asked the price of the crystal egg. Mr. Cave glanced nervously towards the door leading into the parlour, and said five pounds. The clergyman protested that the price was high, to his companion as well as to Mr. Cave—it was, indeed, very much more than Mr. Cave had intended to ask, when he had stocked the article—and an attempt at bargaining ensued. Mr. Cave stepped to the shop-door, and held it open. "Five pounds is my price," he said, as though he wished to save himself the trouble of unprofitable discussion. As he did so, the upper portion of a woman's face appeared above the blind in the glass upper panel of the door leading into the parlour, and stared curiously at the two customers. "Five pounds is my price," said Mr. Cave, with a quiver in his voice.

The swarthy young man had so far remained a spectator, watching Cave keenly. Now he spoke. "Give him five pounds," he said. The clergyman glanced at him to see if he were in earnest, and, when he looked at Mr. Cave again, he saw that the latter's face was white. "It's a lot of money," said the clergyman, and, diving into his pocket, began counting his resources. He had little more than thirty shillings, and he appealed to his companion, with whom he seemed to be on terms of considerable intimacy. This gave Mr. Cave an opportunity of collecting his thoughts, and he began to explain in an agitated manner that the crystal was not, as a matter of fact, entirely free for sale. His two customers were naturally surprised at this, and inquired why he had not thought of that before he began to bargain. Mr. Cave became confused, but he stuck to his story, that the crystal was not in the market that afternoon, that a probable purchaser of it had already appeared. The two, treating this as an attempt to raise the price still further, made as if they would leave the shop. But at this point the parlour door opened, and the owner of the dark fringe and the little eyes appeared.

She was a coarse-featured, corpulent woman, younger and very much larger than Mr. Cave; she walked heavily, and her face was flushed. "That crystal *is* for sale," she said. "And five pounds is a good enough price for it. I can't think what you're about, Cave, not to take the gentleman's offer!"

Mr. Cave, greatly perturbed by the irruption, looked angrily at her over the rims of his spectacles, and, without excessive assurance, asserted his right to manage his business in his own way. An altercation began. The two customers watched the scene with interest and some amusement, occasionally assisting Mrs. Cave with suggestions. Mr. Cave, hard driven, persisted in a confused and impossible story of an enquiry for the crystal that morning, and his agitation became painful. But he stuck to his point with extraordinary persistence. It was the young Oriental who ended this curious controversy. He proposed that they should call again in the course of two days—so as to give the alleged inquirer a fair chance. "And then we must insist," said the clergyman. "Five pounds." Mrs. Cave took it on herself to apologise for her husband, explaining that he was sometimes "a little odd," and as the two customers left, the couple prepared for a free discussion of the incident in all its bearings.

Mrs. Cave talked to her husband with singular directness. The poor little man, quivering with emotion, muddled himself between his stories, maintaining on the one hand that he had another customer in view, and on the other asserting that the crystal was honestly worth ten guineas. "Why did you ask five pounds?" said his wife. "*Do* let me manage my business my own way!" said Mr. Cave.

Mr. Cave had living with him a step-daughter and a step-son, and at supper that night the transaction was rediscussed. None of them had a high opinion of Mr. Cave's business methods, and his action seemed a culminating folly.

"It's my opinion he's refused that crystal before," said the step-son, a loose-limbed lout of eighteen.

"But *five pounds*!" said the step-daughter, an argumentative young woman of six-and-twenty.

Mr. Cave's answers were wretched; he could only mumble weak assertions that he knew his own business best. They drove him from his half-eaten supper into the shop, to close it for the night, his ears aflame and tears of vexation behind his spectacles. "Why had he left the crystal in the window so long? The folly of it!" That was the trouble closest in his mind. For a time he could see no way of evading sale.

After supper his step-daughter and step-son smartened themselves up and went out and his wife retired upstairs to reflect upon the business aspects of the crystal, over a little sugar and lemon and so forth in hot water. Mr. Cave went into the shop, and stayed there until late, ostensibly to make ornamental rockeries for goldfish cases but really for a private purpose that will be better explained later. The next day Mrs. Cave found that the crystal had been removed from the window, and was lying behind some second-hand books on angling. She replaced it in a conspicuous position. But she did not argue further about it, as a nervous headache disinclined her from debate. Mr. Cave was always disinclined. The day passed disagreeably. Mr. Cave was, if anything, more absent-minded than usual, and uncommonly irritable withal. In the afternoon, when his wife was taking her customary sleep, he removed the crystal from the window again.

The next day Mr. Cave had to deliver a consignment of dog-fish at one of the hospital schools, where they were needed for dissection. In his absence Mrs. Cave's mind reverted to the topic of the crystal, and the methods of expenditure suitable to a windfall of five pounds. She had already devised some very agreeable expedients, among others a dress of green silk for herself and a trip to Richmond, when a jangling of the front door bell summoned her into the shop. The customer was an examination coach who came to complain of the non-delivery of certain frogs asked for the previous day. Mrs. Cave did not approve of this particular branch of Mr. Cave's business, and the gentleman, who had called in a somewhat aggressive mood, retired after a brief exchange of words—entirely civil so far as he was concerned. Mrs. Cave's eye then naturally turned to the window; for the sight of the crystal was an assurance of the five pounds and of her dreams. What was her surprise to find it gone!

She went to the place behind the locker on the counter, where she had discovered it the day before. It was not there; and she immediately began an eager search about the shop.

When Mr. Cave returned from his business with the dog-fish, about a quarter to two in the afternoon, he found the shop in some confusion, and his wife, extremely exasperated and on her knees behind the counter, routing among his taxidermic material. Her face came up hot and angry over the counter, as the jangling bell announced his return, and she forthwith accused him of "hiding it."

"Hid *what*?" asked Mr. Cave.

"The crystal!"

At that Mr. Cave, apparently much surprised, rushed to the window. "Isn't it here?" he said. "Great Heavens! what has become of it?"

Just then, Mr. Cave's step-son re-entered the shop from the inner room—he had come home a minute or so before Mr. Cave—and he was blaspheming freely. He was apprenticed to a second-hand furniture dealer down the road, but he had his meals at home, and he was naturally annoyed to find no dinner ready.

But, when he heard of the loss of the crystal, he forgot his meal, and his anger was diverted from his mother to his step-father. Their first idea, of course, was that he had hidden it. But Mr. Cave stoutly denied all knowledge of its fate—freely offering his bedabbled affidavit in the matter—and at last was working up to the point of accusing, first, his wife and then his step-son of having taken it with a view to a private sale. So began an exceedingly acrimonious and emotional discussion, which ended for Mrs. Cave in a peculiar nervous condition midway between hysterics and amuck, and caused the step-son to be half-an-hour late at the furniture establishment in the afternoon. Mr. Cave took refuge from his wife's emotions in the shop.

In the evening the matter was resumed, with less passion and in a judicial spirit, under the presidency of the step-daughter. The supper passed unhappily and culminating in a painful scene. Mr. Cave gave way at last to extreme exasperation, and went out banging the front door violently. The rest of the family, having discussed him with the freedom his absence warranted, hunted the house from garret to cellar, hoping to light upon the crystal.

The next day the two customers called again. They were received by Mrs. Cave almost in tears. It transpired that no one *could* imagine all that she had stood from Cave at various times in her married pilgrimage... She also gave a garbled account of the disappearance. The clergyman and the Oriental laughed silently at one another, and said it was very extraordinary. As Mrs. Cave seemed disposed to give them the complete history of her life they made to leave the shop. Thereupon Mrs. Cave, still clinging to hope, asked for the clergyman's address, so that, if she could get anything out of Cave, she might communicate it. The address was duly given, but apparently was afterwards mislaid. Mrs. Cave can remember nothing about it.

In the evening of that day, the Caves seem to have exhausted their emotions, and Mr. Cave, who had been out in the afternoon, supped in a gloomy isolation that contrasted pleasantly with the impassioned controversy of the previous days. For some time matters were very badly strained in the Cave household, but neither crystal nor customer reappeared.

Now, without mincing the matter, we must admit that Mr. Cave was a liar. He knew perfectly well where the crystal was. It was in the rooms of Mr. Jacoby Wace, Assistant Demonstrator at St. Catherine's Hospital, Westbourne Street. It stood on the sideboard partially covered by a black velvet cloth, and beside a decanter of American whisky. It is from Mr. Wace, indeed, that the particulars upon which this narrative is based were derived. Cave had taken off the thing to the hospital hidden in the dog-fish sack, and there had pressed the young investigator to keep it for him. Mr. Wace was a little dubious at first. His relationship to Cave was peculiar. He had a taste for singular characters, and he had more than once invited the old man to smoke and drink in his rooms, and to unfold his rather amusing views of life in general and of his wife in particular. Mr. Wace had encountered Mrs. Cave, too, on occasions when Mr. Cave was not at home to attend to him. He knew the constant interference to which Cave was subjected, and having weighed the story judicially, he decided to give the crystal a refuge. Mr. Cave promised to explain the reasons for his remarkable affection for the crystal more fully on a later occasion, but he spoke distinctly of seeing visions therein. He called on Mr. Wace the same evening.

He told a complicated story. The crystal he said had come into his possession with other oddments at the forced sale of another curiosity dealer's effects, and not knowing what its value might be, he had ticketed it at ten shillings. It had hung upon his hands at that price for some months, and he was thinking of "reducing the figure," when he made a singular discovery.

At that time his health was very bad—and it must be borne in mind that, throughout all of this experience, his physical condition was one of ebb—and he was in considerable distress by reason of the negligence, the positive ill-treatment even, he received from his wife and step-children. His wife was vain, extravagant, unfeeling, and had a growing taste for private drinking; his step-daughter was mean and over-reaching; and his step-son had conceived a violent dislike for him, and lost no chance of showing it. The requirements of his business pressed heavily upon him, and Mr. Wace does not think that he was altogether free from occasional intemperance. He had begun life in a comfortable position, he was a man of fair education, and he suffered, for weeks at a stretch, from melancholia and insomnia. Afraid to disturb his family, he would slip quietly from his wife's side, when his thoughts became intolerable, and wander about the house. And about three o'clock one morning, late in August, chance directed him into the shop.

The dirty little place was impenetrably black except in one spot, where he perceived an unusual glow of light. Approaching this, he discovered it to be the crystal egg, which was standing on the corner of the counter towards the window. A thin ray smote through a crack in the shutters, impinged upon the object, and seemed as it were to fill its entire interior.

It occurred to Mr. Cave that this was not in accordance with the laws of optics as he had known them in his younger days. He could understand the rays being refracted by the crystal and coming to a focus in its interior, but this diffusion jarred with his physical conceptions. He approached the crystal nearly, peering into it and round it, with a transient revival of the scientific curiosity that in his youth had determined his choice of a calling. He was surprised to find the light not steady, but writhing within the substance of the egg, as though that object was a hollow sphere of some luminous vapour. In moving about to get different points of view, he suddenly found that he had come between it and the ray, and that the crystal none the less remained luminous. Greatly astonished, he lifted it out of the light ray and carried it to the darkest part of the shop. It remained bright for some four or five minutes, when it slowly faded and went out. He placed it in the thin streak of daylight, and its luminousness was almost immediately restored.

So far, at least, Mr. Wace was able to verify the remarkable story of Mr. Cave. He has himself repeatedly held this crystal in a ray of light (which has to be of a less diameter than one millimetre). And in a perfect darkness, such as could be produced by velvet wrapping, the crystal did undoubtedly appear very faintly phosphorescent. It would seem, however, that the luminousness was of some exceptional sort, and not equally visible to all eyes; for Mr. Harbinger—whose name will be familiar to the scientific reader in connection with the Pasteur Institute—was quite unable to see any light whatever. And Mr. Wace's own capacity for its appreciation was out of comparison inferior to that of Mr. Cave's. Even with Mr. Cave the power varied very considerably: his vision was most vivid during states of extreme weakness and fatigue.

Now from the outset this light in the crystal exercised an irresistible fascination upon Mr. Cave. And it says more for his loneliness of soul than a volume of pathetic writing could do, that he told no human being of his curious observations. He seems to have been living in such an atmosphere of petty spite that to admit the existence of a pleasure would have been to risk the loss of it. He found that as the dawn advanced, and the amount of diffused light increased, the crystal became to all appearance non-luminous. And for some time he was unable to see anything in it, except at night-time, in dark corners of the shop.

But the use of an old velvet cloth, which he used as a background for a collection of minerals, occurred to him, and by doubling this, and putting it over his head and hands, he was able to get a sight of the luminous movement within the crystal even in the day-time. He was very cautious lest he should be thus discovered by his wife, and he practised this occupation only in the afternoon, while she was asleep upstairs, and then circumspectly in a hollow under the counter. And one day, turning the crystal about in his hands, he saw something. It came and went like a flash, but it gave him the impression that the object had for a moment opened to him the view of a wide and spacious and strange country; and, turning it about, he did, just as the light faded, see the same vision again.

Now, it would be tedious and unnecessary to state all the phases of Mr. Cave's discovery from this point. Suffice that the effect was this: the crystal, being peered into at an angle of about 137 degrees from the direction of the illuminating ray, gave a clear and consistent picture of a wide and peculiar countryside. It was not dream-like at all; it produced a definite impression of reality, and the better the light the more real and solid it seemed. It was a moving picture: that is to say, certain objects moved in it, but slowly in an orderly manner like real things, and, according as the direction of the lighting and vision changed, the picture changed also. It must, indeed, have been like looking through an oval glass at a view, and turning the glass about to get at different aspects.

Mr. Cave's statements, Mr. Wace assures me, were extremely circumstantial, and entirely free from any of that emotional quality that taints hallucinatory impressions. But it must be remembered that all the efforts of Mr. Wace to see any similar clarity in the faint opalescence of the crystal were wholly unsuccessful, try as he would. The difference in intensity of the impressions by the two men was very great, and it is quite conceivable that what was a view to Mr. Cave was a mere blurred nebulosity to Mr. Wace.

The view, as Mr. Cave described it, was invariably of an extensive plain, and he seemed always to be looking at it from a considerable height, as if from a tower or a mast. To the east and to the west the plain was bounded at a remote distance by vast reddish cliffs, which reminded him of those he had seen in some picture; but what the picture was Mr. Wace was unable to ascertain. These cliffs passed north and south—he could tell the points of the compass by the stars that were visible of a night—receding in an almost illimitable perspective and fading into the mists of the distance before they met. He was nearer the eastern set of cliffs, on the occasion of his first vision the sun was rising over them, and black against the sunlight and pale against their shadow appeared a multitude of soaring forms that Mr. Cave regarded as birds. A vast range of buildings spread below him; he seemed to be looking down upon them; and, as they approached the blurred and refracted edge of the picture, they became indistinct. There were also trees curious in shape, and in colouring, a deep mossy green and an exquisite grey, beside a wide and shining canal. And something great and brilliantly coloured flew across the picture. But the first time Mr. Cave saw these pictures he saw only in flashes, his hands shook, his head moved, the vision came and went, and grew foggy and indistinct. And at first he had the greatest difficulty in finding the picture again once the direction of it was lost.

His next clear vision, which came about a week after the first, the interval having yielded nothing but tantalising glimpses and some useful experience, showed him the view down the length of the valley. The view was different, but he had a curious persuasion, which his subsequent observations abundantly confirmed, that he was regarding this strange world from exactly the same spot, although he was looking in a different direction. The long façade of the great building, whose roof he had looked down upon before, was now receding in perspective. He recognised the roof. In the front of the façade was a terrace of massive proportions and extraordinary length, and down the middle of the terrace, at certain intervals, stood huge but very graceful masts, bearing small shiny objects which reflected the setting sun. The import of these small objects did not occur to Mr. Cave until some time after, as he was describing the scene to Mr. Wace. The terrace overhung a thicket of the most luxuriant and graceful vegetation, and beyond this was a wide grassy lawn on which certain broad creatures, in form like beetles but enormously larger, reposed. Beyond this again was a richly decorated causeway of pinkish stone; and beyond that, and lined with dense *red* weeds, and passing up the valley exactly parallel with the distant cliffs, was a broad and mirror-like expanse of water. The air seemed full of squadrons of great birds, manoeuvring in stately curves; and across the river was a multitude of splendid buildings, richly coloured and glittering with metallic tracery and facets, among a forest of moss-like and lichenous trees. And suddenly something flapped repeatedly across the vision, like the fluttering of a jewelled fan or the beating of a wing, and a face, or rather the upper part of a face with very large eyes, came as it were close to his own and as if on the other side of the crystal. Mr. Cave was so startled and so impressed by the absolute reality of these eyes, that he drew his head back from the crystal to look behind it. He had become so absorbed in watching that he was quite surprised to find himself in the cool darkness of his little shop, and its familiar odour of methyl, mustiness, and decay. And, as he blinked about him, the glowing crystal faded, and went out.

Such were the first general impressions of Mr. Cave. The story is curiously direct and circumstantial. From the outset, when the valley first flashed momentarily on his senses, his imagination was strangely affected, and, as he began to appreciate the details of the scene he saw, his wonder rose to the point of a passion. He went about his business listless and distraught, thinking only of the time when he should be able to return to his watching. And then a few weeks after his first sight of the valley came the two customers, the stress and excitement of their offer, and the narrow escape of the crystal from sale, as I have already told.

Now while the thing was Mr. Cave's secret, it remained a mere wonder, a thing to creep to covertly and peep at, as a child might peep upon a forbidden garden. But Mr. Wace has, for a young scientific investigator, a particularly lucid and consecutive habit of mind. Directly the crystal and its story came to him, and he had satisfied himself, by seeing the phosphorescence with his own eyes, that there really was a certain evidence for Mr. Cave's statements, he proceeded to develop the matter systematically. Mr. Cave was only too eager to come and feast his eyes on this wonderland he saw, and he came every night from half-past eight until half-past ten, and sometimes, in Mr. Wace's absence, during the day. On Sunday afternoons, also, he came. From the outset Mr. Wace made copious notes, and it was due to his scientific method that the relation between the direction from which the initiating ray entered the crystal and the orientation of the picture was proved. And, by covering the crystal in a box perforated only with a small aperture to admit the exciting ray, and by substituting black holland for his buff blinds, he greatly improved the conditions of the observations; so that in a little while they were able to survey the valley in any direction they desired.

So having cleared the way, we may give a brief account of this visionary world within the crystal. The things were in all cases seen by Mr. Cave, and the method of working was invariably for him to watch the crystal and report what he saw, while Mr. Wace (who as a science student had learnt the trick of writing in the dark) wrote a brief note of his report. When the crystal faded, it was put into its box in the proper position and the electric light turned on. Mr. Wace asked questions, and suggested observations to clear up difficult points. Nothing, indeed, could have been less visionary and more matter-of-fact.

The attention of Mr. Cave had been speedily directed to the bird-like creatures he had seen so abundantly present in each of his earlier visions. His first impression was soon corrected, and he considered for a time that they might represent a diurnal species of bat. Then he thought, grotesquely enough, that they might be cherubs. Their heads were round, and curiously human, and it was the eyes of one of them that had so startled him on his second observation. They had broad, silvery wings, not feathered, but glistening almost as brilliantly as new-killed fish and with the same subtle play of colour, and these wings were not built on the plan of bird-wing or bat, Mr. Wace learned, but supported by curved ribs radiating from the body. (A sort of butterfly wing with curved ribs seems best to express their appearance.) The body was small, but fitted with two bunches of prehensile organs, like long tentacles, immediately under the mouth. Incredible as it appeared to Mr. Wace, the persuasion at last became irresistible, that it was these creatures which owned the great quasi-human buildings and the magnificent garden that made the broad valley so splendid. And Mr. Cave perceived that the buildings, with other peculiarities, had no doors, but that the great circular windows, which opened freely, gave the creatures egress and entrance. They would alight upon their tentacles, fold their wings to a smallness almost rod-like, and hop into the interior. But among them was a multitude of smaller-winged creatures, like great dragon-flies and moths and flying beetles, and across the greensward brilliantly coloured gigantic ground-beetles crawled lazily to and fro. Moreover, on the causeways and terraces, large-headed creatures similar to the greater winged flies, but wingless, were visible, hopping busily upon their hand-like tangle of tentacles.

Allusion has already been made to the glittering objects upon masts that stood upon the terrace of the nearer building. It dawned on Mr. Cave, after regarding one of these masts very fixedly on one particularly vivid day, that the glittering object there was a crystal exactly like that into which he peered. And a still more careful scrutiny convinced him that each one in a vista of nearly twenty carried a similar object.

Occasionally one of the large flying creatures would flutter up to one, and, folding its wings and coiling a number of its tentacles about the mast, would regard the crystal fixedly for a space,—sometimes for as long as fifteen minutes. And a series of observations, made at the suggestion of Mr. Wace, convinced both watchers that, so far as this visionary world was concerned, the crystal into which they peered actually stood at the summit of the end-most mast on the terrace, and that on one occasion at least one of these inhabitants of this other world had looked into Mr. Cave's face while he was making these observations.

So much for the essential facts of this very singular story. Unless we dismiss it all as the ingenious fabrication of Mr. Wace, we have to believe one of two things: either that Mr. Cave's crystal was in two worlds at once, and that, while it was carried about in one, it remained stationary in the other, which seems altogether absurd; or else that it had some peculiar relation of sympathy with another and exactly similar crystal in this other world, so that what was seen in the interior of the one in this world was, under suitable conditions, visible to an observer in the corresponding crystal in the other world; and *vice versa*. At present, indeed, we do not know of any way in which two crystals could so come *en rapport,* but nowadays we know enough to understand that the thing is not altogether impossible. This view of the crystals as *en rapport* was the supposition that occurred to Mr. Wace, and to me at least it seems extremely plausible...

And where was this other world? On this, also, the alert intelligence of Mr. Wace speedily threw light. After sunset, the sky darkened rapidly—there was a very brief twilight interval indeed—and the stars shone out. They were recognisably the same as those we see, arranged in the same constellations. Mr. Cave recognised the Bear, the Pleiades, Aldebaran, and Sirius: so that the other world must be somewhere in the solar system, and, at the utmost, only a few hundreds of millions of miles from our own. Following up this clue, Mr. Wace learned that the midnight sky was a darker blue even than our mid-winter sky, and that the sun seemed a little smaller. *And there were two small moons!* "Like our moon but smaller, and quite differently marked," one of which moved so rapidly that its motion was clearly visible as one regarded it. These moons were never high in the sky, but vanished as they rose: that is, every time they revolved they were eclipsed because they were so near their primary planet. And all this answers quite completely, although Mr. Cave did not know it, to what must be the condition of things on Mars.

Indeed, it seems an exceedingly plausible conclusion that peering into this crystal Mr. Cave did actually see the planet Mars and its inhabitants. And, if that be the case, then the evening star that shone so brilliantly in the sky of that distant vision, was neither more nor less than our own familiar earth.

For a time the Martians—if they were Martians—do not seem to have known of Mr. Cave's inspection. Once or twice one would come to peer, and go away very shortly to some other mast, as though the vision was unsatisfactory. During this time Mr. Cave was able to watch the proceedings of these winged people without being disturbed by their attentions, and, although his report is necessarily vague and fragmentary, it is nevertheless very suggestive. Imagine the impression of humanity a Martian observer would get who, after a difficult process of preparation and with considerable fatigue to the eyes, was able to peer at London from the steeple of St. Martin's Church for stretches, at longest, of four minutes at a time. Mr. Cave was unable to ascertain if the winged Martians were the same as the Martians who hopped about the causeways and terraces, and if the latter could put on wings at will. He several times saw certain clumsy bipeds, dimly suggestive of apes, white and partially translucent, feeding among certain of the lichenous trees, and once some of these fled before one of the hopping, round-headed Martians. The latter caught one in its tentacles, and then the picture faded suddenly and left Mr. Cave most tantalisingly in the dark. On another occasion a vast thing, that Mr. Cave thought at first was some gigantic insect, appeared advancing along the causeway beside the canal with extraordinary rapidity. As this drew nearer Mr. Cave perceived that it was a mechanism of shining metals and of extraordinary complexity. And then, when he looked again, it had passed out of sight.

After a time Mr. Wace aspired to attract the attention of the Martians, and the next time that the strange eyes of one of them appeared close to the crystal Mr. Cave cried out and sprang away, and they immediately turned on the light and began to gesticulate in a manner suggestive of signalling. But when at last Mr. Cave examined the crystal again the Martian had departed.

Thus far these observations had progressed in early November, and then Mr. Cave, feeling that the suspicions of the family about the crystal were allayed, began to take it to and fro with him in order that, as occasion arose in the daytime or night, he might comfort himself with what was fast becoming the most real thing in his existence.

In December Mr. Wace's work in connection with a forthcoming examination became heavy, and sittings were reluctantly suspended for a week, and for ten or eleven days—he is not quite sure which—he saw nothing of Cave. He then grew anxious to resume these investigations, and, the stress of his seasonal labours being abated, he went down to Seven Dials. At the corner he noticed a shutter before a bird fancier's window, and then another at a cobbler's. Mr. Cave's shop was closed.

He rapped and the door was opened by the step-son in black. He at once called Mrs. Cave, who was, Mr. Wace could not but observe, in cheap but ample widow's weeds of the most imposing pattern. Without any very great surprise Mr. Wace learnt that Cave was dead and already buried. She was in tears, and her voice was a little thick. She had just returned from Highgate. Her mind seemed occupied with her own prospects and the honourable details of the obsequies, but Mr. Wace was at last able to learn the particulars of Cave's death. He had been found dead in his shop in the early morning, the day after his last visit to Mr. Wace, and the crystal had been clasped in his stone-cold hands. His face was smiling, said Mrs. Cave, and the velvet cloth from the minerals lay on the floor at his feet. He must have been dead five or six hours when he was found.

This came as a great shock to Wace, and he began to reproach himself bitterly for having neglected the plain symptoms of the old man's ill health. But his chief thought was of the crystal. He approached that topic in a gingerly manner, because he knew Mrs. Cave's peculiarities. He was dumbfounded to learn that it was sold.

Mrs. Cave's first impulse, directly Cave's body had been taken upstairs, had been to write to the mad clergyman who had offered five pounds for the crystal, informing him of its recovery; but after a violent hunt in which her daughter joined her, they were convinced of the loss of his address. As they were without the means required to mourn and bury Cave in the elaborate style the dignity of an old Seven Dials inhabitant demands, they had appealed to a friendly fellow-tradesman in Great Portland Street. He had very kindly taken over a portion of the stock at a valuation. The valuation was his own and the crystal egg was included in one of the lots. Mr. Wace, after a few suitable consolatory observations, a little off-handedly proffered perhaps, hurried at once to Great Portland Street. But there he learned that the crystal egg had already been sold to a tall, dark man in grey. And there the material facts in this curious, and to me at least very suggestive, story come abruptly to an end. The Great Portland Street dealer did not know who the tall dark man in grey was, nor had he observed him with sufficient attention to describe him minutely. He did not even know which way this person had gone after leaving the shop. For a time Mr. Wace remained in the shop, trying the dealer's patience with hopeless questions, venting his own exasperation. And at last, realising abruptly that the whole thing had passed out of his hands, had vanished like a vision of the night, he returned to his own rooms, a little astonished to find the notes he had made still tangible and visible upon his untidy table.

His annoyance and disappointment were naturally very great. He made a second call (equally ineffectual) upon the Great Portland

Street dealer, and he resorted to advertisements in such periodicals as were likely to come into the hands of a bric-à-brac collector. He also wrote letters to *The Daily Chronicle* and *Nature,* but both those periodicals, suspecting a hoax, asked him to reconsider his action before they printed, and he was advised that such a strange story, unfortunately so bare of supporting evidence, might imperil his reputation as an investigator. Moreover, the calls of his proper work were urgent. So that after a month or so, save for an occasional reminder to certain dealers, he had reluctantly to abandon the quest for the crystal egg, and from that day to this it remains undiscovered. Occasionally however, he tells me, and I can quite believe him, he has bursts of zeal in which he abandons his more urgent occupation and resumes the search.

Whether or not it will remain lost for ever, with the material and origin of it, are things equally speculative at the present time. If the present purchaser is a collector, one would have expected the inquiries of Mr. Wace to have reached him through the dealers. He has been able to discover Mr. Cave's clergyman and "Oriental"—no other than the Rev. James Parker and the young Prince of Bosso-Kuni in Java. I am obliged to them for certain particulars. The object of the Prince was simply curiosity—and extravagance. He was so eager to buy, because Cave was so oddly reluctant to sell. It is just as possible that the buyer in the second instance was simply a casual purchaser and not a collector at all, and the crystal egg, for all I know, may at the present moment be within a mile of me, decorating a drawing-room or serving as a paper-weight—its remarkable functions all unknown. Indeed, it is partly with the idea of such a possibility that I have thrown this narrative into a form that will give it a chance of being read by the ordinary consumer of fiction.

My own ideas in the matter are practically identical with those of Mr. Wace. I believe the crystal on the mast in Mars and the crystal egg of Mr. Cave's to be in some physical, but at present quite inexplicable, way *en rapport,* and we both believe further that the terrestrial crystal must have been—possibly at some remote date—sent hither from that planet, in order to give the Martians a near view of our affairs. Possibly the fellows to the crystals in the other masts are also on our globe. No theory of hallucination suffices for the facts.

THE NEW ACCELERATOR

Certainly, if ever a man found a guinea when he was looking for a pin it is my good friend Professor Gibberne. I have heard before of investigators overshooting the mark, but never quite to the extent that he has done. He has really, this time at any rate, without any touch of exaggeration in the phrase, found something to revolutionise human life. And that when he was simply seeking an all-round nervous stimulant to bring languid people up to the stresses of these pushful days. I have tasted the stuff now several times, and I cannot do better than describe the effect the thing had on me. That there are astonishing experiences in store for all in search of new sensations will become apparent enough.

Professor Gibberne, as many people know, is my neighbour in Folkestone. Unless my memory plays me a trick, his portrait at various ages has already appeared in *The Strand Magazine*—I think late in 1899; but I am unable to look it up because I have lent that volume to some one who has never sent it back. The reader may, perhaps, recall the high forehead and the singularly long black eyebrows that give such a Mephistophelian touch to his face. He occupies one of those pleasant detached houses in the mixed style that make the western end of the Upper Sandgate Road so interesting. His is the one with the Flemish gables and the Moorish portico, and it is in the room with the mullioned bay window that he works when he is down here, and in which of an evening we have so often smoked and talked together. He is a mighty jester, but, besides, he likes to talk to me about his work; he is one of those men who find a help and stimulus in talking, and so I have been able to follow the conception of the New Accelerator right up from a very early stage. Of course, the greater portion of his experimental work is not done in Folkestone, but in Gower Street, in the fine new laboratory next to the hospital that he has been the first to use.

As everyone knows, or at least as all intelligent people know, the special department in which Gibberne has gained so great and deserved a reputation among physiologists is the action of drugs upon the nervous system. Upon soporifics, sedatives, and anaesthetics he is, I am told, unequalled. He is also a chemist of considerable eminence, and I suppose in the subtle and complex jungle of riddles that centres about the ganglion cell and the axis fibre there are little cleared places of his making, glades of illumination, that, until he sees fit to publish his results, are inaccessible to every other living man. And in the last few years he has been particularly assiduous upon this question of nervous stimulants, and already, before the discovery of the New Accelerator, very successful with them. Medical science has to thank him for at least three distinct and absolutely safe invigorators of unrivalled value to practising men. In cases of exhaustion the preparation known as Gibberne's B Syrup has, I suppose, saved more lives already than any lifeboat round the coast.

"But none of these things begin to satisfy me yet," he told me nearly a year ago. "Either they increase the central energy without affecting the nerves or they simply increase the available energy by lowering the nervous conductivity; and all of them are unequal and local in their operation. One wakes up the heart and viscera and leaves the brain stupefied, one gets at the brain champagne fashion and does nothing good for the solar plexus, and what I want—and what, if it's an earthly possibility, I mean to have—is a stimulant that stimulates all round, that wakes you up for a time from the crown of your head to the tip of your great toe, and makes you go two—or even three to everybody else's one. Eh? That's the thing I'm after."

"It would tire a man," I said.

"Not a doubt of it. And you'd eat double or treble—and all that. But just think what the thing would mean. Imagine yourself with a little phial like this"—he held up a bottle of green glass and marked his points with it—"and in this precious phial is the power to think twice as fast, move twice as quickly, do twice as much work in a given time as you could otherwise do."

"But is such a thing possible?"

"I believe so. If it isn't, I've wasted my time for a year. These various preparations of the hypophosphites, for example, seem to show that something of the sort... Even if it was only one and a half times as fast it would do."

"It *would* do," I said.

"If you were a statesman in a corner, for example, time rushing up against you, something urgent to be done, eh?"

"He could dose his private secretary," I said.

"And gain—double time. And think if *you*, for example, wanted to finish a book."

"Usually," I said, "I wish I'd never begun 'em."

"Or a doctor, driven to death, wants to sit down and think out a case. Or a barrister—or a man cramming for an examination."

"Worth a guinea a drop," said I, "and more—to men like that."

"And in a duel again," said Gibberne, "where it all depends on your quickness in pulling the trigger."

"Or in fencing," I echoed.

"You see," said Gibberne, "if I get it as an all-round thing it will really do you no harm at all—except perhaps to an infinitesimal degree it brings you nearer old age. You will just have lived twice to other people's once—"

"I suppose," I meditated, "in a duel—it would be fair?"

"That's a question for the seconds," said Gibberne.

I harked back further. "And you really think such a thing *is* possible?" I said.

"As possible," said Gibberne, and glanced at something that went throbbing by the window, "as a motorbus. As a matter of fact—"

He paused and smiled at me deeply, and tapped slowly on the edge of his desk with the green phial. "I think I know the stuff... Already I've got something coming." The nervous smile upon his face betrayed the gravity of his revelation. He rarely talked of his actual experimental work unless things were very near the end. "And it may be, it may be—I shouldn't be surprised—it may even do the thing at a greater rate than twice."

"It will be rather a big thing," I hazarded.

"It will be, I think, rather a big thing."

But I don't think he quite knew what a big thing it was to be, for all that.

I remember we had several subsequent talks about the stuff. "The New Accelerator" he called it, and his tone about it grew more confident on each occasion. Sometimes he talked nervously of unexpected physiological results its use might have, and then he would get a bit unhappy; at others he was frankly mercenary, and we debated long and anxiously how the preparation might be turned to commercial account. "It's a good thing," said Gibberne, "a tremendous thing. I know I'm giving the world something, and I think it only reasonable we should expect the world to pay. The dignity of science is all very well, but I think somehow I must have the monopoly of the stuff for, say, ten years. I don't see why *all* the fun in life should go to the dealers in ham."

My own interest in the coming drug certainly did not wane in the time. I have always had a queer twist towards metaphysics in my mind. I have always been given to paradoxes about space and time, and it seemed to me that Gibberne was really preparing no less than the absolute acceleration of life. Suppose a man repeatedly dosed with such a preparation: he would live an active and record life indeed, but he would be an adult at eleven, middle-aged at twenty-five, and by thirty well on the road to senile decay. It seemed to me that so far Gibberne was only going to do for anyone who took his drug exactly what Nature had done for the Jews and Orientals, who are men in their teens and aged by fifty, and quicker in thought and act than we are all the time. The marvel of drugs has always been great to my mind; you can madden a man, calm a man, make him incredibly strong and alert or a helpless log, quicken this passion and allay that, all by means of drugs, and here was a new miracle to be added to this strange armoury of phials the doctors use! But Gibberne was far too eager upon his technical points to enter very keenly into my aspect of the question.

It was the 7th or 8th of August when he told me the distillation that would decide his failure or success for a time was going forward as we talked, and it was on the 10th that he told me the thing was done and the New Accelerator a tangible reality in the world. I met him as I was going up the Sandgate Hill towards Folkestone—I think I was going to get my hair cut; and he came hurrying down to meet me—I suppose he was coming to my house to tell me at once of his success. I remember that his eyes were unusually bright and his face flushed, and I noted even then the swift alacrity of his step.

"It's done," he cried, and gripped my hand, speaking very fast; "it's more than done. Come up to my house and see."

"Really?"

"Really!" he shouted. "Incredibly! Come up and see."

"And it does—twice?"

"It does more, much more. It scares me. Come up and see the stuff. Taste it! Try it! It's the most amazing stuff on earth." He gripped my arm and, walking at such a pace that he forced me into a trot, went shouting with me up the hill. A whole charabancful of people turned and stared at us in unison after the manner of people in charabancs. It was one of those hot, clear days that Folkestone sees so much of, every colour incredibly bright and every outline hard. There was a breeze, of course, but not so much breeze as sufficed under these conditions to keep me cool and dry. I panted for mercy.

"I'm not walking fast, am I?" cried Gibberne, and slackened his pace to a quick march.

"You've been taking some of this stuff," I puffed.

"No," he said. "At the utmost a drop of water that stood in a beaker from which I had washed out the last traces of the stuff. I took some last night, you know. But that is ancient history, now."

"And it goes twice?" I said, nearing his doorway in a grateful perspiration.

"It goes a thousand times, many thousand times!" cried Gibberne, with a dramatic gesture, flinging open his Early English carved oak gate.

"Phew!" said I, and followed him to the door.

"I don't know how many times it goes," he said, with his latch-key in his hand.

"And you—"

"It throws all sorts of light on nervous physiology, it kicks the theory of vision into a perfectly new shape!… Heaven knows how many thousand times. We'll try all that after— The thing is to try the stuff now."

"Try the stuff?" I said, as we went along the passage.

"Rather," said Gibberne, turning on me in his study. "There it is in that little green phial there! Unless you happen to be afraid?"

I am a careful man by nature, and only theoretically adventurous. I *was* afraid. But on the other hand there is pride.

"Well," I haggled. "You say you've tried it?"

"I've tried it," he said, "and I don't look hurt by it, do I? I don't even look livery and I *feel*— "

I sat down. "Give me the potion," I said. "If the worst comes to the worst it will save having my hair cut, and that I think is one of the most hateful duties of a civilised man. How do you take the mixture?"

"With water," said Gibberne, whacking down a carafe.

He stood up in front of his desk and regarded me in his easy chair; his manner was suddenly affected by a touch of the Harley Street specialist. "It's rum stuff, you know," he said.

I made a gesture with my hand.

"I must warn you in the first place as soon as you've got it down to shut your eyes, and open them very cautiously in a minute or so's time. One still sees. The sense of vision is a question of length of vibration, and not of multitude of impacts; but there's a kind of shock to the retina, a nasty giddy confusion just at the time if the eyes are open. Keep 'em shut."

"Shut," I said. "Good!"

"And the next thing is, keep still. Don't begin to whack about. You may fetch something a nasty rap if you do. Remember you will be going several thousand times faster than you ever did before, heart, lungs, muscles, brain—everything—and you will hit hard without knowing it. You won't know it, you know. You'll feel just as you do now. Only everything in the world will seem to be going ever so many thousand times slower than it ever went before. That's what makes it so deuced queer."

"Lor'," I said. "And you mean— "

"You'll see," said he, and took up a measure. He glanced at the material on his desk. "Glasses," he said, "water. All here. Mustn't take too much for the first attempt."

The little phial glucked out its precious contents. "Don't forget what I told you," he said, turning the contents of the measure into a glass in the manner of an Italian waiter measuring whisky. "Sit with the eyes tightly shut and in absolute stillness for two minutes," he said. "Then you will hear me speak."

He added an inch or so of water to the dose in each glass.

"By-the-bye," he said, "don't put your glass down. Keep it in your hand and rest your hand on your knee. Yes—so. And now—"

He raised his glass.

"The New Accelerator," I said.

"The New Accelerator," he answered, and we touched glasses and drank, and instantly I closed my eyes.

You know that blank non-existence into which one drops when one has taken "gas." For an indefinite interval it was like that. Then I heard Gibberne telling me to wake up, and I stirred and opened my eyes. There he stood as he had been standing, glass still in hand. It was empty, that was all the difference.

"Well?" said I.

"Nothing out of the way?"

"Nothing. A slight feeling of exhilaration, perhaps. Nothing more."

"Sounds?"

"Things are still," I said. "By Jove! yes! They *are* still. Except the sort of faint pat, patter, like rain falling on different things. What is it?"

"Analysed sounds," I think he said, but I am not sure. He glanced at the window. "Have you ever seen a curtain before a window fixed in that way before?"

I followed his eyes, and there was the end of the curtain, frozen, as it were, corner high, in the act of flapping briskly in the breeze.

"No," said I; "that's odd."

"And here," he said, and opened the hand that held the glass. Naturally I winced, expecting the glass to smash. But so far from smashing it did not even seem to stir; it hung in mid-air—motionless. "Roughly speaking," said Gibberne, "an object in these latitudes falls 16 feet in the first second. This glass is falling 16 feet in a second now. Only, you see, it hasn't been falling yet for the hundredth part of a second. That gives you some idea of the pace of my Accelerator." And he waved his hand round and round, over and under the slowly sinking glass. Finally he took it by the bottom, pulled it down and placed it very carefully on the table. "Eh?" he said to me, and laughed.

"That seems all right," I said, and began very gingerly to raise myself from my chair. I felt perfectly well, very light and comfortable, and quite confident in my mind. I was going fast all over. My heart, for example, was beating a thousand times a second, but that caused me no discomfort at all. I looked out of the window. An immovable cyclist, head down and with a frozen puff of dust behind his driving-wheel, scorched to overtake a galloping charabanc that did not stir. I gaped in amazement at this incredible spectacle. "Gibberne," I cried, "how long will this confounded stuff last?"

"Heaven knows!" he answered. "Last time I took it I went to bed and slept it off. I tell you, I was frightened. It must have lasted some minutes, I think—it seemed like hours. But after a bit it slows down rather suddenly, I believe."

I was proud to observe that I did not feel frightened—I suppose because there were two of us. "Why shouldn't we go out?" I asked.

"Why not?"

"They'll see us."

"Not they. Goodness, no! Why, we shall be going a thousand times faster than the quickest conjuring trick that was ever done. Come along! Which way shall we go? Window, or door?"

And out by the window we went.

Assuredly of all the strange experiences that I have ever had, or imagined, or read of other people having or imagining, that little raid I made with Gibberne on the Folkestone Leas, under the influence of the New Accelerator, was the strangest and maddest of all. We went out by his gate into the road, and there we made a minute examination of the statuesque passing traffic. The tops of the wheels and some of the legs of the horses of this charabanc, the end of the whip-lash and the lower jaw of the conductor—who was just beginning to yawn—were perceptibly in motion, but all the rest of the lumbering conveyance seemed still. And quite noiseless except for a faint rattling that came from one man's throat! And as parts of this frozen edifice there were a driver, you know, and a conductor, and eleven people! The effect as we walked about the thing began by being madly queer and ended by being—disagreeable. There they were, people like ourselves and yet not like ourselves, frozen in careless attitudes, caught in mid-gesture. A girl and a man smiled at one another, a leering smile that threatened to last for evermore; a woman in a floppy capelline rested her arm on the rail and stared at Gibberne's house with the unwinking stare of eternity; a man stroked his moustache like a figure of wax, and another stretched a tiresome stiff hand with extended fingers towards his loosened hat. We stared at them, we laughed at them, we made faces at them, and then a sort of disgust of them came upon us, and we turned away and walked round in front of the cyclist towards the Leas.

"Goodness!" cried Gibberne, suddenly; "look there!"

He pointed, and there at the tip of his finger and sliding down the air with wings flapping slowly and at the speed of an exceptionally languid snail—was a bee.

And so we came out upon the Leas. There the thing seemed madder than ever. The band was playing in the upper stand, though all the sound it made for us was a low-pitched, wheezy rattle, a sort of prolonged last sigh that passed at times into a sound like the slow, muffled ticking of some monstrous clock. Frozen people stood erect; strange, silent, self-conscious-looking dummies hung unstably in mid-stride, promenading upon the grass. I passed close to a poodle dog suspended in the act of leaping, and watched the slow movement of his legs as he sank to earth. "Lord, look *here*!" cried Gibberne, and we halted for a moment before a magnificent person in white faint-striped flannels, white shoes, and a Panama hat, who turned back to wink at two gaily dressed ladies he had passed. A wink, studied with such leisurely deliberation as we could afford, is an unattractive thing. It loses any quality of alert gaiety, and one remarks that the winking eye does not completely close, that under its drooping lid appears the lower edge of an eyeball and a line of white. "Heaven give me memory," said I, "and I will never wink again."

"Or smile," said Gibberne, with his eye on the lady's answering teeth.

"It's infernally hot, somehow," said I. "Let's go slower."

"Oh, come along!" said Gibberne.

We picked our way among the bath-chairs in the path. Many of the people sitting in the chairs seemed almost natural in their passive poses, but the contorted scarlet of the bandsmen was not a restful thing to see. A purple-faced gentleman was frozen in the midst of a violent struggle to refold his newspaper against the wind; there were many evidences that all these people in their sluggish way were exposed to a considerable breeze, a breeze that had no existence so far as our sensations went. We came out and walked a little way from the crowd, and turned and regarded it. To see all that multitude changed to a picture, smitten rigid, as it were, into a semblance of realistic wax, was impossibly wonderful. It was absurd, of course; but it filled me with an irrational, an exultant sense of superior advantage. Consider the wonder of it! All that I had said and thought and done since the stuff had begun to work in my veins had happened, so far as those people, so far as the world in general went, in the twinkling of an eye. "The New Accelerator—" I began, but Gibberne interrupted me.

"There's that infernal old woman!" he said.

"What old woman?"

"Lives next door to me," said Gibberne. "Has a lapdog that yaps. Gods! The temptation is strong!"

There is something very boyish and impulsive about Gibberne at times. Before I could expostulate with him he had dashed forward, snatched the unfortunate animal out of visible existence, and was running violently with it towards the cliff of the Leas. It was most extraordinary. The little brute, you know, didn't bark or wriggle or make the slightest sign of vitality. It kept quite stiffly in an attitude of somnolent repose, and Gibberne held it by the neck. It was like running about with a dog of wood. "Gibberne," I cried, "put it down!" Then I said something else. "If you run like that, Gibberne," I cried, "you'll set your clothes on fire. Your linen trousers are going brown as it is!"

He clapped his hand on his thigh and stood hesitating on the verge. "Gibberne," I cried, coming up, "put it down. This heat is too much! It's our running so! Two or three miles a second! Friction of the air!"

"What?" he said, glancing at the dog.

"Friction of the air," I shouted. "Friction of the air. Going too fast. Like meteorites and things. Too hot. And, Gibberne! Gibberne! I'm all over pricking and a sort of perspiration. You can see people stirring slightly. I believe the stuff's working off! Put that dog down."

"Eh?" he said.

"It's working off," I repeated. "We're too hot and the stuff's working off! I'm wet through."

He stared at me. Then at the band, the wheezy rattle of whose performance was certainly going faster. Then with a tremendous sweep of the arm he hurled the dog away from him and it went spinning upward, still inanimate and hung at last over the grouped parasols of a knot of chattering people. Gibberne was gripping my elbow. "By Jove!" he cried. "I believe it is! A sort of hot pricking and—yes. That man's moving his pocket-handkerchief! Perceptibly. We must get out of this sharp."

But we could not get out of it sharply enough. Luckily perhaps! For we might have run, and if we had run we should, I believe, have burst into flames. Almost certainly we should have burst into flames! You know we had neither of us thought of that... But before we could even begin to run the action of the drug had ceased. It was the business of a minute fraction of a second. The effect of the New Accelerator passed like the drawing of a curtain, vanished in the movement of a hand. I heard Gibberne's voice in infinite alarm. "Sit down," he said, and flop, down upon the turf at the edge of the Leas I sat—scorching as I sat. There is a patch of burnt grass there still where I sat down. The whole stagnation seemed to wake up as I did so, the disarticulated vibration of the band rushed together into a blast of music, the promenaders put their feet down and walked their ways, the papers and flags began flapping, smiles passed into words, the winker finished his wink and went on his way complacently, and all the seated people moved and spoke.

The whole world had come alive again, was going as fast as we were, or rather we were going no faster than the rest of the world. It was like slowing down as one comes into a railway station. Everything seemed to spin round for a second or two, I had the most transient feeling of nausea, and that was all. And the little dog which had seemed to hang for a moment when the force of Gibberne's arm was expended fell with a swift acceleration clean through a lady's parasol!

That was the saving of us. Unless it was for one corpulent old gentleman in a bath-chair, who certainly did start at the sight of us and afterwards regarded us at intervals with a darkly suspicious eye, and finally, I believe, said something to his nurse about us, I doubt if a solitary person remarked our sudden appearance among them. Plop! We must have appeared abruptly. We ceased to smoulder almost at once, though the turf beneath me was uncomfortably hot. The attention of everyone—including even the Amusements' Association band, which on this occasion, for the only time in its history, got out of tune—was arrested by the amazing fact, and the still more amazing yapping and uproar caused by the fact, that a respectable, over-fed lapdog sleeping quietly to the east of the bandstand should suddenly fall through the parasol of a lady on the west—in a slightly singed condition due to the extreme velocity of its movements through the air. In these absurd days, too, when we are all trying to be as psychic and silly and super-stitious as possible! People got up and trod on other people, chairs were overturned, the Leas policeman ran. How the matter settled itself I do not know—we were much too anxious to disentangle ourselves from the affair and get out of range of the eye of the old gentleman in the bath-chair to make minute inquiries. As soon as we were suffi-ciently cool and sufficiently recovered from our giddiness and nausea and confusion of mind to do so we stood up and, skirting the crowd, di-rected our steps back along the road below the Metropole towards Gibberne's house. But amidst the din I heard very distinctly the gen-tleman who had been sitting beside the lady of the ruptured sunshade using quite unjustifiable threats and language to one of those chair-attendants who have "Inspector" written on their caps. "If you didn't throw the dog," he said, "who *did*?"

The sudden return of movement and familiar noises, and our nat-ural anxiety about ourselves (our clothes were still dreadfully hot, and the fronts of the thighs of Gibberne's white trousers were scorched a drabbish brown), prevented the minute observations I should have liked to make on all these things. Indeed, I really made no observations of any scientific value on that return. The bee, of course, had gone. I looked for the cyclist, but he was already out of sight as we came into the Upper Sandgate Road or hidden from us by traffic; the charabanc, however, with its people now all alive and stirring, was clattering along at a spanking pace almost abreast of the nearer church.

We noted, however, that the window-sill on which we had stepped in getting out of the house was slightly singed, and that the impres-sions of our feet on the gravel of the path were unusually deep.

———

So it was I had my first experience of the New Accelerator. Practically we had been running about and saying and doing all sorts of things in the space of a second or so of time. We had lived half an hour while the band had played, perhaps, two bars. But the effect it had upon us was that the whole world had stopped for our convenient inspection. Con-sidering all things, and particularly considering our rashness in ven-turing out of the house, the experience might certainly have been much more disagreeable than it was. It showed, no doubt, that Gibberne has still much to learn before his preparation is a manageable convenience, but its practicability it certainly demonstrated beyond all cavil.

Since that adventure he has been steadily bringing its use under control, and I have several times, and without the slightest bad result, taken measured doses under his direction; though I must confess I have not yet ventured abroad again while under its influence. I may mention, for example, that this story has been written at one sitting and without interruption, except for the nibbling of some chocolate, by its means. I began at 6:25, and my watch is now very nearly at the minute past the half-hour. The convenience of securing a long, uninterrupted spell of work in the midst of a day full of engagements cannot be exaggerated. Gibberne is now working at the quantitative handling of his preparation, with especial reference to its distinctive effects upon different types of constitution. He then hopes to find a Retarder with which to dilute its present rather excessive potency. The Retarder will, of course, have the reverse effect to the Accelerator; used alone it should enable the patient to spread a few seconds over many hours of ordinary time, and so to maintain an apathetic inaction, a glacier-like absence of alacrity, amidst the most animated or irritating surroundings. The two things together must necessarily work an entire revolution in civilised existence. It is the beginning of our escape from that Time Garment of which Carlyle speaks. While this Accelerator will enable us to concentrate ourselves with tremendous impact upon any moment or occasion that demands our utmost sense and vigour, the Retarder will enable us to pass in passive tranquillity through infinite hardship and tedium. Perhaps I am a little optimistic about the Retarder, which has indeed still to be discovered, but about the Accelerator there is no possible sort of doubt whatever. Its appearance upon the market in a convenient, controllable, and assimilable form is a matter of the next few months. It will be obtainable of all chemists and druggists, in small green bottles, at a high but, considering its extraordinary qualities, by no means excessive price. Gibberne's Nervous Accelerator it will be called, and he hopes to be able to supply it in three strengths: one in 200, one in 900, and one in 2,000, distinguished by yellow, pink, and white labels respectively.

No doubt its use renders a great number of very extraordinary things possible; for, of course, the most remarkable and, possibly, even criminal proceedings may be effected with impunity by thus dodging, as it were, into the interstices of time. Like all potent preparations it will be liable to abuse. We have, however, discussed this aspect of the question very thoroughly, and we have decided that this is purely a matter of medical jurisprudence and altogether outside our province. We shall manufacture and sell the Accelerator, and, as for the consequences—we shall see.

THE STOLEN BODY

Mr. Bessel was the senior partner in the firm of Bessel, Hart, and Brown, of St. Paul's Churchyard, and for many years he was well known among those interested in psychical research as a liberal-minded and conscientious investigator. He was an unmarried man, and instead of living in the suburbs, after the fashion of his class, he occupied rooms in the Albany, near Piccadilly. He was particularly interested in the questions of thought transference and of apparitions of the living, and in November, 1896, he commenced a series of experiments in conjunction with Mr. Vincey, of Staple Inn, in order to test the alleged possibility of projecting an apparition of oneself by force of will through space.

Their experiments were conducted in the following manner: at a prearranged hour Mr. Bessel shut himself in one of his rooms in the Albany and Mr. Vincey in his sitting-room in Staple Inn, and each then fixed his mind as resolutely as possible on the other. Mr. Bessel had acquired the art of self-hypnotism, and, so far as he could, he attempted first to hypnotise himself and then to project himself as a "phantom of the living" across the intervening space of nearly two miles into Mr. Vincey's apartment. On several evenings this was tried without any satisfactory result, but on the fifth or sixth occasion Mr. Vincey did actually see or imagine he saw an apparition of Mr. Bessel standing in his room. He states that the appearance, although brief, was very vivid and real. He noticed that Mr. Bessel's face was white and his expression anxious, and, moreover, that his hair was disordered. For a moment Mr. Vincey, in spite of his state of expectation, was too surprised to speak or move, and in that moment it seemed to him as though the figure glanced over its shoulder and incontinently vanished.

It had been arranged that an attempt should be made to photograph any phantasm seen, but Mr. Vincey had not the instant presence of mind to snap the camera that lay ready on the table beside him, and when he did so he was too late. Greatly elated, however, even by this partial success, he made a note of the exact time, and at once took a cab to the Albany to inform Mr. Bessel of this result.

He was surprised to find Mr. Bessel's outer door standing open to the night, and the inner apartments lit and in an extraordinary disorder. An empty champagne magnum lay smashed upon the floor; its neck had been broken off against the inkpot on the bureau and lay beside it. An octagonal occasional table, which carried a bronze statuette and a number of choice books, had been rudely overturned, and down the primrose paper of the wall inky fingers had been drawn, as it seemed for the mere pleasure of defilement. One of the delicate chintz curtains had been violently torn from its rings and thrust upon the fire, so that the smell of its smouldering filled the room. Indeed the whole place was disarranged in the strangest fashion. For a few minutes Mr. Vincey, who had entered sure of finding Mr. Bessel in his easy chair awaiting him, could scarcely believe his eyes, and stood staring helplessly at these unanticipated things.

Then, full of a vague sense of calamity, he sought the porter at the entrance lodge. "Where is Mr. Bessel?" he asked. "Do you know that all the furniture is broken in Mr. Bessel's room?" The porter said nothing, but, obeying his gestures, came at once to Mr. Bessel's apartment to see the state of affairs. "This settles it," he said, surveying the lunatic confusion. "I didn't know of this. Mr. Bessel's gone off. He's mad!"

He then proceeded to tell Mr. Vincey that about half an hour previously, that is to say, at about the time of Mr. Bessel's apparition in Mr. Vincey's rooms, the missing gentleman had rushed out of the gates of the Albany into Vigo Street, hatless and with disordered hair, and had vanished into the direction of Bond Street. "And as he went past me," said the porter, "he laughed—a sort of gasping laugh, with his mouth open and his eyes glaring—I tell you, sir, he fair scared me!—like this."

According to his imitation it was anything but a pleasant laugh. "He waved his hand, with all his fingers crooked and clawing—like that. And he said, in a sort of fierce whisper, *'Life.'* Just that one word, *'Life!'*"

"Dear me," said Mr. Vincey. "Tut, tut," and "Dear me!" He could think of nothing else to say. He was naturally very much surprised. He turned from the room to the porter and from the porter to the room in the gravest perplexity. Beyond his suggestion that probably Mr. Bessel would come back presently and explain what had happened, their conversation was unable to proceed. "It might be a sudden toothache," said the porter, "a very sudden and violent toothache, jumping on him suddenly-like and driving him wild. I've broken things myself before now in such a case..." He thought. "If it was, why should he say *'life'* to me as he went past?"

Mr. Vincey did not know. Mr. Bessel did not return, and at last Mr. Vincey, having done some more helpless staring, and having addressed a note of brief inquiry and left it in a conspicuous position on the bureau, returned in a very perplexed frame of mind to his own premises in Staple Inn. This affair had given him a shock. He was at a loss to account for Mr. Bessel's conduct on any sane hypothesis. He tried to read, but he could not do so; he went for a short walk, and was so preoccupied that he narrowly escaped a cab at the top of Chancery Lane; and at last—a full hour before his usual time—he went to bed. For a considerable time he could not sleep because of his memory of the silent confusion of Mr. Bessel's apartment, and when at length he did attain an uneasy slumber it was at once disturbed by a very vivid and distressing dream of Mr. Bessel.

He saw Mr. Bessel gesticulating wildly, and with his face white and contorted. And, inexplicably mingled with his appearance, suggested perhaps by his gestures, was an intense fear, an urgency to act. He even believes that he heard the voice of his fellow experimenter calling distressfully to him, though at the time he considered this to be an illusion. The vivid impression remained though Mr. Vincey awoke. For a space he lay awake and trembling in the darkness, possessed with that vague, unaccountable terror of unknown possibilities that comes out of dreams upon even the bravest men. But at last he roused himself, and turned over and went to sleep again, only for the dream to return with enhanced vividness.

He awoke with such a strong conviction that Mr. Bessel was in overwhelming distress and need of help that sleep was no longer possible. He was persuaded that his friend had rushed out to some dire calamity. For a time he lay reasoning vainly against this belief, but at last he gave way to it. He arose, against all reason, lit his gas and dressed, and set out through the deserted streets—deserted, save for a noiseless policeman or so and the early news carts—towards Vigo Street to inquire if Mr. Bessel had returned.

But he never got there. As he was going down Long Acre some unaccountable impulse turned him aside out of that street towards Covent Garden, which was just waking to its nocturnal activities. He saw the market in front of him—a queer effect of glowing yellow lights and busy black figures. He became aware of a shouting, and perceived a figure turn the corner by the hotel and run swiftly towards him. He knew at once that it was Mr. Bessel. But it was Mr. Bessel transfigured. He was hatless and dishevelled, his collar was torn open, he grasped a bone-handled walking-cane near the ferrule end, and his mouth was pulled awry. And he ran, with agile strides, very rapidly. Their encounter was the affair of an instant. "Bessel!" cried Vincey.

The running man gave no sign of recognition either of Mr. Vincey or of his own name. Instead, he cut at his friend savagely with the stick, hitting him in the face within an inch of the eye. Mr. Vincey, stunned and astonished, staggered back, lost his footing, and fell heavily on the pavement. It seemed to him that Mr. Bessel leapt over him as he fell. When he looked again Mr. Bessel had vanished, and a policeman and a number of garden porters and salesmen were rushing past towards Long Acre in hot pursuit.

With the assistance of several passers-by—for the whole street was speedily alive with running people—Mr. Vincey struggled to his feet. He at once became the centre of a crowd greedy to see his injury. A multitude of voices competed to reassure him of his safety, and then to tell him of the behaviour of the madman, as they regarded Mr. Bessel. He had suddenly appeared in the middle of the market screaming "*'Life! Life!'*" striking left and right with a blood-stained walking-stick, and dancing and shouting with laughter at each successful blow. A lad and two women had broken heads, and he had smashed a man's wrist; a little child had been knocked insensible, and for a time he had driven everyone before him, so furious and resolute had his behaviour been. Then he made a raid upon a coffee stall, hurled its paraffin flare through the window of the post office, and fled laughing, after stunning the foremost of the two policemen who had the pluck to charge him.

Mr. Vincey's first impulse was naturally to join in the pursuit of his friend, in order if possible to save him from the violence of the indignant people. But his action was slow, the blow had half stunned him, and while this was still no more than a resolution came the news, shouted through the crowd, that Mr. Bessel had eluded his pursuers. At first Mr. Vincey could scarcely credit this, but the universality of the report, and presently the dignified return of two futile policemen, convinced him. After some aimless inquiries he returned towards Staple Inn, padding a hankerchief to a now very painful nose.

He was angry and astonished and perplexed. It appeared to him indisputable that Mr. Bessel must have gone violently mad in the midst of his experiment in thought transference, but why that should make him appear with a sad white face in Mr. Vincey's dreams seemed a problem beyond solution. He racked his brains in vain to explain this. It seemed to him at last that not simply Mr. Bessel, but the order of things must be insane. But he could think of nothing to do. He shut himself carefully into his room, lit his fire—it was a gas fire with asbestos bricks—and, fearing fresh dreams if he went to bed, remained bathing his injured face, or holding up books in a vain attempt to read, until dawn. Throughout that vigil he had a curious persuasion that Mr. Bessel was endeavouring to speak to him, but he would not let himself attend to any such belief.

About dawn, his physical fatigue asserted itself, and he went to bed and slept at last in spite of dreaming. He rose late, unrested and anxious and in considerable facial pain. The morning papers had no news of Mr. Bessel's aberration—it had come too late for them. Mr. Vincey's perplexities, to which the fever of his bruise added fresh irritation, became at last intolerable, and, after a fruitless visit to the Albany, he went down to St. Paul's Churchyard to Mr. Hart, Mr. Bessel's partner, and so far as Mr. Vincey knew, his nearest friend.

He was surprised to learn that Mr. Hart, although he knew nothing of the outbreak, had also been disturbed by a vision, the very vision that Mr. Vincey had seen—Mr. Bessel, white and dishevelled, pleading earnestly by his gestures for help. That was his impression of the import of his signs. "I was just going to look him up in the Albany when you arrived," said Mr. Hart. "I was so sure of something being wrong with him."

As the outcome of their consultation the two gentlemen decided to inquire at Scotland Yard for news of their missing friend. "He is bound to be laid by the heels," said Mr. Hart. "He can't go on at that pace for long." But the police authorities had not laid Mr. Bessel by the heels. They confirmed Mr. Vincey's overnight experiences and added fresh circumstances, some of an even graver character than those he knew— a list of smashed glass along the upper half of Tottenham Court Road, an attack upon a policeman in Hampstead Road, and an atrocious assault upon a woman. All these outrages were committed between half-past twelve and a quarter to two in the morning, and between those hours—and, indeed, from the very moment of Mr. Bessel's first rush from his rooms at half-past nine in the evening—they could trace the deepening violence of his fantastic career. For the last hour, at least from before one, that is, until a quarter to two, he had run amuck through London, eluding with amazing agility every effort to stop or capture him.

But after a quarter to two he had vanished. Up to that hour witnesses were multitudinous. Dozens of people had seen him, fled from him or pursued him, and then things suddenly came to an end. At a quarter to two he had been seen running down the Euston Road towards Baker Street, flourishing a can of burning colza oil and jerking splashes of flame therefrom at the windows of the houses he passed. But none of the policemen on Euston Road beyond the Waxwork Exhibition, nor any of those in the side streets down which he must have passed had he left the Euston Road, had seen anything of him. Abruptly he disappeared. Nothing of his subsequent doings came to light in spite of the keenest inquiry.

Here was a fresh astonishment for Mr. Vincey. He had found considerable comfort in Mr. Hart's conviction: "He is bound to be laid by the heels before long," and in that assurance he had been able to suspend his mental perplexities. But any fresh development seemed destined to add new impossibilities to a pile already heaped beyond the powers of his acceptance. He found himself doubting whether his memory might not have played him some grotesque trick, debating whether any of these things could possibly have happened; and in the afternoon he hunted up Mr. Hart again to share the intolerable weight on his mind. He found Mr. Hart engaged with a well-known private detective, but as that gentleman accomplished nothing in this case, we need not enlarge upon his proceedings.

All that day Mr. Bessel's whereabouts eluded an unceasingly active inquiry, and all that night. And all that day there was a persuasion in the back of Mr. Vincey's mind that Mr. Bessel sought his attention, and all through the night Mr. Bessel with a tear-stained face of anguish pursued him through his dreams. And whenever he saw Mr. Bessel in his dreams he also saw a number of other faces, vague but malignant, that seemed to be pursuing Mr. Bessel.

It was on the following day, Sunday, that Mr. Vincey recalled certain remarkable stories of Mrs. Bullock, the medium, who was then attracting attention for the first time in London. He determined to consult her. She was staying at the house of that well-known inquirer, Doctor Wilson Paget, and Mr. Vincey, although he had never met that gentleman before, repaired to him forthwith with the intention of invoking her help. But scarcely had he mentioned the name of Bessel when Doctor Paget interrupted him. "Last night—just at the end," he said, "we had a communication."

He left the room, and returned with a slate on which were certain words written in a handwriting, shaky indeed, but indisputably the handwriting of Mr. Bessel!

"How did you get this?" said Mr. Vincey. "Do you mean—?"

"We got it last night," said Doctor Paget. With numerous interruptions from Mr. Vincey, he proceeded to explain how the writing had been obtained. It appears that in her *séances,* Mrs. Bullock passes into a condition of trance, her eyes rolling up in a strange way under her eyelids, and her body becoming rigid. She then begins to talk very rapidly, usually in voices other than her own. At the same time one or both of her hands may become active, and if slates and pencils are provided they will then write messages simultaneously with and quite independently of the flow of words from her mouth. By many she is considered an even more remarkable medium than the celebrated Mrs. Piper. It was one of these messages, the one written by her left hand, that Mr. Vincey now had before him. It consisted of eight words written disconnectedly: "George Bessel...trial excav...Baker Street...

help ... starvation." Curiously enough, neither Doctor Paget nor the two other inquirers who were present had heard of the disappearance of Mr. Bessel—the news of it appeared only in the evening papers of Saturday—and they had put the message aside with many others of a vague and enigmatical sort that Mrs. Bullock has from time to time delivered.

When Doctor Paget heard Mr. Vincey's story, he gave himself at once with great energy to the pursuit of this clue to the discovery of Mr. Bessel. It would serve no useful purpose here to describe the inquiries of Mr. Vincey and himself; suffice it that the clue was a genuine one, and that Mr. Bessel was actually discovered by its aid.

He was found at the bottom of a detached shaft which had been sunk and abandoned at the commencement of the work for the new electric railway near Baker Street Station. His arm and leg and two ribs were broken. The shaft is protected by a hoarding nearly 20 feet high, and over this, incredible as it seems, Mr. Bessel, a stout, middle-aged gentleman, must have scrambled in order to fall down the shaft. He was saturated in colza oil, and the smashed tin lay beside him, but luckily the flame had been extinguished by his fall. And his madness had passed from him altogether. But he was, of course, terribly enfeebled, and at the sight of his rescuers he gave way to hysterical weeping.

In view of the deplorable state of his flat, he was taken to the house of Doctor Hatton in Upper Baker Street. Here he was subjected to a sedative treatment, and anything that might recall the violent crisis through which he had passed was carefully avoided. But on the second day he volunteered a statement.

Since that occasion Mr. Bessel has several times repeated this statement—to myself among other people—varying the details as the narrator of real experiences always does, but never by any chance contradicting himself in any particular. And the statement he makes is in substance as follows.

In order to understand it clearly it is necessary to go back to his experiments with Mr. Vincey before his remarkable attack. Mr. Bessel's first attempts at self-projection, in his experiments with Mr. Vincey, were, as the reader will remember, unsuccessful. But through all of them he was concentrating all his power and will upon getting out of the body—"willing it with all my might," he says. At last, almost against expectation, came success. And Mr. Bessel asserts that he, being alive, did actually, by an effort of will, leave his body and pass into some place or state outside this world.

The release was, he asserts, instantaneous. "At one moment I was seated in my chair, with my eyes tightly shut, my hands gripping the arms of the chair, doing all I could to concentrate my mind on Vincey, and then I perceived myself outside my body—saw my body near me, but certainly not containing me, with the hands relaxing and the head drooping forward on the breast."

Nothing shakes him in his assurance of that release. He describes in a quiet, matter-of-fact way the new sensation he experienced. He felt he had become impalpable—so much he had expected, but he had not expected to find himself enormously large. So, however, it would seem he became. "I was a great cloud—if I may express it that way—anchored to my body. It appeared to me, at first, as if I had discovered a greater self of which the conscious being in my brain was only a little part. I saw the Albany and Piccadilly and Regent Street and all the rooms and places in the houses, very minute and very bright and distinct, spread out below me like a little city seen from a balloon. Every now and then vague shapes like drifting wreaths of smoke made the vision a little indistinct, but at first I paid little heed to them. The thing that astonished me most, and which astonishes me still, is that I saw quite distinctly the insides of the houses as well as the streets, saw little people dining and talking in the private houses, men and women dining, playing billiards, and drinking in restaurants and hotels, and several places of entertainment crammed with people. It was like watching the affairs of a glass hive."

Such were Mr. Bessel's exact words as I took them down when he told me the story. Quite forgetful of Mr. Vincey, he remained for a space observing these things. Impelled by curiosity, he says, he stooped down, and with the shadowy arm he found himself possessed of attempted to touch a man walking along Vigo Street. But he could not do so, though his finger seemed to pass through the man. Something prevented his doing this, but what it was he finds it hard to describe. He compares the obstacle to a sheet of glass.

"I felt as a kitten may feel," he said, "when it goes for the first time to pat its reflection in a mirror." Again and again, on the occasion when I heard him tell this story, Mr. Bessel returned to that comparison of the sheet of glass. Yet it was not altogether a precise comparison, because, as the reader will speedily see, there were interruptions of this generally impermeable resistance, means of getting through the barrier to the material world again. But, naturally, there is a very great difficulty in expressing these unprecedented impressions in the language of everyday experience.

A thing that impressed him instantly, and which weighed upon him throughout all this experience, was the stillness of this place—he was in a world without sound.

At first Mr. Bessel's mental state was an unemotional wonder. His thought chiefly concerned itself with where he might be. He was out of the body—out of his material body, at any rate—but that was not all. He believes, and I for one believe also, that he was somewhere out of space, as we understand it, altogether. By a strenuous effort of will he had passed out of his body into a world beyond this world, a world undreamt of, yet lying so close to it and so strangely situated with regard to it that all things on this earth are clearly visible both from without and from within in this other world about us. For a long time, as it seemed to him, this realisation occupied his mind to the exclusion of all other matters, and then he recalled the engagement with Mr. Vincey, to which this astonishing experience was, after all, but a prelude.

He turned his mind to locomotion in this new body in which he found himself. For a time he was unable to shift himself from his attachment to his earthly carcass. For a time this new strange cloud body of his simply swayed, contracted, expanded, coiled, and writhed with his efforts to free himself, and then quite suddenly the link that bound him snapped. For a moment everything was hidden by what appeared to be whirling spheres of dark vapour, and then through a momentary gap he saw his drooping body collapse limply, saw his lifeless head drop sideways, and found he was driving along like a huge cloud in a strange place of shadowy clouds that had the luminous intricacy of London spread like a model below.

But now he was aware that the fluctuating vapour about him was something more than vapour, and the temerarious excitement of his first essay was shot with fear. For he perceived, at first indistinctly, and then suddenly very clearly, that he was surrounded by *faces*! that each roll and coil of the seeming cloud-stuff was a face. And such faces! Faces of thin shadow, faces of gaseous tenuity. Faces like those faces that glare with intolerable strangeness upon the sleeper in the evil hours of his dreams. Evil, greedy eyes that were full of a covetous curiosity, faces with knit brows and snarling, smiling lips; their vague hands clutched at Mr. Bessel as he passed, and the rest of their bodies was but an elusive streak of trailing darkness. Never a word they said, never a sound from the mouths that seemed to gibber. All about him they pressed in that dreamy silence, passing freely through the dim mistiness that was his body, gathering ever more numerously about him. And the shadowy Mr. Bessel, now suddenly fear-stricken, drove through the silent, active multitude of eyes and clutching hands.

So inhuman were these faces, so malignant their staring eyes, and shadowy, clawing gestures, that it did not occur to Mr. Bessel to attempt intercourse with these drifting creatures. Idiot phantoms, they seemed, children of vain desire, beings unborn and forbidden the boon of being, whose only expressions and gestures told of the envy and craving for life that was their one link with existence.

It says much for his resolution that, amidst the swarming cloud of these noiseless spirits of evil, he could still think of Mr. Vincey. He made a violent effort of will and found himself, he knew not how, stooping towards Staple Inn, saw Vincey sitting attentive and alert in his armchair by the fire.

And clustering also about him, as they clustered ever about all that lives and breathes, was another multitude of these vain voiceless shadows, longing, desiring, seeking some loophole into life.

For a space Mr. Bessel sought ineffectually to attract his friend's attention. He tried to get in front of his eyes, to move the objects in his room, to touch him. But Mr. Vincey remained unaffected, ignorant of the being that was so close to his own. The strange something that Mr. Bessel has compared to a sheet of glass separated them impermeably.

And at last Mr. Bessel did a desperate thing. I have told how that in some strange way he could see not only the outside of a man as we see him, but within. He extended his shadowy hand and thrust his vague black fingers, as it seemed, through the heedless brain.

Then, suddenly, Mr. Vincey started like a man who recalls his attention from wandering thoughts, and it seemed to Mr. Bessel that a little dark-red body situated in the middle of Mr. Vincey's brain swelled and glowed as he did so. Since that experience he has been shown anatomical figures of the brain, and he knows now that this is that useless structure, as doctors call it, the pineal eye. For, strange as it will seem to many, we have, deep in our brains—where it cannot possibly see any earthly light—an eye! At the time this, with the rest of the internal anatomy of the brain, was quite new to him. At the sight of its changed appearance, however, he thrust forth his finger, and, rather fearful still of the consequences, touched this little spot. And instantly Mr. Vincey started, and Mr. Bessel knew that he was seen.

And at that instant it came to Mr. Bessel that evil had happened to his body, and behold! a great wind blew through all that world of shadows and tore him away. So strong was this persuasion that he thought no more of Mr. Vincey, but turned about forthwith, and all the countless faces drove back with him like leaves before a gale. But he returned too late. In an instant he saw the body that he had left inert and collapsed—lying, indeed, like the body of a man just dead—had arisen, had arisen by virtue of some strength and will beyond his own. It stood with staring eyes, stretching its limbs in dubious fashion.

For a moment he watched it in wild dismay, and then he stooped towards it. But the pane of glass had closed against him again, and he was foiled. He beat himself passionately against this, and all about him the spirits of evil grinned and pointed and mocked. He gave way to furious anger. He compares himself to a bird that has fluttered heedlessly into a room and is beating at the window-pane that holds it back from freedom.

And behold! the little body that had once been his was now dancing with delight. He saw it shouting, though he could not hear its shouts; he saw the violence of its movements grow. He watched it fling his cherished furniture about in the mad delight of existence, rend his books apart, smash bottles, drink heedlessly from the jagged fragments, leap and smite in a passionate acceptance of living. He watched these actions in paralysed astonishment. Then once more he hurled himself against the impassable barrier, and then, with all that crew of mocking ghosts about him, hurried back in dire confusion to Vincey to tell him of the outrage that had come upon him.

But the brain of Vincey was now closed against apparitions, and the disembodied Mr. Bessel pursued him in vain as he hurried into Holborn to call a cab. Foiled and terror-stricken, Mr. Bessel swept back again, to find his desecrated body whooping in a glorious frenzy down the Burlington Arcade...

And now the attentive reader begins to understand Mr. Bessel's interpretation of the first part of this strange story. The being whose frantic rush through London had inflicted so much injury and disaster had indeed Mr. Bessel's body, but it was not Mr. Bessel. It was an evil spirit out of that strange world beyond existence, into which Mr. Bessel had so rashly ventured. For twenty hours it held possession of him, and for all those twenty hours the dispossessed spirit-body of Mr. Bessel was going to and fro in that unheard-of middle world of shadows seeking help in vain.

He spent many hours beating at the minds of Mr. Vincey and of his friend Mr. Hart. Each, as we know, he roused by his efforts. But the language that might convey his situation to these helpers across the gulf he did not know; his feeble fingers groped vainly and powerlessly in their brains. Once, indeed, as we have already told, he was able to turn Mr. Vincey aside from his path so that he encountered the stolen body in its career, but he could not make him understand the thing that had happened: he was unable to draw any help from that encounter...

All through those hours the persuasion was overwhelming in Mr. Bessel's mind that presently his body would be killed by its furious tenant, and he would have to remain in this shadow-land for evermore. So that those long hours were a growing agony of fear. And ever as he hurried to and fro in his ineffectual excitement innumerable spirits of that world about him mobbed him and confused his mind. And ever an envious applauding multitude poured after their successful fellow as he went upon his glorious career.

For that, it would seem, must be the life of these bodiless things of this world that is the shadow of our world. Ever they watch, coveting a way into a mortal body, in order that they may descend, as furies and frenzies, as violent lusts and mad, strange impulses, rejoicing in the body they have won. For Mr. Bessel was not the only human soul in that place. Witness the fact that he met first one, and afterwards several shadows of men, men like himself, it seemed, who had lost their bodies even it may be as he had lost his, and wandered, despairingly, in that lost world that is neither life nor death. They could not speak because that world is silent, yet he knew them for men because of their dim human bodies, and because of the sadness of their faces.

But how they had come into that world he could not tell, nor where the bodies they had lost might be, whether they still raved about the earth, or whether they were closed for ever in death against return. That they were the spirits of the dead neither he nor I believe. But Doctor Wilson Paget thinks they are the rational souls of men who are lost in madness on the earth.

At last Mr. Bessel chanced upon a place where a little crowd of such disembodied silent creatures had gathered, and thrusting through them he saw below a brightly lit room, and four or five quiet gentlemen and a woman, a stoutish woman dressed in black bombazine and sitting awkwardly in a chair with her head thrown back. He knew her from her portraits to be Mrs. Bullock, the medium. And he perceived that tracts and structures in her brain glowed and stirred as he had seen the pineal eye in the brain of Mr. Vincey glow. The light was very fitful; sometimes it was a broad illumination, and sometimes merely a faint twilight spot, and it shifted slowly about her brain. She kept on talking and writing with one hand. And Mr. Bessel saw that the crowding shadows of men about him, and a great multitude of the shadow spirits of that shadow-land, were all striving and thrusting to touch the lighted regions of her brain. As one gained her brain or another was thrust away, her voice and the writing of her hand changed. So that what she said was disorderly and confused for the most part; now a fragment of one soul's message, and now a fragment of another's, and now she babbled the insane fancies of the spirit of vain desire. Then Mr. Bessel understood that she spoke for the spirit that had touched her, and he began to struggle very furiously towards her. But he was on the outside of the crowd and at that time he could not reach her, and at last, growing anxious, he went away to find what had happened meanwhile to his body.

For a long time he went to and fro seeking it in vain and fearing that it must have been killed, and then he found it at the bottom of the shaft in Baker Street, writhing furiously and cursing with pain. Its leg and an arm and two ribs had been broken by its fall. Moreover, the evil spirit was angry because his time had been so short and because of the pain—making violent movements and casting his body about.

And at that Mr. Bessel returned with redoubled earnestness to the room where the *séance* was going on, and so soon as he had thrust himself within sight of the place he saw one of the men who stood about the medium looking at his watch as if he meant that the *séance* should presently end. At that a great number of the shadows who had been striving turned away with gestures of despair. But the thought that the *séance* was almost over only made Mr. Bessel the more earnest, and he struggled so stoutly with his will against the others that presently he gained the woman's brain. It chanced that just at that moment it glowed very brightly, and in that instant she wrote the message that Doctor Wilson Paget preserved. And then the other shadows and the cloud of evil spirits about him had thrust Mr. Bessel away from her, and for all the rest of the *séance* he could regain her no more.

So he went back and watched through the long hours at the bottom of the shaft where the evil spirit lay in the stolen body it had maimed, writhing and cursing, and weeping and groaning, and learning the lesson of pain. And towards dawn the thing he had waited for happened, the brain glowed brightly and the evil spirit came out, and Mr. Bessel entered the body he had feared he should never enter again. As he did so, the silence—the brooding silence—ended; he heard the tumult of traffic and the voices of people overhead, and that strange world that is the shadow of our world—the dark and silent shadows of ineffectual desire and the shadows of lost men—vanished clean away.

He lay there for the space of about three hours before he was found. And in spite of the pain and suffering of his wounds, and of the dim damp place in which he lay; in spite of the tears—wrung from him by his physical distress—his heart was full of gladness to know that he was nevertheless back once more in the kindly world of men.

PART TWO

TECHNOLOGICAL AND PREDICTIVE SCIENCE FICTION

INTRODUCTION

People who don't know what science fiction is tend to think science fiction is about the future—technologies that don't exist (yet) and awful cataclysms that haven't happened (yet). Some of it is. But I don't recommend using it as a guide to the future. I'd look hard at the (yet).

Writers of science fiction predicted robots that would do housework, but didn't foresee the computer till they were writing their stories on it. They predicted that we'd be colonizing alien planets by now, but not that we'd have so much trouble just getting to Mars.

The rate of technological invention long ago outstripped the ability of the artist to keep up. Engineers are supposed to be restricted by hard realities, but actually they're free to invent anything the laws of math, physics, and biology allow, which is, after all, a lot. Their minds can fly. They can defy gravity. Storytellers are supposed to be irresponsible, fancy-free; and indeed they may flout the laws of physics, but not the laws of art. They can't defy gravitas. Their inventions are bound to and bounded by the limitations of common experience, ordinary understanding, and human emotion. The kind of thing the real cyberheads disparagingly call wetware. Wetware is clumsy stuff, muddy and intractable, but it's the only stuff you can make stories out of.

Wells was writing his "futuristic" tales before the twentieth century got going, when technology hadn't run so far ahead of the writer—when, indeed, the writer could run ahead of the technology. Three of the five stories in this section are exactly that, the writer telling the engineers where they're going to go. These stories, like many of Jules Verne's, are genuinely predictive.

Since about the time it got called science fiction—the late 1920s—science fiction has not, in fact, been able to predict anything much at all. What science fiction can do and does do is offer not predictions but warnings, speculations, and alternatives.

Much of the strength of Wells's predictive visions lies there: as warnings, as visions of power out of control, as dreams of Armageddon.

—

"The Argonauts of the Air" was published in 1895, eight years before the Wright brothers took off at Kitty Hawk. It tells of the first trial of a flying machine—the word *aeroplane* or *airplane* wasn't current then.

The preparations, the machinery, the flight are splendidly, starkly imagined. Although the author speaks of the conquest of the air as being perhaps "costlier than the greatest war," his mood is adventurous, hopeful. Man will fly: it is only a matter of time. Less time, possibly, than he expected.

"In the Abyss" was written decades before William Beebe went that first half-mile down in his bathysphere. The details of the imagined technology are explicit and convincing, as is the descent into the depths of the sea. What the explorer of the abyss discovers there is a little less plausible. Though explained in the finest deadpan fake-scientific lingo ("descendants like ourselves of the great Theriomorpha of the New Red Sandstone age"), the creatures of the deep belong to Wells's cheerfully spooky mode. I doubt he really thought we'd meet them.

"The Star" is the purest example of a kind of story that has been written on its model ever since. Nothing fantastic or implausible: a perfectly possible event. No protagonists, no individual experience. A little necessary scientific jargon, then simple description, immense in scope, rapid in pace, of catastrophe approaching the whole earth. And a few final paragraphs of wry and unexpected summing-up. Wells wrote it in 1897. I doubt its brevity and intensity have been equaled.

He included "The Star" in his 1913 selection of his own short stories, but omitted the "Argonauts of the Air," "In the Abyss," and the next story here, "The Land Ironclads." He could not have imagined how poignant his predictions, both on the nail and amiss, might seem to people a hundred years later.

"The Land Ironclads," published in 1903, demands some imaginative repositioning on the part of the reader. It's not easy to pretend the First World War won't happen for ten years yet, and that the word *tank* means nothing but a container for liquids. It may take a little mental stretch to see what the argument about "Manhood *Versus* Machinery" meant—and means.

The last story in this section, "A Dream of Armageddon"—technological, predictive, terrible—a story about air war—was written in 1901. Still two years to go before Kitty Hawk. And the whole twentieth century and all its wars to come. Here the engineering and the visionary imaginations merge into something approaching prophecy.

Wells now has the words *aeroplane* and *propellor,* though the things did not exist (yet).

But war existed.

He tells his tale as a dream recounted by a chance acquaintance to the narrator, thus doubly distancing the emotional, almost hysterical story, which is weirdly complicated by the narrator's trivial questions, by interruptions from the dreamer's memories of the waking world, and by the narrator's awareness of all that is going on around the conversation. "A Dream of Armageddon" is a troubled, troubling story, half out of control, not easy to get out of your head.

The Argonauts of the Air

One saw Monson's Flying-Machine from the windows of the trains passing either along the South-Western main line or along the line between Wimbledon and Worcester Park,—to be more exact, one saw the huge scaffoldings which limited the flight of the apparatus. They rose over the tree-tops, a massive alley of interlacing iron and timber, and an enormous web of ropes and tackle, extending the best part of two miles. From the Leatherhead branch this alley was foreshortened and in part hidden by a hill with villas; but from the main line one had it in profile, a complex tangle of girders and curving bars, very impressive to the excursionists from Portsmouth and Southampton and the West. Monson had taken up the work where Maxim had left it, had gone on at first with an utter contempt for the journalistic wit and ignorance that had irritated and hampered his predecessor, and had spent (it was said) rather more than half his immense fortune upon his experiments. The results, to an impatient generation, seemed inconsiderable. When some five years had passed after the growth of the colossal iron groves at Worcester Park, and Monson still failed to put in a fluttering appearance over Trafalgar Square, even the Isle of Wight trippers felt their liberty to smile. And such intelligent people as did not consider Monson a fool stricken with the mania for invention, denounced him as being (for no particular reason) a self-advertising quack.

Yet now and again a morning trainload of season-ticket holders would see a white monster rush headlong through the airy tracery of guides and bars, and hear the further stays, nettings, and buffers snap, creak, and groan with the impact of the blow. Then there would be an efflorescence of black-set white-rimmed faces along the sides of the train, and the morning papers would be neglected for a vigorous discussion of the possibility of flying (in which nothing new was ever said by any chance), until the train reached Waterloo, and its cargo of season-ticket holders dispersed themselves over London. Or the fathers and mothers in some multitudinous train of weary excursionists returning exhausted from a day of rest by the sea, would find the dark fabric, standing out against the evening sky, useful in diverting some bilious child from its introspection, and be suddenly startled by the swift transit of a huge black flapping shape that strained upward against the guides. It was a great and forcible thing beyond dispute, and excellent for conversation; yet, all the same, it was but flying in leading-strings, and most of those who witnessed it scarcely counted its flight as flying. More of a switchback it seemed to the run of the folk.

Monson, I say, did not trouble himself very keenly about the opinions of the press at first. But possibly he, even, had formed but a poor idea of the time it would take before the tactics of flying were mastered, the swift assured adjustment of the big soaring shape to every gust and chance movement of the air; nor had he clearly reckoned the money this prolonged struggle against gravitation would cost him. And he was not so pachydermatous as he seemed. Secretly he had his periodical bundles of cuttings sent him by Romeike, he had his periodical reminders from his banker; and if he did not mind the initial ridicule and scepticism, he felt the growing neglect as the months went by and the money dribbled away. Time was when Monson had sent the enterprising journalist, keen after readable matter, empty from his gates. But when the enterprising journalist ceased from troubling, Monson was anything but satisfied in his heart of hearts. Still day by day the work went on, and the multitudinous subtle difficulties of the steering diminished in number. Day by day, too, the money trickled away, until his balance was no longer a matter of hundreds of thousands, but of tens. And at last came an anniversary.

Monson, sitting in the little drawing-shed, suddenly noticed the date on Woodhouse's calendar.

"It was five years ago today that we began," he said to Woodhouse suddenly.

"Is it?" said Woodhouse.

"It's the alterations play the devil with us," said Monson, biting a paper-fastener.

The drawings for the new vans to the hinder screw lay on the table before him as he spoke. He pitched the mutilated brass paper-fastener into the waste-paper basket and drummed with his fingers. "These alterations! Will the mathematicians ever be clever enough to save us all this patching and experimenting? Five years—learning by rule of thumb, when one might think that it was possible to calculate the whole thing out beforehand. The cost of it! I might have hired three senior wranglers for life. But they'd only have developed some beautifully useless theorems in pneumatics. What a time it has been, Woodhouse!"

"These mouldings will take three weeks," said Woodhouse. "At special prices."

"Three weeks!" said Monson, and sat drumming.

"Three weeks certain," said Woodhouse, an excellent engineer, but no good as a comforter. He drew the sheets towards him and began shading a bar.

Monson stopped drumming, and began to bite his finger-nails, staring the while at Woodhouse's head.

"How long have they been calling this Monson's Folly?" he said suddenly.

"*Oh!* Year or so," said Woodhouse carelessly, without looking up.

Monson sucked the air in between his teeth, and went to the window. The stout iron columns carrying the elevated rails upon which the start of the machine was made rose up close by, and the machine was hidden by the upper edge of the window. Through the grove of iron pillars, red painted and ornate with rows of bolts, one had a glimpse of the pretty scenery towards Esher. A train went gliding noiselessly across the middle distance, its rattle drowned by the hammering of the workmen overhead. Monson could imagine the grinning faces at the windows of the carriages. He swore savagely under his breath, and dabbed viciously at a blowfly that suddenly became noisy on the window-pane.

"What's up?" said Woodhouse, staring in surprise at his employer.

"I'm about sick of this."

Woodhouse scratched his cheek. "Oh!" he said, after an assimilating pause. He pushed the drawing away from him.

"Here these fools...I'm trying to conquer a new element—trying to do a thing that will revolutionise life. And instead of taking an intelligent interest, they grin and make their stupid jokes, and call me and my appliances names."

"Asses!" said Woodhouse, letting his eye fall again on the drawing.

The epithet, curiously enough, made Monson wince. "I'm about sick of it, Woodhouse, anyhow," he said, after a pause.

Woodhouse shrugged his shoulders.

"There's nothing for it but patience, I suppose," said Monson, sticking his hands in his pockets. "I've started. I've made my bed, and I've got to lie on it. I can't go back. I'll see it through, and spend every penny I have and every penny I can borrow. But I tell you, Woodhouse, I'm infernally sick of it, all the same. If I'd paid a tenth part of the money towards some political greaser's expenses—I'd have been a baronet before this."

Monson paused. Woodhouse stared in front of him with a blank expression he always employed to indicate sympathy, and tapped his pencil-case on the table. Monson stared at him for a minute.

"Oh, *damn!*" said Monson suddenly, and abruptly rushed out of the room.

Woodhouse continued his sympathetic rigour for perhaps half a minute. Then he sighed and resumed the shading of the drawings. Something had evidently upset Monson. Nice chap, and generous, but difficult to get on with. It was the way with every amateur who had anything to do with engineering—wanted everything finished at once. But Monson had usually the patience of the expert. Odd he was so irritable. Nice and round that aluminium rod did look now! Woodhouse threw back his head, and put it, first this side and then that, to appreciate his bit of shading better.

"Mr. Woodhouse," said Hooper, the foreman of the labourers, putting his head in at the door.

"Hullo!" said Woodhouse, without turning round.

"Nothing happened, sir?" said Hooper.

"Happened?" said Woodhouse.

"The governor just been up the rails swearing like a tornader."

"Oh!" said Woodhouse.

"It ain't like him, sir."

"No?"

"And I was thinking perhaps—"

"Don't think," said Woodhouse, still admiring the drawings.

Hooper knew Woodhouse, and he shut the door suddenly with a vicious slam. Woodhouse stared stonily before him for some further minutes, and then made an ineffectual effort to pick his teeth with his pencil. Abruptly he desisted, pitched that old, tried, and stumpy servitor across the room, got up, stretched himself, and followed Hooper.

He looked ruffled—it was visible to every workman he met. When a millionaire who has been spending thousands on experiments that employ quite a little army of people suddenly indicates that he is sick of the undertaking, there is almost invariably a certain amount of mental friction in the ranks of the little army he employs. And even before he indicates his intentions there are speculations and murmurs, a watching of faces and a study of straws. Hundreds of people knew before the day was out that Monson was ruffled, Woodhouse ruffled, Hooper ruffled. A workman's wife, for instance (whom Monson had never seen), decided to keep her money in the savings-bank instead of buying a velveteen dress. So far-reaching are even the casual curses of a millionaire.

Monson found a certain satisfaction in going on the works and behaving disagreeably to as many people as possible. After a time even that palled upon him, and he rode off the grounds, to every one's relief there, and through the lanes south-eastward, to the infinite tribulation of his house steward at Cheam.

And the immediate cause of it all, the little grain of annoyance that had suddenly precipitated all this discontent with his life-work was— these trivial things that direct all our great decisions!—half a dozen ill-considered remarks made by a pretty girl, prettily dressed, with a beautiful voice and something more than prettiness in her soft-grey eyes. And of these half-dozen remarks, two words especially— "Monson's Folly." She had felt she was behaving charmingly to Monson; she reflected the next day how exceptionally effective she had been, and no one would have been more amazed than she, had she learned the effect she had left on Monson's mind. I hope, considering everything, that she never knew.

"How are you getting on with your flying-machine?" she asked. ("I wonder if I shall ever meet any one with the sense not to ask that," thought Monson.) "It will be very dangerous at first, will it not?" ("Thinks I'm afraid.") "Jorgon is going to play presently; have you heard him before?" ("My mania being attended to, we turn to rational conversation.") Gush about Jorgon; gradual decline of conversation, ending with—"You must let me know when your flying-machine is finished, Mr. Monson, and then I will consider the advisability of taking a ticket." ("One would think I was still playing inventions in the nursery.") But the bitterest thing she said was not meant for Monson's ears. To Phlox, the novelist, she was always conscientiously brilliant. "I have been talking to Mr. Monson, and he can think of nothing, positively nothing, but that flying-machine of his. Do you know, all his workmen call that place of his 'Monson's Folly'? He is quite impossible. It is really very, very sad. I always regard him myself in the light of sunken treasure—the Lost Millionaire, you know."

She was pretty and well educated,—indeed, she had written an epigrammatic novelette; but the bitterness was that she was typical. She summarised what the world thought of the man who was working sanely, steadily, and surely towards a more tremendous revolution in the appliances of civilisation, a more far-reaching alteration in the ways of humanity than has ever been effected since history began. They did not even take him seriously. In a little while he would be proverbial. "I *must* fly now," he said on his way home, smarting with a sense of absolute social failure. "I must fly soon. If it doesn't come off soon, by God! I shall run amuck."

He said that before he had gone through his pass-book and his litter of papers. Inadequate as the cause seems, it was that girl's voice and the expression of her eyes that precipitated his discontent. But certainly the discovery that he had no longer even one hundred thousands pounds' worth of realisable property behind him was the poison that made the wound deadly.

It was the next day after this that he exploded upon Woodhouse and his workmen, and thereafter his bearing was consistently grim for three weeks, and anxiety dwelt in Cheam and Ewell, Malden, Morden, and Worcester Park, places that had thriven mightily on his experiments.

Four weeks after that first swearing of his, he stood with Woodhouse by the reconstructed machine as it lay across the elevated railway, by means of which it gained its initial impetus. The new propeller glittered a brighter white than the rest of the machine, and a gilder, obedient to a whim of Monson's, was picking out the aluminium bars with gold. And looking down the long avenue between the ropes (gilded now with the sunset), one saw red signals, and two miles away an ant-hill of workmen busy altering the last falls of the run into a rising slope.

"I'll *come*," said Woodhouse. "I'll come right enough. But I tell you it's infernally foolhardy. If only you would give another year—"

"I tell you I won't. I tell you the thing works. I've given years enough—"

"It's not that," said Woodhouse. "We're all right with the machine. But it's the steering—"

"Haven't I been rushing, night and morning, backwards and forwards, through this squirrel's cage? If the thing steers true here, it will steer true all across England. It's just funk, I tell you, Woodhouse. We could have gone a year ago. And besides—"

"Well?" said Woodhouse.

"The money!" snapped Monson over his shoulder.

"Hang it! I never thought of the money," said Woodhouse, and then, speaking now in a very different tone to that with which he had said the words before, he repeated, "I'll come. Trust me."

Monson turned suddenly, and saw all that Woodhouse had not the dexterity to say, shining on his sunset-lit face. He looked for a moment, then impulsively extended his hand. "Thanks," he said.

"All right," said Woodhouse, gripping the hand, and with a queer softening of his features. "Trust me."

Then both men turned to the big apparatus that lay with its flat wings extended upon the carrier, and stared at it meditatively. Monson, guided perhaps by a photographic study of the flight of birds, and by Lilienthal's methods, had gradually drifted from Maxim's shapes towards the bird form again. The thing, however, was driven by a huge screw behind in the place of the tail; and so hovering, which needs an almost vertical adjustment of a flat tail, was rendered impossible. The body of the machine was small, almost cylindrical, and pointed. Forward and aft on the pointed ends were two small petroleum engines for the screw, and the navigators sat deep in a canoe-like recess, the foremost one steering, and being protected by a low screen, with two plate-glass windows, from the blinding rush of air. On either side a monstrous flat framework with a curved front border could be adjusted so as either to lie horizontally, or to be tilted upward or down. These wings worked rigidly together, or, by releasing a pin, one could be tilted through a small angle independently of its fellow. The front edge of either wing could also be shifted back so as to diminish the wing-area about one-sixth. The machine was not only not designed to hover, but it was also incapable of fluttering. Monson's idea was to get into the air with the initial rush of the apparatus, and then to skim, much as a playing-card may be skimmed, keeping up the rush by means of the screw at the stern. Rooks and gulls fly enormous distances in that way with scarcely a perceptible movement of the wings. The bird really drives along on an aerial switchback. It glides slanting downward for a space, until it has gained considerable momentum, and then altering the inclination of its wings, glides up again almost to its original altitude. Even a Londoner who has watched the birds in the aviary in Regent's Park knows that.

But the bird is practising this art from the moment it leaves its nest. It has not only the perfect apparatus, but the perfect instinct to use it. A man off his feet has the poorest skill in balancing. Even the simple trick of the bicycle costs him some hours of labour. The instantaneous adjustments of the wings, the quick response to a passing breeze, the swift recovery of equilibrium, the giddy, eddying movements that require such absolute precision—all that he must learn, learn with infinite labour and infinite danger, if ever he is to conquer flying. The flying-machine that will start off some fine day, driven by neat "little levers," with a nice open deck like a liner, and all loaded up with bombshells and guns, is the easy dreaming of a literary man. In lives and in treasure the cost of the conquest of the empire of the air may even exceed all that has been spent in man's great conquest of the sea. Certainly it will be costlier than the greatest war that has ever devastated the world.

No one knew these things better than these two practical men. And they knew they were in the front rank of the coming army. Yet there is hope even in a forlorn hope. Men are killed outright in the reserves sometimes, while others who have been left for dead in the thickest corner crawl out and survive.

"If we miss these meadows"—said Woodhouse presently in his slow way.

"My dear chap," said Monson, whose spirits had been rising fitfully during the last few days, "we mustn't miss these meadows. There's a quarter of a square mile for us to hit, fences removed, ditches levelled. We shall come down all right—rest assured. And if we don't—"

"Ah!" said Woodhouse. "If we don't!"

Before the day of the start, the newspaper people got wind of the alterations at the northward end of the framework, and Monson was cheered by a decided change in the comments Romeike forwarded him. "He will be off some day," said the papers. "He will be off some day," said the South-Western season-ticket holders one to another; the seaside excursionists, the Saturday-to-Monday trippers from Sussex and Hampshire and Dorset and Devon, the eminent literary people from Haslemere, all remarked eagerly one to another, "He will be off some day," as the familiar scaffolding came in sight. And actually, one bright morning, in full view of the ten-past-ten train from Basingstoke, Monson's flying-machine started on its journey.

They saw the carrier running swiftly along its rail, and the white and gold screw spinning in the air. They heard the rapid rumble of wheels, and a thud as the carrier reached the buffers at the end of its run. Then a whirr as the Flying-Machine was shot forward into the networks. All that the majority of them had seen and heard before. The thing went with a drooping flight through the framework and rose again, and then every beholder shouted, or screamed, or yelled, or shrieked after his kind. For instead of the customary concussion and stoppage, the Flying-Machine flew out of its five years' cage like a bolt from a crossbow, and drove slantingly upward into the air, curved round a little, so as to cross the line, and soared in the direction of Wimbledon Common.

It seemed to hang momentarily in the air and grow smaller, then it ducked and vanished over the clustering blue tree-tops to the east of Coombe Hill, and no one stopped staring and gasping until long after it had disappeared.

That was what the people in the train from Basingstoke saw. If you had drawn a line down the middle of that train, from engine to guard's van, you would not have found a living soul on the opposite side to the flying-machine. It was a mad rush from window to window as the thing crossed the line. And the engine-driver and stoker never took their eyes off the low hills about Wimbledon, and never noticed that they had run clean through Coombe and Malden and Raynes Park, until, with returning animation, they found themselves pelting, at the most indecent pace, into Wimbledon station.

From the moment when Monson had started the carrier with a *"Now!"* neither he nor Woodhouse said a word. Both men sat with clenched teeth. Monson had crossed the line with a curve that was too sharp, and Woodhouse had opened and shut his white lips; but neither spoke. Woodhouse simply gripped his seat, and breathed sharply through his teeth, watching the blue country to the west rushing past, and down, and away from him. Monson knelt at his post forward, and his hands trembled on the spoked wheel that moved the wings. He could see nothing before him but a mass of white clouds in the sky.

The machine went slanting upward, travelling with an enormous speed still, but losing momentum every moment. The land ran away underneath with diminishing speed.

"Now!" said Woodhouse at last, and with a violent effort Monson wrenched over the wheel and altered the angle of the wings. The machine seemed to hang for half a minute motionless in mid-air, and then he saw the hazy blue house-covered hills of Kilburn and Hampstead jump up before his eyes and rise steadily, until the little sunlit dome of the Albert Hall appeared through his windows. For a moment he scarcely understood the meaning of this upward rush of the horizon, but as the nearer and nearer houses came into view, he realised what he had done. He had turned the wings over too far, and they were swooping steeply downward towards the Thames.

The thought, the question, the realisation were all the business of a second of time. "Too much!" gasped Woodhouse. Monson brought the wheel half-way back with a jerk, and forthwith the Kilburn and Hampstead ridge dropped again to the lower edge of his windows. They had been a thousand feet above Coombe and Malden station; fifty seconds after they whizzed, at a frightful pace, not eighty feet above the East Putney station, on the Metropolitan District line, to the screaming astonishment of a platformful of people. Monson flung up the vans against the air, and over Fulham they rushed up their atmospheric switchback again, steeply—too steeply. The buses went floundering across the Fulham Road, the people yelled.

Then down again, too steeply still, and the distant trees and houses about Primrose Hill leapt up across Monson's window, and then suddenly he saw straight before him the greenery of Kensington Gardens and the towers of the Imperial Institute. They were driving straight down upon South Kensington. The pinnacles of the Natural History Museum rushed up into view. There came one fatal second of swift thought, a moment of hesitation. Should he try and clear the towers, or swerve eastward?

He made a hesitating attempt to release the right wing, left the catch half-released, and gave a frantic clutch at the wheel.

The nose of the machine seemed to leap up before him. The wheel pressed his hand with irresistible force, and jerked itself out of his control.

Woodhouse, sitting crouched together, gave a hoarse cry, and sprang up towards Monson. "Too far!" he cried, and then he was clinging to the gunwale for dear life, and Monson had been jerked clean overhead, and was falling backwards upon him.

So swiftly had the thing happened that barely a quarter of the people going to and fro in Hyde Park, and Brompton Road, and the Exhibition Road saw anything of the aerial catastrophe. A distant winged shape had appeared above the clustering houses to the south, had fallen and risen, growing larger as it did so; had swooped swiftly down towards the Imperial Institute, a broad spread of flying wings, had swept round in a quarter circle, dashed eastward, and then suddenly sprang vertically into the air. A black object shot out of it, and came spinning downward. A man! Two men clutching each other! They came whirling down, separated as they struck the roof of the Students' Club, and bounded off into the green bushes on its southward side.

For perhaps half a minute, the pointed stem of the big machine still pierced vertically upward, the screw spinning desperately. For one brief instant, that yet seemed an age to all who watched, it had hung motionless in mid-air. Then a spout of yellow flame licked up its length from the stern engine, and swift, swifter, swifter, and flaring like a rocket, it rushed down upon the solid mass of masonry which was formerly the Royal College of Science. The big screw of white and gold touched the parapet, and crumpled up like wet linen. Then the blazing spindle-shaped body smashed and splintered, smashing and splintering in its fall, upon the north-westward angle of the building.

But the crash, the flame of blazing paraffin that shot heavenward from the shattered engines of the machine, the crushed horrors that were found in the garden beyond the Students' Club, the masses of yellow parapet and red brick that fell headlong into the roadway, the running to and fro of people like ants in a broken ant-hill, the galloping of fire-engines, the gathering of crowds—all these things do not belong to this story, which was written only to tell how the first of all successful flying-machines was launched and flew. Though he failed, and failed disastrously, the record of Monson's work remains—a sufficient monument—to guide the next of that band of gallant experimentalists who will sooner or later master this great problem of flying. And between Worcester Park and Malden there still stands that portentous avenue of iron-work, rusting now, and dangerous here and there, to witness to the first desperate struggle for man's right of way through the air.

In the Abyss

The lieutenant stood in front of the steel sphere and gnawed a piece of pine splinter. "What do you think of it, Steevens?" he asked.

"It's an idea," said Steevens, in the tone of one who keeps an open mind.

"I believe it will smash—flat," said the lieutenant.

"He seems to have calculated it all out pretty well," said Steevens, still impartial.

"But think of the pressure," said the lieutenant. "At the surface of the water it's fourteen pounds to the inch, thirty feet down it's double that; sixty, treble; ninety, four times; nine hundred, forty times; five thousand, three hundred—that's a mile—it's two hundred and forty times fourteen pounds; that's—let's see—thirty hundredweight—a ton and a half, Steevens; *a ton and a half* to the square inch. And the ocean where he's going is five miles deep. That's seven and a half—"

"Sounds a lot," said Steevens, "but it's jolly thick steel."

The lieutenant made no answer, but resumed his pine splinter. The object of their conversation was a huge ball of steel, having an exterior diameter of perhaps nine feet. It looked like the shot for some Titanic piece of artillery. It was elaborately nested in a monstrous scaffolding built into the framework of the vessel, and the gigantic spars that were presently to sling it overboard gave the stern of the ship an appearance that had raised the curiosity of every decent sailor who had sighted it, from the Pool of London to the Tropic of Capricorn. In two places, one above the other, the steel gave place to a couple of circular windows of enormously thick glass, and one of these, set in a steel frame of great solidity, was now partially unscrewed. Both the men had seen the interior of this globe for the first time that morning. It was elaborately padded with air cushions, with little studs sunk between bulging pillows to work the simple mechanism of the affair. Everything was elaborately padded, even the Myers apparatus which was to absorb carbonic acid and replace the oxygen inspired by its tenant, when he had crept in by the glass manhole, and had been screwed in. It was so elaborately padded that a man might have been fired from a gun in it with perfect safety. And it had need to be, for presently a man was to crawl in through that glass manhole, to be screwed up tightly, and to be flung overboard, and to sink down—down—down, for five miles, even as the lieutenant said. It had taken the strongest hold of his imagination; it made him a bore at mess; and he found Steevens, the new arrival aboard, a godsend to talk to about it, over and over again.

"It's my opinion," said the lieutenant, "that that glass will simply bend in and bulge and smash, under a pressure of that sort. Daubrée has made rocks run like water under big pressure—and, you mark my words—"

"If the glass did break in," said Steevens, "what then?"

"The water would shoot in like a jet of iron. Have you ever felt a straight jet of high pressure water? It would hit as hard as a bullet. It would simply smash him and flatten him. It would tear down his throat, and into his lungs; it would blow in his ears—"

"What a detailed imagination you have!" protested Steevens, who saw things vividly.

"It's a simple statement of the inevitable," said the lieutenant.

"And the globe?"

"Would just give out a few little bubbles, and it would settle down comfortably against the day of judgment, among the oozes and the bottom clay—with poor Elstead spread over his own smashed cushions like butter over bread."

He repeated his sentence as though he liked it very much. "Like butter over bread," he said.

"Having a look at the jigger?" said a voice, and Elstead stood behind them, spick and span in white, with a cigarette between his teeth, and his eyes smiling out of the shadow of his ample hat-brim. "What's that about bread and butter, Weybridge! Grumbling as usual about the insufficient pay of naval officers? It won't be more than a day now before I start. We are to get the slings ready to-day. This clean sky and gentle swell is just the kind of thing for swinging off a dozen tons of lead and iron, isn't it?"

"It won't affect you much," said Weybridge.

"No. Seventy or eighty feet down, and I shall be there in a dozen seconds, there's not a particle moving, though the wind shriek itself hoarse up above, and the water lifts halfway to the clouds. No. Down there—" He moved to the side of the ship and the other two followed him. All three leant forward on their elbows and stared down into the yellow-green water.

"Peace," said Elstead, finishing his thought aloud.

"Are you dead certain that clockwork will act?" asked Weybridge presently.

"It has worked thirty-five times," said Elstead. "It's bound to work."

"But if it doesn't?"

"Why shouldn't it?"

"I wouldn't go down in that confounded thing," said Weybridge, "for twenty thousand pounds."

"Cheerful chap you are," said Elstead, and spat sociably at a bubble below.

"I don't understand yet how you mean to work the thing," said Steevens.

"In the first place, I'm screwed into the sphere," said Elstead, "and when I've turned the electric light off and on three times to show I'm cheerful, I'm swung out over the stern by that crane, with all those big lead sinkers slung below me. The top lead weight has a roller carrying a hundred fathoms of strong cord rolled up, and that's all that joins the sinkers to the sphere, except the slings that will be cut when the affair is dropped. We use cord rather than wire rope because it's easier to cut and more buoyant—necessary points, as you will see.

"Through each of these lead weights you notice there is a hole, and an iron rod will be run through that and will project six feet on the lower side. If that rod is rammed up from below, it knocks up a lever and sets the clockwork in motion at the side of the cylinder on which the cord winds.

"Very well. The whole affair is lowered gently into the water, and the slings are cut. The sphere floats,—with the air in it, it's lighter than water,—but the lead weights go down straight and the cord runs out. When the cord is all paid out, the sphere will go down too, pulled down by the cord."

"But why the cord?" asked Steevens. "Why not fasten the weights directly to the sphere?"

"Because of the smash down below. The whole affair will go rushing down, mile after mile, at a headlong pace at last. It would be knocked to pieces on the bottom if it wasn't for that cord. But the weights will hit the bottom, and directly they do, the buoyancy of the sphere will come into play. It will go on sinking slower and slower; come to a stop at last, and then begin to float upward again.

"That's where the clockwork comes in. Directly the weights smash against the sea bottom, the rod will be knocked through and will kick up the clockwork, and the cord will be rewound on the reel. I shall be lugged down on the sea bottom. There I shall stay for half an hour, with the electric light on, looking about me. Then the clockwork will release a spring knife, the cord will be cut, and up I shall rush again, like a soda-water bubble. The cord itself will help the flotation."

"And if you should chance to hit a ship?" said Weybridge.

"I should come up at such a pace, I should go clean through it," said Elstead, "like a cannon ball. You needn't worry about that."

"And suppose some nimble crustacean should wriggle into your clockwork—"

"It would be a pressing sort of invitation for me to stop," said Elstead, turning his back on the water and staring at the sphere.

———

They had swung Elstead overboard by eleven o'clock. The day was serenely bright and calm, with the horizon lost in haze. The electric glare in the little upper compartment beamed cheerfully three times. Then they let him down slowly to the surface of the water, and a sailor in the stern chains hung ready to cut the tackle that held the lead weights and the sphere together. The globe, which had looked so large on deck, looked the smallest thing conceivable under the stern of the ship. It rolled a little, and its two dark windows, which floated uppermost, seemed like eyes turned up in round wonderment at the people who crowded the rail. A voice wondered how Elstead liked the rolling. "Are you ready?" sang out the commander. "Ay, ay, sir!" "Then let her go!"

The rope of the tackle tightened against the blade and was cut, and an eddy rolled over the globe in a grotesquely helpless fashion. Some-one waved a handkerchief, someone else tried an ineffectual cheer, a middy was counting slowly, "Eight, nine, ten!" Another roll, then with a jerk and a splash the thing righted itself.

It seemed to be stationary for a moment, to grow rapidly smaller, and then the water closed over it, and it became visible, enlarged by re-fraction and dimmer, below the surface. Before one could count three it had disappeared. There was a flicker of white light far down in the water, that diminished to a speck and vanished. Then there was noth-ing but a depth of water going down into blackness, through which a shark was swimming.

Then suddenly the screw of the cruiser began to rotate, the water was crickled, the shark disappeared in a wrinkled confusion, and a tor-rent of foam rushed across the crystalline clearness that had swallowed up Elstead. "What's the idee?" said one A.B. to another.

"We're going to lay off about a couple of miles, 'fear he should hit us when he comes up," said his mate.

The ship steamed slowly to her new position. Aboard her almost every one who was unoccupied remained watching the breathing swell into which the sphere had sunk. For the next half-hour it is doubtful if a word was spoken that did not bear directly or indirectly on Elstead. The December sun was now high in the sky, and the heat very considerable.

"He'll be cold enough down there," said Weybridge. "They say that below a certain depth sea water's always just about freezing."

"Where'll he come up?" asked Steevens. "I've lost my bearings."

"That's the spot," said the commander, who prided himself on his omniscience. He extended a precise finger south-eastward. "And this, I reckon, is pretty nearly the moment," he said. "He's been thirty-five minutes."

"How long does it take to reach the bottom of the ocean?" asked Steevens.

"For a depth of five miles, and reckoning—as we did—an accelera-tion of two feet per second, both ways, is just about three-quarters of a minute."

"Then he's overdue," said Weybridge.

"Pretty nearly," said the commander. "I suppose it takes a few min-utes for that cord of his to wind in."

"I forgot that," said Weybridge, evidently relieved.

And then began the suspense. A minute slowly dragged itself out, and no sphere shot out of the water. Another followed, and nothing broke the low oily swell. The sailors explained to one another that little point about the winding-in of the cord. The rigging was dotted with expectant faces. "Come up, Elstead!" called one hairy-chested salt impatiently, and the others caught it up, and shouted as though they were waiting for the curtain of a theatre to rise.

The commander glanced irritably at them.

"Of course, if the acceleration's less than two," he said, "he'll be all the longer. We aren't absolutely certain that was the proper figure. I'm no slavish believer in calculations."

Steevens agreed concisely. No one on the quarterdeck spoke for a couple of minutes. Then Steevens's watchcase clicked.

When, twenty-one minutes after, the sun reached the zenith, they were still waiting for the globe to reappear, and not a man aboard had dared to whisper that hope was dead. It was Weybridge who first gave expression to that realisation. He spoke while the sound of eight bells still hung in the air. "I always distrusted that window," he said quite suddenly to Steevens.

"Good God!" said Steevens; "you don't think—?"

"Well!" said Weybridge, and left the rest to his imagination.

"I'm no great believer in calculations myself," said the commander dubiously, "so that I'm not altogether hopeless yet." And at midnight the gunboat was steaming in a spiral round the spot where the globe had sunk, and the white beam of the electric light fled and halted and swept discontentedly onward again over the waste of phosphorescent waters under the little stars.

"If his window hasn't burst and smashed him," said Weybridge, "then it's a cursed sight worse, for his clockwork has gone wrong, and he's alive now, five miles under our feet, down there in the cold and dark, anchored in that little bubble of his, where never a ray of light has shone or a human being lived, since the waters were gathered together. He's there without food, feeling hungry and thirsty and scared, wondering whether he'll starve or stifle. Which will it be? The Myers apparatus is running out, I suppose. How long do they last?

"Good heavens!" he exclaimed; "what little things we are! What daring little devils! Down there, miles and miles of water—all water, and all this empty water about us and this sky. Gulfs!" He threw his hands out, and as he did so, a little white streak swept noiselessly up the sky, travelled more slowly, stopped, became a motionless dot, as though a new star had fallen up into the sky. Then it went sliding back again and lost itself amidst the reflections of the stars and the white haze of the sea's phosphorescence.

At the sight he stopped, arm extended and mouth open. He shut his mouth, opened it again, and waved his arms with an impatient gesture. Then he turned, shouted, "El-stead ahoy!" to the first watch, and went at a run to Lindley and the search-light. "I saw him," he said. "Starboard there! His light's on, and he's just shot out of the water. Bring the light round. We ought to see him drifting, when he lifts on the swell."

But they never picked up the explorer until dawn. Then they almost ran him down. The crane was swung out and a boat's crew hooked the chain to the sphere. When they had shipped the sphere, they unscrewed the manhole and peered into the darkness of the interior (for the electric light chamber was intended to illuminate the water about the sphere, and was shut off entirely from its general cavity).

The air was very hot within the cavity, and the indiarubber at the lip of the manhole was soft. There was no answer to their eager questions and no sound of movement within. Elstead seemed to be lying motionless, crumpled up in the bottom of the globe. The ship's doctor crawled in and lifted him out to the men outside. For a moment or so they did not know whether Elstead was alive or dead. His face, in the yellow light of the ship's lamps, glistened with perspiration. They carried him down to his own cabin.

He was not dead, they found, but in a state of absolute nervous collapse, and besides cruelly bruised. For some days he had to lie perfectly still. It was a week before he could tell his experiences.

Almost his first words were that he was going down again. The sphere would have to be altered, he said, in order to allow him to throw off the cord if need be, and that was all. He had had the most marvellous experience. "You thought I should find nothing but ooze," he said. "You laughed at my explorations, and I've discovered a new world!" He told his story in disconnected fragments, and chiefly from the wrong end, so that it is impossible to retell it in his words. But what follows is the narrative of his experience.

It began atrociously, he said. Before the cord ran out, the thing kept rolling over. He felt like a frog in a football. He could see nothing but the crane and the sky overhead, and with an occasional glimpse of the people on the ship's rail. He couldn't tell a bit which way the thing would roll next. Suddenly he would find his feet going up, and try to step, and over he went rolling, head over heels, and just anyhow, on the padding. Any other shape would have been more comfortable, but no other shape was to be relied upon under the huge pressure of the nethermost abyss.

Suddenly the swaying ceased; the globe righted, and when he had picked himself up, he saw the water all about him greeny-blue, with an attenuated light filtering down from above, and a shoal of little floating things went rushing up past him, as it seemed to him, towards the light. And even as he looked, it grew darker and darker, until the water above was as dark as the midnight sky, albeit of a greener shade, and the water below black. And little transparent things in the water developed a faint glint of luminosity, and shot past him in faint greenish streaks.

And the feeling of falling! It was just like the start of a lift, he said, only it kept on. One has to imagine what that means, that keeping on. It was then of all times that Elstead repented of his adventure. He saw the chances against him in an altogether new light. He thought of the big cuttle-fish people knew to exist in the middle waters, the kind of things they find half-digested in whales at times, or floating dead and rotten and half-eaten by fish. Suppose one caught hold and wouldn't let go. And had the clockwork really been sufficiently tested? But whether he wanted to go or to go back mattered not the slightest now.

In fifty seconds everything was as black as night outside, except where the beam from his light struck through the waters, and picked out every now and then some fish or scrap of sinking matter. They flashed by too fast for him to see what they were. Once he thinks he passed a shark. And then the sphere began to get hot by friction against the water. They had underestimated this, it seems.

The first thing he noticed was that he was perspiring, and then he heard a hissing growing louder under his feet, and saw a lot of little bubbles—very little bubbles they were—rushing upward like a fan through the water outside. Steam! He felt the window, and it was hot. He turned on the minute glow-lamp that lit his own cavity, looked at the padded watch by the studs, and saw he had been travelling now for two minutes. It came into his head that the window would crack through the conflict of temperatures, for he knew the bottom water is very near freezing.

Then suddenly the floor of the sphere seemed to press against his feet, the rush of bubbles outside grew slower and slower, and the hissing diminished. The sphere rolled a little. The window had not cracked, nothing had given, and he knew that the dangers of sinking, at any rate, were over.

In another minute or so he would be on the floor of the abyss. He thought, he said, of Steevens and Weybridge and the rest of them five miles overhead, higher to him than the very highest clouds that ever floated over land are to us, steaming slowly and staring down and wondering what had happened to him.

He peered out of the window. There were no more bubbles now, and the hissing had stopped. Outside there was a heavy blackness—as black as black velvet—except where the electric light pierced the empty water and showed the colour of it—a yellow-green. Then three things like shapes of fire swam into sight, following each other through the water. Whether they were little and near or big and far off he could not tell.

Each was outlined in a bluish light almost as bright as the lights of a fishing smack, a light which seemed to be smoking greatly, and all along the sides of them were specks of this, like the lighter portholes of a ship. Their phosphorescence seemed to go out as they came into the radiance of his lamp, and he saw then that they were little fish of some strange sort, with huge heads, vast eyes, and dwindling bodies and tails. Their eyes were turned towards him, and he judged they were following him down. He supposed they were attracted by his glare.

Presently others of the same sort joined them. As he went on down, he noticed that the water became of a pallid colour, and that little specks twinkled in his ray like motes in a sunbeam. This was probably due to the clouds of ooze and mud that the impact of his leaden sinkers had disturbed.

By the time he was drawn down to the lead weights he was in a dense fog of white that his electric light failed altogether to pierce for more than a few yards, and many minutes elapsed before the hanging sheets of sediment subsided to any extent. Then, lit by his light and by the transient phosphorescence of a distant shoal of fishes, he was able to see under the huge blackness of the super-incumbent water an undulating expanse of greyish-white ooze, broken here and there by tangled thickets of a growth of sea lilies, waving hungry tentacles in the air.

Farther away were the graceful, translucent outlines of a group of gigantic sponges. About this floor there were scattered a number of bristling flattish tufts of rich purple and black, which he decided must be some sort of sea-urchin, and small, large-eyed or blind things having a curious resemblance, some to woodlice, and others to lobsters, crawled sluggishly across the track of the light and vanished into the obscurity again, leaving furrowed trails behind them.

Then suddenly the hovering swarm of little fishes veered about and came towards him as a flight of starlings might do. They passed over him like a phosphorescent snow, and then he saw behind them some larger creature advancing towards the sphere.

At first he could see it only dimly, a faintly moving figure remotely suggestive of a walking man, and then it came into the spray of light that the lamp shot out. As the glare struck it, it shut its eyes, dazzled. He stared in rigid astonishment.

It was a strange vertebrated animal. Its dark purple head was dimly suggestive of a chameleon, but it had such a high forehead and such a braincase as no reptile ever displayed before; the vertical pitch of its face gave it a most extraordinary resemblance to a human being.

Two large and protruding eyes projected from sockets in chameleon fashion, and it had a broad reptilian mouth with horny lips beneath its little nostrils. In the position of the ears were two huge gill-covers, and out of these floated a branching tree of coralline filaments, almost like the tree-like gills that very young rays and sharks possess.

But the humanity of the face was not the most extraordinary thing about the creature. It was a biped; its almost globular body was poised on a tripod of two frog-like legs and a long thick tail, and its fore limbs, which grotesquely caricatured the human hand, much as a frog's do, carried a long shaft of bone, tipped with copper. The colour of the creature was variegated; its head, hands, and legs were purple; but its skin, which hung loosely upon it, even as clothes might do, was a phosphorescent grey. And it stood there blinded by the light.

At last this unknown creature of the abyss blinked its eyes open, and, shading them with its disengaged hand, opened its mouth and gave vent to a shouting noise, articulate almost as speech might be, that penetrated even the steel case and padded jacket of the sphere. How a shouting may be accomplished without lungs Elstead does not profess to explain. It then moved sideways out of the glare into the mystery of shadow that bordered it on either side, and Elstead felt rather than saw that it was coming towards him. Fancying the light had attracted it, he turned the switch that cut off the current. In another moment something soft dabbed upon the steel, and the globe swayed.

Then the shouting was repeated, and it seemed to him that a distant echo answered it. The dabbing recurred, and the globe swayed and ground against the spindle over which the wire was rolled. He stood in the blackness and peered out into the everlasting night of the abyss. And presently he saw, very faint and remote, other phosphorescent quasi-human forms hurrying towards him.

Hardly knowing what he did, he felt about in his swaying prison for the stud of the exterior electric light, and came by accident against his own small glow-lamp in its padded recess. The sphere twisted, and then threw him down; he heard shouts like shouts of surprise, and when he rose to his feet, he saw two pairs of stalked eyes peering into the lower window and reflecting his light.

In another moment hands were dabbing vigorously at his steel casing, and there was a sound, horrible enough in his position, of the metal protection of the clockwork being vigorously hammered. That, indeed, sent his heart into his mouth, for if these strange creatures succeeded in stopping that, his release would never occur. Scarcely had he thought as much when he felt the sphere sway violently, and the floor of it press hard against his feet. He turned off the small glow-lamp that lit the interior, and sent the ray of the large light in the separate compartment out into the water. The sea-floor and the man-like creatures had disappeared, and a couple of fish chasing each other dropped suddenly by the window.

He thought at once that these strange denizens of the deep sea had broken the rope, and that he had escaped. He drove up faster and faster, and then stopped with a jerk that sent him flying against the padded roof of his prison. For half a minute, perhaps, he was too astonished to think.

Then he felt that the sphere were spinning slowly, and rocking, and it seemed to him that it was also being drawn through the water. By crouching close to the window, he managed to make his weight effective and roll that part of the sphere downward, but he could see nothing save the pale ray of his light striking down ineffectively into the darkness. It occurred to him that he would see more if he turned the lamp off, and allowed his eyes to grow accustomed to the profound obscurity.

In this he was wise. After some minutes the velvety blackness became a translucent blackness, and then, far away, and as faint as the zodiacal light of an English summer evening, he saw shapes moving below. He judged these creatures had detached his cable, and were towing him along the sea bottom.

And then he saw something faint and remote across the undulations of the submarine plain, a broad horizon of pale luminosity that extended this way and that way as far as the range of his little window permitted him to see. To this he was being towed, as a balloon might be towed by men out of the open country into a town. He approached it very slowly, and very slowly the dim irradiation was gathered together into more definite shapes.

It was nearly five o'clock before he came over this luminous area, and by that time he could make out an arrangement suggestive of streets and houses grouped about a vast roofless erection that was grotesquely suggestive of a ruined abbey. It was spread out like a map below him. The houses were all roofless enclosures of walls, and their substance being, as he afterwards saw, of phosphorescent bones, gave the place an appearance as if it were built of drowned moonshine.

Among the inner caves of the place waving trees of crinoid stretched their tentacles, and tall, slender, glassy sponges shot like shining minarets and lilies of filmy light out of the general glow of the city. In the open spaces of the place he could see a stirring movement as of crowds of people, but he was too many fathoms above them to distinguish the individuals in those crowds.

Then slowly they pulled him down, and as they did so, the details of the place crept slowly upon his apprehension. He saw that the courses of the cloudy buildings were marked out with beaded lines of round objects, and then he perceived that at several points below him, in broad open spaces, were forms like the encrusted shapes of ships.

Slowly and surely he was drawn down, and the forms below him became brighter, clearer, more distinct. He was being pulled down, he perceived, towards the large building in the centre of the town, and he could catch a glimpse ever and again of the multitudinous forms that were lugging at his cord. He was astonished to see that the rigging of one of the ships, which formed such a prominent feature of the place, was crowded with a host of gesticulating figures regarding him, and then the walls of the great building rose about him silently, and hid the city from his eyes.

And such walls they were, of water-logged wood, and twisted wire-rope, and iron spars, and copper, and the bones and skulls of dead men. The skulls ran in zigzag lines and spirals and fantastic curves over the building; and in and out of their eye-sockets, and over the whole surface of the place, lurked and played a multitude of silvery little fishes.

Suddenly his ears were filled with a low shouting and a noise like the violent blowing of horns, and this gave place to a fantastic chant. Down the sphere sank, past the huge pointed windows, through which he saw vaguely a great number of these strange, ghost-like people regarding him, and at last he came to rest, as it seemed, on a kind of altar that stood in the centre of the place.

And now he was at such a level that he could see these strange people of the abyss plainly once more. To his astonishment, he perceived that they were prostrating themselves before him, all save one, dressed as it seemed in a robe of placoid scales, and crowned with a luminous diadem, who stood with his reptilian mouth opening and shutting, as though he led the chanting of the worshippers.

A curious impulse made Elstead turn on his small glow-lamp again, so that he became visible to these creatures of the abyss, albeit the glare made them disappear forthwith into night. At this sudden sight of him, the chanting gave place to a tumult of exultant shouts; and Elstead, being anxious to watch them, turned his light off again, and vanished from before their eyes. But for a time he was too blind to make out what they were doing, and when at last he could distinguish them, they were kneeling again. And thus they continued worshipping him, without rest or intermission, for a space of three hours.

Most circumstantial was Elstead's account of this astounding city and its people, these people of perpetual night, who have never seen sun or moon or stars, green vegetation, nor any living, air-breathing creatures, who know nothing of fire, nor any light but the phosphorescent light of living things.

Startling as is his story, it is yet more startling to find that scientific men, of such eminence as Adams and Jenkins, find nothing incredible in it. They tell me they see no reason why intelligent, water-breathing, vertebrated creatures, inured to a low temperature and enormous pressure, and of such a heavy structure, that neither alive nor dead would they float, might not live upon the bottom of the deep sea, and quite unsuspected by us, descendants like ourselves of the great Theriomorpha of the New Red Sandstone age.

We should be known to them, however, as strange, meteoric creatures, wont to fall catastrophically dead out of the mysterious blackness of their watery sky. And not only we ourselves, but our ships, our metals, our appliances, would come raining down out of the night. Sometimes sinking things would smite down and crush them, as if it were the judgment of some unseen power above, and sometimes would come things of the utmost rarity or utility, or shapes of inspiring suggestion. One can understand, perhaps, something of their behaviour at the descent of a living man, if one thinks what a barbaric people might do, to whom an enhaloed, shining creature came suddenly out of the sky.

At one time or another Elstead probably told the officers of the *Ptarmigan* every detail of his strange twelve hours in the abyss. That he also intended to write them down is certain, but he never did, and so unhappily we have to piece together the discrepant fragments of his story from the reminiscences of Commander Simmons, Weybridge, Steevens, Lindley, and the others.

We see the thing darkly in fragmentary glimpses—the huge ghostly building, the bowing, chanting people, with their dark chameleon-like heads and faintly luminous clothing, and Elstead, with his light turned on again, vainly trying to convey to their minds that the cord by which the sphere was held was to be severed. Minute after minute slipped away, and Elstead, looking at his watch, was horrified to find that he had oxygen only for four hours more. But the chant in his honour kept on as remorselessly as if it was the marching song of his approaching death.

The manner of his release he does not understand, but to judge by the end of cord that hung from the sphere, it had been cut through by rubbing against the edge of the altar. Abruptly the sphere rolled over, and he swept up, out of their world, as an ethereal creature clothed in a vacuum would sweep through our own atmosphere back to its native ether again. He must have torn out of their sight as a hydrogen bubble hastens upward from our air. A strange ascension it must have seemed to them.

The sphere rushed up with even greater velocity than, when weighted with the lead sinkers, it had rushed down. It became exceedingly hot. It drove up with the windows uppermost, and he remembers the torrent of bubbles frothing against the glass. Every moment he expected this to fly. Then suddenly something like a huge wheel seemed to be released in his head, the padded compartment began spinning about him, and he fainted. His next recollection was of his cabin, and of the doctor's voice.

But that is the substance of the extraordinary story that Elstead related in fragments to the officers of the *Ptarmigan*. He promised to write it all down at a later date. His mind was chiefly occupied with the improvement of his apparatus, which was effected at Rio.

It remains only to tell that on February 2, 1896, he made his second descent into the ocean abyss, with the improvements his first experience suggested. What happened we shall probably never know. He never returned. The *Ptarmigan* beat about over the point of his submersion, seeking him in vain for thirteen days. Then she returned to Rio, and the news was telegraphed to his friends. So the matter remains for the present. But it is hardly probable that no further attempt will be made to verify his strange story of these hitherto unsuspected cities of the deep sea.

THE STAR

It was on the first day of the new year that the announcement was made, almost simultaneously from three observatories, that the motion of the planet Neptune, the outermost of all the planets that wheel about the sun, had become very erratic. Ogilvy had already called attention to a suspected retardation in its velocity in December. Such a piece of news was scarcely calculated to interest a world the greater portion of whose inhabitants were unaware of the existence of the planet Neptune, nor outside the astronomical profession did the subsequent discovery of a faint remote speck of light in the region of the perturbed planet cause any very great excitement. Scientific people, however, found the intelligence remarkable enough, even before it became known that the new body was rapidly growing larger and brighter, that its motion was quite different from the orderly progress of the planets, and that the deflection of Neptune and its satellite was becoming now of an unprecedented kind.

Few people without a training in science can realise the huge isolation of the solar system. The sun with its specks of planets, its dust of planetoids, and its impalpable comets, swims in a vacant immensity that almost defeats the imagination. Beyond the orbit of Neptune there is space, vacant so far as human observation has penetrated, without warmth or light or sound, blank emptiness, for twenty million times a million miles. That is the smallest estimate of the distance to be traversed before the very nearest of the stars is attained. And, saving a few comets more unsubstantial than the thinnest flame, no matter had ever to human knowledge crossed this gulf of space, until early in the twentieth century this strange wanderer appeared. A vast mass of matter it was, bulky, heavy, rushing without warning out of the black mystery of the sky into the radiance of the sun. By the second day it was clearly visible to any decent instrument, as a speck with a barely sensible diameter, in the constellation Leo near Regulus. In a little while an opera glass could attain it.

On the third day of the new year the newspaper readers of two hemispheres were made aware for the first time of the real importance of this unusual apparition in the heavens. "A Planetary Collision," one London paper headed the news, and proclaimed Duchaine's opinion that this strange new planet would probably collide with Neptune. The leader writers enlarged upon the topic. So that in most of the capitals of the world, on January 3rd, there was an expectation, however vague, of some imminent phenomenon in the sky; and as the night followed the sunset round the globe, thousands of men turned their eyes skyward to see—the old familiar stars just as they had always been.

Until it was dawn in London and Pollux setting and the stars overhead grown pale. The winter's dawn it was, a sickly filtering accumulation of daylight, and the light of gas and candles shone yellow in the windows to show where people were astir. But the yawning policeman saw the thing, the busy crowds in the markets stopped agape, workmen going to their work betimes, milkmen, the drivers of news-carts, dissipation going home jaded and pale, homeless wanderers, sentinels on their beats, and in the country, labourers trudging afield, poachers slinking home, all over the dusky quickening country it could be seen— and out at sea by seamen watching for the day—a great white star, come suddenly into the westward sky!

Brighter it was than any star in our skies; brighter than the evening star at its brightest. It still glowed out white and large, no mere twinkling spot of light, but a small round clear shining disc, an hour after the day had come. And where science has not reached, men stared and feared, telling one another of the wars and pestilences that are foreshadowed by these fiery signs in the Heavens. Sturdy Boers, dusky

Hottentots, Gold Coast negroes, Frenchmen, Spaniards, Portuguese, stood in the warmth of the sunrise watching the setting of this strange new star.

And in a hundred observatories there had been suppressed excitement, rising almost to shouting pitch, as the two remote bodies had rushed together, and a hurrying to and fro to gather photographic apparatus and spectroscope, and this appliance and that, to record this novel astonishing sight, the destruction of a world. For it was a world, a sister planet of our earth, far greater than our earth indeed, that had so suddenly flashed into flaming death. Neptune it was, had been struck, fairly and squarely, by the strange planet from outer space and the heat of the concussion had incontinently turned two solid globes into one vast mass of incandescence. Round the world that day, two hours before the dawn, went the pallid great white star, fading only as it sank westward and the sun mounted above it. Everywhere men marvelled at it, but of all those who saw it none could have marvelled more than those sailors, habitual watchers of the stars, who far away at sea had heard nothing of its advent and saw it now rise like a pigmy moon and climb zenithward and hang overhead and sink westward with the passing of the night.

And when next it rose over Europe everywhere were crowds of watchers on hilly slopes, on house-roofs, in open spaces, staring eastward for the rising of the great new star. It rose with a white glow in front of it, like the glare of a white fire, and those who had seen it come into existence the night before cried out at the sight of it. "It is larger," they cried. "It is brighter!" And, indeed the moon a quarter full and sinking in the west was in its apparent size beyond comparison, but scarcely in all its breadth had it as much brightness now as the little circle of the strange new star.

"It is brighter!" cried the people clustering in the streets. But in the dim observatories the watchers held their breath and peered at one another. *"It is nearer,"* they said. *"Nearer!"*

And voice after voice repeated, "It is nearer," and the clicking telegraph took that up, and it trembled along telephone wires, and in a thousand cities grimy compositors fingered the type. "It is nearer." Men writing in offices, struck with a strange realisation, flung down their pens; men talking in a thousand places suddenly came upon a grotesque possibility in those words, "It is nearer." It hurried along awakening streets, it was shouted down the frost-stilled ways of quiet villages, men who had read these things from the throbbing tape stood in yellow-lit doorways shouting the news to the passers-by. "It is nearer." Pretty women, flushed and glittering, heard the news told jestingly between the dances, and feigned an intelligent interest they did not feel. "Nearer! Indeed. How curious! How very, very clever people must be to find out things like that!"

Lonely tramps faring through the wintry night murmured those words to comfort themselves—looking skyward. "It has need to be nearer, for the night's as cold as charity. Don't seem much warmth from it if it *is* nearer, all the same."

"What is a new star to me?" cried the weeping woman kneeling beside her dead.

The schoolboy, rising early for his examination work, puzzled it out for himself—with the great white star, shining broad and bright through the frost-flowers of his window. "Centrifugal, centripetal," he said, with his chin on his fist. "Stop a planet in its flight, rob it of its centrifugal force, what then? Centripetal has it, and down it falls into the sun! And this—!"

"Do *we* come in the way? I wonder—"

The light of that day went the way of its brethren, and with the later watches of the frosty darkness rose the strange star again. And it was now so bright that the waxing moon seemed but a pale yellow ghost of itself, hanging huge in the sunset. In a South African city a great man had married, and the streets were alight to welcome his return with his bride. "Even the skies have illuminated," said the flatterer. Under Capricorn, two negro lovers, daring the wild beasts and evil spirits, for love of one another, crouched together in a cane brake where the fireflies hovered. "That is our star," they whispered, and felt strangely comforted by the sweet brilliance of its light.

The master mathematician sat in his private room and pushed the papers from him. His calculations were already finished. In a small white phial there still remained a little of the drug that had kept him awake and active for four long nights. Each day, serene, explicit, patient as ever, he had given his lecture to his students, and then had come back at once to this momentous calculation. His face was grave, a little drawn and hectic from his drugged activity. For some time he seemed lost in thought. Then he went to the window, and the blind went up with a click. Half-way up the sky, over the clustering roofs, chimneys and steeples of the city, hung the star.

He looked at it as one might look into the eyes of a brave enemy. "You may kill me," he said after a silence. "But I can hold you—and all the universe for that matter—in the grip of this little brain. I would not change. Even now."

He looked at the little phial. "There will be no need of sleep again," he said. The next day at noon, punctual to the minute, he entered his lecture theatre, put his hat on the end of the table as his habit was, and carefully selected a large piece of chalk. It was a joke among his students that he could not lecture without that piece of chalk to fumble in his fingers, and once he had been stricken to impotence by their hiding his supply. He came and looked under his grey eyebrows at the rising tiers of young fresh faces, and spoke with his accustomed studied commonness of phrasing. "Circumstances have arisen—circumstances beyond my control," he said and paused, "which will debar me from completing the course I had designed. It would seem, gentlemen, if I may put the thing clearly and briefly, that—Man has lived in vain."

The students glanced at one another. Had they heard aright? Mad? Raised eyebrows and grinning lips there were, but one or two faces remained intent upon his calm grey-fringed face. "It will be interesting," he was saying, "to devote this morning to an exposition, so far as I can make it clear to you, of the calculations that have led me to this conclusion. Let us assume—"

He turned towards the blackboard, meditating a diagram in the way that was usual to him. "What was that about 'lived in vain'?" whispered one student to another. "Listen," said the other, nodding towards the lecturer.

And presently they began to understand.

That night the star rose later, for its proper eastward motion had carried it some way across Leo towards Virgo, and its brightness was so great that the sky became a luminous blue as it rose, and every star was hidden in its turn, save only Jupiter near the zenith, Capella, Aldebaran, Sirius and the pointers of the Bear. It was very white and beautiful. In many parts of the world that night a pallid halo encircled it about. It was perceptibly larger; in the clear refractive sky of the tropics it seemed as if it were nearly a quarter the size of the moon. The frost was still on the ground in England, but the world was as brightly lit as if it were midsummer moonlight. One could see to read quite ordinary print by that cold clear light, and in the cities the lamps burnt yellow and wan.

And everywhere the world was awake that night, and throughout Christendom a sombre murmur hung in the keen air over the country side like the belling of bees in the heather, and this murmurous tumult grew to a clangour in the cities. It was the tolling of the bells in a million belfry towers and steeples, summoning the people to sleep no more, to sin no more, but to gather in their churches and pray. And overhead, growing larger and brighter as the earth rolled on its way and the night passed, rose the dazzling star.

And the streets and houses were alight in all the cities, the shipyards glared, and whatever roads led to high country were lit and crowded all night long. And in all the seas about the civilised lands, ships with throbbing engines, and ships with bellying sails, crowded with men and living creatures, were standing out to ocean and the north. For already the warning of the master mathematician had been telegraphed all over the world, and translated into a hundred tongues. The new planet and Neptune, locked in a fiery embrace, were whirling headlong, ever faster and faster towards the sun. Already every second this blazing mass flew a hundred miles, and every second its terrific velocity increased. As it flew now, indeed, it must pass a hundred million of miles wide of the earth and scarcely affect it. But near its destined path, as yet only slightly perturbed, spun the mighty planet Jupiter and his moons sweeping splendid round the sun. Every moment now the attraction between the fiery star and the greatest of the planets grew stronger. And the result of the attraction? Inevitably Jupiter would be deflected from his orbit into an elliptical path, and the burning star, swung by his attraction wide of its sunward rush, would "describe a curved path" and perhaps collide with, and certainly pass very close to, our earth. "Earthquakes, volcanic outbreaks, cyclones, sea waves, floods, and a steady rise in temperature to I know not what limit"—so prophesied the master mathematician.

And overhead, to carry out his words, lonely and cold and livid, blazed the star of the coming doom.

To many who stared at it that night until their eyes ached, it seemed that it was visibly approaching. And that night, too, the weather changed, and the frost that had gripped all Central Europe and France and England softened towards a thaw.

But you must not imagine because I have spoken of people praying through the night and people going aboard ships and people fleeing towards mountainous country that the whole world was already in a terror because of the star. As a matter of fact, use and wont still ruled the world, and save for the talk of idle moments and the splendour of the night, nine human beings out of ten were still busy at their common occupations. In all the cities the shops, save one here and there, opened and closed at their proper hours, the doctor and the undertaker plied their trades, the workers gathered in the factories, soldiers drilled, scholars studied, lovers sought one another, thieves lurked and fled, politicians planned their schemes. The presses of the newspapers roared through the nights, and many a priest of this church and that would not open his holy building to further what he considered a foolish panic. The newspapers insisted on the lesson of the year 1000—for then, too, people had anticipated the end. The star was no star—mere gas—a comet; and were it a star it could not possibly strike the earth. There was no precedent for such a thing. Common sense was sturdy everywhere, scornful, jesting, a little inclined to persecute the obdurate fearful. That night, at seven-fifteen by Greenwich time, the star would be at its nearest to Jupiter. Then the world would see the turn things would take. The master mathematician's grim warnings were treated by many as so much mere elaborate self-advertisement. Common sense at last, a little heated by argument, signified its unalterable convictions by going to bed. So, too, barbarism and savagery, already tired of the novelty, went about their mighty business, and save for a howling dog here and there, the beast world left the star unheeded.

And yet, when at last the watchers in the European States saw the star rise, an hour later it is true, but no larger than it had been the night before, there were still plenty awake to laugh at the master mathematician—to take the danger as if it had passed.

But hereafter the laughter ceased. The star grew—it grew with a terrible steadiness hour after hour, a little larger each hour, a little nearer the midnight zenith, and brighter and brighter, until it had turned night into a second day. Had it come straight to the earth instead of in a curved path, had it lost no velocity to Jupiter, it must have

leapt the intervening gulf in a day, but as it was it took five days altogether to come by our planet. The next night it had become a third the
size of the moon before it set to English eyes, and the thaw was assured. It rose over America near the size of the moon, but blinding
white to look at, and *hot;* and a breath of hot wind blew now with its rising and gathering strength, and in Virginia, and Brazil, and down the
St. Lawrence valley, it shone intermittently through a driving reek of
thunder-clouds, flickering violet lightning, and hail unprecedented. In
Manitoba was a thaw and devastating floods. And upon all the mountains of the earth the snow and ice began to melt that night, and all the
rivers coming out of high country flowed thick and turbid, and soon—
in their upper reaches—with swirling trees and the bodies of beasts
and men. They rose steadily, steadily in the ghostly brilliance, and
came trickling over their banks at last, behind the flying population of
their valleys.

And along the coast of Argentina and up the South Atlantic the
tides were higher than had ever been in the memory of man, and the
storms drove the waters in many cases scores of miles inland, drowning whole cities. And so great grew the heat during the night that the
rising of the sun was like the coming of a shadow. The earthquakes
began and grew until all down America from the Arctic Circle to Cape
Horn, hillsides were sliding, fissures were opening, and houses and
walls crumbling to destruction. The whole side of Cotopaxi slipped
out in one vast convulsion, and a tumult of lava poured out so high and
broad and swift and liquid that in one day it reached the sea.

So the star, with the wan moon in its wake, marched across the Pacific, trailed the thunderstorms like the hem of a robe, and the growing tidal wave that toiled behind it, frothing and eager, poured over
island and island and swept them clear of men. Until that wave came
at last—in a blinding light and with the breath of a furnace, swift and
terrible it came—a wall of water, fifty feet high, roaring hungrily, upon
the long coasts of Asia, and swept inland across the plains of China.
For a space the star, hotter now and larger and brighter than the sun in
its strength, showed with pitiless brilliance the wide and populous
country; towns and villages with their pagodas and trees, roads, wide
cultivated fields, millions of sleepless people staring in helpless terror
at the incandescent sky; and then, low and growing, came the murmur
of the flood. And thus it was with millions of men that night—a flight

no-whither, with limbs heavy with heat and breath fierce and scant, and the flood like a wall swift and white behind. And then death.

China was lit glowing white, but over Japan and Java and all the islands of Eastern Asia the great star was a ball of dull red fire because of the steam and smoke and ashes the volcanoes were spouting forth to salute its coming. Above was the lava, hot gases and ash, and below the seething floods, and the whole earth swayed and rumbled with the earthquake shocks. Soon the immemorial snows of Thibet and the Himalaya were melting and pouring down by ten million deepening converging channels upon the plains of Burma and Hindustan. The tangled summits of the Indian jungles were aflame in a thousand places, and below the hurrying waters around the stems were dark objects that still struggled feebly and reflected the blood-red tongues of fire. And in a rudderless confusion a multitude of men and women fled down the broad river-ways to that one last hope of men—the open sea.

Larger grew the star, and larger, hotter, and brighter with a terrible swiftness now. The tropical ocean had lost its phosphorescence, and the whirling steam rose in ghostly wreaths from the black waves that plunged incessantly, speckled with storm-tossed ships.

And then came a wonder. It seemed to those who in Europe watched for the rising of the star that the world must have ceased its rotation. In a thousand open spaces of down and upland the people who had fled thither from the floods and the falling houses and sliding slopes of hill watched for that rising in vain. Hour followed hour through a terrible suspense, and the star rose not. Once again men set their eyes upon the old constellations they had counted lost to them forever. In England it was hot and clear overhead, though the ground quivered perpetually, but in the tropics, Sirius and Capella and Aldebaran showed through a veil of steam. And when at last the great star rose near ten hours late, the sun rose close upon it, and in the centre of its white heart was a disc of black.

Over Asia it was the star had begun to fall behind the movement of the sky, and then suddenly, as it hung over India, its light had been veiled. All the plain of India from the mouth of the Indus to the mouths of the Ganges was a shallow waste of shining water that night, out of which rose temples and palaces, mounds and hills, black with people. Every minaret was a clustering mass of people, who fell one by one into the turbid waters, as heat and terror overcame them. The whole land seemed a-wailing, and suddenly there swept a shadow across that furnace of despair, and a breath of cold wind, and a gathering of clouds, out of the cooling air. Men looking up, near blinded, at the star, saw that a black disc was creeping across the light. It was the moon, coming between the star and the earth. And even as men cried to God at this respite, out of the East with a strange inexplicable swiftness sprang the sun. And then star, sun and moon rushed together across the heavens.

So it was that presently, to the European watchers, star and sun rose close upon each other, drove headlong for a space and then slower, and at last came to rest, star and sun merged into one glare of flame at the zenith of the sky. The moon no longer eclipsed the star but was lost to sight in the brilliance of the sky. And though those who were still alive regarded it for the most part with that dull stupidity that hunger, fatigue, heat and despair engender, there were still men who could perceive the meaning of these signs. Star and earth had been at their nearest, had swung about one another, and the star had passed. Already it was receding, swifter and swifter, in the last stage of its headlong journey downward into the sun.

And then the clouds gathered, blotting out the vision of the sky, the thunder and lightning wove a garment round the world; all over the earth was such a downpour of rain as men had never before seen, and where the volcanoes flared red against the cloud canopy there descended torrents of mud. Everywhere the waters were pouring off the land, leaving mud-silted ruins, and the earth littered like a storm-worn beach with all that had floated, and the dead bodies of the men and brutes, its children. For days the water streamed off the land, sweeping away soil and trees and houses in the way, and piling huge dykes and scooping out Titanic gullies over the country side. Those were the days of darkness that followed the star and the heat. All through them, and for many weeks and months, the earthquakes continued.

But the star had passed, and men, hunger-driven and gathering courage only slowly, might creep back to their ruined cities, buried granaries, and sodden fields. Such few ships as had escaped the storms of that time came stunned and shattered and sounding their way cautiously through the new marks and shoals of once familiar ports. And as the storms subsided men perceived that everywhere the days were hotter than of yore, and the sun larger, and the moon, shrunk to a third of its former size, took now fourscore days between its new and new.

But of the new brotherhood that grew presently among men, of the saving of laws and books and machines, of the strange change that had come over Iceland and Greenland and the shores of Baffin's Bay, so that the sailors there presently found them green and gracious, and could scarce believe their eyes, this story does not tell. Nor of the movement of mankind now that the earth was hotter, northward and southward towards the poles of the earth. It concerns itself only with the coming and the passing of the Star.

The Martian astronomers—for there are astronomers on Mars, although they are very different beings from men—were naturally profoundly interested by these things. They saw them from their own standpoint of course. "Considering the mass and temperature of the missile that was flung through our solar system into the sun," one wrote, "it is astonishing what a little damage the earth, which it missed so narrowly, has sustained. All the familiar continental markings and the masses of the seas remain intact, and indeed the only difference seems to be a shrinkage of the white discoloration (supposed to be frozen water) round either pole." Which only shows how small the vastest of human catastrophes may seem, at a distance of a few million miles.

THE LAND IRONCLADS

1

The young lieutenant lay beside the war correspondent and admired the idyllic calm of the enemy's lines through his field-glass.

"So far as I can see," he said at last, "one man."

"What's he doing?" asked the war correspondent.

"Field-glass at us," said the young lieutenant.

"And this is war!"

"No," said the young lieutenant; "it's Bloch."

"The game's a draw."

"No! They've got to win or else they lose. A draw's a win for our side."

They had discussed the political situation fifty times or so, and the war correspondent was weary of it. He stretched out his limbs. "Aaai s'pose it *is!*" he yawned.

Flut!

"What was that?"

"Shot at us."

The war correspondent shifted to a slightly lower position. "No one shot at him," he complained.

"I wonder if they think we shall get so bored we shall go home?"

The war correspondent made no reply.

"There's the harvest, of course..."

They had been there a month. Since the first brisk movements after the declaration of war things had gone slower and slower, until it seemed as though the whole machine of events must have run down. To begin with, they had had almost a scampering time; the invader had come across the frontier on the very dawn of the war in half-a-dozen parallel columns behind a cloud of cyclists and cavalry, with a general air of coming straight on the capital, and the defender horsemen had held him up, and peppered him and forced him to open out to out-flank, and had then bolted to the next position in the most approved style, for a couple of days, until in the afternoon, bump! they had the invader against their prepared lines of defence. He did not suffer so much as had been hoped and expected: he was coming on, it seemed, with his eyes open, his scouts winded the guns, and down he sat at once without the shadow of an attack and began grubbing trenches for him-self, as though he meant to sit down there to the very end of time. He was slow, but much more wary than the world had been led to expect, and he kept convoys tucked in and shielded his slow-marching in-fantry sufficiently well to prevent any heavy adverse scoring.

"But he ought to attack," the young lieutenant had insisted.

"He'll attack us at dawn, somewhere along the lines. You'll get the bayonets coming into the trenches just about when you can see," the war correspondent had held until a week ago.

The young lieutenant winked when he said that.

When one early morning the men the defenders sent to lie out five hundred yards before the trenches, with a view to the unexpected emptying of magazines into any night attack, gave way to causeless panic and blazed away at nothing for ten minutes, the war correspon-dent understood the meaning of that wink.

"What would you do if you were the enemy?" said the war corre-spondent, suddenly.

"If I had men like I've got now?"

"Yes."

"Take those trenches."

"How?"

"Oh—dodges! Crawl out half-way at night before moonrise and get into touch with the chaps we send out. Blaze at 'em if they tried to shift, and so bag some of 'em in the daylight. Learn that patch of ground by heart, lie all day in squatty holes, and come on nearer next night. There's a bit over there, lumpy ground, where they could get across to rushing distance—easy. In a night or so. It would be a mere game for our fellows; it's what they're made for... Guns! Shrapnel and stuff wouldn't stop good men who meant business."

"Why don't *they* do that?"

"Their men aren't brutes enough; that's the trouble. They're a crowd of devitalised townsmen, and that's the truth of the matter. They're clerks, they're factory hands, they're students, they're civilised men. They can write, they can talk, they can make and do all sorts of things, but they're poor amateurs at war. They've got no physical staying power, and that's the whole thing. They've never slept in the open one night in their lives; they've never drunk anything but the purest water-company water; they've never gone short of three meals a day since they left their feeding-bottles. Half their cavalry never cocked leg over horse till it enlisted six months ago. They ride their horses as though they were bicycles—you watch 'em! They're fools at the game, and they know it. Our boys of fourteen can give their grown men points... Very well—"

The war correspondent mused on his face with his nose between his knuckles.

"If a decent civilisation," he said, "cannot produce better men for war than—" He stopped with belated politeness. "I mean—"

"Than our open-air life," said the young lieutenant.

"Exactly," said the war correspondent. "Then civilisation has to stop."

"It looks like it," the young lieutenant admitted.

"Civilisation has science, you know," said the war correspondent. "It invented and it makes the rifles and guns and things you use."

"Which our nice healthy hunters and stockmen and so on, rowdy-dowdy cowpunchers and nigger-whackers, can use ten times better than— *What's that?*"

"What?" said the war correspondent, and then seeing his companion busy with his field-glass he produced his own: "Where?" said the war correspondent, sweeping the enemy's lines.

"It's nothing," said the young lieutenant, still looking.

"What's nothing?"

The young lieutenant put down his glass and pointed. "I thought

I saw something there, behind the stems of those trees. Something black. What it was I don't know."

The war correspondent tried to get even by intense scrutiny.

"It wasn't anything," said the young lieutenant, rolling over to regard the darkling evening sky, and generalised: "There never will be anything any more for ever. Unless—"

The war correspondent looked inquiry.

"They may get their stomachs wrong, or something—living without proper drains."

A sound of bugles came from the tents behind. The war correspondent slid backward down the sand and stood up. "Boom!" came from somewhere far away to the left. "Halloa!" he said, hesitated, and crawled back to peer again. "Firing at this time is jolly bad manners."

The young lieutenant was uncommunicative for a space.

Then he pointed to the distant clump of trees again. "One of our big guns. They were firing at that," he said.

"The thing that wasn't anything?"

"Something over there, anyhow."

Both men were silent, peering through their glasses for a space. "Just when it's twilight," the lieutenant complained. He stood up.

"I might stay here a bit," said the war correspondent.

The lieutenant shook his head. "There's nothing to see," he apologised, and then went down to where his little squad of sun-brown, loose-limbed men had been yarning in the trench. The war correspondent stood up also, glanced for a moment at the business-like bustle below him, gave perhaps twenty seconds to those enigmatical trees again, then turned his face towards the camp.

He found himself wondering whether his editor would consider the story of how somebody thought he saw something black behind a clump of trees, and how a gun was fired at this illusion by somebody else, too trivial for public consumption.

"It's the only gleam of a shadow of interest," said the war correspondent, "for ten whole days.

"No," he said presently; "I'll write that other article, 'Is War Played Out?'"

He surveyed the darkling lines in perspective, the tangle of trenches one behind another, one commanding another, which the defender had made ready. The shadows and mists swallowed up their receding contours, and here and there a lantern gleamed, and here and there knots of men were busy about small fires. "No troops on earth could do it...," he said.

He was depressed. He believed that there were other things in life better worth having than proficiency in war; he believed that in the heart of civilisation, for all its stresses, its crushing concentrations of forces, its injustice and suffering, there lay something that might be the hope of the world; and the idea that any people by living in the open air, hunting perpetually, losing touch with books and art and all the things that intensify life, might hope to resist and break that great development to the end of time, jarred on his civilised soul.

Apt to his thought came a file of the defender soldiers and passed him in the gleam of a swinging lamp that marked the way.

He glanced at their red-lit faces, and one shone out for a moment, a common type of face in the defender's ranks: ill-shaped nose, sensuous lips, bright clear eyes full of alert cunning, slouch hat cocked on one side and adorned with the peacock's plume of the rustic Don Juan turned soldier, a hard brown skin, a sinewy frame, an open, tireless stride, and a master's grip on the rifle.

The war correspondent returned their salutations and went on his way.

"Louts," he whispered. "Cunning, elementary louts. And they are going to beat the townsmen at the game of war!"

From the red glow among the nearer tents came first one and then half-a-dozen hearty voices, bawling in a drawling unison the words of a particularly slab and sentimental patriotic song.

"Oh, *go* it!" muttered the war correspondent, bitterly.

2

It was opposite the trenches called after Hackbone's Hut that the battle began. There the ground stretched broad and level between the lines, with scarcely shelter for a lizard, and it seemed to the startled, just-awakened men who came crowding into the trenches that this was one more proof of that inexperience of the enemy of which they had heard so much. The war correspondent would not believe his ears at first, and swore that he and the war artist, who, still imperfectly roused, was trying to put on his boots by the light of a match held in his hand, were the victims of a common illusion. Then, after putting his head in a bucket of cold water, his intelligence came back as he towelled. He listened. "Gollys!" he said; "that's something more than scare firing this time. It's like ten thousand carts on a bridge of tin."

There came a sort of enrichment to that steady uproar. "Machine-guns!"

Then, "Guns!"

The artist, with one boot on, thought to look at his watch, and went to it hopping.

"Half an hour from dawn," he said. "You were right about their attacking, after all..."

The war correspondent came out of the tent, verifying the presence of chocolate in his pocket as he did so. He had to halt for a moment or so until his eyes were toned down to the night a little. "Pitch!" he said. He stood for a space to season his eyes before he felt justified in striking out for a black gap among the adjacent tents. The artist coming out behind him fell over a tent-rope. It was half-past two o'clock in the morning of the darkest night in time, and against a sky of dull black silk the enemy was talking search-lights, a wild jabber of search-lights. "He's trying to blind our riflemen," said the war correspondent with a flash, and waited for the artist and then set off with a sort of discreet haste again. "Whoa!" he said, presently. "Ditches!"

They stopped.

"It's the confounded search-lights," said the war correspondent.

They saw lanterns going to and fro, near by, and men falling in to march down to the trenches. They were for following them, and then the artist began to get his night eyes. "If we scramble this," he said, "and it's only a drain, there's a clear run up to the ridge." And that way they took. Lights came and went in the tents behind, as the men turned out, and ever and again they came to broken ground and staggered and stumbled. But in a little while they drew near the crest. Something that sounded like the impact of a tremendous railway accident happened in the air above them, and the shrapnel bullets seethed about them like a sudden handful of hail. "Right-ho!" said the war correspondent, and soon they judged they had come to the crest and stood in the midst of a world of great darkness and frantic glares, whose principal fact was sound.

Right and left of them and all about them was the uproar, an army-full of magazine fire, at first chaotic and monstrous, and then, eked out by little flashes and gleams and suggestions, taking the beginnings of a shape. It looked to the war correspondent as though the enemy must have attacked in line and with his whole force—in which case he was either being or was already annihilated.

"Dawn and the dead," he said, with his instinct for headlines. He said this to himself, but afterwards by means of shouting he conveyed an idea to the artist. "They must have meant it for a surprise," he said.

It was remarkable how the firing kept on. After a time he began to perceive a sort of rhythm in this inferno of noise. It would decline— decline perceptibly, droop towards something that was comparatively a pause—a pause of inquiry. "Aren't you all dead yet?" this pause seemed to say. The flickering fringe of rifle-flashes would become attenuated and broken, and the "whack-bang" of the enemy's big guns two miles away there would come up out of the deeps. Then suddenly, east or west of them, something would startle the rifles to a frantic outbreak again.

The war correspondent taxed his brain for some theory of conflict that would account for this, and was suddenly aware that the artist and he were vividly illuminated. He could see the ridge on which they stood, and before them in black outline a file of riflemen hurrying down towards the nearer trenches. It became visible that a light rain was falling, and farther away towards the enemy was a clear space with men—"Our men?"—running across it in disorder. He saw one of those men throw up his hands and drop. And something else black and shining loomed up on the edge of the beam-coruscating flashes; and behind it and far away a calm, white eye regarded the world. "Whit, whit, whit," sang something in the air, and then the artist was running for cover, with the war correspondent behind him. "Bang" came shrapnel, bursting close at hand as it seemed, and our two men were lying flat in a dip in the ground, and the light and everything had gone again, leaving a vast note of interrogation upon the light.

The war correspondent came within bawling range. "What the deuce was it? Shooting our men down!"

"Black," said the artist, "and like a fort. Not two hundred yards from the first trench."

He sought for comparisons in his mind. "Something between a big blockhouse and a giant's dishcover," he said.

"And they were running!" said the war correspondent.

"*You'd* run if a thing like that, with a search-light to help it, turned up like a prowling nightmare in the middle of the night."

They crawled to what they judged the edge of the dip and lay regarding the unfathomable dark. For a space they could distinguish nothing, and then a sudden convergence of the search-lights of both sides brought the strange thing out again.

In that flickering pallor it had the effect of a large and clumsy black insect, an insect the size of an iron-clad cruiser, crawling obliquely to the first line of trenches and firing shots out of portholes in its side. And on its carcass the bullets must have been battering with more than the passionate violence of hail on a roof of tin.

Then in the twinkling of an eye the curtain of the dark had fallen again and the monster had vanished, but the crescendo of musketry marked its approach to the trenches.

They were beginning to talk about the thing to each other, when a flying bullet kicked dirt into the artist's face, and they decided abruptly to crawl down into the cover of the trenches. They had got down with an unobtrusive persistence into the second line, before the dawn had grown clear enough for anything to be seen. They found themselves in a crowd of expectant riflemen, all noisily arguing about what would happen next. The enemy's contrivance had done execution upon the outlying men, it seemed, but they did not believe it would do any more. "Come the day and we'll capture the lot of them," said a burly soldier.

"Them?" said the war correspondent.

"They say there's a regular string of 'em, crawling along the front of our lines... Who cares?"

The darkness filtered away so imperceptibly that at no moment could one declare decisively that one could see. The search-lights ceased to sweep hither and thither. The enemy's monsters were dubious patches of darkness upon the dark, and then no longer dubious, and so they crept out into distinctness. The war correspondent, munching chocolate absent-mindedly, beheld at last a spacious picture of battle under the cheerless sky, whose central focus was an array of fourteen or fifteen huge clumsy shapes lying in perspective on the very edge of the first line of trenches, at intervals of perhaps three hundred yards, and evidently firing down upon the crowded riflemen. They were so close in that the defender's guns had ceased, and only the first line of trenches was in action.

The second line commanded the first, and as the light grew, the war correspondent could make out the riflemen who were fighting these monsters, crouched in knots and crowds behind the transverse banks that crossed the trenches against the eventuality of an enfilade. The trenches close to the big machines were empty save for the crumpled suggestions of dead and wounded men; the defenders had been driven right and left as soon as the prow of a land ironclad had looked up over the front of the trench. The war correspondent produced his field-glass, and was immediately a centre of inquiry from the soldiers about him.

They wanted to look, they asked questions, and after he had announced that the men across the traverses seemed unable to advance or retreat, and were crouching under cover rather than fighting, he found it advisable to loan his glasses to a burly and incredulous corporal. He heard a strident voice, and found a lean and sallow soldier at his back talking to the artist.

"There's chaps down there caught," the man was saying. "If they retreat they got to expose themselves, and the fire's too straight…"

"They aren't firing much, but every shot's a hit."

"Who?"

"The chaps in that thing. The men who're coming up—"

"Coming up where?"

"We're evacuating them trenches where we can. Our chaps are coming back up the zigzags… No end of 'em hit… But when we get clear our turn'll come. Rather! Those things won't be able to cross a trench or get into it; and before they can get back our guns'll smash 'em up. Smash 'em right up. See?" A brightness came into his eyes. "Then we'll have a go at the beggars inside…," he said.

The war correspondent thought for a moment, trying to realise the idea. Then he set himself to recover his field-glasses from the burly corporal…

The daylight was getting clearer now. The clouds were lifting, and a gleam of lemon-yellow amidst the level masses to the east portended sunrise. He looked again at the land ironclad. As he saw it in the bleak, grey dawn, lying obliquely upon the slope and on the very lip of the foremost trench, the suggestion of a stranded vessel was very strong indeed. It might have been from eighty to a hundred feet long—it was about two hundred and fifty yards away—its vertical side was ten feet high or so, smooth for that height, and then with a complex patterning under the eaves of its flattish turtle cover. This patterning was a close inter-lacing of portholes, rifle barrels, and telescope tubes—sham and real—indistinguishable one from the other. The thing had come into such a position as to enfilade the trench, which was empty now, so far as he could see, except for two or three crouching knots of men and the tumbled dead. Behind it, across the plain, it had scored the grass with a train of linked impressions, like the dotted tracings sea-things leave in sand. Left and right of that track dead men and wounded men were scattered—men it had picked off as they fled back from the invader's lines. And now it lay with its head projecting a little over the trench it had won, as if it were a single sentient thing planning the next phase of its attack...

He lowered his glasses and took a more comprehensive view of the situation. These creatures of the night had evidently won the first line of trenches and the fight had come to a pause. In the increasing light he could make out by a stray shot or a chance exposure that the defender's marksmen were lying thick in the second and third line of trenches up towards the low crest of the position, and in such of the zigzags as gave them a chance of a converging fire. The men about him were talking of guns. "We're in the line of the big guns at the crest, but they'll soon shift one to pepper them," the lean man said, reassuringly.

"Whup," said the corporal.

"Bang! bang! bang! Whir-r-r-r!" it was a sort of nervous jump, and all the rifles were going off by themselves. The war correspondent found himself and the artist, two idle men crouching behind a line of preoccupied backs, of industrious men discharging magazines. The monster had moved. It continued to move regardless of the hail that splashed its skin with bright new specks of lead. It was singing a mechanical little ditty to itself, "Tuf-tuf, tuf-tuf, tuf-tuf," and squirting out little jets of steam behind. It had humped itself up, as a limpet does before it crawls; it had lifted its skirt and displayed along the length of it—*feet*! They were thick, stumpy feet, between knobs and buttons in shape—flat, broad things, reminding one of the feet of elephants or the legs of caterpillars; and then, as the skirt rose higher, the war correspondent, scrutinising the thing through his glasses again, saw that these feet hung, as it were, on the rims of wheels. His thoughts whirled back to Victoria Street, Westminster, and he saw himself in the piping times of peace, seeking matter for an interview.

"Mr.—Mr. Diplock," he said; "and he called them Pedrails...Fancy meeting them here!"

The marksman beside him raised his head and shoulders in a speculative mood to fire more certainly—it seemed so natural to assume the attention of the monster must be distracted by this trench before it—and was suddenly knocked backwards by a bullet through his neck. His feet flew up, and he vanished out of the margin of the watcher's field of vision. The war correspondent grovelled tighter, but after a glance behind him at a painful little confusion, he resumed his field-glass, for the thing was putting down its feet one after the other, and hoisting itself farther and farther over the trench. Only a bullet in the head could have stopped him looking just then.

The lean man with the strident voice ceased firing to turn and reiterate his point. "They can't possibly cross," he bawled. "They—"

"Bang! Bang! Bang! Bang!"—drowned everything.

The lean man continued speaking for a word or so, then gave it up, shook his head to enforce the impossibility of anything crossing a trench like the one below, and resumed business once more.

And all the while that great bulk was crossing. When the war correspondent turned his glass on it again it had bridged the trench, and its queer feet were rasping away at the farther bank, in the attempt to get a hold there. It got its hold. It continued to crawl until the greater bulk of it was over the trench—until it was all over. Then it paused for a moment, adjusted its skirt a little nearer the ground, gave an unnerving "toot, toot," and came on abruptly at a pace of, perhaps, six miles an hour straight up the gentle slope towards our observer.

The war correspondent raised himself on his elbow and looked a natural inquiry at the artist.

For a moment the men about him stuck to their position and fired furiously. Then the lean man in a mood of precipitancy slid backwards, and the war correspondent said "Come along" to the artist, and led the movement along the trench.

As they dropped down, the vision of a hillside of trench being rushed by a dozen vast cockroaches disappeared for a space, and instead was one of a narrow passage, crowded with men, for the most part receding, though one or two turned or halted. He never turned back to see the nose of the monster creep over the brow of the trench; he never even troubled to keep in touch with the artist. He heard the "whit" of bullets about him soon enough, and saw a man before him stumble and drop, and then he was one of a furious crowd fighting to get into a transverse zigzag ditch that enabled the defenders to get under cover up and down the hill. It was like a theatre panic. He gathered from signs and fragmentary words that on ahead another of these monsters had also won to the second trench.

He lost his interest in the general course of the battle for a space altogether; he became simply a modest egotist, in a mood of hasty circumspection, seeking the farthest rear, amidst a dispersed multitude of disconcerted riflemen similarly employed. He scrambled down through trenches, he took his courage in both hands and sprinted across the open, he had moments of panic when it seemed madness not to be quadrupedal, and moments of shame when he stood up and faced about to see how the fight was going. And he was one of many thousand very similar men that morning. On the ridge he halted in a knot of scrub, and was for a few minutes almost minded to stop and see things out.

The day was now fully come. The grey sky had changed to blue, and of all the cloudy masses of the dawn there remained only a few patches of dissolving fleeciness. The ridge was not, perhaps, more than a hundred feet or so above the general plain, but in this flat region it sufficed to give the effect of extensive view. Away on the north side of the ridge, little and far, were the camps, the ordered wagons, all the gear of a big army; with officers galloping about and men doing aimless things. Here and there men were falling in, however, and the cavalry was forming up on the plain beyond the tents. The bulk of men who had been in the trenches were still on the move to the rear, scattered like sheep without a shepherd over the farther slopes. Here and there were little rallies and attempts to wait and do—something vague; but the general drift was away from any concentration. There on the southern side was the elaborate lacework of trenches and defences, across which these iron turtles, fourteen of them spread out over a line of perhaps three miles, were now advancing as fast as a man could trot, and methodically shooting down and breaking up any persistent knots of resistance. Here and there stood little clumps of men, outflanked and unable to get away, showing the white flag, and the invader's cyclist infantry was advancing now across the open, in open order but unmolested to complete the work of the machines. Surveyed at large, the defenders already looked a beaten army. A mechanism that was effectually ironclad against bullets, that could at a pinch cross a thirty-foot trench, and that seemed able to shoot out rifle-bullets with unerring precision, was clearly an inevitable victor against anything but rivers, precipices, and guns.

He looked at his watch. "Half-past four! Lord! What things can happen in two hours. Here's the whole blessed army being walked over, and at half-past two—

"And even now our blessed louts haven't done a thing with their guns!"

He scanned the ridge right and left of him with his glasses. He turned again to the nearest land ironclad, advancing now obliquely to him and not three hundred yards away, and then scanned the ground over which he must retreat if he was not to be captured.

"They'll do nothing," he said, and glanced again at the enemy.

And then from far away to the left came the thud of a gun, followed very rapidly by a rolling gun-fire.

He hesitated and decided to stay.

3

The defender had relied chiefly upon his rifles in the event of an assault. His guns he kept concealed at various points upon and behind the ridge ready to bring them into action against any artillery preparations for an attack on the part of his antagonist. The situation had rushed upon him with the dawn, and by the time the gunners had their guns ready for motion, the land ironclads were already in among the foremost trenches. There is a natural reluctance to fire into one's own broken men, and many of the guns, being intended simply to fight an advance of the enemy's artillery, were not in positions to hit anything in the second line of trenches. After that the advance of the land ironclads was swift. The defender-general found himself suddenly called upon to invent a new sort of warfare, in which guns were to fight alone amidst broken and retreating infantry. He had scarcely thirty minutes in which to think it out. He did not respond to the call, and what happened that morning was that the advance of the land ironclads forced the fight, and each gun and battery made what play its circumstances dictated. For the most part it was poor play.

Some of the guns got in two or three shots, some one or two, and the percentage of misses was unusually high. The howitzers, of course, did nothing. The land ironclads in each case followed much the same tactics. As soon as a gun came into play the monster turned itself almost end-on, so as to minimise the chances of a square hit, and made not for the gun, but for the nearest point on its flank from which the gunners could be shot down. Few of the hits scored were very effectual; only one of the things was disabled, and that was the one that fought the three batteries attached to the brigade on the left wing. Three that were hit when close upon the guns were clean shot through without being put out of action. Our war correspondent did not see that one momentary arrest of the tide of victory on the left; he saw only the very ineffectual fight of half-battery 96B close at hand upon his right. This he watched some time beyond the margin of safety.

Just after he heard the three batteries opening up upon his left he became aware of the thud of horses' hoofs from the sheltered side of the slope, and presently saw first one and then two other guns galloping into position along the north side of the ridge, well out of sight of the great bulk that was now creeping obliquely towards the crest and cutting up the lingering infantry beside it and below, as it came.

The half-battery swung round into line—each gun describing its curve—halted, unlimbered, and prepared for action...

"Bang!"

The land ironclad had become visible over the brow of the hill, and just visible as a long black back to the gunners. It halted, as though it hesitated.

The two remaining guns fired, and then their big antagonist had swung round and was in full view, end-on, against the sky, coming at a rush.

The gunners became frantic in their haste to fire again. They were so near the war correspondent could see the expression of their excited faces through his field-glass. As he looked he saw a man drop, and realised for the first time that the ironclad was shooting.

For a moment the big black monster crawled with an accelerated pace towards the furiously active gunners. Then, as if moved by a generous impulse, it turned its full broadside to their attack, and scarcely forty yards away from them. The war correspondent turned his field-glass back to the gunners and perceived it was now shooting down the men about the guns with the most deadly rapidity.

Just for a moment it seemed splendid, and then it seemed horrible. The gunners were dropping in heaps about their guns. To lay a hand on a gun was death. "Bang!" went the gun on the left, a hopeless miss, and that was the only second shot the half-battery fired. In another moment half-a-dozen surviving artillerymen were holding up their hands amidst a scattered muddle of dead and wounded men, and the fight was done.

The war correspondent hesitated between stopping in his scrub and waiting for an opportunity to surrender decently, or taking to an adjacent gully he had discovered. If he surrendered it was certain he would get no copy off; while, if he escaped, there were all sorts of chances. He decided to follow the gully, and take the first offer in the confusion beyond the camp of picking up a horse.

4

Subsequent authorities have found fault with the first land ironclads in many particulars, but assuredly they served their purpose on the day of their appearance. They were essentially long, narrow, and very strong steel frameworks carrying the engines, and borne upon eight pairs of big pedrail wheels, each about ten feet in diameter, each a driving wheel and set upon long axles free to swivel round a common axis. This arrangement gave them the maximum of adaptability to the contours of the ground. They crawled level along the ground with one foot high upon a hillock and another deep in a depression, and they could hold themselves erect and steady sideways upon even a steep hillside. The engineers directed the engines under the command of the captain, who had look-out points at small ports all round the upper edge of the adjustable skirt of twelve-inch iron-plating which protected the whole affair, and who could also raise or depress a conning-tower set about the portholes through the centre of the iron top cover. The riflemen each occupied a small cabin of peculiar construction, and these cabins were slung along the sides of and before and behind the great main framework, in a manner suggestive of the slinging of the seats of an Irish jaunting-car. Their rifles, however, were very different pieces of apparatus from the simple mechanisms in the hands of their adversaries.

These were in the first place automatic, ejected their cartridges and loaded again from a magazine each time they fired, until the ammunition store was at an end, and they had the most remarkable sights imaginable, sights which threw a bright little camera-obscura picture into the light-tight box in which the rifleman sat below. This camera-obscura picture was marked with two crossed lines, and whatever was covered by the intersection of these two lines, that the rifle hit. The sighting was ingeniously contrived. The rifleman stood at the table with a thing like an elaboration of a draughtsman's dividers in his hand, and he opened and closed these dividers, so that they were always at the apparent height—if it was an ordinary-sized man—of the man he wanted to kill. A little twisted strand of wire like an electric-light wire ran from this implement up to the gun, and as the dividers opened and shut the sights went up or down. Changes in the clearness of the atmosphere, due to changes of moisture, were met by an ingenious use of that meteorologically sensitive substance, catgut, and when the land ironclad moved forward the sights got a compensatory deflection in the direction of its motion. The rifleman stood up in his pitch-dark chamber and watched the little picture before him. One hand held the dividers for judging distance, and the other grasped a big knob like a door-handle. As he pushed this knob about the rifle above swung to correspond, and the picture passed to and fro like an agitated panorama. When he saw a man he wanted to shoot he brought him up to the cross-lines, and then pressed a finger upon a little push like an electric bell-push, conveniently placed in the centre of the knob. Then the man was shot. If by any chance the rifleman missed his target he moved the knob a trifle, or readjusted his dividers, pressed the push, and got him the second time.

This rifle and its sights protruded from a porthole, exactly like a great number of other portholes that ran in a triple row under the eaves of the cover of the land ironclad. Each porthole displayed a rifle and sight in dummy, so that the real ones could only be hit by a chance shot, and if one was, then the young man below said "Pshaw!" turned on an electric light, lowered the injured instrument into his camera, replaced the injured part, or put up a new rifle if the injury was considerable.

You must conceive these cabins as hung clear above the swing of the axles, and inside the big wheels upon which the great elephant-like feet were hung and behind these cabins along the centre of the monster ran a central gallery into which they opened, and along which worked the big compact engines. It was like a long passage into which this throbbing machinery had been packed, and the captain stood about the middle, close to the ladder that led to his conning-tower, and directed the silent, alert engineers—for the most part by signs. The throb and noise of the engines mingled with the reports of the rifles and the intermittent clangour of the bullet hail upon the armour. Ever and again he would touch the wheel that raised his conning-tower, step up his ladder until his engineers could see nothing of him above the waist, and then come down again with orders. Two small electric lights were all the illumination of this space—they were placed to make him most clearly visible to his subordinates; the air was thick with the smell of oil and petrol, and had the war correspondent been suddenly transferred from the spacious dawn outside to the bowels of this apparatus he would have thought himself fallen into another world.

The captain, of course, saw both sides of the battle. When he raised his head into his conning-tower there were the dewy sunrise, the amazed and disordered trenches, the flying and falling soldiers, the depressed-looking groups of prisoners, the beaten guns; when he bent down again to signal "half speed," "quarter speed," "half circle round toward the right," or what not, he was in the oil-smelling twilight of the ill-lit engine-room. Close beside him on either side was the mouthpiece of a speaking-tube, and ever and again he would direct one side or other of his strange craft to "concentrate fire forward on gunners," or to "clear out trench about a hundred yards on our right front."

He was a young man, healthy enough but by no means suntanned, and of a type of feature and expression that prevails in His Majesty's Navy: alert, intelligent, quiet. He and his engineers and his riflemen all went about their work, calm and reasonable men. They had none of that flapping strenuousness of the half-wit in a hurry, that excessive strain upon the blood-vessels, that hysteria of effort which is so frequently regarded as the proper state of mind for heroic deeds.

For the enemy these young engineers were defeating they felt a certain qualified pity and a quite unqualified contempt. They regarded these big, healthy men they were shooting down precisely as these same big, healthy men might regard some inferior kind of nigger. They despised them for making war; despised their bawling patriotisms and their emotionality profoundly; despised them, above all, for the petty cunning and the almost brutish want of imagination their method of fighting displayed. "If they *must* make war," these young men thought, "why in thunder don't they do it like sensible men?" They resented the assumption that their own side was too stupid to do anything more than play their enemy's game, that they were going to play this costly folly according to the rules of unimaginative men. They resented being forced to the trouble of making man-killing machinery; resented the alternative of having to massacre these people or endure their truculent yappings; resented the whole unfathomable imbecility of war.

Meanwhile, with something of the mechanical precision of a good clerk posting a ledger, the riflemen moved their knobs and pressed their buttons...

The captain of Land Ironclad Number Three had halted on the crest close to his captured half-battery. His lined-up prisoners stood hard by and waited for the cyclists behind to come for them. He surveyed the victorious morning through his conning-tower.

He read the general's signals. "Five and Four are to keep among the guns to the left and prevent any attempt to recover them. Seven and Eleven and Twelve, stick to the guns you have got; Seven, get into position to command the guns taken by Three. Then we're to do something else, are we? Six and One, quicken up to about ten miles an hour and walk round behind that camp to the levels near the river—we shall bag the whole crowd of them," interjected the young man. "Ah, here we are! Two and Three, Eight and Nine, Thirteen and Fourteen, space out to a thousand yards, wait for the word, and then go slowly to cover the advance of the cyclist infantry against any charge of mounted troops. That's all right. But where's Ten? Halloa! Ten to repair and get movable as soon as possible. They've broken up Ten!"

The discipline of the new war machines was business-like rather than pedantic, and the head of the captain came down out of the conning-tower to tell his men. "I say, you chaps there. They've broken up Ten. Not badly, I think; but anyhow, he's stuck."

But that still left thirteen of the monsters in action to finish up the broken army.

The war correspondent stealing down his gully looked back and saw them all lying along the crest and talking fluttering congratulatory flags to one another. Their iron sides were shining golden in the light of the rising sun.

5

The private adventures of the war correspondent terminated in surrender about one o'clock in the afternoon, and by that time he had stolen a horse, pitched off it, and narrowly escaped being rolled upon; found the brute had broken its leg, and shot it with his revolver. He had spent some hours in the company of a squad of dispirited riflemen, had quarrelled with them about topography at last, and gone off by himself in a direction that should have brought him to the banks of the river and didn't. Moreover, he had eaten all his chocolate and found nothing in the whole world to drink. Also, it had become extremely hot. From behind a broken, but attractive, stone wall he had seen far away in the distance the defender-horsemen trying to charge cyclists in open order, with land ironclads outflanking them on either side. He had discovered the cyclists could retreat over open turf before horsemen with a sufficient margin of speed to allow of frequent dismounts and much terribly effective sharp-shooting; and he had a sufficient persuasion that those horsemen, having charged their hearts out, had halted just beyond his range of vision and surrendered. He had been urged to sudden activity by a forward movement of one of those machines that had threatened to enfilade his wall. He had discovered a fearful blister on his heel.

He was now in a scrubby gravelly place, sitting down and meditating on his pocket-handkerchief, which had in some extraordinary way become in the last twenty-four hours extremely ambiguous in hue. "It's the whitest thing I've got," he said.

He had known all along that the enemy was east, west, and south of him, but when he heard land ironclads Numbers One and Six talking in their measured, deadly way not half a mile to the north he decided to make his own little unconditional peace without any further risks. He was for hoisting his white flag to a bush and taking up a position of modest obscurity near it until some one came along. He became aware of voices, clatter, and the distinctive noises of a body of horse, quite near, and he put his handkerchief in his pocket again and went to see what was going forward.

The sound of firing ceased, and then as he drew near he heard the deep sounds of many simple, coarse, but hearty and noble-hearted soldiers of the old school swearing with vigour.

He emerged from his scrub upon a big level plain, and far away a fringe of trees marked the banks of the river.

In the centre of the picture was a still intact road bridge, and a big railway bridge a little to the right. Two land ironclads rested, with a general air of being long, harmless sheds, in a pose of anticipatory peacefulness right and left of the picture, completely commanding two miles and more of the river levels. Emerged and halted a few yards from the scrub was the remainder of the defender's cavalry, dusty, a little disordered and obviously annoyed, but still a very fine show of men. In the middle distance three or four men and horses were receiving medical attendance, and nearer a knot of officers regarded the distant novelties in mechanism with profound distaste. Every one was very distinctly aware of the twelve other ironclads, and of the multitude of townsmen soldiers, on bicycles or afoot, encumbered now by prisoners and captured war-gear but otherwise thoroughly effective, who were sweeping like a great net in their rear.

"Checkmate," said the war correspondent, walking out into the open. "But I surrender in the best of company. Twenty-four hours ago I thought war was impossible—and these beggars have captured the whole blessed army! Well! Well!" He thought of his talk with the young lieutenant. "If there's no end to the surprises of science, the civilised people have it, of course. As long as their science keeps going they will necessarily be ahead of open-country men. Still..." He wondered for a space what might have happened to the young lieutenant.

The war correspondent was one of those inconsistent people who always want the beaten side to win. When he saw all these burly, suntanned horsemen, disarmed and dismounted and lined up; when he saw their horses unskilfully led away by the singularly not equestrian cyclists to whom they had surrendered; when he saw these truncated Paladins watching this scandalous sight, he forgot altogether that he had called these men "cunning louts" and wished them beaten not four-and-twenty hours ago. A month ago he had seen that regiment in its pride going forth to war, and had been told of its terrible prowess, how it could charge in open order with each man firing from his saddle, and sweep before it anything else that ever came out to battle in any sort of order, foot or horse. And it had had to fight a few score of young men in atrociously unfair machines!

"Manhood *Versus* Machinery" occurred to him as a suitable headline. Journalism curdles all one's mind to phrases.

He strolled as near the lined-up prisoners as the sentinels seemed disposed to permit, and surveyed them and compared their sturdy proportions with those of their lightly built captors.

"Smart degenerates," he muttered. "Anaemic cockneydom."

The surrendered officers came quite close to him presently, and he could hear the colonel's high-pitched tenor. The poor gentleman had spent three years of arduous toil upon the best material in the world perfecting that shooting from the saddle charge, and he was inquiring with phrases of blasphemy, natural in the circumstances, what one could be expected to do against this suitably consigned ironmongery.

"Guns," said some one.

"Big guns they can walk round. You can't shift big guns to keep pace with them, and little guns in the open they rush. I saw 'em rushed. You might do a surprise now and then—assassinate the brutes, perhaps—"

"You might make things like 'em."

"What? *More* ironmongery? Us ... ?"

"I'll call my article," meditated the war correspondent, " 'Mankind *Versus* Ironmongery,' and quote the old boy at the beginning."

And he was much too good a journalist to spoil his contrast by remarking that the half-dozen comparatively slender young men in blue pyjamas who were standing about their victorious land ironclad, drinking coffee and eating biscuits, had also in their eyes and carriage something not altogether degraded below the level of a man.

A Dream of Armageddon

The man with the white face entered the carriage at Rugby. He moved slowly in spite of the urgency of his porter, and even while he was still on the platform I noted how ill he seemed. He dropped into the corner over against me with a sigh, made an incomplete attempt to arrange his travelling shawl, and became motionless, with his eyes staring vacantly. Presently he was moved by a sense of my observation, looked up at me, and put out a spiritless hand for his newspaper. Then he glanced again in my direction.

I feigned to read. I feared I had unwittingly embarrassed him, and in a moment I was surprised to find him speaking.

"I beg your pardon?" said I.

"That book," he repeated, pointing a lean finger, "is about dreams."

"Obviously," I answered, for it was Fortnum-Roscoe's *Dream States*, and the title was on the cover.

He hung silent for a space as if he sought words. "Yes," he said at last, "but they tell you nothing."

I did not catch his meaning for a second.

"They don't know," he added.

I looked a little more attentively at his face.

"There are dreams," he said, "and dreams."

That sort of proposition I never dispute.

"I suppose—" He hesitated. "Do you ever dream? I mean vividly."

"I dream very little," I answered. "I doubt if I have three vivid dreams a year."

"Ah!" he said, and seemed for a moment to collect his thoughts.

"Your dreams don't mix with your memories?" he asked abruptly. "You don't find yourself in doubt; did this happen or did it not?"

"Hardly ever. Except just for a momentary hesitation now and then. I suppose few people do."

"Does *he* say——" He indicated the book.

"Says it happens at times and gives the usual explanation about intensity of impression and the like to account for its not happening as a rule. I suppose you know something of these theories——"

"Very little—except that they are wrong."

His emaciated hand played with the strap of the window for a time. I prepared to resume reading, and that seemed to precipitate his next remark. He leant forward almost as though he would touch me.

"Isn't there something called consecutive dreaming—that goes on night after night?"

"I believe there is. There are cases given in most books on mental trouble."

"Mental trouble! Yes. I dare say there are. It's the right place for them. But what I mean——" He looked at his bony knuckles. "Is that sort of thing always dreaming? *Is* it dreaming? Or is it something else? Mightn't it be something else?"

I should have snubbed his persistent conversation but for the drawn anxiety of his face. I remember now the look of his faded eyes and the lids red stained—perhaps you know that look.

"I'm not just arguing about a matter of opinion," he said. "The thing's killing me."

"Dreams?"

"If you call them dreams. Night after night. Vivid!—so vivid... this——" (he indicated the landscape that went streaming by the window) "seems unreal in comparison! I can scarcely remember who I am, what business I am on..."

He paused. "Even now——"

"The dream is always the same—do you mean?" I asked.

"It's over."

"You mean?"

"I died."

"Died?"

"Smashed and killed, and now, so much of me as that dream was, is dead. Dead for ever. I dreamt I was another man, you know, living in a different part of the world and in a different time. I dreamt that night after night. Night after night I woke into that other life. Fresh scenes and fresh happenings—until I came upon the last—"

"When you died?"

"When I died."

"And since then—"

"No," he said. "Thank God! That was the end of the dream..."

It was clear I was in for this dream. And after all, I had an hour before me, the light was fading fast, and Fortnum-Roscoe has a dreary way with him. "Living in a different time," I said. "Do you mean in some different age?"

"Yes."

"Past?"

"No—to come—to come."

"The year three thousand, for example?"

"I don't know what year it was. I did when I was asleep, when I was dreaming, that is, but not now—not now that I am awake. There's a lot of things I have forgotten since I woke out of these dreams, though I knew them at the time when I was—I suppose it was dreaming. They called the year differently from our way of calling the year... What *did* they call it?" He put his hand to his forehead. "No," said he, "I forget."

He sat smiling weakly. For a moment I feared he did not mean to tell me his dream. As a rule I hate people who tell their dreams, but this struck me differently. I proffered assistance even. "It began—" I suggested.

"It was vivid from the first. I seemed to wake up in it suddenly. And it's curious that in these dreams I am speaking of I never remembered this life I am living now. It seemed as if the dream life was enough while it lasted. Perhaps—but I will tell you how I find myself when I do my best to recall it all. I don't remember anything clearly until I found myself sitting in a sort of loggia looking out over the sea. I had been dozing, and suddenly I woke up—fresh and vivid—not a bit dream-like—because the girl had stopped fanning me."

"The girl?"

"Yes, the girl. You must not interrupt or you will put me out."

He stopped abruptly. "You won't think I'm mad?" he said.

"No," I answered; "you've been dreaming. Tell me your dream."

"I woke up, I say, because the girl had stopped fanning me. I was not surprised to find myself there or anything of that sort, you understand. I did not feel I had fallen into it suddenly. I simply took it up at that point. Whatever memory I had of *this* life, this nineteenth-century life, faded as I woke, vanished like a dream. I knew all about myself, knew that my name was no longer Cooper but Hedon, and all about my position in the world. I've forgotten a lot since I woke—there's a want of connection—but it was all quite clear and matter of fact then."

He hesitated again, gripping the window strap, putting his face forward and looking up to me appealingly.

"This seems bosh to you?"

"No, no!" I cried. "Go on. Tell me what this loggia was like."

"It was not really a loggia—I don't know what to call it. It faced south. It was small. It was all in shadow except the semicircle above the balcony that showed the sky and sea and the corner where the girl stood. I was on a couch—it was a metal couch with light striped cushions—and the girl was leaning over the balcony with her back to me. The light of the sunrise fell on her ear and cheek. Her pretty white neck and the little curls that nestled there, and her white shoulder were in the sun, and all the grace of her body was in the cool blue shadow. She was dressed—how can I describe it? It was easy and flowing. And altogether there she stood, so that it came to me how beautiful and desirable she was, as though I had never seen her before. And when at last I sighed and raised myself upon my arm she turned her face to me—"

He stopped.

"I have lived three-and-fifty years in this world. I have had mother, sisters, friends, wife and daughters—all their faces, the play of their faces, I know. But the face of this girl—it is much more real to me. I can bring it back into memory so that I see it again—I could draw it or paint it. And after all—"

He stopped—but I said nothing.

"The face of a dream—the face of a dream. She was beautiful. Not that beauty which is terrible, cold, and worshipful, like the beauty of a saint; nor that beauty that stirs fierce passions; but a sort of radiation, sweet lips that soften into smiles, and grave grey eyes. And she moved gracefully, she seemed to have part with all pleasant and gracious things—"

He stopped, and his face was downcast and hidden. Then he looked up at me and went on, making no further attempt to disguise his absolute belief in the reality of his story.

"You see, I had thrown up my plans and ambitions, thrown up all I had ever worked for or desired for her sake. I had been a master man away there in the north, with influence and property and a great reputation, but none of it had seemed worth having beside her. I had come to the place, this city of sunny pleasures, with her, and left all those things to wreck and ruin just to save a remnant at least of my life. While I had been in love with her before I knew that she had any care for me, before I had imagined that she would dare—that we should dare, all my life had seemed vain and hollow, dust and ashes. It *was* dust and ashes. Night after night and through the long days I had longed and desired—my soul had beaten against the thing forbidden!

"But it is impossible for one man to tell another just these things. It's emotion, it's a tint, a light that comes and goes. Only while it's there, everything changes, everything. The thing is I came away and left them in their crisis to do what they could."

"Left whom?" I asked, puzzled.

"The people up in the north there. You see—in this dream, anyhow—I had been a big man, the sort of man men come to trust in, to group themselves about. Millions of men who had never seen me were ready to do things and risk things because of their confidence in me. I had been playing that game for years, that big laborious game, that vague, monstrous political game amidst intrigues and betrayals, speech and agitation. It was a vast weltering world, and at last I had a sort of leadership against the Gang—you know it was called the Gang—a sort of compromise of scoundrelly projects and base ambitions and vast public emotional stupidities and catch-words—the Gang that kept the world noisy and blind year by year, and all the while that it was drifting, drifting towards infinite disaster. But I can't expect you to understand the shades and complications of the year—the year something or other ahead. I had it all—down to the smallest details—in my dream. I suppose I had been dreaming of it before I awoke, and the fading outline of some queer new development I had imagined still hung about me as I rubbed my eyes. It was some grubby affair that made me thank God for the sunlight. I sat up on the couch and remained looking at the woman and rejoicing—rejoicing that I had come away out of all that tumult and folly and violence before it was too late. After all, I thought, this is life—love and beauty, desire and delight, are they not worth all those dismal struggles for vague, gigantic ends. And I blamed myself for having ever sought to be a leader when I might have given my days to love. But then, thought I, if I had not spent my early days sternly and austerely, I might have wasted myself upon vain and worthless women, and at the thought all my being went out in love and tenderness to my dear mistress, my dear lady, who had come at last and compelled me—compelled me by her invincible charm for me—to lay that life aside.

" 'You are worth it,' I said, speaking without intending her to hear; 'you are worth it, my dearest one; worth pride and praise and all things. Love! to have *you* is worth them all together.' And at the murmur of my voice she turned about.

" 'Come and see,' she cried—I can hear her now—'come and see the sunrise upon Monte Solaro.'

"I remember how I sprang to my feet and joined her at the balcony. She put a white hand upon my shoulder and pointed towards great masses of limestone, flushing, as it were, into life. I looked. But first I noted the sunlight on her face caressing the lines of her cheeks and neck. How can I describe to you the scene we had before us? We were at Capri—"

"I have been there," I said. "I have clambered up Monte Solaro and drunk *vero Capri*—muddy stuff like cider—at the summit."

"Ah!" said the man with the white face; "then perhaps you can tell me—you will know if this was indeed Capri. For in this life I have never been there. Let me describe it. We were in a little room, one of a vast multitude of little rooms, very cool and sunny, hollowed out of the limestone of a sort of cape, very high above the sea. The whole island, you know, was one enormous hotel, complex beyond explaining, and on the other side there were miles of floating hotels, and huge floating stages to which the flying machines came. They called it a pleasure city. Of course, there was none of that in your time—rather, I should say, *is* none of that *now*. Of course. Now!—yes.

"Well, this room of ours was at the extremity of the cape, so that one could see east and west. Eastward was a great cliff—a thousand feet high perhaps—coldly grey except for one bright edge of gold, and beyond it the Isle of the Sirens, and a falling coast that faded and passed into the hot sunrise. And when one turned to the west, distinct and near was a little bay, a scimitar of beach still in shadow. And out of that shadow rose Solaro straight and tall, flushed and golden crested, like a beauty throned, and the white moon was floating behind her in the sky. And before us from east to west stretched the many-tinted sea all dotted with sailing boats.

"To the eastward, of course, these little boats were grey and very minute and clear, but to the westward they were little boats of gold—shining gold—almost like little flames. And just below us was a rock with an arch worn through it. The blue sea-water broke to green and foam all round the rock, and a galley came gliding out of the arch."

"I know that rock," I said. "I was nearly drowned there. It is called the Faraglioni."

"*I Faraglioni?* Yes, *she* called it that," answered the man with the white face. "There was some story—but that—"

He put his hand to his forehead again. "No," he said, "I forget that story.

"Well, that is the first thing I remember, the first dream I had, that shaded room and the beautiful air and sky and that dear lady of mine, with her shining arms and her graceful robe, and how we sat and talked in half whispers to one another. We talked in whispers not because there was anyone to hear, but because there was still such a freshness of mind between us that our thoughts were a little frightened, I think, to find themselves at last in words. And so they went softly.

"Presently we were hungry and we went from our apartment, going by a strange passage with a moving floor, until we came to the great breakfast room—there was a fountain and music. A pleasant and joyful place it was, with its sunlight and splashing, and the murmur of plucked strings. And we sat and ate and smiled at one another, and I would not heed a man who was watching me from a table near by.

"And afterwards we went on to the dancing-hall. But I cannot describe that hall. The place was enormous—larger than any building you have ever seen—and in one place there was the old gate of Capri, caught into the wall of a gallery high overhead. Light girders, stems and threads of gold, burst from the pillars like fountains, streamed like an Aurora across the roof and interlaced, like—like conjuring tricks.

All about the great circle for the dancers there were beautiful figures, strange dragons, and intricate and wonderful grotesques bearing lights. The place was inundated with artificial light that shamed the newborn day. And as we went through the throng the people turned about and looked at us, for all through the world my name and face were known, and how I had suddenly thrown up pride and struggle to come to this place. And they looked also at the lady beside me, though half the story of how at last she had come to me was unknown or mistold. And few of the men who were there, I know, but judged me a happy man, in spite of all the shame and dishonour that had come upon my name.

"The air was full of music, full of harmonious scents, full of the rhythm of beautiful motions. Thousands of beautiful people swarmed about the hall, crowded the galleries, sat in a myriad recesses; they were dressed in splendid colours and crowned with flowers; thousands danced about the great circle beneath the white images of the ancient gods, and glorious processions of youths and maidens came and went. We two danced, not the dreary monotonies of your days—of this time, I mean—but dances that were beautiful, intoxicating. And even now I can see my lady dancing—dancing joyously. She danced, you know, with a serious face; she danced with a serious dignity, and yet she was smiling at me and caressing me—smiling and caressing with her eyes.

"The music was different," he murmured. "It went—I cannot describe it; but it was infinitely richer and more varied than any music that has ever come to me awake.

"And then—it was when we had done dancing—a man came to speak to me. He was a lean, resolute man, very soberly clad for that place, and already I had marked his face watching me in the breakfasting hall, and afterwards as we went along the passage I had avoided his eye. But now, as we sat in an alcove, smiling at the pleasure of all the people who went to and fro across the shining floor, he came and touched me, and spoke to me so that I was forced to listen. And he asked that he might speak to me for a while apart.

" 'No,' I said. 'I have no secrets from this lady. What do you want to tell me?'

"He said it was a trivial matter, or at least a dry matter, for a lady to hear.

" 'Perhaps for me to hear,' said I.

"He glanced at her, as though almost he would appeal to her. Then he asked me suddenly if I had heard of a great and avenging declaration that Evesham had made. Now, Evesham had always before been the man next to myself in the leadership of that great party in the north. He was a forcible, hard, and tactless man, and only I had been able to control and soften him. It was on his account even more than my own, I think, that the others had been so dismayed at my retreat. So this question about what he had done reawakened my old interest in the life I had put aside just for a moment.

" 'I have taken no heed of any news for many days,' I said. 'What has Evesham been saying?'

"And with that the man began, nothing loth, and I must confess even I was struck by Evesham's reckless folly in the wild and threatening words he had used. And this messenger they had sent to me not only told me of Evesham's speech, but went on to ask counsel and to point out what need they had of me. While he talked, my lady sat a little forward and watched his face and mine.

"My old habits of scheming and organising reasserted themselves. I could even see myself suddenly returning to the north, and all the dramatic effect of it. All that this man said witnessed to the disorder of the party indeed, but not to its damage. I should go back stronger than I had come. And then I thought of my lady. You see—how can I tell you? There were certain peculiarities of our relationship—as things are I need not tell you about that—which would render her presence with me impossible. I should have had to leave her; indeed, I should have had to renounce her clearly and openly, if I was to do all that I could do in the north. And the man knew *that*, even as he talked to her and me, knew it as well as she did, that my steps to duty were—first, separation, then abandonment. At the touch of that thought my dream of a return was shattered. I turned on the man suddenly, as he was imagining his eloquence was gaining ground with me.

" 'What have I to do with these things now?' I said. 'I have done with them. Do you think I am coquetting with your people in coming here?'

" 'No,' he said; 'but—'

" 'Why cannot you leave me alone. I have done with these things. I have ceased to be anything but a private man.'

" 'Yes,' he answered. 'But have you thought?—this talk of war, these reckless challenges, these wild aggressions—'

"I stood up.

" 'No,' I cried. 'I won't hear you. I took count of all those things, I weighed them—and I have come away.'

"He seemed to consider the possibility of persistence. He looked from me to where the lady sat regarding us.

" 'War,' he said, as if he were speaking to himself, and then turned slowly from me and walked away.

"I stood, caught in the whirl of thoughts his appeal had set going.

"I heard my lady's voice.

" 'Dear,' she said; 'but if they have need of you—'

"She did not finish her sentence, she let it rest there. I turned to her sweet face, and the balance of my mood swayed and reeled.

" 'They want me only to do the thing they dare not do themselves,' I said. 'If they distrust Evesham they must settle with him themselves.'

"She looked at me doubtfully.

" 'But war—,' she said.

"I saw a doubt on her face that I had seen before, a doubt of herself and me, the first shadow of the discovery that, seen strongly and completely, must drive us apart for ever.

"Now I was an older mind than hers, and I could sway her to this belief or that.

" 'My dear one,' I said, 'you must not trouble over these things. There will be no war. Certainly there will be no war. The age of wars is past. Trust me to know the justice of this case. They have no right upon me, dearest, and no one has a right upon me. I have been free to choose my life, and I have chosen this.'

" 'But *war*—,' she said.

"I sat down beside her. I put an arm behind her and took her hand in mine. I set myself to drive that doubt away—I set myself to fill her mind with pleasant things again. I lied to her, and in lying to her I lied also to myself. And she was only too ready to believe me, only too ready to forget.

"Very soon the shadow had gone again, and we were hastening to our bathing-place in the Grotta del Bove Marino, where it was our custom to bathe every day. We swam and splashed one another, and in that buoyant water I seemed to become something lighter and stronger than a man. And at last we came out dripping and rejoicing and raced among the rocks. And then I put on a dry bathing-dress, and we sat to bask in the sun, and presently I nodded, resting my head against her knee, and she put her hand upon my hair and stroked it softly and I dozed. And behold! as it were with the snapping of the string of a violin, I was awakening, and I was in my own bed in Liverpool, in the life of today.

"Only for a time I could not believe that all these vivid moments had been no more than the substance of a dream.

"In truth, I could not believe it a dream for all the sobering reality of things about me. I bathed and dressed as it were by habit, and as I shaved I argued why I of all men should leave the woman I loved to go back to fantastic politics in the hard and strenuous north. Even if Evesham did force the world back to war, what was that to me? I was a man with the heart of a man, and why should I feel the responsibility of a deity for the way the world might go?

"You know that it is not quite the way I think about affairs, about my real affairs. I am a solicitor, you know, with a point of view.

"The vision was so real, you must understand, so utterly unlike a dream that I kept perpetually recalling trivial irrelevant details; even the ornament of a book-cover that lay on my wife's sewing-machine in the breakfast-room recalled with the utmost vividness the gilt line that ran about the seat in the alcove where I had talked with the messenger from my deserted party. Have you ever heard of a dream that had a quality like that?"

"Like—?"

"So that afterwards you remembered details you had forgotten."

I thought. I had never noticed the point before, but he was right.

"Never," I said. "That is what you never seem to do with dreams."

"No," he answered. "But that is just what I did. I am a solicitor, you must understand, in Liverpool, and I could not help wondering what the clients and business people I found myself talking to in my office would think if I told them suddenly I was in love with a girl who would be born a couple of hundred years or so hence, and worried about the politics of my great-great-great-grand-children. I was chiefly busy that day negotiating a ninety-nine-year building lease. It was a private builder in a hurry, and we wanted to tie him in every possible way. I had an interview with him, and he showed a certain want of temper that sent me to bed still irritated. That night I had no dream. Nor did I dream the next night, at least, to remember.

"Something of that intense reality of conviction vanished. I began to feel sure it *was* a dream. And then it came again.

"When the dream came again, nearly four days later, it was very different. I think it certain that four days had also elapsed in the dream. Many things had happened in the north, and the shadow of them was back again between us, and this time it was not so easily dispelled. I began I know with moody musings. Why, in spite of all, should I go back, go back for all the rest of my days to toil and stress, insults and perpetual dissatisfaction, simply to save hundreds of millions of common people, whom I did not love, whom too often I could do no other than despise, from the stress and anguish of war and infinite misrule? And after all I might fail. *They* all sought their own narrow ends, and why should not I—why should not I also live as a man? And out of such thoughts her voice summoned me, and I lifted my eyes.

"I found myself awake and walking. We had come out above the Pleasure City, we were near the summit of Monte Solaro and looking towards the bay. It was the late afternoon and very clear. Far away to the left Ischia hung in a golden haze between sea and sky, and Naples was coldly white against the hills, and before us was Vesuvius with a tall and slender streamer feathering at last towards the south, and the ruins of Torre Annunziata and Castellamare glittering and near."

I interrupted suddenly: "You have been to Capri, of course?"

"Only in this dream," he said, "only in this dream. All across the bay beyond Sorrento were the floating palaces of the Pleasure City moored and chained. And northward were the broad floating stages that received the aeroplanes. Aeroplanes fell out of the sky every afternoon, each bringing its thousands of pleasure-seekers from the uttermost parts of the earth to Capri and its delights. All these things, I say, stretched below.

"But we noticed them only incidentally because of an unusual sight that evening had to show. Five war aeroplanes that had long slumbered useless in the distant arsenals of the Rhinemouth were manoeuvring now in the eastward sky. Evesham had astonished the world by producing them and others, and sending them to circle here and there. It was the threat material in the great game of bluff he was playing, and it had taken even me by surprise. He was one of those incredibly stupid energetic people who seem sent by heaven to create disasters. His energy to the first glance seemed so wonderfully like capacity! But he had no imagination, no invention, only a stupid, vast, driving force of will, and a mad faith in his stupid idiot 'luck' to pull him through. I remember how we stood out upon the headland watching the squadron circling far away, and how I weighed the full meaning of the sight, seeing clearly the way things must go. And then even it was not too late. I might have gone back, I think, and saved the world. The people of the north would follow me, I knew, granted only that in one thing I respected their moral standards. The east and south would trust me as they would trust no other northern man. And I knew I had only to put it to her and she would have let me go ... Not because she did not love me!

"Only I did not want to go; my will was all the other way about. I had so newly thrown off the incubus of responsibility: I was still so fresh a renegade from duty that the daylight clearness of what I *ought* to do had no power at all to touch my will. My will was to live, to gather pleasures and make my dear lady happy. But though this sense of vast neglected duties had no power to draw me, it could make me silent and preoccupied, it robbed the days I had spent of half their brightness and roused me into dark meditations in the silence of the night. And as I stood and watched Evesham's aeroplanes sweep to and fro—those birds of infinite ill omen—she stood beside me watching me, perceiving the trouble indeed, but not perceiving it clearly—her eyes questioning my face, her expression shaded with perplexity. Her face was grey because the sunset was fading out of the sky. It was no fault of hers that she held me. She had asked me to go from her, and again in the night-time and with tears she had asked me to go.

"At last it was the sense of her that roused me from my mood. I turned upon her suddenly and challenged her to race down the mountain slopes. 'No,' she said, as if I jarred with her gravity; but I was resolved to end that gravity, and made her run—no one can be very grey and sad who is out of breath—and when she stumbled I ran with my hand beneath her arm. We ran down past a couple of men, who turned back staring in astonishment at my behaviour—they must have recognised my face. And half-way down the slope came a tumult in the air, clang-clank, clang-clank, and we stopped, and presently over the hill-crest those war things came flying one behind the other."

The man seemed hesitating on the verge of a description.

"What were they like?" I asked.

"They had never fought," he said. "They were just like our ironclads are nowadays; they had never fought. No one knew what they might do, with excited men inside them; few even cared to speculate. They were great driving things shaped like spear-heads without a shaft, with a propeller in the place of the shaft."

"Steel?"

"Not steel."

"Aluminium?"

"No, no, nothing of that sort. An alloy that was very common—as common as brass, for example. It was called—let me see—" He squeezed his forehead with the fingers of one hand. "I am forgetting everything," he said.

"And they carried guns?"

"Little guns, firing high explosive shells. They fired the guns backwards, out of the base of the leaf, so to speak, and rammed with the beak. That was the theory, you know, but they had never been fought. No one could tell exactly what was going to happen. And meanwhile I suppose it was very fine to go whirling through the air like a flight of young swallows, swift and easy. I guess the captains tried not to think too clearly what the real thing would be like. And these flying war machines, you know, were only one sort of the endless war contrivances that had been invented and had fallen into abeyance during the long peace. There were all sorts of these things that people were routing out and furbishing up; infernal things, silly things; things that had never been tried; big engines, terrible explosives, great guns. You know the silly way of the ingenious sort of men who make these things; they turn 'em out as beavers build dams, and with no more sense of the rivers they're going to divert and the lands they're going to flood!

"As we went down the winding stepway to our hotel again, in the twilight, I foresaw it all: I saw how clearly and inevitably things were driving for war in Evesham's silly, violent hands, and I had some inkling of what war was bound to be under these new conditions. And even then, though I knew it was drawing near the limit of my opportunity, I could find no will to go back."

He sighed.

"That was my last chance.

"We didn't go into the city until the sky was full of stars, so we walked out upon the high terrace, to and fro, and—she counselled me to go back.

" 'My dearest,' she said, and her sweet face looked up to me, 'this is Death. This life you lead is Death. Go back to them, go back to your duty—'

"She began to weep, saying, between her sobs, and clinging to my arm as she said it, 'Go back—go back.'

"Then suddenly she fell mute, and, glancing down at her face, I read in an instant the thing she had thought to do. It was one of those moments when one *sees*.

" 'No!' I said.

" 'No?' she asked, in surprise, and I think a little fearful at the answer to her thought.

" 'Nothing,' I said, 'shall send me back. Nothing! I have chosen. Love, I have chosen, and the world must go. Whatever happens I will live this life—I will live for *you!* It—nothing shall turn me aside; nothing, my dear one. Even if you died—even if you died—'

" 'Yes?' she murmured, softly.

" 'Then—I also would die.'

"And before she could speak again I began to talk, talking eloquently—as I *could* do in that life—talking to exalt love, to make the life we were living seem heroic and glorious; and the thing I was deserting something hard and enormously ignoble that it was a fine thing to set aside. I bent all my mind to throw that glamour upon it, seeking not only to convert her but myself to that. We talked, and she clung to me, torn too between all that she deemed noble and all that she knew was sweet. And at last I did make it heroic, made all the thickening disaster of the world only a sort of glorious setting to our unparalleled love, and we two poor foolish souls strutted there at last, clad in that splendid delusion, drunken rather with that glorious delusion, under the still stars.

"And so my moment passed.

"It was my last chance. Even as we went to and fro there, the leaders of the south and east were gathering their resolve, and the hot answer that shattered Evesham's bluffing for ever, took shape and waited. And all over Asia, and the ocean, and the South, the air and the wires were throbbing with their warnings to prepare—prepare.

"No one living, you know, knew what war was; no one could imagine, with all these new inventions, what horror war might bring. I believe most people still believed it would be a matter of bright uniforms and shouting charges and triumphs and flags and bands—in a time when half the world drew its food supply from regions ten thousand miles away—"

The man with the white face paused. I glanced at him, and his face was intent on the floor of the carriage. A little railway station, a string of loaded trucks, a signal-box, and the back of a cottage, shot by the carriage window, and a bridge passed with a clap of noise, echoing the tumult of the train.

"After that," he said, "I dreamt often. For three weeks of nights that dream was my life. And the worst of it was there were nights when I could not dream, when I lay tossing on a bed in *this* accursed life; and *there*—somewhere lost to me—things were happening—momentous, terrible things... I lived at nights—my days, my waking days, this life I am living now, became a faded, far-away dream, a drab setting, the cover of the book."

He thought.

"I could tell you all, tell you every little thing in the dream, but as to what I did in the daytime—no, I could not tell—I do not remember. My memory—my memory has gone. The business of life slips from me—"

He leant forward, and pressed his hands upon his eyes. For a long time he said nothing.

"And then?" said I.

"The war burst like a hurricane."

He stared before him at unspeakable things.

"And then?" I urged again.

"One touch of unreality," he said, in a low tone of a man who speaks to himself, "and they would have been nightmares. But they were not nightmares—they were not nightmares. *No!*"

He was silent for so long that it dawned upon me that there was a danger of losing the rest of the story. But he went on talking again in the same tone of questioning self-communion.

"What was there to do but flight? I had not thought the war would touch Capri—I had seemed to see Capri as being out of it all, as the contrast to it all; but two nights after the whole place was shouting and bawling, every woman almost and every other man wore a badge—

Evesham's badge—and there was no music but a jangling war-song over and over again, and everywhere men enlisting, and in the dancing halls they were drilling. The whole island was awhirl with rumours; it was said, again and again, that fighting had begun. I had not expected this. I had seen so little of the life of pleasure that I had failed to reckon with this violence of the amateurs. And as for me, I was out of it. I was like a man who might have prevented the firing of a magazine. The time had gone. I was no one; the vainest stripling with a badge counted for more than I. The crowd jostled us and bawled in our ears; that accursed song deafened us; a woman shrieked at my lady because no badge was on her, and we two went back to our own place again, ruffled and insulted—my lady white and silent, and I aquiver with rage. So furious was I, I could have quarrelled with her if I could have found one shade of accusation in her eyes.

"All my magnificence had gone from me. I walked up and down our rock cell, and outside was the darkling sea and a light to the southward that flared and passed and came again.

" 'We must get out of this place,' I said over and over. 'I have made my choice, and I will have no hand in these troubles. I will have nothing of this war. We have taken our lives out of all these things. This is no refuge for us. Let us go.'

"And the next day we were already in flight from the war that covered the world.

"And all the rest was Flight—all the rest was Flight."

He mused darkly.

"How much was there of it?"

He made no answer.

"How many days?"

His face was white and drawn and his hands were clenched. He took no heed of my curiosity.

I tried to draw him back to his story with questions.

"Where did you go?" I said.

"When?"

"When you left Capri."

"South-west," he said, and glanced at me for a second. "We went in a boat."

"But I should have thought an aeroplane?"

"They had been seized."

I questioned him no more. Presently I thought he was beginning again. He broke out in an argumentative monotone:

"But why should it be? If, indeed, this battle, this slaughter and stress *is* life, why have we this craving for pleasure and beauty? If there *is* no refuge, if there is no place of peace, and if all our dreams of quiet places are a folly and a snare, why have we such dreams? Surely it was no ignoble cravings, no base intentions, had brought us to this; it was Love had isolated us. Love had come to me with her eyes and robed in her beauty, more glorious than all else in life, in the very shape and colour of life, and summoned me away. I had silenced all the voices, I had answered all the questions—I had come to her. And suddenly there was nothing but War and Death!"

I had an inspiration. "After all," I said, "it could have been only a dream."

"A dream!" he cried, flaming upon me, "a dream—when, even now—"

For the first time he became animated. A faint flush crept into his cheek. He raised his open hand and clenched it, and dropped it to his knee. He spoke, looking away from me, and for all the rest of the time he looked away. "We are but phantoms," he said, "and the phantoms of phantoms, desires like cloud shadows and wills of straw that eddy in the wind; the days pass, use and wont carry us through as a train carries the shadow of its lights—so be it! But one thing is real and certain, one thing is no dreamstuff, but eternal and enduring. It is the centre of my life, and all other things about it are subordinate or altogether vain. I loved her, that woman of a dream. And she and I are dead together!

"A dream! How can it be a dream, when it has drenched a living life with unappeasable sorrow, when it makes all that I have lived for and cared for, worthless and unmeaning?

"Until that very moment when she was killed I believed we had still a chance of getting away," he said. "All through the night and morning that we sailed across the sea from Capri to Salerno, we talked of escape. We were full of hope, and it clung about us to the end, hope for the life together we should lead, out of it all, out of the battle and struggle, the wild and empty passions, the empty arbitrary 'thou shalt' and 'thou shalt not' of the world. We were uplifted, as though our quest was a holy thing, as though love for one another was a mission . . .

"Even when from our boat we saw the fair face of that great rock

Capri—already scarred and gashed by the gun emplacements and hiding-places that were to make it a fastness—we reckoned nothing of the imminent slaughter, though the fury of preparation hung about in puffs and clouds of dust at a hundred points amidst the grey; but, indeed, I made a text of that and talked. There, you know, was the rock, still beautiful for all its scars, with its countless windows and arches and ways, tier upon tier, for a thousand feet, a vast carving of grey, broken by vine-clad terraces and lemon and orange groves and masses of agave and prickly pear, and puffs of almond blossom. And out under the archway that is built over the Marina Piccola other boats were coming; and as we came round the cape and within sight of the mainland, another string of boats came into view, driving before the wind towards the south-west. In a little while a multitude had come out, the remoter just specks of ultramarine in the shadow of the eastward cliff.

" 'It is love and reason,' I said, 'fleeing from all this madness of war.'

"And though we presently saw a squadron of aeroplanes flying across the southern sky we did not heed it. There it was—a line of dots in the sky—and then more, dotting the south-eastern horizon, and then still more, until all that quarter of the sky was stippled with blue specks. Now they were all thin little strokes of blue, and now one and now a multitude would heel and catch the sun and become short flashes of light. They came, rising and falling and growing larger like some huge flight of gulls or rooks or such-like birds, moving with a marvellous uniformity, and ever as they drew nearer they spread over a greater width of sky. The southward wing flung itself in an arrow-headed cloud athwart the sun. And then suddenly they swept round to the eastward and streamed eastward, growing smaller and smaller and clearer and clearer again until they vanished from the sky. And after that we noted to the northward and very high Evesham's fighting machines hanging high over Naples like an evening swarm of gnats.

"It seemed to have no more to do with us than a flight of birds.

"Even the mutter of guns far away in the south-east seemed to us to signify nothing...

"Each day, each dream after that, we were still exalted, still seeking that refuge where we might live and love. Fatigue had come upon us, pain and many distresses. For though we were dusty and stained by our toilsome tramping, and half starved and with the horror of the dead men we had seen and the flight of the peasants—for very soon a gust of fighting swept up the peninsula—with these things haunting our minds it still resulted only in a deepening resolution to escape. Oh, but she was brave and patient! She who had never faced hardship and exposure had courage for herself—and me. We went to and fro seeking an outlet, over a country all commandeered and ransacked by the gathering hosts of war. Always we went on foot. At first there were other fugitives, but we did not mingle with them. Some escaped northward, some were caught in the torrent of peasantry that swept along the main roads; many gave themselves into the hands of the soldiery and were sent northward. Many of the men were impressed. But we kept away from these things; we had brought no money to bribe a passage north, and I feared for my lady at the hands of these conscript crowds. We had landed at Salerno, and we had been turned back from Cava, and we had tried to cross towards Taranto by a pass over Monte Alburno, but we had been driven back for want of food, and so we had come down among the marshes by Paestum, where those great temples stand alone. I had some vague idea that by Paestum it might be possible to find a boat or something, and take once more to sea. And there it was the battle overtook us.

"A sort of soul-blindness had me. Plainly I could see that we were being hemmed in; the great net of that giant Warfare had us in its toils. Many times we had seen the levies that had come down from the north going to and fro, and had come upon them in the distance amidst the mountains making ways for the ammunition and preparing the mounting of the guns. Once we fancied they had fired at us, taking us for spies—at any rate a shot had gone shuddering by us. Several times we had hidden in woods from hovering aeroplanes.

"But all these things do not matter now, these nights of flight and pain... We were in an open place near those great temples at Paestum at last, on a blank stony place dotted with spiky bushes, empty and desolate and so flat that a grove of eucalyptus far away showed to the feet of its stems. How I can see it! My lady was sitting down under a bush resting a little, for she was very weak and weary, and I was standing up watching to see if I could tell the distance of the firing that came and went. They were still, you know, fighting far from each other, with those terrible new weapons that had never before been used: guns that would carry beyond sight, and aeroplanes that would do— What *they* would do no man could foretell.

"I knew that we were between the two armies, and that they drew together. I knew we were in danger, and that we could not stop there and rest!

"Though all these things were in my mind, they were in the background. They seemed to be affairs beyond our concern. Chiefly, I was thinking of my lady. An aching distress filled me. For the first time she had owned herself beaten and had fallen a-weeping. Behind me I could hear her sobbing, but I would not turn round to her because I knew she had need of weeping, and had held herself so far and so long for me. It was well, I thought, that she would weep and rest and then we would toil on again, for I had no inkling of the thing that hung so near. Even now I can see her as she sat there, her lovely hair upon her shoulder, can mark again the deepening hollow of her cheek.

" 'If we had parted,' she said, 'if I had let you go.'

" 'No,' I said. 'Even now, I do not repent. I will not repent; I made my choice, and I will hold on to the end.'

"And then—

"Overhead in the sky flashed something and burst, and all about us I heard the bullets making a noise like a handful of peas suddenly thrown. They chipped the stones about us, and whirled fragments from the bricks and passed..."

He put his hand to his mouth, and then moistened his lips.

"At the flash I had turned about...

"You know—she stood up—

"She stood up, you know, and moved a step towards me—

"As though she wanted to reach me—

"And she had been shot through the heart."

He stopped and stared at me. I felt all that foolish incapacity an Englishman feels on such occasions. I met his eyes for a moment, and then stared out of the window. For a long space we kept silence. When at last I looked at him he was sitting back in his corner, his arms folded, and his teeth gnawing at his knuckles.

He bit his nail suddenly, and stared at it.

"I carried her," he said, "towards the temples, in my arms—as though it mattered. I don't know why. They seemed a sort of sanctuary, you know; they had lasted so long, I suppose.

"She must have died almost instantly. Only—I talked to her—all the way."

Silence again.

"I have seen those temples," I said abruptly, and indeed he had brought those still, sunlit arcades of worn sandstone very vividly before me.

"It was the brown one, the big brown one. I sat down on a fallen pillar and held her in my arms... Silent after the first babble was over. And after a little while the lizards came out and ran about again, as though nothing unusual was going on, as though nothing had changed... It was tremendously still there, the sun high and the shadows still; even the shadows of the weeds upon the entablature were still—in spite of the thudding and banging that went all about the sky.

"I seem to remember that the aeroplanes came up out of the south, and that the battle went away to the west. One aeroplane was struck, and overset and fell. I remember that—though it didn't interest me in the least. It didn't seem to signify. It was like a wounded gull, you know—flapping for a time in the water. I could see it down the aisle of the temple—a black thing in the bright blue water.

"Three or four times shells burst about the beach, and then that ceased. Each time that happened all the lizards scuttled in and hid for a space. That was all the mischief done, except that once a stray bullet gashed the stone hard by—made just a fresh bright surface.

"As the shadows grew longer, the stillness seemed greater.

"The curious thing," he remarked, with the manner of a man who makes a trivial conversation, "is that I didn't *think*—I didn't think at all. I sat with her in my arms amidst the stones—in a sort of lethargy—stagnant.

"And I don't remember waking up. I don't remember dressing that day. I know I found myself in my office, with my letters all slit open in front of me, and how I was struck by the absurdity of being there, seeing that in reality I was sitting, stunned, in that Paestum Temple with a dead woman in my arms. I read my letters like a machine. I have forgotten what they were about."

He stopped, and there was a long silence.

Suddenly I perceived that we were running down the incline from Chalk Farm to Euston. I started at this passing of time. I turned on him with a brutal question, in the tone of "Now or never."

"And did you dream again?"

"Yes."

He seemed to force himself to finish. His voice was very low.

"Once more, and as it were only for a few instants. I seemed to have suddenly awakened out of a great apathy, to have risen into a sitting position, and the body lay there on the stones beside me. A gaunt body. Not her, you know. So soon—it was not her . . .

"I may have heard voices. I do not know. Only I knew clearly that men were coming into the solitude and that that was a last outrage.

"I stood up and walked through the temple, and then there came into sight—first one man with a yellow face, dressed in a uniform of dirty white, trimmed with blue, and then several, climbing to the crest of the old wall of the vanished city, and crouching there. They were little bright figures in the sunlight, and there they hung, weapon in hand, peering cautiously before them.

"And further away I saw others and then more at another point in the wall. It was a long lax line of men in open order.

"Presently the man I had first seen stood up and shouted a command, and his men came tumbling down the wall and into the high weeds towards the temple. He scrambled down with them and led them. He came facing towards me, and when he saw me he stopped.

"At first I had watched these men with a mere curiosity, but when I had seen they meant to come to the temple I was moved to forbid them. I shouted to the officer.

" 'You must not come here,' I cried, '*I* am here. I am here with my dead.'

"He stared, and then shouted a question back to me in some unknown tongue.

"I repeated what I had said.

"He shouted again, and I folded my arms and stood still. Presently he spoke to his men and came forward. He carried a drawn sword.

"I signed to him to keep away, but he continued to advance. I told him again very patiently and clearly: 'You must not come here. These are old temples and I am here with my dead.'

"Presently he was so close I could see his face clearly. It was a narrow face, with dull grey eyes, and a black moustache. He had a scar on his upper lip, and he was dirty and unshaven. He kept shouting unintelligible things, questions, perhaps, at me.

"I know now that he was afraid of me, but at the time that did not occur to me. As I tried to explain to him, he interrupted me in imperious tones, bidding me, I suppose, stand aside.

"He made to go past me, and I caught hold of him.

"I saw his face change at my grip.

" 'You fool,' I cried. 'Don't you know? She is dead!'

"He started back. He looked at me with cruel eyes. I saw a sort of exultant resolve leap into them—delight. Then, suddenly, with a scowl, he swept his sword back—*so*—and thrust."

He stopped abruptly.

I became aware of a change in the rhythm of the train. The brakes lifted their voices and the carriage jarred and jerked. This present world insisted upon itself, became clamorous. I saw through the steamy window huge electric lights glaring down from tall masts upon a fog, saw rows of stationary empty carriages passing by; and then a signal-box, hoisting its constellation of green and red into the murky London twilight, marched after them. I looked again at his drawn features.

"He ran me through the heart. It was with a sort of astonishment—no fear, no pain—but just amazement, that I felt it pierce me, felt the sword drive home into my body. It didn't hurt, you know. It didn't hurt at all."

The yellow platform lights came into the field of view, passing first rapidly, then slowly, and at last stopping with a jerk. Dim shapes of men passed to and fro without.

"Euston!" cried a voice.

"Do you mean—?"

"There was no pain, no sting or smart. Amazement and then darkness sweeping over everything. The hot, brutal face before me, the face of the man who had killed me, seemed to recede. It swept out of existence—"

"Euston!" clamoured the voices outside; "Euston!"

The carriage door opened admitting a flood of sound, and a porter stood regarding us. The sounds of doors slamming, and the hoof-clatter of cab-horses, and behind these things the featureless remote roar of the London cobble-stones, came to my ears. A truckload of lighted lamps blazed along the platform.

"A darkness, a flood of darkness that opened and spread and blotted out all things."

"Any luggage, sir?" said the porter.

"And that was the end?" I asked.

He seemed to hesitate. Then, almost inaudibly, he answered, *"No."*

"You mean?"

"I couldn't get to her. She was there on the other side of the temple— And then—"

"Yes," I insisted. "Yes?"

"Nightmares," he cried; "nightmares indeed! My God! Great birds that fought and tore."

PART THREE

HORROR STORIES

Horror, as a genre, is enduringly popular both in fiction and film, maybe because we like the luxury of feeling real fear while knowing there's no real cause for it—as if one could eat a whole hot fudge sundae and lick the spoon, knowing it was a pure, sugar-free, fat-free illusion. The late nineteenth and early twentieth century was a good period for horror stories, and Wells added his grue to the brew.

In "The Lord of the Dynamos," the young H. G. Wells seems to be parading a bland conviction of white "civilized" superiority to vaguely "Asiatic" races, and he uses the word *nigger* in indirect discourse. If you stop reading at that word, you will miss the fact that the writer's sympathy is with the black man, not the white one who beats him. It is not an agreeable story; it is crude, shocking, cynical, and powerful. There is a good deal of violence in Wells's early work; both *The Time Machine* and *The First Men in the Moon* are full of grotesque and rather superfluous killings. At least the deaths in "The Lord of the Dynamos" are quite essential to the story. And I will attest that, having read the tale at ten years old or so, I have remembered poor Azuma-zi and the hum and throb of the dynamo for the next sixty.

I wanted to include "The Empire of the Ants," not because it's a very good story, but because it's so clearly an ancestor of so many movies about unpleasant insects with imperialistic ambitions. But there wasn't room for both it and "The Valley of Spiders," and the latter tale seemed more truly imaginative. It is boldly told, throwing us together with men whose motives and passions we must guess at, in a strange, cobwebby landscape.

THE LORD OF THE DYNAMOS

The chief attendant of the three dynamos that buzzed and rattled at Camberwell and kept the electric railway going, came out of Yorkshire, and his name was James Holroyd. He was a practical electrician but fond of whisky, a heavy, red-haired brute with irregular teeth. He doubted the existence of the Deity but accepted Carnot's cycle, and he had read Shakespeare and found him weak in chemistry. His helper came out of the mysterious East, and his name was Azuma-zi. But Holroyd called him Pooh-bah. Holroyd liked a nigger help because he would stand kicking—a habit with Holroyd—and did not pry into the machinery and try to learn the ways of it. Certain odd possibilities of the negro mind brought into abrupt contact with the crown of our civilisation Holroyd never fully realised, though just at the end he got some inkling of them.

To define Azuma-zi was beyond ethnology. He was, perhaps, more negroid than anything else, though his hair was curly rather than frizzy, and his nose had a bridge. Moreover, his skin was brown rather than black, and the whites of his eyes were yellow. His broad cheekbones and narrow chin gave his face something of the viperine V. His head, too, was broad behind, and low and narrow at the forehead, as if his brain had been twisted round in the reverse way to a European's. He was short of stature and still shorter of English. In conversation he made numerous odd noises of no known marketable value, and his infrequent words were carved and wrought into heraldic grotesqueness. Holroyd tried to elucidate his religious beliefs, and—especially after whisky—lectured to him against superstition and missionaries. Azuma-zi, however, shirked the discussion of his gods, even though he was kicked for it.

Azuma-zi had come, clad in white but insufficient raiment, out of the stoke-hole of the *Lord Clive,* from the Straits Settlements and beyond, into London. He had heard even in his youth of the greatness and riches of London, where all the women are white and fair and even the beggars in the streets are white; and he had arrived, with newly earned gold coins in his pocket, to worship at the shrine of civilisation. The day of his landing was a dismal one; the sky was dun, and a wind-worried drizzle filtered down to the greasy streets, but he plunged boldly into the delights of Shadwell, and was presently cast up, shattered in health, civilised in costume, penniless, and, except in matters of the direst necessity, practically a dumb animal, to toil for James Holroyd, and to be bullied by him in the dynamo shed at Camberwell. And to James Holroyd bullying was a labour of love.

There were three dynamos with their engines at Camberwell. The two that have been there since the beginning are small machines; the larger one was new. The smaller machines made a reasonable noise; their straps hummed over the drums, every now and then the brushes buzzed and fizzled, and the air churned steadily "whoo! whoo! whoo!" between their poles. One was loose in its foundations and kept the shed vibrating. But the big dynamo drowned these little noises altogether with the sustained drone of its iron core, which somehow set part of the ironwork humming. The place made the visitor's head reel with the throb, throb, throb of the engines, the rotation of the big wheels, the spinning ball-valves, the occasional spittings of the steam, and over all the deep, unceasing, surging note of the big dynamo. This last noise was from an engineering point of view a defect, but Azuma-zi accounted it unto the monster for mightiness and pride.

If it were possible we would have the noises of that shed always about the reader as he reads, we would tell all our story to such an accompaniment. It was a steady stream of din, from which the ear picked out first one thread and then another; there was the intermittent snorting, panting, and seething of the steam-engines, the suck and thud of their pistons, the dull beat on the air as the spokes of the great driving wheels came round, a note the leather straps made as they ran tighter and looser, and a fretful tumult from the dynamos; and, over all, sometimes inaudible, as the ear tired of it, and then creeping back upon the senses again, was this trombone note of the big machine. The floor never felt steady and quiet beneath one's feet, but quivered and jarred. It was a confusing, unsteady place, and enough to send anyone's thoughts jerking into odd zigzags. And for three months, while the big strike of the engineers was in progress, Holroyd who was a blackleg, and Azuma-zi who was a mere black, were never out of the stir and eddy of it, but slept and fed in the little wooden shanty between the shed and the gates.

Holroyd delivered a theological lecture on the text of his big machine soon after Azuma-zi came. He had to shout to be heard in the din. "Look at that," said Holroyd; "where's your 'eathen idol to match 'im?" And Azuma-zi looked. For a moment Holroyd was inaudible, and then Azuma-zi heard: "Kill a hundred men. Twelve per cent on the ordinary shares," said Holroyd, "and that's something like a Gord."

Holroyd was proud of his big dynamo, and expatiated upon its size and power to Azuma-zi until heaven knows what odd currents of thought that and the incessant whirling and shindy set up within the curly black cranium. He would explain in the most graphic manner the dozen or so ways in which a man might be killed by it, and once he gave Azuma-zi a shock as a sample of its quality. After that, in the breathing times of his labour—it was heavy labour, being not only his own, but most of Holroyd's—Azuma-zi would sit and watch the big machine. Now and then the brushes would sparkle and spit blue flashes, at which Holroyd would swear, but all the rest was as smooth and rhythmic as breathing. The band ran shouting over the shaft, and ever behind one as one watched was the complacent thud of the piston. So it lived all day in this big airy shed, with him and Holroyd to wait upon it; not prisoned up and slaving to drive a ship as the other engines he knew—mere captive devils of the British Solomon—had been, but a machine enthroned. Those two smaller dynamos Azuma-zi by force of contrast despised; the large one he privately christened the Lord of the Dynamos. They were fretful and irregular, but the big dynamo was steady. How great it was! How serene and easy in its working! Greater and calmer even than the Buddhas he had seen at Rangoon, and yet not motionless, but living! The great black coils spun, spun, spun, the rings ran round under the brushes, and the deep note of its coil steadied the whole. It affected Azuma-zi queerly.

Azuma-zi was not fond of labour. He would sit about and watch the Lord of the Dynamos while Holroyd went away to persuade the yard porter to get whisky, although his proper place was not in the dynamo shed but behind the engines, and, moreover, if Holroyd caught him skulking he got hit for it with a rod of stout copper wire. He would go and stand close to the colossus, and look up at the great leather band running overhead. There was a black patch on the band that came round, and it pleased him somehow among all the clatter to watch this return again and again. Odd thoughts spun with the whirl of it. Scientific people tell us that savages give souls to rocks and trees—and a machine is a thousand times more alive than a rock or a tree. And Azuma-zi was practically a savage still; the veneer of civilisation lay no deeper than his slop suit, his bruises, and the coal grime on his face and hands. His father before him had worshipped a meteoric stone; kindred blood, it may be, had splashed the broad wheels of Juggernaut.

He took every opportunity Holroyd gave him of touching and handling the great dynamo that was fascinating him. He polished and cleaned it until the metal parts were blinding in the sun. He felt a mysterious sense of service in doing this. He would go up to it and touch its spinning coils gently. The gods he had worshipped were all far away. The people in London hid their gods.

At last his dim feelings grew more distinct and took shape in thoughts, and at last in acts. When he came into the roaring shed one morning he salaamed to the Lord of the Dynamos, and then, when Holroyd was away, he went and whispered to the thundering machine that he was its servant, and prayed it to have pity on him and save him from Holroyd. As he did so a rare gleam of light came in through the open archway of the throbbing machine-shed, and the Lord of the Dynamos, as he whirled and roared, was radiant with pale gold. Then Azuma-zi knew that his service was acceptable to his Lord. After that he did not feel so lonely as he had done, and he had indeed been very much alone in London. Even when his work-time was over, which was rare, he loitered about the shed.

The next time Holroyd maltreated him, Azuma-zi went presently to the Lord of the Dynamos and whispered, "Thou seest, O my Lord!" and the angry whirr of the machinery seemed to answer him. Thereafter it appeared to him that whenever Holroyd came into the shed a different note mingled with the sounds of the dynamo. "My Lord bides his time," said Azuma-zi to himself. "The iniquity of the fool is not yet ripe." And he waited and watched for the reckoning. One day there was evidence of short circuiting, and Holroyd, making an unwary examination—it was in the afternoon—got a rather severe shock. Azuma-zi from behind the engine saw him jump off and curse at the peccant coil.

"He is warned," said Azuma-zi to himself. "Surely my Lord is very patient."

Holroyd had at first initiated his "nigger" into such elementary conceptions of the dynamo's working as would enable him to take temporary charge of the shed in his absence. But when he noticed the manner in which Azuma-zi hung about the monster he became suspicious. He dimly perceived his assistant was "up to something," and connecting him with the anointing of the coils with oil that had rotted the varnish in one place, he issued an edict, shouted above the confusion of the machinery, "Don't 'ee go nigh that big dynamo any more, Pooh-bah, or a'll take thy skin off!" Besides, if it pleased Azuma-zi to be near the big machine, it was plain sense and decency to keep him away from it.

Azuma-zi obeyed at the time, but later he was caught bowing before the Lord of the Dynamos. At which Holroyd twisted his arm and kicked him as he turned to go away. As Azuma-zi presently stood behind the engine and glared at the back of the hated Holroyd, the noises of the machinery took a new rhythm and sounded like four words in his native tongue.

It is hard to say exactly what madness is. I fancy Azuma-zi was mad. The incessant din and whirl of the dynamo shed may have churned up his little store of knowledge and big store of superstitious fancy, at last, into something akin to frenzy. At any rate, when the idea of making Holroyd a sacrifice to the Dynamo Fetich was thus suggested to him, it filled him with a strange tumult of exultant emotion.

That night the two men and their black shadows were alone in the shed together. The shed was lit with one big arc-light and winked and flickered purple. The shadows lay black behind the dynamos, the ball governors of the engines whirled from light to darkness, and their pistons beat loud and steadily. The world outside seen through the open end of the shed seemed incredibly dim and remote. It seemed absolutely silent, too, since the riot of the machinery drowned every external sound. Far away was the black fence of the yard with grey shadowy houses behind, and above was the deep blue sky and the pale little stars. Azuma-zi suddenly walked across the centre of the shed above which the leather bands were running, and went into the shadow by the big dynamos. Holroyd heard a click, and the spin of the armature changed.

"What are you dewin' with that switch?" he bawled in surprise. "Han't I told you—"

Then he saw the set expression of Azuma-zi's eyes as the Asiatic came out of the shadow towards him.

In another moment the two men were grappling fiercely in front of the great dynamo.

"You coffee-headed fool!" gasped Holroyd, with a brown hand at his throat. "Keep off those contact rings." In another moment he was tripped and reeling back upon the Lord of the Dynamos. He instinctively loosened his grip upon his antagonist to save himself from the machine.

The messenger, sent in furious haste from the station to find out what had happened in the dynamo shed, met Azuma-zi at the porter's lodge by the gate. Azuma-zi tried to explain something, but the messenger could make nothing of the black's incoherent English, and hurried on to the shed. The machines were all noisily at work, and nothing seemed to be disarranged. There was, however, a queer smell of singed hair. Then he saw an odd-looking crumpled mass clinging to the front of the big dynamo, and, approaching, recognised the distorted remains of Holroyd.

The man stared and hesitated a moment. Then he saw the face, and shut his eyes convulsively. He turned on his heel before he opened them, so that he should not see Holroyd again, and went out of the shed to get advice and help.

When Azuma-zi saw Holroyd die in the grip of the Great Dynamo he had been a little scared about the consequences of his act. Yet he felt strangely elated, and knew that the favour of the Lord Dynamo was upon him. His plan was already settled when he met the man coming from the station, and the scientific manager who speedily arrived on the scene jumped at the obvious conclusion of suicide. This expert scarcely noticed Azuma-zi except to ask a few questions. Did he see Holroyd kill himself? Azuma-zi explained he had been out of sight at the engine furnace until he heard a difference in the noise from the dynamo. It was not a difficult examination, being untinctured by suspicion.

The distorted remains of Holroyd, which the electrician removed from the machine, were hastily covered by the porter with a coffee-stained tablecloth. Somebody, by a happy inspiration, fetched a medical man. The expert was chiefly anxious to get the machine at work again, for seven or eight trains had stopped midway in the stuffy tunnels of the electric railway. Azuma-zi, answering or misunderstanding the questions of the people who had by authority or impudence come into the shed, was presently sent back to the stoke-hole by the scientific manager. Of course a crowd collected outside the gates of the yard—a crowd, for no known reason, always hovers for a day or two near the scene of a sudden death in London—two or three reporters percolated somehow into the engine shed, and one even got to Azuma-zi; but the scientific expert cleared them out again, being himself an amateur journalist.

Presently the body was carried away, and public interest departed with it. Azuma-zi remained very quietly at his furnace, seeing over and over again in the coals a figure that wriggled violently and became still. An hour after the murder, to anyone coming into the shed things would have looked exactly as if nothing remarkable had ever happened there. Peeping presently from his engine-room the black saw the Lord Dynamo spin and whirl beside his little brothers, and the driving-wheels were beating round and the steam in the pistons went thud, thud, exactly as it had been earlier in the evening. After all, from the mechanical point of view it had been a most insignificant incident—the mere temporary deflection of a current. But now the slender form and slender shadow of the scientific manager replaced the sturdy outline of Holroyd travelling up and down the lane of light upon the vibrating floor under the straps between the engines and the dynamos.

"Have I not served my Lord?" said Azuma-zi audibly from his shadow, and the note of the great dynamo rang out full and clear. As he looked at the big whirling mechanism the strange fascination of it that had been a little in abeyance since Holroyd's death resumed its sway.

Never had Azuma-zi seen a man killed so swiftly and pitilessly. The big humming machine had slain its victim without wavering for a second from its steady beating. It was indeed a mighty god.

The unconscious scientific manager stood with his back to him, scribbling on a piece of paper. His shadow lay at the foot of the monster.

Was the Lord Dynamo still hungry? His servant was ready.

Azuma-zi made a stealthy step forward; then stopped. The scientific manager suddenly ceased his writing, walked down the shed to the endmost of the dynamos, and began to examine the brushes.

Azuma-zi hesitated, and then slipped across noiselessly into the shadow by the switch. There he waited. Presently the manager's footsteps could be heard returning. He stopped in his old position, unconscious of the stoker crouching ten feet away from him. Then the big dynamo suddenly fizzled, and in another moment Azuma-zi had sprung out of the darkness upon him.

The scientific manager was gripped round the body and swung towards the big dynamo. Kicking with his knee and forcing his antagonist's head down with his hands, he loosened the grip on his waist and swung round away from the machine. Then the black grasped him again, putting a curly head against his chest, and they swayed and panted as it seemed for an age or so. Then the scientific manager was impelled to catch a black ear in his teeth and bite furiously. The black yelled hideously.

They rolled over on the floor, and the black, who had apparently slipped from the vice of the teeth or parted with some ear—the scientific manager wondered which at the time—tried to throttle him. The scientific manager was making some ineffectual efforts to claw something with his hands and to kick, when the welcome sound of quick footsteps sounded on the floor. The next moment Azuma-zi had left him and darted towards the big dynamo. There was a splutter amid the roar.

The officer of the company who had entered stood staring as Azuma-zi caught the naked terminals in his hands, gave one horrible convulsion, and then hung motionless from the machine, his face violently distorted.

"I'm jolly glad you came in when you did," said the scientific manager, still sitting on the floor.

He looked at the still quivering figure. "It is not a nice death to die, apparently—but it is quick."

The official was still staring at the body. He was a man of slow apprehension.

There was a pause.

The scientific manager got up on his feet rather awkwardly. He ran his fingers along his collar thoughtfully, and moved his head to and fro several times.

"Poor Holroyd! I see now." Then almost mechanically he went towards the switch in the shadow and turned the current into the railway circuit again. As he did so the singed body loosened its grip upon the machine and fell forward on its face. The core of the dynamo roared out loud and clear, and the armature beat the air.

So ended prematurely the worship of the Dynamo Deity, perhaps the most short-lived of all religions. Yet withal it could at least boast a Martyrdom and a Human Sacrifice.

THE VALLEY OF SPIDERS

Towards mid-day the three pursuers came abruptly round a bend in the torrent bed upon the sight of a very broad and spacious valley. The difficult and winding trench of pebbles along which they had tracked the fugitives for so long, expanded to a broad slope, and with a common impulse the three men left the trail, and rode to a low eminence set with olive-dun trees, and there halted, the two others, as became them, a little behind the man with the silver-studded bridle.

For a space they scanned the great expanse below them with eager eyes. It spread remoter and remoter, with only a few clusters of sere thorn bushes here and there, and the dim suggestions of some now waterless ravine to break its desolation of yellow grass. Its purple distances melted at last into the bluish slopes of the further hills—hills it might be of a greener kind—and above them invisibly supported, and seeming indeed to hang in the blue, were the snow-clad summits of mountains—that grew larger and bolder to the north-westward as the sides of the valley drew together. And westward the valley opened until a distant darkness under the sky told where the forests began. But the three men looked neither east nor west, but only steadfastly across the valley.

The gaunt man with the scarred lip was the first to speak. "Nowhere," he said, with a sigh of disappointment in his voice. "But after all, they had a full day's start."

"They don't know we are after them," said the little man on the white horse.

"*She* would know," said the leader bitterly, as if speaking to himself.

"Even then they can't go fast. They've got no beast but the mule, and all today the girl's foot has been bleeding—"

The man with the silver bridle flashed a quick intensity of rage on him. "Do you think I haven't seen that?" he snarled.

"It helps, anyhow," whispered the little man to himself.

The gaunt man with the scarred lip stared impassively. "They can't be over the valley," he said. "If we ride hard—"

He glanced at the white horse and paused.

"Curse all white horses!" said the man with the silver bridle, and turned to scan the beast his curse included.

The little man looked down between the melancholy ears of his steed.

"I did my best," he said.

The two others stared again across the valley for a space. The gaunt man passed the back of his hand across the scarred lip.

"Come up!" said the man who owned the silver bridle, suddenly. The little man started and jerked his rein, and the horse hoofs of the three made a multitudinous faint pattering upon the withered grass as they turned back towards the trail...

They rode cautiously down the long slope before them, and so came through a waste of prickly twisted bushes and strange dry shapes of horny branches that grew amongst the rocks, into the level below. And there the trail grew faint, for the soil was scanty, and the only herbage was this scorched dead straw that lay upon the ground. Still, by hard scanning, by leaning beside the horses' necks and pausing ever and again, even these white men could contrive to follow after their prey.

There were trodden places, bent and broken blades of the coarse grass, and ever and again the sufficient intimation of a footmark. And once the leader saw a brown smear of blood where the half-caste girl may have trod. And at that under his breath he cursed her for a fool.

The gaunt man checked his leader's tracking, and the little man on the white horse rode behind, a man lost in a dream. They rode one after another, the man with the silver bridle led the way, and they spoke never a word. After a time it came to the little man on the white horse that the world was very still. He started out of his dream. Besides the minute noises of their horses and equipment, the whole great valley kept the brooding quiet of a painted scene.

Before him went his master and his fellow, each intently leaning forward to the left, each impassively moving with the paces of his horse; their shadows went before them—still, noiseless, tapering attendants; and nearer a crouched cool shape was his own. He looked about him. What was it had gone? Then he remembered the reverberation from the banks of the gorge and the perpetual accompaniment of shifting, jostling pebbles. And, moreover—? There was no breeze. That was it! What a vast, still place it was, a monotonous afternoon slumber. And the sky open and blank, except for a sombre veil of haze that had gathered in the upper valley.

He straightened his back, fretted with his bridle, puckered his lips to whistle, and simply sighed. He turned in his saddle for a time, and stared at the throat of the mountain gorge out of which they had come. Blank! Blank slopes on either side, with never a sign of a decent beast or tree—much less a man. What a land it was! What a wilderness! He dropped again into his former pose.

It filled him with a momentary pleasure to see a wry stick of purple black flash out into the form of a snake, and vanish amidst the brown. After all, the infernal valley *was* alive. And then, to rejoice him still more, came a breath across his face, a whisper that came and went, the faintest inclination of a stiff black-antlered bush upon a crest, the first intimations of a possible breeze. Idly he wetted his finger, and held it up.

He pulled up sharply to avoid a collision with the gaunt man, who had stopped at fault upon the trail. Just at that guilty moment he caught his master's eye looking towards him.

For a time he forced an interest in the tracking. Then, as they rode on again, he studied his master's shadow and hat and shoulder appearing and disappearing behind the gaunt man's nearer contours. They had ridden four days out of the very limits of the world into this desolate place, short of water, with nothing but a strip of dried meat under their saddles, over rocks and mountains, where surely none but these fugitives had ever been before—for *that*!

And all this was for a girl, a mere wilful child! And the man had whole cityfuls of people to do his basest bidding—girls, women! Why in the name of passionate folly *this* one in particular? asked the little man, and scowled at the world, and licked his parched lips with a blackened tongue. It was the way of the master, and that was all he knew. Just because she sought to evade him...

His eye caught a whole row of high plumed canes bending in unison, and then the tails of silk that hung before his neck flapped and fell. The breeze was growing stronger. Somehow it took the stiff stillness out of things—and that was well.

"Hullo!" said the gaunt man.

All three stopped abruptly.

"What?" asked the master. "What?"

"Over there," said the gaunt man, pointing up the valley.

"What?"

"Something coming towards us."

And as he spoke a yellow animal crested a rise and came bearing down upon them. It was a big wild dog, coming before the wind, tongue out, at a steady pace, and running with such an intensity of purpose that he did not seem to see the horseman he approached. He ran with his nose up, following, it was plain, neither scent nor quarry. As he drew nearer the little man felt for his sword. "He's mad," said the gaunt rider.

"Shout!" said the little man and shouted.

The dog came on. Then when the little man's blade was already out, it swerved aside and went panting by them and past. The eyes of the little man followed its flight. "There was no foam," he said. For a space the man with the silver-studded bridle stared up the valley. "Oh, come on!" he cried at last. "What does it matter?" and jerked his horse into movement again.

The little man left the insoluble mystery of a dog that fled from nothing but the wind, and lapsed into profound musings on human character. "Come on!" he whispered to himself. "Why should it be given to one man to say 'Come on!' with that stupendous violence of effect. Always, all his life, the man with the silver bridle has been saying that. If *I* said it—!" thought the little man. But people marvelled when the master was disobeyed even in the wildest things. This half-caste girl seemed to him, seemed to everyone, mad—blasphemous almost. The little man, by way of comparison, reflected on the gaunt rider with the scarred lip, as stalwart as his master, as brave and, indeed, perhaps braver, and yet for him there was obedience, nothing but to give obedience duly and stoutly...

Certain sensations of the hands and knees called the little man back to more immediate things. He became aware of something. He rode up beside his gaunt fellow. "Do you notice the horses?" he said in an undertone.

The gaunt face looked interrogation.

"They don't like this wind," said the little man, and dropped behind as the man with the silver bridle turned upon him.

"It's all right," said the gaunt-faced man.

They rode on again for a space in silence. The foremost two rode downcast upon the trail, the hindmost man watched the haze that crept down the vastness of the valley, nearer and nearer, and noted how the wind grew in strength moment by moment. Far away on the left he saw a line of dark bulks—wild hog perhaps, galloping down the valley, but of that he said nothing, nor did he remark again upon the uneasiness of the horses.

And then he saw first one and then a second great white ball, a great shining white ball like a gigantic head of thistledown, that drove before the wind athwart the path. These balls soared high in the air, and dropped and rose again and caught for a moment, and hurried on and passed, but at the sight of them the restlessness of the horses increased.

Then presently he saw that more of these drifting globes—and then soon very many more—were hurrying towards him down the valley.

They became aware of a squealing. Athwart the path a huge boar rushed, turning his head but for one instant to glance at them, and then hurling on down the valley again. And at that, all three stopped and sat in their saddles, staring into the thickening haze that was coming upon them.

"If it were not for this thistledown—" began the leader.

But now a big globe came drifting past within a score of yards of them. It was really not an even sphere at all, but a vast, soft, ragged, filmy thing, a sheet gathered by the corners, an aerial jelly-fish, as it were, but rolling over and over as it advanced, and trailing long, cobwebby threads and streamers that floated in its wake.

"It isn't thistledown," said the little man.

"I don't like the stuff," said the gaunt man.

And they looked at one another.

"Curse it!" cried the leader. "The air's full of it up there. If it keeps on at this pace long, it will stop us altogether."

An instinctive feeling, such as lines out a herd of deer at the approach of some ambiguous thing, prompted them to turn their horses to the wind, ride forward for a few paces, and stare at that advancing multitude of floating masses. They came on before the wind with a sort of smooth swiftness, rising and falling noiselessly, sinking to earth, rebounding high, soaring—all with a perfect unanimity, with a still, deliberate assurance.

Right and left of the horsemen the pioneers of this strange army passed. At one that rolled along the ground, breaking shapelessly and trailing out reluctantly into long grappling ribbons and bands, all three horses began to shy and dance. The master was seized with a sudden, unreasonable impatience. He cursed the drifting globes roundly. "Get on!" he cried; "get on! What do these things matter? How *can* they matter? Back to the trail!" He fell swearing at his horse and sawed the bit across its mouth.

He shouted aloud with rage. "I will follow that trail, I tell you," he cried. "Where is the trail?"

He gripped the bridle of his prancing horse and searched amidst the grass. A long and clinging thread fell across his face, a grey streamer dropped about his bridle arm, some big, active thing with many legs ran down the back of his head. He looked up to discover one of those grey masses anchored as it were above him by these things and flapping out ends as a sail flaps when a boat comes about—but noiselessly.

He had an impression of many eyes, of a dense crew of squat bodies, of long, many-jointed limbs hauling at their mooring ropes to bring the thing down upon him. For a space he stared up, reining in his prancing horse with the instinct born of years of horsemanship. Then the flat of a sword smote his back, and a blade flashed overhead and cut the drifting balloon of spider-web free, and the whole mass lifted softly and drove clear and away.

"Spiders!" cried the voice of the gaunt man. "The things are full of big spiders! Look, my lord!"

The man with the silver bridle still followed the mass that drove away.

"Look, my lord!"

The master found himself staring down at a red smashed thing on the ground that, in spite of partial obliteration, could still wriggle unavailing legs. Then when the gaunt man pointed to another mass that bore down upon them, he drew his sword hastily. Up the valley now it was like a fog bank torn to rags. He tried to grasp the situation.

"Ride for it!" the little man was shouting. "Ride for it down the valley."

What happened then was like the confusion of a battle. The man with the silver bridle saw the little man go past him slashing furiously at imaginary cobwebs, saw him cannon into the horse of the gaunt man and hurl it and its rider to earth. His own horse went a dozen paces before he could rein it in. Then he looked up to avoid imaginary dangers, and then back again to see a horse rolling on the ground, the gaunt man standing and slashing over it at a rent and fluttering mass of grey that streamed and wrapped about them both. And thick and fast as thistledown on waste land on a windy day in July, the cobweb masses were coming on.

The little man had dismounted, but he dared not release his horse. He was endeavouring to lug the struggling brute back with the strength of one arm, while with the other he slashed aimlessly. The tentacles of a second grey mass had entangled themselves with the struggle, and this second grey mass came to its moorings, and slowly sank.

The master set his teeth, gripped his bridle, lowered his head, and spurred his horse forward. The horse on the ground rolled over, there was blood and moving shapes upon the flanks, and the gaunt man suddenly leaving it, ran forward towards his master, perhaps ten paces. His legs were swathed and encumbered with grey; he made ineffectual movements with his sword. Grey streamers waved from him; there was a thin veil of grey across his face. With his left hand he beat at something on his body, and suddenly he stumbled and fell. He struggled to rise, and fell again, and suddenly, horribly, began to howl, "Oh—ohoo, ohooh!"

The master could see the great spiders on him, and others upon the ground.

As he strove to force his horse nearer to this gesticulating, screaming grey object that struggled up and down, there came a clatter of hoofs, and the little man, in act of mounting, swordless, balanced on his belly athwart the white horse, and clutching its mane, whirled past. And again a clinging thread of grey gossamer swept across the master's face. All about him, and over him, it seemed this drifting, noiseless cobweb circled and drew nearer him...

To the day of his death he never knew just how the event of that moment happened. Did he, indeed, turn his horse, or did it really of its own accord stampede after its fellow? Suffice it that in another second he was galloping full tilt down the valley with his sword whirling furiously overhead. And all about him on the quickening breeze, the spiders' air-ships, their air bundles and air sheets, seemed to him to hurry in a conscious pursuit.

Clatter, clatter, thud, thud—the man with the silver bridle rode, heedless of his direction, with his fearful face looking up now right, now left, and his sword arm ready to slash. And a few hundred yards ahead of him, with a tail of torn cobweb trailing behind him, rode the little man on the white horse, still but imperfectly in the saddle. The reeds bent before them, the wind blew fresh and strong, over his shoulder the master could see the webs hurrying to overtake...

He was so intent to escape the spiders' webs that only as his horse gathered together for a leap did he realise the ravine ahead. And then he realised it only to misunderstand and interfere. He was leaning forward on his horse's neck and sat up and back all too late.

But if in his excitement he had failed to leap, at any rate he had not forgotten how to fall. He was horseman again in mid-air. He came off clear with a mere bruise upon his shoulder, and his horse rolled, kicking spasmodic legs, and lay still. But the master's sword drove its point into the hard soil, and snapped clean across, as though Chance refused him any longer as her Knight, and the splintered end missed his face by an inch or so.

He was on his feet in a moment, breathlessly scanning the onrushing spider-webs. For a moment he was minded to run, and then thought of the ravine, and turned back. He ran aside once to dodge one drifting terror, and then he was swiftly clambering down the precipitous sides, and out of the touch of the gale.

There under the lee of the dry torrent's steeper banks he might crouch, and watch these strange, grey masses pass and pass in safety till the wind fell, and it became possible to escape. And there for a long time he crouched, watching the strange, grey, ragged masses trail their streamers across his narrowed sky.

Once a stray spider fell into the ravine close beside him—a full foot it measured from leg to leg, and its body was half a man's hand—and after he had watched its monstrous alacrity of search and escape for a little while, and tempted it to bite his broken sword, he lifted up his iron heeled boot and smashed it into a pulp. He swore as he did so, and for a time sought up and down for another.

Then presently, when he was surer these spider swarms could not drop into the ravine, he found a place where he could sit down, and sat and fell into deep thought and began after his manner to gnaw his knuckles and bite his nails. And from this he was moved by the coming of the man with the white horse.

He heard him long before he saw him, as a clattering of hoofs, stumbling footsteps, and a reassuring voice. Then the little man appeared, a rueful figure, still with a tail of white cobweb trailing behind him. They approached each other without speaking, without a salutation. The little man was fatigued and shamed to the pitch of hopeless bitterness, and came to a stop at last, face to face with his seated master. The latter winced a little under his dependant's eye. "Well?" he said at last, with no pretence of authority.

"You left him?"

"My horse bolted."

"I know. So did mine."

He laughed at his master mirthlessly.

"I say my horse bolted," said the man who once had a silver-studded bridle.

"Cowards both," said the little man.

The other gnawed his knuckle through some meditative moments, with his eye on his inferior.

"Don't call me a coward," he said at length.

"You are a coward like myself."

"A coward possibly. There is a limit beyond which every man must fear. That I have learnt at last. But not like yourself. That is where the difference comes in."

"I never could have dreamt you would have left him. He saved your life two minutes before... Why are you our lord?"

The master gnawed his knuckles again, and his countenance was dark.

"No man calls me a coward," he said. "No... A broken sword is better than none... One spavined white horse cannot be expected to carry two men a four days' journey. I hate white horses, but this time it cannot be helped. You begin to understand me?... I perceive that you are minded, on the strength of what you have seen and fancy, to taint my reputation. It is men of your sort who unmake kings. Besides which—I never liked you."

"My lord!" said the little man.

"No," said the master. *"No!"*

He stood up sharply as the little man moved. For a minute perhaps they faced one another. Overhead the spiders' balls went driving. There was a quick movement among the pebbles; a running of feet, a cry of despair, a gasp and a blow ...

———

Towards nightfall the wind fell. The sun set in a calm serenity, and the man who had once possessed the silver bridle came at last very cautiously and by an easy slope out of the ravine again; but now he led the white horse that once belonged to the little man. He would have gone back to his horse to get his silver-mounted bridle again, but he feared night and a quickening breeze might still find him in the valley, and besides he disliked greatly to think he might discover his horse all swathed in cobwebs and perhaps unpleasantly eaten.

And as he thought of those cobwebs and of all the dangers he had been through, and the manner in which he had been preserved that day, his hand sought a little reliquary that hung about his neck, and he clasped it for a moment with heartfelt gratitude. As he did so his eyes went across the valley.

"I was hot with passion," he said, "and now she has met her reward. They also, no doubt—"

And behold! Far away out of the wooded slopes across the valley, but in the clearness of the sunset distinct and unmistakable, he saw a little spire of smoke.

At that his expression of serene resignation changed to an amazed anger. Smoke? He turned the head of the white horse about, and hesitated. And as he did so a little rustle of air went through the grass about him. Far away upon some reeds swayed a tattered sheet of grey. He looked at the cobwebs; he looked at the smoke.

"Perhaps, after all, it is not them," he said at last.

But he knew better.

After he had stared at the smoke for some time, he mounted the white horse.

As he rode, he picked his way amidst stranded masses of web. For some reason there were many dead spiders on the ground, and those that lived feasted guiltily on their fellows. At the sound of his horse's hoofs they fled.

Their time had passed. From the ground, without either a wind to carry them or a winding sheet ready, these things, for all their poison, could do him no evil.

He flicked with his belt at those he fancied came too near. Once, where a number ran together over a bare place, he was minded to dismount and trample them with his boots, but this impulse he overcame. Ever and again he returned in his saddle, and looked back at the smoke.

"Spiders," he muttered over and over again. "Spiders! Well, well... The next time I must spin a web."

PART FOUR

FANTASIES

INTRODUCTION

Fantasy is the aged aunt, science fiction is the up-to-date nephew who shows Auntie how to do email. Science fiction explains its wonders, rationalizes them, and shows effect following from cause, because its daddy is Realism. Aunt Fantasy doesn't give a hoot. For all she cares, cause follows from effect. She tells her impossible tales shamelessly, knowing she has reasons that reason knows not of.

Young H. G. Wells took the nephew around town, got to know him well, and in fact showed him the ropes and gave him a good start in life. But Wells was familiar also with Auntie and her great old house set in its immense garden, which you enter by a door in a wall, and whose forking paths lead back and back through time to the world outside time.

Five of the six fantasies in this section can be related to old tales or traditions of folklore and myth, the stories we tell over and over in every language, changing their clothes and props as the ages change.

Fantasy of course includes ghosts and nightmares of all kinds. "The Story of the Late Mr. Elvesham" might well have gone with the Horror Stories, but I put it here because its aim seems less to gross out the reader than to explore metaphorically a fear we all have, a horror that happens to everybody. Its relation to Oscar Wilde's *Dorian Gray* is interesting and probably purely coincidental.

Wells called "The Man Who Could Work Miracles" a "Pantoum in Prose." A pantoum is a highly repetitive poetic form that ends up, in a sense, where it began, which gives us the cue. Otherwise, this funny romp of a story is a kind of cosmic enlargement of the folktale about the man who gets three wishes, and wishes for sausages, and his wife scolds him so hard for wasting a wish on something so stupid that he wishes the sausages were stuck on the end of her nose, and then...

"The Magic Shop" is an endearing story told in a rather gentler tone than Wells mostly used. How many fantasies have their beginning in a shop, a little shop, with an odd shopkeeper, and something odd for sale? It is almost a genre in itself.

The tale of Mr. Skelmersdale is a riff on the ballad of Tam Lin, the man stolen away by the Fair Folk, a story that seems to lie very deep in the English imagination. Told lamely and inarticulately by the ordinary young man who keeps the general store in a village, it gains a particular poignancy, showing a deep strangeness in the heart of the commonplace, glimpsed, and irrecoverably lost.

The yearning for another world, barely seen and then lost, comes up again and again in Wells's fiction, never more explicitly than in "The Door in the Wall." Is that other, sweeter world real or unreal? Is it unattainable, or just on the other side of a door we can open if we choose?

The last story of this group, "The Presence by the Fire," is a kind of antifantasy or lament for the death of a fantasy. It draws, briefly and with the simplest means, a vivid picture of grief and the loss of consolation.

THE STORY OF THE LATE
MR. ELVESHAM

I set this story down, not expecting it will be believed, but, if possible, to prepare a way of escape for the next victim. He perhaps may profit by my misfortune. My own case, I know, is hopeless, and I am now in some measure prepared to meet my fate.

My name is Edward George Eden. I was born at Trentham, in Staffordshire, my father being employed in the gardens there. I lost my mother when I was three years old and my father when I was five, my uncle, George Eden, then adopting me as his own son. He was a single man, self-educated, and well-known in Birmingham as an enterprising journalist; he educated me generously, fired my ambition to succeed in the world, and at his death, which happened four years ago, left me his entire fortune, a matter of about five hundred pounds after all outgoing charges were paid. I was then eighteen. He advised me in his will to expend the money in completing my education. I had already chosen the profession of medicine, and through his posthumous generosity, and my good fortune in a scholarship competition, I became a medical student at University College, London. At the time of the beginning of my story I lodged at 11A University Street, in a little upper room, very shabbily furnished, and draughty, overlooking the back of Shoolbred's premises. I used this little room both to live in and sleep in, because I was anxious to eke out my means to the very last shillingsworth.

I was taking a pair of shoes to be mended at a shop in the Totten-ham Court Road when I first encountered the little old man with the yellow face, with whom my life has now become so inextricably en-tangled. He was standing on the kerb, and staring at the number on the door in a doubtful way, as I opened it. His eyes—they were dull grey eyes, and reddish under the rims—fell to my face, and his countenance immediately assumed an expression of corrugated amiability.

"You come," he said, "apt to the moment. I had forgotten the num-ber of your house. How do you do, Mr. Eden?"

I was a little astonished at his familiar address, for I had never set eyes on the man before. I was annoyed, too, at his catching me with my boots under my arm. He noticed my lack of cordiality.

"Wonder who the deuce I am, eh? A friend, let me assure you. I have seen you before, though you haven't seen me. Is there anywhere where I can talk to you?"

I hesitated. The shabbiness of my room upstairs was not a matter for every stranger. "Perhaps," said I, "we might walk down the street. I'm unfortunately prevented—" My gesture explained the sentence before I had spoken it.

"The very thing," he said, and faced this way and then that. "The street? Which way shall we go?" I slipped my boots down in the pas-sage. "Look here!" he said abruptly; "this business of mine is a rigma-role. Come and lunch with me, Mr. Eden. I'm an old man, a very old man, and not good at explanations, and what with my piping voice and the clatter of the traffic—"

He laid a persuasive skinny hand that trembled a little upon my arm.

I was not so old that an old man might not treat me to a lunch. Yet at the same time I was not altogether pleased by this abrupt invitation. "I had rather—" I began. "But *I* had rather," he said, catching me up, "and a certain civility is surely due to my grey hairs." And so I con-sented, and went away with him.

He took me to Blavitski's; I had to walk slowly to accommodate my-self to his paces; and over such a lunch as I had never tasted before, he fended off my leading questions, and I took a better note of his ap-pearance. His clean-shaven face was lean and wrinkled, his shrivelled lips fell over a set of false teeth, and his white hair was thin and rather long; he seemed small to me—though, indeed, most people seemed small to me—and his shoulders were rounded and bent. And, watching him, I could not help but observe that he too was taking note of me, running his eyes, with a curious touch of greed in them, over me from my broad shoulders to my sun-tanned hands and up to my freckled face again. "And now," said he, as we lit our cigarettes, "I must tell you of the business in hand.

"I must tell you, then, that I am an old man, a very old man." He paused momentarily. "And it happens that I have money that I must presently be leaving, and never a child have I to leave it to." I thought of the confidence trick, and resolved I would be on the alert for the vestiges of my five hundred pounds. He proceeded to enlarge on his loneliness, and the trouble he had to find a proper disposition of his money. "I have weighed this plan and that plan, charities, institutions, and scholarships, and libraries, and I have come to this conclusion at last,"—he fixed his eyes on my face,—"that I will find some young fellow, ambitious, pure-minded, and poor, healthy in body and healthy in mind, and, in short, make him my heir, give him all that I have." He repeated, "Give him all that I have. So that he will suddenly be lifted out of all the trouble and struggle in which his sympaties have been educated, to freedom and influence."

I tried to seem disinterested. With a transparent hypocrisy, I said, "And you want my help, my professional services maybe, to find that person."

He smiled and looked at me over his cigarette, and I laughed at his quiet exposure of my modest pretence.

"What a career such a man might have!" he said. "It fills me with envy to think how I have accumulated that another man may spend—

"But there are conditions, of course, burdens to be imposed. He must, for instance, take my name. You cannot expect everything without some return. And I must go into all the circumstances of his life before I can accept him. He *must* be sound. I must know his heredity, how his parents and grandparents died, have the strictest inquiries made into his private morals—"

This modified my secret congratulations a little. "And do I understand," said I, "that I—?"

"Yes," he said, almost fiercely. "You. *You.*"

I answered never a word. My imagination was dancing wildly, my innate scepticism was useless to modify its transports. There was not a particle of gratitude in my mind—I did not know what to say nor how to say it. "But why me in particular?" I said at last.

He had chanced to hear of me from Professor Haslar, he said, as a typically sound and sane young man, and he wished, as far as possible, to leave his money where health and integrity were assured.

That was my first meeting with the little old man. He was mysterious about himself; he would not give his name yet, he said, and after I had answered some questions of his, he left me at the Blavitski portal. I noticed that he drew a handful of gold coins from his pocket when it came to paying for the lunch. His insistence upon bodily health was curious. In accordance with an arrangement we had made I applied that day for a life policy in the Loyal Insurance Company for a large sum, and I was exhaustively overhauled by the medical advisers of that company in the subsequent week. Even that did not satisfy him, and he insisted I must be re-examined by the great Doctor Henderson. It was Friday in Whitsun week before he came to a decision. He called me down quite late in the evening,—nearly nine it was,—from cramming chemical equations for my Preliminary Scientific examinations. He was standing in the passage under the feeble gas-lamp, and his face was a grotesque interplay of shadows. He seemed more bowed than when I had first seen him, and his cheeks had sunk in a little.

His voice shook with emotion. "Everything is satisfactory, Mr. Eden," he said. "Everything is quite, quite satisfactory. And this night of all nights, you must dine with me and celebrate your—accession." He was interrupted by a cough. "You won't have long to wait, either," he said, wiping his handkerchief across his lips, and gripping my hand with his long bony claw that was disengaged. "Certainly not very long to wait."

We went into the street and called a cab. I remember every incident of that drive vividly, the swift, easy motion, the contrast of gas and oil and electric light, the crowds of people in the streets, the place in Regent Street to which we went, and the sumptuous dinner we were served with there. I was disconcerted at first by the well-dressed waiter's glances at my rough clothes, bothered by the stones of the olives, but as the champagne warmed my blood, my confidence revived. At first the old man talked of himself. He had already told me his name in the cab; he was Egbert Elvesham, the great philosopher, whose name I had known since I was a lad at school. It seemed incredible to me that this man, whose intelligence had so early dominated mine, this great abstraction, should suddenly realise itself as this decrepit, familiar figure. I dare say every young fellow who had suddenly fallen among celebrities has felt something of my disappointment. He told me now of the future that the feeble streams of his life would presently leave dry for me, houses, copyrights, investments; I had never suspected that philosophers were so rich. He watched me drink and eat with a touch of envy. "What a capacity for living you have!" he said; and then, with a sigh, a sigh of relief I could have thought it, "It will not be long."

"Ay," said I, my head swimming now with champagne; "I have a future perhaps—of a fairly agreeable sort, thanks to you. I shall now have the honour of your name. But you have a past. Such a past as is worth all my future."

He shook his head and smiled, as I thought with half-sad appreciation of my flattering admiration. "That future," he said; "would you in truth change it?" The waiter came with liqueurs. "You will not perhaps mind taking my name, taking my position, but would you indeed—willingly—take my years?"

"With your achievements," said I gallantly.

He smiled again. "Kümmel—both," he said to the waiter, and turned his attention to a little paper packet he had taken from his pocket. "This hour," said he, "this after-dinner hour is the hour of small things. Here is a scrap of my unpublished wisdom." He opened the packet with his shaking yellow fingers, and showed a little pinkish powder on the paper. "This," said he—"well, you must guess what it is. But Kümmel—put but a dash of this powder in it—is Himmel." His large greyish eyes watched mine with an inscrutable expression.

It was a bit of a shock to me to find this great teacher gave his mind to the flavour of liqueurs. However, I feigned a great interest in his weakness, for I was drunk enough for such small sycophancy.

He parted the powder between the little glasses, and rising suddenly with a strange unexpected dignity, held out his hand towards me. I imitated his action, and the glasses rang. "To a quick succession," said he, and raised his glass towards his lips.

"Not that," I said hastily. "Not that."

He paused, with the liqueur at the level of his chin, and his eyes blazing into mine.

"To a long life," said I.

He hesitated. "To a long life," said he, with a sudden bark of laughter, and with eyes fixed on one another we tilted the little glasses. His eyes looked straight into mine, and as I drained the stuff off, I felt a curiously intense sensation. The first touch of it set my brain in a furious tumult; I seemed to feel an actual physical stirring in my skull, and a seething humming filled my ears. I did not notice the flavour in my mouth, the aroma that filled my throat; I saw only the grey intensity of his gaze that burnt into mine. The draught, the mental confusion, the noise and stirring in my head, seemed to last an interminable time. Curious vague impressions of half-forgotten things danced and vanished on the edge of my consciousness. At last he broke the spell. With a sudden explosive sigh he put down his glass.

"Well?" he said.

"It's glorious," said I, though I had not tasted the stuff.

My head was spinning. I sat down. My brain was chaos. Then my perception grew clear and minute as though I saw things in a concave mirror. His manner seemed to have changed into something nervous and hasty. He pulled out his watch and grimaced at it. "Eleven-seven! And to-night I must—Seven—twenty-five. Waterloo! I must go at once." He called for the bill, and struggled with his coat. Officious waiters came to our assistance. In another moment I was wishing him good-bye, over the apron of a cab, and still with an absurd feeling of minute distinctness, as though—how can I express it?—I not only saw but *felt* through an inverted opera-glass.

"That stuff," he said. He put his hand to his forehead. "I ought not to have given it to you. It will make your head split tomorrow. Wait a minute. Here." He handed me out a little flat thing like a seidlitz-powder. "Take that in water as you are going to bed. The other thing was a drug. Not till you're ready to go to bed, mind. It will clear your head. That's all. One more shake—Futurus!"

I gripped his shrivelled claw. "Good-bye," he said, and by the droop of his eyelids I judged he too was a little under the influence of that brain-twisting cordial.

He recollected something else with a start, felt in his breast-pocket, and produced another packet, this time a cylinder the size and shape of a shaving-stick. "Here," said he. "I'd almost forgotten. Don't open this until I come tomorrow—but take it now."

It was so heavy that I well-nigh dropped it. "All ri'!" said I, and he grinned at me through the cab window as the cabman flicked his horse into wakefulness. It was a white packet he had given me, with red seals at either end and along its edge. "If this isn't money," said I, "it's platinum or lead."

I stuck it with elaborate care into my pocket, and with a whirling brain walked home through the Regent Street loiterers and the dark back streets beyond Portland Road. I remember the sensations of that walk very vividly, strange as they were. I was still so far myself that I could notice my strange mental state, and wonder whether this stuff I had had was opium—a drug beyond my experience. It is hard now to describe the peculiarity of my mental strangeness—mental doubling vaguely expresses it. As I was walking up Regent Street I found in my mind a queer persuasion that it was Waterloo station, and had an odd impulse to get into the Polytechnic as a man might get into a train. I put a knuckle in my eye, and it was Regent Street. How can I express it? You see a skilful actor looking quietly at you, he pulls a grimace, and lo!—another person. Is it too extravagant if I tell you that it seemed to me as if Regent Street had, for the moment, done that? Then, being persuaded it was Regent Street again, I was oddly muddled about some fantastic reminiscences that cropped up. "Thirty years ago," thought I, "it was here that I quarrelled with my brother." Then I burst out laughing, to the astonishment and encouragement of a group of night prowlers. Thirty years ago I did not exist, and never in my life had I boasted a brother. The stuff was surely liquid folly, for the poignant regret for that lost brother still clung to me. Along Portland Road the madness took another turn. I began to recall vanished shops, and to compare the street with what it used to be. Confused, troubled thinking was comprehensible enough after the drink I had taken, but what puzzled me were these curiously vivid phantasmal memories that had crept into my mind; and not only the memories that had crept in, but also the memories that had slipped out. I stopped opposite Stevens's, the natural history dealer, and cudgelled my brains to think what he had to do with me. A bus went by, and sounded exactly like the rumbling of a train. I seemed to be dipped into some dark, remote pit for the recollection. "Of course," said I, at last, "he has promised me three frogs tomorrow. Odd I should have forgotten."

Do they still show children dissolving views? In those I remember one view would begin like a faint ghost, and grow and oust another. In just that way it seemed to me that a ghostly set of new sensations was struggling with those of my ordinary self.

I went on through Euston Road to Tottenham Court Road, puzzled, and a little frightened, and scarcely noticed the unusual way I was taking, for commonly I used to cut through the intervening network of back streets. I turned into University Street, to discover that I had forgotten my number. Only by a strong effort did I recall 11A, and even then it seemed to me that it was a thing some forgotten person had told me. I tried to steady my mind by recalling the incidents of the dinner, and for the life of me I could conjure up no picture of my host's face; I saw him only as a shadowy outline, as one might see oneself reflected in a window through which one was looking. In his place, however, I had a curious exterior vision of myself sitting at a table, flushed, bright-eyed, and talkative.

"I must take this other powder," said I. "This is getting impossible."

I tried the wrong side of the hall for my candle and the matches, and had a doubt of which landing my room might be on. "I'm drunk," I said, "that's certain," and blundered needlessly on the staircase to sustain the proposition.

At the first glance my room seemed unfamiliar. "What rot!" I said, and stared about me. I seemed to bring myself back by the effort and the odd phantasmal quality passed into a concrete familiar. There was the old looking-glass, with my notes on the albumens stuck in the corner of the frame, my old everyday suit of clothes pitched about the floor. And yet it was not so real after all. I felt an idiotic persuasion trying to creep into my mind, as it were, that I was in a railway carriage in a train just stopping, that I was peering out of the window at some unknown station. I gripped the bed-rail firmly to reassure myself. "It's clairvoyance, perhaps," I said. "I must write to the Psychical Research Society."

I put the rouleau on my dressing-table, sat on my bed and began to take off my boots. It was as if the picture of my present sensations was painted over some other picture that was trying to show through. "Curse it!" said I; "my wits are going, or am I in two places at once?" Half-undressed, I tossed the powder into a glass and drank it off. It effervesced, and became a fluorescent amber colour. Before I was in bed my mind was already tranquillised. I felt the pillow at my cheek, and thereupon I must have fallen asleep.

———

I awoke abruptly out of a dream of strange beasts, and found myself lying on my back. Probably everyone knows that dismal emotional dream from which one escapes, awake indeed but strangely cowed. There was a curious taste in my mouth, a tired feeling in my limbs, a sense of cutaneous discomfort. I lay with my head motionless on my pillow, expecting that my feeling of strangeness and terror would probably pass away, and that I should then doze off again to sleep. But instead of that, my uncanny sensations increased. At first I could perceive nothing wrong about me. There was a faint light in the room, so faint that it was the very next thing to darkness, and the furniture stood out in it as vague blots of absolute darkness. I stared with my eyes just over the bedclothes.

It came into my mind that someone had entered the room to rob me of my rouleau of money, but after lying for some moments, breathing regularly to simulate sleep, I realised this was mere fancy. Nevertheless, the uneasy assurance of something wrong kept fast hold of me. With an effort I raised my head from the pillow, and peered about me at the dark. What it was I could not conceive. I looked at the dim shapes around me, the greater and lesser darknesses that indicated curtains, table, fireplace, bookshelves, and so forth. Then I began to perceive something unfamiliar in the forms of the darkness. Had the bed turned round? Yonder should be the bookshelves, and something shrouded and pallid rose there, something that would not answer to the bookshelves, however I looked at it. It was far too big to be my shirt thrown on a chair.

Overcoming a childish terror, I threw back the bedclothes and thrust my leg out of bed. Instead of coming out of my truckle-bed upon the floor, I found my foot scarcely reached the edge of the mattress. I made another step, as it were, and sat up on the edge of the bed. By the side of my bed should be the candle, and the matches upon the broken chair. I put out my hand and touched—nothing. I waved my hand in the darkness, and it came against some heavy hanging, soft and thick in texture, which gave a rustling noise at my touch. I grasped this and pulled it; it appeared to be a curtain suspended over the head of my bed.

I was now thoroughly awake, and beginning to realise that I was in a strange room. I was puzzled. I tried to recall the overnight circumstances, and I found them now, curiously enough, vivid in my memory: the supper, my reception of the little packages, my wonder whether I was intoxicated, my slow undressing, the coolness to my flushed face of my pillow. I felt a sudden distrust. Was that last night, or the night before? At any rate, this room was strange to me, and I could not imagine how I had got into it. The dim, pallid outline was growing paler, and I perceived it was a window, with the dark shape of an oval toilet-glass against the weak intimation of the dawn that filtered through the blind. I stood up, and was surprised by a curious feeling of weakness and unsteadiness. With trembling hands outstretched, I walked slowly towards the window, getting, nevertheless, a bruise on the knee from a chair by the way. I fumbled round the glass, which was large, with handsome brass sconces, to find the blind-cord. I could not find any. By chance I took hold of the tassel, and with a click of a spring the blind ran up.

I found myself looking out upon a scene that was altogether strange to me. The night was overcast, and through the flocculent grey of the heaped clouds there filtered a faint half-light of dawn. Just at the edge of the sky, the cloud-canopy had a blood-red rim. Below, everything was dark and indistinct, dim hills in the distance, a vague mass of buildings running up into pinnacles, trees like spilt ink, and below the window a tracery of black bushes and pale grey paths. It was so unfamiliar that for the moment I thought myself still dreaming. I felt the toilet-table; it appeared to be made of some polished wood, and was rather elaborately furnished—there were little cut-glass bottles and a brush upon it. There was also a queer little object, horse-shoe-shaped it felt, with smooth, hard projections lying in a saucer. I could find no matches nor candlestick.

I turned my eyes to the room again. Now the blind was up, faint spectres of its furnishing came out of the darkness. There was a huge curtained bed, and the fireplace at its foot had a large white mantel with something of the shimmer of marble.

I leant against the toilet-table, shut my eyes and opened them again, and tried to think. The whole thing was far too real for dreaming. I was inclined to imagine there was still some hiatus in my memory as a consequence of my draught of that strange liqueur; that I had come into my inheritance perhaps, and suddenly lost my recollection of everything since my good fortune had been announced. Perhaps if I waited a little, things would be clearer to me again. Yet my dinner with old Elvesham was now singularly vivid and recent. The champagne, the observant waiters, the powder, and the liqueurs—I could have staked my soul it all happened a few hours ago.

And then occurred a thing so trivial and yet so terrible to me that I shiver now to think of that moment. I spoke aloud. I said, "How the devil did I get here?" ... *And the voice was not my own.*

It was not my own, it was thin, the articulation was slurred, the resonance of my facial bones was different. Then to reassure myself I ran one hand over the other, and felt loose folds of skin, the bony laxity of age. "Surely," I said in that horrible voice that had somehow established itself in my throat, "surely this thing is a dream!" Almost as quickly as if I did it involuntarily, I thrust my fingers into my mouth. My teeth had gone. My finger-tips ran on the flaccid surface of an even row of shrivelled gums. I was sick with dismay and disgust.

I felt then a passionate desire to see myself, to realise at once in its full horror the ghastly change that had come upon me. I tottered to the mantel, and felt along it for matches. As I did so, a barking cough sprang up in my throat, and I clutched the thick flannel nightdress I found about me. There were no matches there, and I suddenly realised that my extremities were cold. Sniffing and coughing, whimpering a little perhaps, I fumbled back to bed. "It is surely a dream," I whimpered to myself as I clambered back, "surely a dream." It was a senile repetition. I pulled the bedclothes over my shoulders, over my ears, I thrust my withered hand under the pillow, and determined to compose myself to sleep. Of course it was a dream. In the morning the dream would be over, and I should wake up strong and vigorous again to my youth and studies. I shut my eyes, breathed regularly, and, finding myself wakeful, began to count slowly through the powers of three.

But the thing I desired would not come. I could not get to sleep. And the persuasion of the inexorable reality of the change that had happened to me grew steadily. Presently I found myself with my eyes wide open, the powers of three forgotten, and my skinny fingers upon my shrivelled gums. I was indeed, suddenly and abruptly, an old man. I had in some unaccountable manner fallen through my life and come to old age, in some way I had been cheated of all the best of my life, of love, of struggle, of strength and hope. I grovelled into the pillow and tried to persuade myself that such hallucination was possible. Imperceptibly, steadily, the dawn grew clearer.

At last, despairing of further sleep, I sat up in bed and looked about me. A chill twilight rendered the whole chamber visible. It was spacious and well-furnished, better furnished than any room I had ever slept in before. A candle and matches became dimly visible upon a little pedestal in a recess. I threw back the bedclothes, and shivering with the rawness of the early morning, albeit it was summertime, I got out and lit the candle. Then, trembling horribly so that the extinguisher rattled on its spike, I tottered to the glass and saw—*Elvesham's face!* It was none the less horrible because I had already dimly feared as much. He had already seemed physically weak and pitiful to me, but seen now, dressed only in a coarse flannel nightdress that fell apart and showed the stringy neck, seen now as my own body, I cannot describe its desolate decrepitude. The hollow cheeks, the straggling tail of dirty grey hair, the rheumy bleared eyes, the quivering, shrivelled lips, the lower displaying a gleam of the pink interior lining, and those horrible dark gums showing. You who are mind and body together at your natural years, cannot imagine what this fiendish imprisonment meant to me. To be young and full of the desire and energy of youth, and to be caught, and presently to be crushed in this tottering ruin of a body…

But I wander from the course of my story. For some time I must have been stunned at this change that had come upon me. It was daylight when I did so far gather myself together as to think. In some inexplicable way I had been changed, though how, short of magic, the thing had been done, I could not say. And as I thought, the diabolical ingenuity of Elvesham came home to me. It seemed plain to me that as I found myself in his, so he must be in possession of *my* body, of my strength that is, and my future. But how to prove it? Then as I thought, the thing became so incredible even to me, that my mind reeled, and I had to pinch myself, to feel my toothless gums, to see myself in the glass, and touch the things about me before I could steady myself to face the facts again. Was all life hallucination? Was I indeed Elvesham, and he me? Had I been dreaming of Eden overnight? Was there any Eden? But if I was Elvesham, I should remember where I was on the previous morning, the name of the town in which I lived, what happened before the dream began. I struggled with my thoughts. I recalled the queer doubleness of my memories overnight. But now my mind was clear. Not the ghost of any memories but those proper to Eden could I raise.

"This way lies insanity!" I cried in my piping voice. I staggered to my feet, dragged my feeble, heavy limbs to the washhand-stand, and plunged my grey head into a basin of cold water. Then, towelling myself, I tried again. It was no good. I felt beyond all question that I was indeed Eden, not Elvesham. But Eden in Elvesham's body!

Had I been a man of any other age, I might have given myself up to my fate as one enchanted. But in these sceptical days miracles do not pass current. Here was some trick of psychology. What a drug and a steady stare could do, a drug and a steady stare, or some similar treatment, could surely undo. Men have lost their memories before. But to exchange memories as one does umbrellas! I laughed. Alas! not a healthy laugh, but a wheezing, senile titter. I could have fancied old Elvesham laughing at my plight, and a gust of petulant anger, unusual to me, swept across my feelings. I began dressing eagerly in the clothes I found lying about on the floor, and only realised when I was dressed that it was an evening suit I had assumed. I opened the wardrobe and found some ordinary clothes, a pair of plaid trousers, and an old-fashioned dressing-gown. I put a venerable smoking-cap on my venerable head, and, coughing a little from my exertions, tottered out upon the landing.

It was then perhaps a quarter to six, and the blinds were closely drawn and the house quite silent. The landing was a spacious one, a broad, richly carpeted staircase went down into the darkness of the hall below, and before me a door ajar showed me a writing-desk, a revolving bookcase, the back of a study chair, and a fine array of bound books, shelf upon shelf.

"My study," I mumbled, and walked across the landing. Then at the sound of my voice a thought struck me, and I went back to the bedroom and put in the set of false teeth. They slipped in with the ease of old habit. "That's better," said I, gnashing them, and so returned to the study.

The drawers of the writing-desk were locked. Its revolving top was also locked. I could see no indications of the keys, and there were none in the pockets of my trousers. I shuffled back at once to the bedroom, and went through the dress suit, and afterwards the pockets of all the garments I could find. I was very eager; and one might have imagined that burglars had been at work, to see my room when I had done. Not only were there no keys to be found, but not a coin, nor a scrap of paper—save only the receipted bill of the overnight dinner.

A curious weariness asserted itself. I sat down and stared at the garments flung here and there, their pockets turned inside out. My first frenzy had already flickered out. Every moment I was beginning to realise the immense intelligence of the plans of my enemy, to see more and more clearly the hopelessness of my position. With an effort I rose and hurried into the study again. On the staircase was a housemaid pulling up the blinds. She stared, I think, at the expression of my face. I shut the door of the study behind me, and, seizing a poker, began an attack upon the desk. That is how they found me. The cover of the desk was split, the lock smashed, the letters torn out of the pigeon-holes and tossed about the room. In my senile rage I had flung about the pens and other such light stationery, and overturned the ink. Moreover, a large vase upon the mantel had got broken—I do not know how. I could find no cheque-book, no money, no indications of the slightest use for the recovery of my body. I was battering madly at the drawers, when the butler, backed by two women-servants, intruded upon me.

———

That simply is the story of my change. No one will believe my frantic assertions. I am treated as one demented, and even at this moment I am under restraint. But I am sane, absolutely sane, and to prove it I have sat down to write this story minutely as the thing happened to me. I appeal to the reader, whether there is any trace of insanity in the style or method of the story he has been reading. I am a young man locked away in an old man's body. But the clear fact is incredible to everyone. Naturally I appear demented to those who will not believe this, naturally I do not know the names of my secretaries, of the doctors who come to see me, of my servants and neighbours, of this town (wherever it is) where I find myself. Naturally I lose myself in my own house, and suffer inconveniences of every sort. Naturally I ask the oddest questions. Naturally I weep and cry out, and have paroxysms of despair. I have no money and no cheque-book. The bank will not recognise my signature, for I suppose that, allowing for the feeble muscles I now have, my handwriting is still Eden's. These people about me will not let me go to the bank personally. It seems, indeed, that there is no bank in this town, and that I have taken an account in some part of London. It seems that Elvesham kept the name of his solicitor secret from all his household—I can ascertain nothing. Elvesham was, of course, a profound student of mental science, and all my declarations of the facts of the case merely confirm the theory that my insanity is the outcome of overmuch brooding upon psychology. Dreams of the personal identity indeed! Two days ago I was a healthy youngster, with all life before me; now I am a furious old man, unkempt and desperate and miserable, prowling about a great luxurious strange house, watched, feared, and avoided as a lunatic by everyone about me. And in London is Elvesham beginning life again in a vigorous body, and with all the accumulated knowledge and wisdom of threescore and ten. He has stolen my life.

What has happened I do not clearly know. In the study are volumes of manuscript notes referring chiefly to the psychology of memory, and parts of what may be either calculations or ciphers in symbols absolutely strange to me. In some passages there are indications that he was also occupied with the philosophy of mathematics. I take it he has transferred the whole of his memories, the accumulation that makes up his personality, from this old withered brain of his to mine, and, similarly, that he has transferred mine to his discarded tenement. Practically, that is, he has changed bodies. But how such a change may be possible is without the range of my philosophy. I have been a materialist for all my thinking life, but here, suddenly, is a clear case of man's detachability from matter.

One desperate experiment I am about to try. I sit writing here before putting the matter to issue. This morning, with the help of a table-knife that I had secreted at breakfast, I succeeded in breaking open a fairly obvious secret drawer in this wrecked writing-desk. I discovered nothing save a little green glass phial containing a white powder. Round the neck of the phial was a label, and thereon was written this one word, *"Release."* This may be—is most probably, poison. I can understand Elvesham placing poison in my way, and I should be sure that it was his intention so to get rid of the only living witness against him, were it not for this careful concealment. The man has practically solved the problem of immortality. Save for the spite of chance, he will live in my body until it has aged, and then, again, throwing that aside, he will assume some other victim's youth and strength. When one remembers his heartlessness, it is terrible to think of the ever-growing experience, that... How long has he been leaping from body to body?... But I tire of writing. The powder appears to be soluble in water. The taste is not unpleasant.

—

There the narrative found upon Mr. Elvesham's desk ends. His dead body lay between the desk and the chair. The latter had been pushed back, probably by his last convulsions. The story was written in pencil, and in a crazy hand quite unlike his usual minute characters. There remains only two curious facts to record. Indisputably there was some connection between Eden and Elvesham, since the whole of Elvesham's property was bequeathed to the young man. But he never inherited. When Elvesham committed suicide, Eden was, strangely enough, already dead. Twenty-four hours before, he had been knocked down by a cab and killed instantly, at the crowded crossing at the intersection of Gower Street and Euston Road. So that the only human being who could have thrown light upon this fantastic narrative is beyond the reach of questions.

THE MAN WHO COULD
WORK MIRACLES

A PANTOUM IN PROSE

It is doubtful whether the gift was innate. For my own part, I think it came to him suddenly. Indeed, until he was thirty he was a sceptic, and did not believe in miraculous powers. And here, since it is the most convenient place, I must mention that he was a little man, and had eyes of a hot brown, very erect red hair, a moustache with ends that he twisted up, and freckles. His name was George McWhirter Fotheringay—not the sort of name by any means to lead to any expectation of miracles—and he was clerk at Gomshott's. He was greatly addicted to assertive argument. It was while he was asserting the impossibility of miracles that he had his first intimation of his extraordinary powers. This particular argument was being held in the bar of the Long Dragon, and Toddy Beamish was conducting the opposition by a monotonous but effective "So *you* say," that drove Mr. Fotheringay to the very limit of his patience.

There were present, besides these two, a very dusty cyclist, landlord Cox, and Miss Maybridge, the perfectly respectable and rather portly barmaid of the Dragon. Miss Maybridge was standing with her back to Mr. Fotheringay, washing glasses; the others were watching him, more or less amused by the present ineffectiveness of the assertive method. Goaded by the Torres Vedras tactics of Mr. Beamish, Mr. Fotheringay determined to make an unusual rhetorical effort.

"Looky here, Mr. Beamish," said Mr. Fotheringay. "Let us clearly understand what a miracle is. It's something contrariwise to the course of nature done by power of Will, something what couldn't happen without being specially willed."

"So *you* say," said Mr. Beamish, repulsing him.

Mr. Fotheringay appealed to the cyclist, who had hitherto been a silent auditor, and received his assent—given with a hesitating cough and a glance at Mr. Beamish. The landlord would express no opinion, and Mr. Fotheringay, returning to Mr. Beamish, received the unexpected concession of a qualified assent to his definition of a miracle.

"For instance," said Mr. Fotheringay, greatly encouraged. "Here would be a miracle. That lamp, in the natural course of nature, couldn't burn like that upsy-down, could it, Beamish?"

"*You* say it couldn't," said Beamish.

"And you?" said Fotheringay. "You don't mean to say—eh?"

"No," said Beamish reluctantly. "No, it couldn't."

"Very well," said Mr. Fotheringay. "Then here comes someone, as it might be me, along here, and stands as it might be here, and says to that lamp, as I might do, collecting all my will—'Turn upsy-down without breaking, and go on burning steady,' and—Hullo!"

It was enough to make anyone say "Hullo!" The impossible, the incredible, was visible to them all. The lamp hung inverted in the air, burning quietly with its flame pointing down. It was as solid, as indisputable as ever a lamp was, the prosaic common lamp of the Long Dragon bar.

Mr. Fotheringay stood with an extended forefinger and knitted brows of one anticipating a catastrophic smash. The cyclist, who was sitting next to the lamp, ducked and jumped across the bar. Everybody jumped, more or less. Miss Maybridge turned and screamed. For nearly three seconds the lamp remained still. A faint cry of mental distress came from Mr. Fotheringay. "I can't keep it up," he said, "any longer." He staggered back, and the inverted lamp suddenly flared, fell against the corner of the bar, bounced aside, smashed upon the floor, and went out.

It was lucky it had a metal receiver, or the whole place would have been in a blaze. Mr. Cox was the first to speak, and his remark, shorn of needless excrescences, was to the effect that Fotheringay was a fool. Fotheringay was beyond disputing even so fundamental a proposition as that! He was astonished beyond measure at the thing that had occurred. The subsequent conversation threw absolutely no light on the matter so far as Fotheringay was concerned; the general opinion not only followed Mr. Cox very closely but very vehemently. Everyone accused Fotheringay of a silly trick, and presented him to himself as a foolish destroyer of comfort and security. His mind was in a tornado of perplexity, he was himself inclined to agree with them, and he made a remarkably ineffectual opposition to the proposal of his departure.

He went home flushed and heated, coat-collar crumpled, eyes smarting and ears red. He watched each of the ten street lamps nervously as he passed it. It was only when he found himself alone in his little bedroom in Church Row that he was able to grapple seriously with his memories of the occurrence, and ask, "What on earth happened?"

He had removed his coat and boots, and was sitting on the bed with his hands in his pockets repeating the text of his defence for the seventeenth time, "*I* didn't want the confounded thing to upset," when it occurred to him that at the precise moment he had said the commanding words he had inadvertently willed the thing he said, and that when he had seen the lamp in the air he had felt that it depended on him to maintain it there without being clear how this was to be done. He had not a particularly complex mind, or he might have stuck for a time at that "inadvertently willed," embracing, as it does, the abstrusest problems of voluntary action; but as it was, the idea came to him with a quite acceptable haziness. And from that, following, as I must admit, no clear logical path, he came to the test of experiment.

He pointed resolutely to his candle and collected his mind, though he felt he did a foolish thing. "Be raised up," he said. But in a second that feeling vanished. The candle was raised, hung in the air one giddy moment, and as Mr. Fotheringay gasped, fell with a smash on his toilet-table, leaving him in darkness save for the expiring glow of its wick.

For a time Mr. Fotheringay sat in the darkness, perfectly still. "It did happen, after all," he said. "And 'ow I'm to explain it I *don't* know." He sighed heavily, and began feeling in his pockets for a match. He could find none, and he rose and groped about the toilet-table. "I wish I had a match," he said. He resorted to his coat, and there were none there, and then it dawned upon him that miracles were possible even with matches. He extended a hand and scowled at it in the dark. "Let there be a match in that hand," he said. He felt some light object fall across his palm, and his fingers closed upon a match.

After several ineffectual attempts to light this, he discovered it was a safety-match. He threw it down, and then it occurred to him that he might have willed it lit. He did, and perceived it burning in the midst of his toilet-table mat. He caught it up hastily, and it went out. His perception of possibilities enlarged, and he felt for and replaced the candle in its candlestick. "Here! *you* be lit," said Mr. Fotheringay, and forthwith the candle was flaring, and he saw a little black hole in the toilet-cover, with a wisp of smoke rising from it. For a time he stared from this to the little flame and back, and then looked up and met his own gaze in the looking glass. By this help he communed with himself in silence for a time.

"How about miracles now?" said Mr. Fotheringay at last, addressing his reflection.

The subsequent meditations of Mr. Fotheringay were of a severe but confused description. So far as he could see, it was a case of pure willing with him. The nature of his first experiences disinclined him for any further experiments except for the most cautious type. But he lifted a sheet of paper, and turned a glass of water pink and then green, and he created a snail, which he miraculously annihilated, and got himself a miraculous new toothbrush. Somewhen in the small hours he had reached the fact that his will-power must be of a particularly rare and pungent quality, a fact of which he had certainly had inklings before, but no certain assurance. The scare and perplexity of his first discovery was now qualified by pride in this evidence of singularity and by vague intimations of advantage. He became aware that the church clock was striking one, and as it did not occur to him that his daily duties at Gomshott's might be miraculously dispensed with, he resumed undressing, in order to get to bed without further delay. As he struggled to get his shirt over his head, he was struck with a brilliant idea. "Let me be in bed," he said, and found himself so. "Undressed," he stipulated; and, finding the sheets cold, added hastily, "and in my nightshirt—no, in a nice soft woollen nightshirt. Ah!" he said with immense enjoyment. "And now let me be comfortably asleep…"

He awoke at his usual hour and was pensive all through breakfast-time, wondering whether his overnight experience might not be a particularly vivid dream. At length his mind turned again to cautious experiments. For instance, he had three eggs for breakfast; two his landlady had supplied, good, but shoppy, and one was a delicious fresh goose-egg, laid, cooked, and served by his extraordinary will. He hurried off to Gomshott's in a state of profound but carefully concealed excitement, and only remembered the shell of the third egg when his landlady spoke of it that night. All day he could do no work because of this astonishingly new self-knowledge, but this caused him no inconvenience, because he made up for it miraculously in his last ten minutes.

As the day wore on his state of mind passed from wonder to elation, albeit the circumstances of his dismissal from the Long Dragon were still disagreeable to recall, and a garbled account of the matter that had reached his colleagues led to some badinage. It was evident he must be careful how he lifted frangible articles, but in other ways his gift promised more and more as he turned it over in his mind. He intended among other things to increase his personal property by unostentatious acts of creation. He called into existence a pair of very splendid diamond studs, and hastily annihilated them again as young Gomshott came across the counting-house to his desk. He was afraid young Gomshott might wonder how he had come by them. He saw quite clearly the gift required caution and watchfulness in its exercise, but so far as he could judge the difficulties attending its mastery would be no greater than those he had already faced in the study of cycling. It was that analogy, perhaps, quite as much as the feeling that he would be unwelcome in the Long Dragon, that drove him out after supper into the lane beyond the gas-works, to rehearse a few miracles in private.

There was possibly a certain want of originality in his attempts, for apart from his will-power Mr. Fotheringay was not a very exceptional man. The miracle of Moses's rod came to his mind, but the night was dark and unfavourable to the proper control of large miraculous snakes. Then he recollected the story of "Tannhäuser" that he had read on the back of the Philharmonic programme. That seemed to him singularly attractive and harmless. He stuck his walking-stick—a very nice Poona-Penang lawyer—into the turf that edged the footpath, and commanded the dry wood to blossom. The air was immediately full of the scent of roses, and by means of a match he saw for himself that this beautiful miracle was indeed accomplished. His satisfaction was ended by advancing footsteps. Afraid of a premature discovery of his powers, he addressed the blossoming stick hastily: "Go back." What he meant was "Change back"; but of course he was confused. The stick receded at a considerable velocity, and incontinently came a cry of anger and a bad word from the approaching person. "Who are you throwing brambles at, you fool?" cried a voice. "That got me on the shin."

"I'm sorry, old chap," said Mr. Fotheringay, and then realising the awkward nature of the explanation, caught nervously at his moustache. He saw Winch, one of the three Immering constables, advancing.

"What d'yer mean by it?" asked the constable. "Hullo! It's you, is it? The gent that broke the lamp at the Long Dragon!"

"I don't mean anything by it," said Mr. Fotheringay. "Nothing at all."

"What d'yer do it for then?"

"Oh, bother!" said Mr. Fotheringay.

"Bother indeed! D'yer know that stick hurt? What d'yer do it for, eh?"

For the moment Mr. Fotheringay could not think what he had done it for. His silence seemed to irritate Mr. Winch. "You've been assaulting the police, young man, this time. That's what *you* done."

"Look here, Mr. Winch," said Mr. Fotheringay, annoyed and confused, "I'm very sorry. The fact is—"

"Well?"

He could think of no way but the truth. "I was working a miracle." He tried to speak in an off-hand way, but try as he would he couldn't.

"Working a—! 'Ere, don't you talk rot. Working a miracle, indeed! Miracle! Well, that's downright funny! Why, you's the chap that don't believe in miracles...Fact is, this is another of your silly conjuring tricks—that's what this is. Now, I tell you—"

But Mr. Fotheringay never heard what Mr. Winch was going to tell him. He realised he had given himself away, flung his valuable secret to all the winds of heaven. A violent gust of irritation swept him to action. He turned on the constable swiftly and fiercely. "Here," he said, "I've had enough of this, I have! I'll show you a silly conjuring trick, I will! Go to Hades! Go, now!"

He was alone!

Mr. Fotheringay performed no more miracles that night, nor did he trouble to see what had become of his flowering stick. He returned to the town, scared and very quiet, and went to his bedroom. "Lord!" he said, "it's a powerful gift—an extremely powerful gift. I didn't hardly mean as much as that. Not really … I wonder what Hades is like!"

He sat on the bed taking off his boots. Struck by a happy thought he transferred the constable to San Francisco, and without any more interference with normal causation went soberly to bed. In the night he dreamt of the anger of Winch.

The next day Mr. Fotheringay heard two interesting items of news. Someone had planted a most beautiful climbing rose against the elder Mr. Gomshott's private house in the Lullaborough Road, and the river as far as Rawling's Mill was to be dragged for Constable Winch.

Mr. Fotheringay was abstracted and thoughtful all the day, and performed no miracles except certain provisions for Winch, and the miracle of completing his day's work with punctual perfection in spite of all the bee-swarm of thoughts that hummed through his mind. And the extraordinary abstraction and meekness of his manner was remarked by several people, and made a matter for jesting. For the most part he was thinking of Winch.

On Sunday evening he went to chapel, and oddly enough, Mr. Maydig, who took a certain interest in occult matters, preached about "things that are not lawful." Mr. Fotheringay was not a regular chapel goer, but the system of assertive scepticism, to which I have already alluded, was now very much shaken. The tenor of the sermon threw an entirely new light on these novel gifts, and he suddenly decided to consult Mr. Maydig immediately after the service. So soon as that was determined, he found himself wondering why he had not done so before.

Mr. Maydig, a lean, excitable man with quite remarkably long wrists and neck, was gratified at a request for a private conversation from a young man whose carelessness in religious matters was a subject for general remark in the town. After a few necessary delays, he conducted him to the study of the Manse, which was contiguous to the chapel, seated him comfortably, and, standing in front of a cheerful fire—his legs threw a Rhodian arch of shadow on the opposite wall—requested Mr. Fotheringay to state his business.

At first Mr. Fotheringay was a little abashed, and found some difficulty in opening the matter. "You will scarcely believe me, Mr. May-dig, I am afraid"—and so forth for some time. He tried a question at last, and asked Mr. Maydig his opinion of miracles.

Mr. Maydig was still saying "Well" in an extremely judicial tone, when Mr. Fotheringay interrupted again: "You don't believe, I suppose, that some common sort of person—like myself, for instance—as it might be sitting here now, might have some sort of twist inside him that made him able to do things by his will."

"It's possible," said Mr. Maydig. "Something of the sort, perhaps, is possible."

"If I might make free with something here, I think I might show you by a sort of experiment," said Mr. Fotheringay. "Now, take that tobacco-jar on the table, for instance. What I want to know is whether what I am going to do with it is a miracle or not. Just half a minute, Mr. Maydig, please."

He knitted his brows, pointed to the tobacco-jar and said: "Be a bowl of vi'lets."

The tobacco-jar did as it was ordered.

Mr. Maydig started violently at the change, and stood looking from the thaumaturgist to the bowl of flowers. He said nothing. Presently he ventured to lean over the table and smell the violets; they were fresh-picked and very fine ones. Then he stared at Mr. Fotheringay again.

"How did you do that?" he asked.

Mr. Fotheringay pulled his moustache. "Just told it—and there you are. Is that a miracle, or is it black art, or what is it? And what do you think's the matter with me? That's what I want to ask."

"It's a most extraordinary occurrence."

"And this day last week I knew no more that I could do things like that than you did. It came quite sudden. It's something odd about my will, I suppose, and that's as far as I can see."

"Is *that*—the only thing. Could you do other things besides that?"

"Lord, yes!" said Mr. Fotheringay. "Just anything." He thought, and suddenly recalled a conjuring entertainment he had seen. "Here!" He pointed. "Change into a bowl of fish—no, not that—change into a glass bowl full of water with goldfish swimming in it. That's better! You see that, Mr. Maydig?"

"It's astonishing. It's incredible. You are either a most extraordi-nary . . . But no—"

"I could change it into anything," said Mr. Fotheringay. "Just anything. Here! be a pigeon, will you?"

In another moment a blue pigeon was fluttering round the room and making Mr. Maydig duck every time it came near him. "Stop there, will you," said Mr. Fotheringay; and the pigeon hung motionless in the air. "I could change it back to a bowl of flowers," he said, and after replacing the pigeon on the table worked that miracle. "I expect you will want your pipe in a bit," he said, and restored the tobacco-jar.

Mr. Maydig had followed all these later changes in a sort of ejaculatory silence. He stared at Mr. Fotheringay and, in a very gingerly manner, picked up the tobacco-jar, examined it, replaced it on the table. *"Well!"* was the only expression of his feelings.

"Now, after that it's easier to explain what I came about," said Mr. Fotheringay; and proceeded to a lengthy and involved narrative of his strange experiences, beginning with the affair of the lamp in the Long Dragon and complicated by persistent allusions to Winch. As he went on, the transient pride Mr. Maydig's consternation had caused passed away; he became the very ordinary Mr. Fotheringay of everyday intercourse again. Mr. Maydig listened intently, the tobacco-jar in his hand, and his bearing changed also with the course of the narrative. Presently, while Mr. Fotheringay was dealing with the miracle of the third egg, the minister interrupted with a fluttering extended hand—

"It is possible," he said. "It is credible. It is amazing, of course, but it reconciles a number of difficulties. The power to work miracles is a gift—a peculiar quality like genius or second sight—hitherto it has come very rarely and to exceptional people. But in this case...I have always wondered at the miracles of Mahomet, and at Yogis' miracles, and the miracles of Madame Blavatsky. But, of course! Yes, it is simply a gift! It carries out so beautifully the arguments of that great thinker"—Mr. Maydig's voice sank—"his Grace the Duke of Argyll. Here we plumb some profounder law—deeper than the ordinary laws of nature. Yes—yes. Go on. Go on!"

Mr. Fotheringay proceeded to tell of his misadventure with Winch, and Mr. Maydig, no longer overawed or scared, began to jerk his limbs about and interject astonishment. "It's this what troubled me most," proceeded Mr. Fotheringay; "it's this I'm most mijitly in want of advice for; of course he's at San Francisco—wherever San Francisco may be—but of course it's awkward for both of us, as you'll see, Mr. Maydig. I don't see how he can understand what has happened, and I dare say he's scared and exasperated something tremendous, and trying to get at me. I dare say he keeps on starting off to come here. I send him back, by a miracle, every few hours, when I think of it. And of course, that's a thing he won't be able to understand, and it's bound to annoy him; and, of course, if he takes a ticket every time it will cost him a lot of money. I done the best I could for him, but of course it's difficult for him to put himself in my place. I thought afterwards that his clothes might have got scorched, you know—if Hades is all it's supposed to be—before I shifted him. In that case I suppose they'd have locked him up in San Francisco. Of course I willed him a new suit of clothes on him directly I thought of it. But, you see, I'm already in a deuce of a tangle—"

Mr. Maydig looked serious. "I see you are in a tangle. Yes, it's a difficult position. How you are to end it…" He became diffuse and inconclusive.

"However, we'll leave Winch for a little and discuss the larger question. I don't think this is a case of the black art or anything of the sort. I don't think there is any taint of criminality about it all, Mr. Fotheringay—none whatever, unless you are suppressing material facts. No, it's miracles—pure miracles—miracles, if I may say so, of the very highest class."

He began to pace the hearthrug and gesticulate, while Mr. Fotheringay sat with his arm on the table and his head on his arm, looking worried. "I don't see how I'm to manage about Winch," he said.

"A gift of working miracles—apparently a very powerful gift," said Mr. Maydig, "will find a way about Winch—never fear. My dear sir, you are a most important man—a man of the most astonishing possibilities. As evidence, for example! And in other ways, the things you may do…"

"Yes, *I've* thought of a thing or two," said Mr. Fotheringay. "But—some of the things came a bit twisty. You saw that fish at first? Wrong sort of bowl and wrong sort of fish. And I thought I'd ask someone."

"A proper course," said Mr. Maydig, "a very proper course—altogether the proper course." He stopped and looked at Mr. Fotheringay.

"It's practically an unlimited gift. Let us test your powers, for instance. If they really *are*... if they really are all they seem to be."

And so, incredible as it may seem, in the study of the little house behind the Congregational Chapel, on the evening of Sunday, Nov. 10, 1896, Mr. Fotheringay, egged on and inspired by Mr. Maydig, began to work miracles. The reader's attention is specially and definitely called to the date. He will object, probably has already objected, that certain points in this story are improbable, that if any things of the sort already described had indeed occurred, they would have been in all the papers a year ago. The details immediately following he will find particularly hard to accept, because among other things they involve the conclusion that he or she, the reader in question, must have been killed in a violent and unprecedented manner more than a year ago. Now a miracle is nothing if not improbable, and as a matter of fact the reader *was* killed in a violent and unprecedented manner a year ago. In the subsequent course of this story that will become perfectly clear and credible, as every right-minded and reasonable reader will admit. But this is not the place for the end of the story, being but little beyond the hither side of the middle. And at first the miracles worked by Mr. Fotheringay were timid little miracles—little things with the cups and parlour fitments, as feeble as the miracles of Theosophists, and, feeble as they were, they were received with awe by his collaborator. He would have preferred to settle the Winch business out of hand, but Mr. Maydig would not let him. But after they had worked a dozen of these domestic trivialities, their sense of power grew, their imagination began to show signs of stimulation, and their ambition enlarged. Their first larger enterprise was due to hunger and the negligence of Mrs. Minchin, Mr. Maydig's housekeeper. The meal to which the minister conducted Mr. Fotheringay was certainly ill-laid and uninviting as refreshment for two industrious miracle-workers; but they were seated, and Mr. Maydig was descanting in sorrow rather than in anger upon his housekeeper's shortcomings, before it occurred to Mr. Fotheringay that an opportunity lay before him. "Don't you think, Mr. Maydig," he said, "if it isn't a liberty, I—"

"My dear Mr. Fotheringay! Of course! No—I didn't think."

Mr. Fotheringay waved his hand. "What shall we have?" he said, in a large, inclusive spirit, and, at Mr. Maydig's order, revised the supper very thoroughly. "As for me," he said, eyeing Mr. Maydig's selection, "I am always particularly fond of a tankard of stout and a nice Welsh rarebit, and I'll order that. I ain't much given to Burgundy," and forthwith stout and Welsh rarebit promptly appeared at his command. They sat long at their supper, talking like equals, as Mr. Fotheringay presently perceived with a glow of surprise and gratification, of all the miracles they would presently do. "And, by the bye, Mr. Maydig," said Mr. Fotheringay, "I might perhaps be able to help you—in a domestic way."

"Don't quite follow," said Mr. Maydig, pouring out a glass of miraculous old Burgundy.

Mr. Fotheringay helped himself to a second Welsh rarebit out of vacancy, and took a mouthful. "I was thinking," he said, "I might be able (*chum, chum*) to work (*chum, chum*) a miracle with Mrs. Minchin (*chum, chum*)—make her a better woman."

Mr. Maydig put down the glass and looked doubtful. "She's—she strongly objects to interference, you know, Mr. Fotheringay. And—as a matter of fact—it's well past eleven and she's probably in bed and asleep. Do you think, on the whole—"

Mr. Fotheringay considered these objections. "I don't see that it shouldn't be done in her sleep."

For a time Mr. Maydig opposed the idea, and then he yielded. Mr. Fotheringay issued his orders, and a little less at their ease, perhaps, the two gentlemen proceeded with their repast. Mr. Maydig was enlarging on the changes he might expect in his housekeeper next day, with an optimism that seemed even to Mr. Fotheringay's super senses a little forced and hectic, when a series of confused noises from upstairs began. Their eyes exchanged interrogations, and Mr. Maydig left the room hastily. Mr. Fotheringay heard him calling up to his housekeeper and then his footsteps going softly up to her.

In a minute or so the minister returned, his step light, his face radiant. "Wonderful!" he said, "and touching! Most touching!"

He began pacing the hearthrug. "A repentance—a most touching repentance—through the crack of the door. Poor woman! A most wonderful change! She had got up. She must have got up at once. She had got up out of her sleep to smash a private bottle of brandy in her box. And to confess it too!... But this gives us—it opens—a most amazing vista of possibilities. If we can work this miraculous change in *her.*"

"The thing's unlimited seemingly," said Mr. Fotheringay. "And about Mr. Winch—"

"Altogether unlimited." And from the hearthrug Mr. Maydig, waving the Winch difficulty aside, unfolded a series of wonderful proposals—proposals he invented as he went along.

Now what those proposals were does not concern the essentials of this story. Suffice it that they were designed in a spirit of infinite benevolence, the sort of benevolence that used to be called postprandial. Suffice it, too, that the problem of Winch remained unsolved. Nor is it necessary to describe how far that series got to its fulfilment. There were astonishing changes. The small hours found Mr. Maydig and Mr. Fotheringay careering across the chilly market-square under the still moon, in a sort of ecstasy of thaumaturgy, Mr. Maydig all flap and gesture, Mr. Fotheringay short and bristling, and no longer abashed at his greatness. They had reformed every drunkard in the Parliamentary division, changed all the beer and alcohol to water (Mr. Maydig had overruled Mr. Fotheringay on this point), they had, further, greatly improved the railway communication of the place, drained Flinder's swamp, improved the soil of One Tree Hill, and cured the Vicar's wart. And they were going to see what could be done with the injured pier at South Bridge. "The place," gasped Mr. Maydig, "won't be the same place tomorrow. How surprised and thankful everyone will be!" And just at that moment the church clock struck three.

"I say," said Mr. Fotheringay, "that's three o'clock! I must be getting back. I've got to be at business by eight. And besides, Mrs. Wimms—"

"We're only beginning," said Mr. Maydig, full of the sweetness of unlimited power. "We're only beginning. Think of all the good we're doing. When people wake—"

"But—," said Mr. Fotheringay.

Mr. Maydig gripped his arm suddenly. His eyes were bright and wild. "My dear chap," he said, "there's no hurry. Look"—he pointed to the moon at the zenith—"Joshua!"

"Joshua?" said Mr. Fotheringay.

"Joshua," said Mr. Maydig. "Why not? Stop it."

Mr. Fotheringay looked at the moon.

"That's a bit tall," he said after a pause.

"Why not?" said Mr. Maydig. "Of course it doesn't stop. You stop the rotation of the earth, you know. Time stops. It isn't as if we were doing harm."

"H'm!" said Mr. Fotheringay. "Well." He sighed. "I'll try. Here—"

He buttoned up his jacket and addressed himself to the habitable globe, with as good an assumption of confidence as lay in his power. "Jest stop rotating, will you," said Mr. Fotheringay.

Incontinently he was flying head over heels through the air at the rate of dozens of miles a minute. In spite of the innumerable circles he was describing per second, he thought; for thought is wonderful—sometimes as sluggish as flowing pitch, sometimes as instantaneous as light. He thought in a second, and willed. "Let me come down safe and sound. Whatever else happens, let me down safe and sound."

He willed it only just in time, for his clothes, heated by his rapid flight through the air, were already beginning to singe. He came down with a forcible, but by no means injurious bump in what appeared to be a mound of fresh-turned earth. A large mass of metal and masonry, extraordinarily like the clock-tower in the middle of the market-square, hit the earth near him, ricochetted over him, and flew into stonework, bricks, and masonry, like a bursting bomb. A hurtling cow hit one of the larger blocks and smashed like an egg. There was a crash that made all the most violent crashes of his past life seem like the sound of falling dust, and this was followed by a descending series of lesser crashes. A vast wind roared throughout earth and heaven, so that he could scarcely lift his head to look. For a while he was too breathless and astonished even to see where he was or what had happened. And his first movement was to feel his head and reassure himself that his streaming hair was still his own.

"Lord!" gasped Mr. Fotheringay, scarce able to speak for the gale, "I've had a squeak! What's gone wrong? Storms and thunder. And only a minute ago a fine night. It's Maydig set me on to this sort of thing. *What* a mind! If I go on fooling in this way I'm bound to have a thundering accident!...

"Where's Maydig?

"What a confounded mess everything's in!"

He looked about him so far as his flapping jacket would permit. The appearance of things was really extremely strange. "The sky's all right anyhow," said Mr. Fotheringay. "And that's about all that is all right. And even there it looks like a terrific gale coming up. But there's the moon overhead. Just as it was now. Bright as midday. But as for the rest— Where's the village? Where's—where's anything? And what on earth set this wind a-blowing? *I* didn't order no wind."

Mr. Fotheringay struggled to get to his feet in vain, and after one failure, remained on all fours, holding on. He surveyed the moonlit world to leeward, with the tails of his jacket streaming over his head. "There's something seriously wrong," said Mr. Fotheringay. "And what it is—goodness knows."

Far and wide nothing was visible in the white glare through the haze of dust that drove before a screaming gale but tumbled masses of earth and heaps of inchoate ruins, no trees, no houses, no familiar shapes, only a wilderness of disorder vanishing at last into the darkness beneath the whirling columns and streamers, the lightnings and thunderings of a swiftly rising storm. Near him in the livid glare was something that might once have been an elm-tree, a smashed mass of splinters, shivered from boughs to base, and further, a twisted mass of iron girders—only too evidently the viaduct—rose out of the piled confusion.

You see, when Mr. Fotheringay had arrested the rotation of the solid globe, he had made no stipulation concerning the trifling movables upon its surface. And the earth spins so fast that the surface at its equator is travelling at rather more than a thousand miles an hour, and in these latitudes at more than half that pace. So that the village, and Mr. Maydig, and Mr. Fotheringay, and everybody and everything had been jerked violently forward at about nine miles per second—that is to say, much more violently than if they had been fired out of a cannon. And every human being, every living creature, every house, and every tree—all the world as we know it—had been so jerked and smashed and utterly destroyed. That was all.

These things Mr. Fotheringay did not, of course, fully appreciate. But he perceived that his miracle had miscarried, and with that a great disgust of miracles came upon him. He was in darkness now, for the clouds had swept together and blotted out his momentary glimpse of the moon, and the air was full of fitful struggling tortured wraiths of hail. A great roaring of wind and waters filled earth and sky, and, peering under his hand through the dust and sleet to windward, he saw by the play of the lightnings a vast wall of water pouring towards him.

"Maydig!" screamed Mr. Fotheringay's feeble voice amid the elemental uproar. "Here!—Maydig!"

"Stop!" cried Mr. Fotheringay to the advanced water. "Oh, for goodness' sake, stop!"

"Just a moment," said Mr. Fotheringay to the lightnings and thunder. "Stop jest a moment while I collect my thoughts... And now what shall I do?" he said. "What *shall* I do? Lord! I wish Maydig was about."

"I know," said Mr. Fotheringay. "And for goodness' sake let's have it right *this* time."

He remained on all fours leaning against the wind, very intent to have everything right.

"Ah!" he said. "Let nothing what I'm going to order happen until I say 'Off!'... Lord! I wish I'd thought of that before!"

He lifted his little voice against the whirlwind, shouting louder and louder in the vain desire to hear himself speak. "Now then!—here goes! Mind about that what I said just now. In the first place, when all I've got to say is done, let me lose my miraculous power, let my will become just like anybody else's will, and all these dangerous miracles be stopped. I don't like them. I'd rather I didn't work 'em. Ever so much. That's the first thing. And the second is—let me be back just before the miracles begin; let everything be just as it was before that blessed lamp turned up. It's a big job, but it's the last. Have you got it? No more miracles, everything as it was—me back in the Long Dragon just before I drank my half-pint. That's it! Yes."

He dug his fingers into the mould, closed his eyes, and said, "Off!"

Everything became perfectly still. He perceived that he was standing erect.

"So *you* say," said a voice.

He opened his eyes. He was in the bar of the Long Dragon, arguing about miracles with Toddy Beamish. He had a vague sense of some great thing forgotten that instantaneously passed. You see, except for the loss of his miraculous powers, everything was back as it had been; his mind and memory therefore were now just as they had been at the time when this story began. So that he knew absolutely nothing of all that is told here, knows nothing of all that is told here to this day. And among other things, of course, he still did not believe in miracles.

"I tell you that miracles, properly speaking, can't possibly happen," he said, "whatever you like to hold. And I'm prepared to prove it up to the hilt."

"That's what *you* think," said Toddy Beamish, and "Prove it if you can."

"Looky here, Mr. Beamish," said Mr. Fotheringay. "Let us clearly understand what a miracle is. It's something contrariwise to the course of nature done by power of Will..."

THE MAGIC SHOP

I had seen the Magic Shop from afar several times; I had passed it once or twice, a shop window of alluring little objects, magic balls, magic hens, wonderful cones, ventriloquist dolls, the material of the basket trick, packs of cards that *looked* all right, and all that sort of thing, but never had I thought of going in until one day, almost without warning, Gip hauled me by my finger right up to the window, and so conducted himself that there was nothing for it but to take him in. I had not thought the place was there, to tell the truth—a modest-sized frontage in Regent Street, between the picture shop and the place where the chicks run about just out of patent incubators—but there it was sure enough. I had fancied it was down nearer the Circus, or round the corner in Oxford Street, or even in Holborn; always over the way and a little inaccessible it had been, with something of the mirage in its position; but here it was now quite indisputably, and the fat end of Gip's pointing finger made a noise upon the glass.

"If I was rich," said Gip, dabbing a finger at the Disappearing Egg, "I'd buy myself that. And that"—which was The Crying Baby, Very Human—"and that," which was a mystery, and called, so a neat card asserted, "Buy One and Astonish Your Friends."

"Anything," said Gip, "will disappear under one of those cones. I have read about it in a book.

"And there, dadda, is a Vanishing Halfpenny—only they've put it this way up so's we can't see how it's done."

Gip, dear boy, inherits his mother's breeding, and he did not propose to enter the shop or worry in any way; only, you know, quite unconsciously he lugged my finger doorward, and he made his interest clear.

"That," he said, and pointed to the Magic Bottle.

"If you had that?" I said; at which promising inquiry he looked up with a sudden radiance.

"I could show it to Jessie," he said, thoughtful as ever of others.

"It's less than a hundred days to your birthday, Gibbles," I said, and laid my hand on the door-handle.

Gip made no answer, but his grip tightened on my finger, and so we came into the shop.

It was no common shop this; it was a magic shop, and all the prancing precedence Gip would have taken in the matter of mere toys was wanting. He left the burden of the conversation to me.

It was a little, narrow shop, not very well lit, and the door-bell pinged again with a plaintive note as we closed it behind us. For a moment or so we were alone and could glance about us. There was a tiger in *papier-mâché* on the glass case that covered the low counter—a grave, kind-eyed tiger that waggled his head in a methodical manner; there were several crystal spheres, a china hand holding magic cards, a stock of magic fish-bowls in various sizes, and an immodest magic hat that shamelessly displayed its springs. On the floor were magic mirrors; one to draw you out long and thin, one to swell your head and vanish your legs, and one to make you short and fat like a draught; and while we were laughing at these the shopman, as I suppose, came in.

At any rate, there he was behind the counter—a curious, sallow, dark man, with one ear larger than the other and a chin like the toe-cap of a boot.

"What can we have the pleasure?" he said, spreading his long, magic fingers on the glass case; and so with a start we were aware of him.

"I want," I said, "to buy my little boy a few simple tricks."

"Legerdemain?" he asked. "Mechanical? Domestic?"

"Anything amusing?" said I.

"Um!" said the shopman, and scratched his head for a moment as if thinking. Then, quite distinctly, he drew from his head a glass ball. "Something in this way?" he said, and held it out.

The action was unexpected. I had seen the trick done at entertainments endless times before—it's part of the common stock of conjurers—but I had not expected it here. "That's good," I said, with a laugh.

"Isn't it?" said the shopman.

Gip stretched out his disengaged hand to take this object and found merely a blank palm.

"It's in your pocket," said the shopman, and there it was!

"How much will that be?" I asked.

"We make no charge for glass balls," said the shopman, politely. "We get them"—he picked one out of his elbow as he spoke—"free." He produced another from the back of his neck, and laid it beside its predecessor on the counter. Gip regarded his glass ball sagely, then directed a look of inquiry at the two on the counter, and finally brought his round-eyed scrutiny to the shopman, who smiled. "You may have those too," said the shopman, "and if you *don't* mind, one from my mouth—*so!*"

Gip counselled me mutely for a moment, and then in a profound silence put away the four balls, resumed my reassuring finger, and nerved himself for the next event.

"We get all our smaller tricks in that way," the shopman remarked.

I laughed in the manner of one who subscribes to a jest. "Instead of going to the wholesale shop," I said. "Of course, it's cheaper."

"In a way," the shopman said. "Though we pay in the end. But not so heavily—as people suppose... Our larger tricks, and our daily provisions and all the other things we want, we get out of that hat... And you know, sir, if you'll excuse my saying it, there *isn't* a wholesale shop, not for Genuine Magic goods, sir. I don't know if you noticed our inscription—the Genuine Magic shop." He drew a business-card from his cheek and handed it to me. "Genuine," he said, with his finger on the word, and added, "there is absolutely no deception, sir."

He seemed to be carrying out the joke pretty thoroughly, I thought.

He turned to Gip with a smile of remarkable affability. "You, you know, are the Right Sort of Boy."

I was surprised at his knowing that, because, in the interests of discipline, we keep it rather a secret even at home; but Gip received it in unflinching silence, keeping a steadfast eye on him.

"It's only the Right Sort of Boy gets through that doorway."

And as if by way of illustration, there came a rattling at the door, and a squeaking little voice could be faintly heard. "Nyar! I *warn* a' go in there, dadda, I WARN 'a go in there. Ny-a-a-ah!" and then the accents of a down-trodden parent, urging consolations and propitiations. "It's locked, Edward," he said.

"But it isn't," said I.

"It is, sir," said the shopman, "always—for that sort of child," and as he spoke we had a glimpse of the other youngster, a small, white face, pallid from sweet-eating and over-sapid food, and distorted by evil passions, a ruthless little egotist, pawing at the enchanted pane. "It's no good, sir," said the shopman, as I moved, with my natural helpfulness, doorward, and presently the spoilt child was carried off howling.

"How do you manage that?" I said, breathing more freely.

"Magic!" said the shopman, with a careless wave of the hand, and behold! sparks of coloured fire flew out of his fingers and vanished into the shadows of the shop.

"You were saying," he said, addressing himself to Gip, "before you came in, that you would like one of our 'Buy One and Astonish Your Friends' boxes?"

Gip, after a gallant effort, said, "Yes."

"It's in your pocket."

And leaning over the counter—he really had an extraordinarily long body—this amazing person produced the article in the customary conjurer's manner. "Paper," he said, and took a sheet out of the empty hat with the springs; "string," and behold his mouth was a string-box, from which he drew an unending thread, which when he had tied his parcel he bit off—and, it seemed to me, swallowed the ball of string. And then he lit a candle at the nose of one of the ventriloquist's dummies, stuck one of his fingers (which had become sealing-wax red) into the flame, and so sealed the parcel. "Then there was the Disappearing Egg," he remarked, and produced one from within my coat-breast and packed it, and also The Crying Baby, Very Human. I handed each parcel to Gip as it was ready, and he clasped them to his chest.

He said very little, but his eyes were eloquent; the clutch of his arms was eloquent. He was the playground of unspeakable emotions. These, you know, were *real* Magics.

Then, with a start, I discovered something moving about in my hat—something soft and jumpy. I whipped it off, and a ruffled pigeon—no doubt a confederate—dropped out and ran on the counter, and went, I fancy, into a cardboard box behind the *papier-mâché* tiger.

"Tut, tut!" said the shopman, dexterously relieving me of my head-dress; "careless bird, and—as I live—nesting!"

He shook my hat, and shook out into his extended hand two or three eggs, a large marble, a watch, about half-a-dozen of the inevitable glass balls, and then crumpled, crinkled paper, more and more and more, talking all the time of the way in which people neglect to brush their hats *inside* as well as out, politely, of course, but with a certain personal application. "All sorts of things accumulate, sir... Not *you*, of course, in particular... Nearly every customer... Astonishing what they carry about with them..." The crumpled paper rose and billowed on the counter more and more and more, until he was nearly hidden from us, until he was altogether hidden, and still his voice went on and on. "We none of us know what the fair semblance of a human being may conceal, sir. Are we all then no better than brushed exteriors, whited sepulchres—"

His voice stopped—exactly like when you hit a neighbour's gramophone with a well-aimed brick, the same instant silence, and the rustle of the paper stopped, and everything was still...

"Have you done with my hat?" I said, after an interval.

There was no answer.

I stared at Gip, and Gip stared at me; and there were our distortions in the magic mirrors, looking very rum, and grave, and quiet...

"I think we'll go now," I said. "Will you tell me how much all this comes to...?

"I say," I said, on a rather louder note, "I want the bill; and my hat, please."

It might have been a sniff from behind the paper pile...

"Let's look behind the counter, Gip," I said. "He's making fun of us."

I led Gip round the head-wagging tiger, and what do you think there was behind the counter? No one at all! Only my hat on the floor, and a common conjurer's lop-eared white rabbit lost in meditation, and looking as stupid and crumpled as only a conjurer's rabbit can do. I resumed my hat, and the rabbit lolloped a lollop or so out of my way.

"Dadda!" said Gip, in a guilty whisper.

"What is it, Gip?" I said.

"I *do* like this shop, dadda."

"So should I," I said to myself, "if the counter wouldn't suddenly extend itself to shut one off from the door." But I didn't call Gip's attention to that. "Pussy!" he said, with a hand out to the rabbit as it came lolloping past us; "Pussy, do Gip a magic!" and his eyes followed it as it squeezed through a door I had certainly not remarked a moment before. Then this door opened wider, and the man with one ear larger than the other appeared again. He was smiling still, but his eye met mine with something between amusement and defiance. "You'd like to see our showroom, sir," he said, with an innocent suavity. Gip tugged my finger forward. I glanced at the counter and met the shopman's eye again. I was beginning to think the magic just a little too genuine. "We haven't *very* much time," I said. But somehow we were inside the showroom before I could finish that.

"All goods of the same quality," said the shopman, rubbing his flexible hands together, "and that is the Best. Nothing in the place that isn't genuine Magic, and warranted thoroughly rum. Excuse me, sir!"

I felt him pull at something that clung to my coatsleeve, and then I saw he held a little, wriggling red demon by the tail—the little creature bit and fought and tried to get at his hand—and in a moment he tossed it carelessly behind a counter. No doubt the thing was only an image of twisted indiarubber, but for the moment—! And his gesture was exactly that of a man who handles some petty biting bit of vermin. I glanced at Gip, but Gip was looking at a magic rocking-horse. I was glad he hadn't seen the thing. "I say," I said, in an undertone, and indicating Gip and the red demon with my eyes, "you haven't many things like *that* about, have you?"

"None of ours! Probably brought it with you," said the shopman—also in an undertone, and with a more dazzling smile than ever. "Astonishing what people *will* carry about with them unawares!" And then to Gip, "Do you see anything you fancy here?"

There were many things that Gip fancied there.

He turned to this astonishing tradesman with mingled confidence and respect. "Is that a Magic Sword?" he said.

"A Magic Toy Sword. It neither bends, breaks, nor cuts the fingers. It renders the bearer invincible in battle against anyone under eighteen. Half-a-crown to seven and sixpence, according to size. These panoplies on cards are for juvenile knights-errant and very useful—shield of safety, sandals of swiftness, helmet of invisibility."

"Oh, dadda!" gasped Gip.

I tried to find out what they cost, but the shopman did not heed me.

He had got Gip now; he had got him away from my finger; he had embarked upon the exposition of all his confounded stock, and nothing was going to stop him. Presently I saw with a qualm of distrust and something very like jealousy that Gip had hold of this person's finger as usually he has hold of mine. No doubt the fellow was interesting, I thought, and had an interestingly faked lot of stuff, really *good* faked stuff, still—

I wandered after them, saying very little, but keeping an eye on this prestidigital fellow. After all, Gip was enjoying it. And no doubt when the time came to go we should be able to go quite easily.

It was a long, rambling place, that showroom, a gallery broken up by stands and stalls and pillars, with archways leading off to other departments, in which the queerest-looking assistants loafed and stared at one, and with perplexing mirrors and curtains. So perplexing, indeed, were these that I was presently unable to make out the door by which we had come.

The shopman showed Gip magic trains that ran without steam or clockwork, just as you set the signals, and then some very, very valuable boxes of soldiers that all came alive directly you took off the lid and said—I myself haven't a very quick ear and it was a tongue-twisting sound, but Gip—he has his mother's ear—got it in no time. "Bravo!" said the shopman, putting the men back into the box unceremoniously and handing it to Gip. "Now," said the shopman, and in a moment Gip had made them all alive again.

"You'll take that box?" asked the shopman.

"We'll take that box," said I, "unless you charge its full value. In which case it would need a Trust Magnate—"

"Dear heart! *No!*" and the shopman swept the little men back again, shut the lid, waved the box in the air, and there it was, in brown paper, tied up and—*with Gip's full name and address on the paper!*

The shopman laughed at my amazement.

"This is the genuine magic," he said. "The real thing."

"It's almost too genuine for my taste," I said again.

After that he fell to showing Gip tricks, odd tricks, and still odder the way they were done. He explained them, he turned them inside out, and there was the dear little chap nodding his busy bit of a head in the sagest manner.

I did not attend as well as I might. "Hey, presto!" said the Magic Shopman, and then would come the clear, small "Hey, presto!" of the boy. But I was distracted by other things. It was being borne in upon me just how tremendously rum this place was; it was, so to speak, inundated by a sense of rumness. There was something vaguely rum about the fixtures even, about the ceiling, about the floor, about the casually distributed chairs. I had a queer feeling that whenever I wasn't looking at them straight they went askew, and moved about, and played a noiseless puss-in-the-corner behind my back. And the cornice had a serpentine design with masks—masks altogether too expressive for proper plaster.

Then abruptly my attention was caught by one of the odd-looking assistants. He was some way off and evidently unaware of my presence—I saw a sort of three-quarter length of him over a pile of toys and through an arch—and, you know, he was leaning against a pillar in an idle sort of way doing the most horrid things with his features! The particular horrid thing he did was with his nose. He did it just as though he was idle and wanted to amuse himself. First of all it was a short, blobby nose, and then suddenly he shot it out like a telescope, and then out it flew and became thinner and thinner until it was like a long, red, flexible whip. Like a thing in a nightmare it was! He flourished it about and flung it forth as a fly-fisher flings his line.

My instant thought was that Gip mustn't see him. I turned about, and there was Gip quite preoccupied with the shopman, and thinking no evil. They were whispering together and looking at me. Gip was standing on a stool, and the shopman was holding a sort of big drum in his hand.

"Hide and seek, dadda!" cried Gip. "You're He!"

And before I could do anything to prevent it, the shopman had clapped the big drum over him.

I saw what was up directly. "Take that off," I cried, "this instant! You'll frighten the boy. Take it off!"

The shopman with the unequal ears did so without a word, and held the big cylinder towards me to show its emptiness. And the stool was vacant! In that instant my boy had utterly disappeared...

You know, perhaps, that sinister something that comes like a hand out of the unseen and grips your heart about. You know it takes your common self away and leaves you tense and deliberate, neither slow nor hasty, neither angry nor afraid. So it was with me.

I came up to this grinning shopman and kicked his stool aside.

"Stop this folly!" I said. "Where is my boy?"

"You see," he said, still displaying the drum's interior, "there is no deception—"

I put out my hand to grip him, and he eluded me by a dexterous movement. I snatched again, and he turned from me and pushed open a door to escape. "Stop!" I said, and he laughed, receding. I leapt after him—into utter darkness.

Thud!

"Lor' bless my 'eart! I didn't see you coming, sir!"

I was in Regent Street, and I had collided with a decent-looking working man; and a yard away, perhaps, and looking extremely perplexed with himself, was Gip. There was some sort of apology, and then Gip had turned and come to me with a bright little smile, as though for a moment he had missed me.

And he was carrying four parcels in his arm!

He secured immediate possession of my finger.

For the second I was rather at a loss. I stared round to see the door of the magic shop, and, behold, it was not there! There was no door, no shop, nothing, only the common pilaster between the shop where they sell pictures and the window with the chicks . . . !

I did the only thing possible in that mental tumult; I walked straight to the kerbstone and held up my umbrella for a cab.

"'Ansoms," said Gip, in a note of culminating exultation.

I helped him in, recalled my address with an effort, and got in also. Something unusual proclaimed itself in my tail-coat pocket, and I felt and discovered a glass ball. With a petulant expression I flung it into the street.

Gip said nothing.

For a space neither of us spoke.

"Dadda!" said Gip, at last, "that *was* a proper shop!"

I came round with that to the problem of just how the whole thing had seemed to him. He looked completely undamaged—so far, good; he was neither scared nor unhinged, he was simply tremendously satisfied with the afternoon's entertainment, and there in his arms were the four parcels.

Confound it! what could be in them?

"Um!" I said. "Little boys can't go to shops like that every day."

He received this with his usual stoicism, and for a moment I was sorry I was his father and not his mother, and so couldn't suddenly there, *coram publico*, in our hansom, kiss him. After all, I thought, the thing wasn't so very bad.

But it was only when we opened the parcels that I really began to be reassured. Three of them contained boxes of soldiers, quite ordinary lead soldiers, but of so good a quality as to make Gip altogether forget that originally these parcels had been Magic Tricks of the only genuine sort, and the fourth contained a kitten, a little living white kitten, in excellent health and appetite and temper.

I saw this unpacking with a sort of provisional relief. I hung about in the nursery for quite an unconscionable time...

That happened six months ago. And now I am beginning to believe it is all right. The kitten had only the magic natural to all kittens, and the soldiers seem as steady a company as any colonel could desire. And Gip—?

The intelligent parent will understand that I have to go cautiously with Gip.

But I went so far as this one day. I said, "How would you like your soldiers to come alive, Gip, and march about by themselves?"

"Mine do," said Gip. "I just have to say a word I know before I open the lid."

"Then they march about alone?"

"Oh, *quite*, dadda. I shouldn't like them if they didn't do that."

I displayed no unbecoming surprise, and since then I have taken occasion to drop in upon him once or twice, unannounced, when the soldiers were about, but so far I have never discovered them performing in anything like a magical manner...

It's so difficult to tell.

There's also a question of finance. I have an incurable habit of paying bills. I have been up and down Regent Street several times, looking for that shop. I am inclined to think, indeed, that in that matter honour is satisfied, and that, since Gip's name and address are known to them, I may very well leave it to these people, whoever they may be, to send in their bill in their own time.

Mr. Skelmersdale in Fairyland

"There's a man in that shop," said the Doctor, "who has been in Fairyland."

"Nonsense!" I said, and stared back at the shop. It was the usual village shop, post-office, telegraph wire on its brow, zinc pans and brushes outside, boots, shirtings, and potted meats in the window. "Tell me about it," I said, after a pause.

"*I* don't know," said the Doctor. "He's an ordinary sort of lout—Skelmersdale is his name. But everybody about here believes it like Bible truth."

I reverted presently to the topic.

"I know nothing about it," said the Doctor, "and I don't *want* to know. I attended him for a broken finger—Married and Single cricket match—and that's when I struck the nonsense. That's all. But it shows you the sort of stuff I have to deal with, anyhow, eh? Nice to get modern sanitary ideas into a people like this!"

"Very," I said in a mildly sympathetic tone, and he went on to tell me about that business of the Bonham drain. Things of that kind, I observe, are apt to weigh on the minds of Medical Officers of Health. I was as sympathetic as I knew how, and when he called the Bonham people "asses," I said they were "thundering asses," but even that did not allay him.

Afterwards, later in the summer, an urgent desire to seclude myself, while finishing my chapter on Spiritual Pathology—it was really, I believe, stiffer to write than it is to read—took me to Bignor. I lodged at a farmhouse, and presently found myself outside that little general shop again, in search of tobacco. "Skelmersdale," said I to myself at the sight of it, and went in.

I was served by a short, but shapely, young man, with a fair downy complexion, good, small teeth, blue eyes, and a languid manner. I scrutinised him curiously. Except for a touch of melancholy in his expression, he was nothing out of the common. He was in the shirt-sleeves and tucked-up apron of his trade, and a pencil was thrust behind his inoffensive ear. Athwart his black waistcoat was a gold chain, from which dangled a bent guinea.

"Nothing more today, sir?" he inquired. He leant forward over my bill as he spoke.

"Are you Mr. Skelmersdale?" said I.

"I am, sir," he said, without looking up.

"Is it true that you have been in Fairyland?"

He looked up at me for a moment with wrinkled brows, with an aggrieved, exasperated face. "O SHUT it!" he said, and, after a moment of hostility, eye to eye, he went on adding up my bill. "Four, six and a half," he said, after a pause. "Thank you, sir."

So, unpropitiously, my acquaintance with Mr. Skelmersdale began.

Well, I got from that to confidence—through a series of toilsome efforts. I picked him up again in the Village Room, where of a night I went to play billiards after my supper, and mitigate the extreme seclusion from my kind that was so helpful to work during the day. I contrived to play with him and afterwards to talk with him. I found the one subject to avoid was Fairyland. On everything else he was open and amiable in a commonplace sort of way, but on that he had been worried—it was a manifest taboo. Only once in the room did I hear the slightest allusion to his experience in his presence, and that was by a cross-grained farm hand who was losing to him. Skelmersdale had run a break into double figures, which, by the Bignor standards, was uncommonly good play. "Steady on!" said his adversary. "None of your fairy flukes!"

Skelmersdale stared at him for a moment, cue in hand, then flung it down and walked out of the room.

"Why can't you leave 'im alone?" said a respectable elder who had been enjoying the game, and in the general murmur of disapproval, the grin of satisfied wit faded from the ploughboy's face.

I scented my opportunity. "What's this joke," said I, "about Fairyland?"

"'Taint no joke about Fairyland, not to young Skelmersdale," said the respectable elder, drinking.

A little man with rosy cheeks was more communicative. "They *do* say, sir," he said, "that they took him into Aldington Knoll an' kep' him there a matter of three weeks."

And with that the gathering was well under weigh. Once one sheep had started, others were ready enough to follow, and in a little time I had at least the exterior aspect of the Skelmersdale affair. Formerly, before he came to Bignor, he had been in that very similar little shop at Aldington Corner, and there whatever it was did happen had taken place. The story was clear that he had stayed out late one night on the Knoll and vanished for three weeks from the sight of men, and had returned with "his cuffs as clean as when he started," and his pockets full of dust and ashes. He returned in a state of moody wretchedness that only slowly passes away, and for many days he would give no account of where it was he had been. The girl he was engaged to at Clapton Hill tried to get it out of him, and threw him over partly because he refused, and partly because, as she said, he fairly gave her the "'ump." And then when, some time after, he let out to someone carelessly that he had been in Fairyland and wanted to go back, and when the thing spread and the simple badinage of the countryside came into play, he threw up his situation abruptly, and came to Bignor to get out of the fuss. But as to what had happened in Fairyland none of these people knew. There the gathering in the Village Room went to pieces like a pack at fault. One said this, and another said that.

Their air in dealing with this marvel was ostensibly critical and sceptical, but I could see a considerable amount of belief showing through their guarded qualifications. I took a line of intelligent interest, tinged with a reasonable doubt of the whole story.

"If Fairyland's inside Aldington Knoll," I said, "why don't you dig it out?"

"That's what I says," said the young ploughboy.

"There's a-many have tried to dig on Aldington Knoll," said the respectable elder, solemnly, "one time and another. But there's none as goes about today to tell what they got by digging."

The unanimity of vague belief that surrounded me was rather impressive; I felt there must surely be *something* at the root of so much conviction, and the already pretty keen curiosity I felt about the real facts of the case was distinctly whetted. If these real facts were to be got from anyone, they were to be got from Skelmersdale himself; and I set myself, therefore, still more assiduously to efface the first bad impression I had made and win his confidence to the pitch of voluntary speech. In that endeavour I had a social advantage. Being a person of affability and no apparent employment, and wearing tweeds and knickerbockers, I was naturally classed as an artist in Bignor, and in the remarkable code of social precedence prevalent in Bignor an artist ranks considerably higher than a grocer's assistant. Skelmersdale, like too many of his class, is something of a snob; he had told me to "SHUT it" only under sudden, excessive provocation, and with, I am certain, a subsequent repentance; he was, I knew, quite glad to be seen walking about the village with me. In due course, he accepted the proposal of a pipe and whisky in my rooms readily enough, and there, scenting by some happy instinct that there was trouble of the heart in this, and knowing that confidences beget confidences, I plied him with much of interest and suggestion from my real and fictitious past. And it was after the third whisky of the third visit of that sort, if I remember rightly, *àpropos* of some artless expansion of a little affair that had touched and left me in my teens, that he did at last, of his own free will and motion, break the ice. "It was like that with me," he said, "over there at Aldington. It's just that that's so rum. First I didn't care a bit and it was all her, and afterwards, when it was too late, it was, in a manner of speaking, all me."

I forbore to jump upon this allusion, and so he presently threw out another, and in a little while he was making it as plain as daylight that the one thing he wanted to talk about now was this Fairyland adventure he had sat tight upon for so long. You see, I'd done the trick with him, and from being just another half-incredulous, would-be facetious stranger, I had, by all my wealth of shameless self-exposure, become the possible confidant. He had been bitten by the desire to show that he, too, had lived and felt many things, and the fever was upon him.

He was certainly confoundedly allusive at first, and my eagerness to clear him up with a few precise questions was only equalled and controlled by my anxiety not to get to this sort of thing too soon. But in another meeting or so the basis of confidence was complete; and from first to last I think I got most of the items and aspects—indeed, I got quite a number of times over almost everything that Mr. Skelmersdale, with his very limited powers of narration, will ever be able to tell. And so I come to the story of his adventure, and I piece it all together again. Whether it really happened, whether he imagined it or dreamt it, or fell upon it in some strange hallucinatory trance, I do not profess to say. But that he invented it I will not for one moment entertain. The man simply and honestly believes the thing happened as he says it happened; he is transparently incapable of any lie so elaborate and sustained, and in the belief of the simple, yet often keenly penetrating, rustic minds about him I find a very strong confirmation of his sincerity. He believes—and nobody can produce any positive fact to falsify his belief. As for me, with this much of endorsement, I transmit his story—I am a little old now to justify or explain.

He says he went to sleep on Aldington Knoll about ten o'clock one night—it was quite possibly Midsummer night, though he has never thought of the date, and he cannot be sure within a week or so—and it was a fine night and windless, with a rising moon. I have been at the pains to visit this Knoll since his story grew up under my persuasions, and once I went there in the twilight summer moonrise on what was, perhaps, a similar night to that of his adventure. Jupiter was great and splendid above the moon, and in the north and north-west the sky was green and vividly bright over the sunken sun. The Knoll stands out bare and bleak under the sky, but surrounded at a little distance by dark thickets, and as I went up towards it there was a mighty starting and scampering of ghostly or quite invisible rabbits. Just over the crown of the Knoll, but nowhere else, was a multitudinous thin trumpeting of midges. The Knoll is, I believe, an artificial mound, the tumulus of some great prehistoric chieftain, and surely no man ever chose a more spacious prospect for a sepulchre. Eastward one sees along the hills to Hythe, and thence across the Channel to where, thirty miles and more, perhaps, away, the great white lights by Gris Nez and Boulogne wink and pass and shine. Westward lies the whole tumbled valley of the Weald, visible as far as Hindhead and Leith Hill, and the valley of the Stour opens the Downs in the north to interminable hills beyond Wye. All Romney Marsh lies southward at one's feet, Dymchurch and Romney and Lydd, Hastings and its hill are in the middle distance, and the hills multiply vaguely far beyond where Eastbourne rolls up to Beachy Head.

And out upon all this it was that Skelmersdale wandered, being troubled in his earlier love affair, and as he says, "not caring *where* he went." And there he sat down to think it over, and so, sulking and grieving, was overtaken by sleep. And so he fell into the fairies' power.

The quarrel that had upset him was some trivial matter enough between himself and the girl at Clapton Hill to whom he was engaged. She was a farmer's daughter, said Skelmersdale, and "very respectable," and no doubt an excellent match for him; but both girl and lover were very young and with just that mutual jealousy, that intolerantly keen edge of criticism, that irrational hunger for a beautiful perfection, that life and wisdom do presently and most mercifully dull. What the precise matter of quarrel was I have no idea. She may have said she liked men in gaiters when he hadn't any gaiters on, or he may have said he liked her better in a different sort of hat, but however it began, it got by a series of clumsy stages to bitterness and tears. She no doubt got tearful and smeary, and he grew dusty and drooping, and she parted with invidious comparisons, grave doubts whether she ever had *really* cared for him, and a clear certainty she would never care again. And with this sort of thing upon his mind he came out upon Aldington Knoll grieving, and presently, after a long interval, perhaps, quite inexplicably, fell asleep.

He woke to find himself on a softer turf than ever he had slept on before, and under the shade of very dark trees that completely hid the sky. Always, indeed, in Fairyland the sky is hidden, it seems. Except for one night when the fairies were dancing, Mr. Skelmersdale, during all his time with them, never saw a star. And of that night I am in doubt whether he was in Fairyland proper or out where the rings and rushes are, in those low meadows near the railway line at Smeeth.

But it was light under these trees for all that, and on the leaves and amidst the turf shone a multitude of glow-worms, very bright and fine. Mr. Skelmersdale's first impression was that he was *small*, and the next that quite a number of people still smaller were standing all about him. For some reason, he says, he was neither surprised nor frightened, but sat up quite deliberately and rubbed the sleep out of his eyes. And there all about him stood the smiling elves who had caught him sleeping under their privileges and had brought him into Fairyland.

What these elves were like I failed to gather, so vague and imperfect is his vocabulary, and so unobservant of all minor detail does he seem to have been. They were clothed in something very light and beautiful, that was neither wool, nor silk, nor leaves, nor the petals of flowers. They stood all about him as he sat and waked, and down the glade towards him, down a glow-worm avenue and fronted by a star, came at once that Fairy Lady who is the chief personage of his memory and tale. Of her I gathered more. She was clothed in filmy green, and about her little waist was a broad silver girdle. Her hair waved back from her forehead on either side; there were curls not too wayward and yet astray, and on her brow was a little tiara, set with a single star. Her sleeves were some sort of open sleeves that gave little glimpses of her arms; her throat, I think, was a little displayed, because he speaks of the beauty of her neck and chin. There was a necklace of coral about her white throat, and in her breast a coral-coloured flower. She had the soft lines of a little child in her chin and cheeks and throat. And her eyes, I gather, were of a kindled brown, very soft and straight and sweet under her level brows. You see by these particulars how greatly this lady must have loomed in Mr. Skelmersdale's picture. Certain things he tried to express and could not express: "the way she moved," he said several times; and I fancy a sort of demure joyousness radiated from this Lady.

And it was in the company of this delightful person, as the guest and chosen companion of this delightful person, that Mr. Skelmersdale set out to be taken into the intimacies of Fairyland. She welcomed him gladly and a little warmly—I suspect a pressure of his hand in both of hers and a lit face to his. After all, ten years ago young Skelmersdale may have been a very comely youth. And once she took his arm, and once, I think, she led him by the hand adown the glade that the glow-worms lit.

Just how things chanced and happened there is no telling from Mr. Skelmersdale's disarticulated skeleton of description. He gives little unsatisfactory glimpses of strange corners and doings, of places where there were many fairies together, of "toadstool things that shone pink," of fairy food, of which he could only say "you should have tasted it!" and of fairy music, "like a little musical box," that came out of nodding flowers. There was a great open place where fairies rode and raced on "things," but what Mr. Skelmersdale meant by "these here things they rode," there is no telling. Larvae, perhaps, or crickets, or the little beetles that elude us so abundantly. There was a place where water splashed and gigantic king-cups grew, and there in the hotter times the fairies bathed together. There were games being played and dancing and much elvish love-making, too, I think, among the moss branch thickets. There can be no doubt that the Fairy Lady made love to Mr. Skelmersdale, and no doubt either that this young man set himself to resist her. A time came, indeed, when she sat on a bank beside him, in a quiet secluded place "all smelling of vi'lets," and talked to him of love.

"When her voice went low and she whispered," said Mr. Skelmersdale, "and laid 'er 'and on my 'and, you know, and came close with a soft, warm friendly way she 'ad, it was as much as I could do to keep my 'ead."

It seems he kept his head to a certain limited unfortunate extent. He saw " 'ow the wind was blowing," he says, and so, sitting there in a place all smelling of violets, with the touch of this lovely Fairy Lady about him, Mr. Skelmersdale broke it to her gently—that he was engaged!

She had told him she loved him dearly, that he was a sweet human lad for her, and whatever he would ask of her he should have—even his heart's desire.

And Mr. Skelmersdale, who, I fancy, tried hard to avoid looking at her little lips as they just dropped apart and came together, led up to the more intimate question by saying he would like enough capital to start a little shop. He'd just like to feel, he said, he had money enough to do that. I imagine a little surprise in those brown eyes he talked about, but she seemed sympathetic for all that, and she asked him many questions about the little shop, "laughing like" all the time. So he got to the complete statement of his affianced position, and told her all about Millie.

"All?" said I.

"Everything," said Mr. Skelmersdale, "just who she was, and where she lived, and everything about her. I sort of felt I 'ad to all the time, I did."

"Whatever you want you shall have, said the Fairy Lady. That's as good as done. You *shall* feel you have the money just as you wish. And now, you know—*you must kiss me.*"

And Mr. Skelmersdale pretended not to hear the latter part of her remark, and said she was very kind. That he really didn't deserve she should be so kind. And—

The Fairy Lady suddenly came quite close to him and whispered, "Kiss me!"

"And," said Mr. Skelmersdale, "like a fool, I did."

There are kisses and kisses, I am told, and this must have been quite the other sort from Millie's resonant signals of regard. There was something magic in that kiss; assuredly it marked a turning point. At any rate, this is one of the passages that he thought sufficiently important to describe most at length. I have tried to get it right, I have tried to disentangle it from the hints and gestures through which it came to me, but I have no doubt that it was all different from my telling and far finer and sweeter, in the soft filtered light and the subtly stirring silences of the fairy glades. The Fairy Lady asked him more about Millie, and was she very lovely, and so on—a great many times. As to Millie's loveliness, I conceive him answering that she was "all right." And then, or on some such occasion, the Fairy Lady told him she had fallen in love with him as he slept in the moonlight, and so he had been brought into Fairyland, and she had thought, not knowing of Millie, that perhaps he might chance to love her. "But now you know you can't," she said, "so you must stop with me just a little while, and then you must go back to Millie." She told him that, and you know Skelmersdale was already in love with her, but the pure inertia of his mind kept him in the way he was going. I imagine him sitting in a sort of stupefaction amidst all these glowing beautiful things, answering about his Millie and the little shop he projected and the need of a horse and cart ... And that absurd state of affairs must have gone on for days and days. I see this little lady, hovering about him and trying to amuse him, too dainty to understand his complexity and too tender to let him go. And he, you know, hypnotised as it were by his earthly position, went his way with her hither and thither, blind to everything in Fairyland but this wonderful intimacy that had come to him. It is hard, it is impossible, to give in print the effect of her radiant sweetness shining through the jungle of poor Skelmersdale's rough and broken sentences. To me, at least, she shone clear amidst the muddle of his story like a glow-worm in a tangle of weeds.

There must have been many days of things while all this was happening—and once, I say, they danced under the moonlight in the fairy rings that stud the meadows near Smeeth—but at last it all came to an end. She led him into a great cavernous place, lit by "a red nightlight sort of thing," where there were coffers piled on coffers, and cups and golden boxes, and a great heap of what certainly seemed to all Mr. Skelmersdale's senses—coined gold. There were little gnomes amidst this wealth, who saluted her at her coming, and stood aside. And suddenly she turned on him there with brightly shining eyes.

"And now," she said, "you have been kind to stay with me so long, and it is time I let you go: You must go back to your Millie. You must go back to your Millie, and here—just as I promised you—they will give you gold."

"She choked like," said Mr. Skelmersdale. "At that, I had a sort of feeling—" (he touched his breastbone) "as though I was fainting here. I felt pale, you know, and shivering, and even then—I 'adn't a thing to say."

He paused. "Yes," I said.

The scene was beyond his describing. But I know that she kissed him good-bye.

"And you said nothing?"

"Nothing," he said. "I stood like a stuffed calf. She just looked back once, you know, and stood smiling like and crying—I could see the shine of her eyes—and then she was gone, and there was all these little fellows bustling about me, stuffing my 'ands and my pockets and the back of my collar and everywhere with gold."

And then it was, when the Fairy Lady had vanished, that Mr. Skelmersdale really understood and knew. He suddenly began plucking out the gold they were thrusting upon him, and shouting out to them to prevent their giving him more. " 'I don't *want* yer gold,' I said. 'I 'aven't done yet. I'm not going. I want to speak to that Fairy Lady again.' I started off to go after her and they held me back. Yes, stuck their little 'ands against my middle and shoved me back. They kept giving me more and more gold until it was running all down my trouser legs and dropping out of my 'ands. 'I don't *want* yer gold,' I says to them, 'I want just to speak to the Fairy Lady again.' "

"And did you?"

"It came to a tussle."

"Before you saw her?"

"I didn't see her. When I got out from them she wasn't anywhere to be seen."

So he ran in search of her out of this red-lit cave, down a long grotto, seeking her, and thence he came out in a great and desolate place athwart which a swarm of will-o'-the-wisps were flying to and fro. And about him elves were dancing in derision, and the little gnomes came out of the cave after him, carrying gold in handfuls and casting it after him, shouting, "Fairy love and fairy gold! Fairy love and fairy gold!"

And when he heard these words, came a great fear that it was all over, and he lifted up his voice and called to her by her name, and suddenly set himself to run down the slope from the mouth of the cavern, through a place of thorns and briers, calling after her very loudly and often. The elves danced about him unheeded, pinching him and pricking him, and the will-o'-the-wisps circled round him and dashed into his face, and the gnomes pursued him shouting and pelting him with fairy gold. As he ran with all this strange rout about him and distracting him, suddenly he was knee-deep in a swamp, and suddenly he was amidst thick twisted roots, and he caught his foot in one and stumbled and fell...

He fell and he rolled over, and in that instant he found himself sprawling upon Aldington Knoll, all lonely under the stars.

He sat up sharply at once, he says, and found he was very stiff and cold, and his clothes were damp with dew. The first pallor of dawn and a chilly wind were coming up together. He could have believed the whole thing a strangely vivid dream until he thrust his hand into his side pocket and found it stuffed with ashes. Then he knew for certain it was fairy gold they had given him. He could feel all their pinches and pricks still, though there was never a bruise upon him. And in that manner, and so suddenly, Mr. Skelmersdale came out of Fairyland back into this world of men. Even then he fancied the thing was but the matter of a night until he returned to the shop at Aldington Corner and discovered amidst their astonishment that he had been away three weeks.

"Lor! the trouble I 'ad!" said Mr. Skelmersdale.

"How?"

"Explaining. I suppose you've never had anything like that to explain."

"Never," I said, and he expatiated for a time on the behaviour of this person and that. One name he avoided for a space.

"And Millie?" said I at last.

"I didn't seem to care a bit for seeing Millie," he said.

"I expect she seemed changed?"

"Everyone was changed. Changed for good. Everyone seemed big, you know, and coarse. And their voices seemed loud. Why, the sun, when it rose in the morning, fair hit me in the eye!"

"And Millie?"

"I didn't want to see Millie."

"And when you did?"

"I came up against her Sunday, coming out of church. 'Where you been?' she said, and I saw there was a row. *I* didn't care if there was. I seemed to forget about her even while she was there a-talking to me. She was just nothing. I couldn't make out whatever I 'ad seen in 'er ever, or what there could 'ave been. Sometimes when she wasn't about, I did get back a little, but never when she was there. Then it was always the other came up and blotted her out... Any'ow, it didn't break her heart."

"Married?" I asked.

"Married 'er cousin," said Mr. Skelmersdale, and reflected on the pattern of the tablecloth for a space.

When he spoke again it was clear that his former sweetheart had clean vanished from his mind, and that the talk had brought back the Fairy Lady triumphant in his heart. He talked of her—soon he was letting out the oddest things, queer love secrets it would be treachery to repeat. I think, indeed, that was the queerest thing in the whole affair, to hear that neat little grocer man after his story was done, with a glass of whisky beside him and a cigar between his fingers, witnessing, with sorrow still, though now, indeed, with a time blunted anguish, of the inappeasable hunger of the heart that presently came upon him. "I couldn't eat," he said, "I couldn't sleep. I made mistakes in orders and got mixed with change. There she was day and night, drawing me and drawing me. Oh, I wanted her. Lord! how I wanted her! I was up there, most evenings I was up there on the Knoll, often even when it rained. I used to walk over the Knoll and round it and round it, calling for them to let me in. Shouting. Near blubbering I was at times. Daft I was and miserable. I kept on saying it was all a mistake. And every Sunday afternoon I went up there, wet and fine, though I knew as well as you do it wasn't no good by day. And I've tried to go to sleep there."

He stopped sharply and decided to drink some whisky.

"I've tried to go to sleep there," he said, and I could swear his lips trembled. "I've tried to go to sleep there, often and often. And, you know, I couldn't, sir—never. I've thought if I could go to sleep there, there might be something... But I've sat up there and laid up there, and I couldn't—not for thinking and longing. It's the longing... I've tried—"

He blew, drank up the rest of his whisky spasmodically, stood up suddenly and buttoned his jacket, staring closely and critically at the cheap oleographs beside the mantel meanwhile. The little black note-book in which he recorded the orders of his daily round projected stiffly from his breast pocket. When all the buttons were quite done, he patted his chest and turned on me suddenly. "Well," he said, "I must be going."

There was something in his eyes and manner that was too difficult for him to express in words. "One gets talking," he said at last at the door, and smiled wanly, and so vanished from my eyes. And that is the tale of Mr. Skelmersdale in Fairyland just as he told it to me.

The Door in the Wall

1

One confidential evening, not three months ago, Lionel Wallace told me this story of the Door in the Wall. And at the time I thought that so far as he was concerned it was a true story.

He told it me with such a direct simplicity of conviction that I could not do otherwise than believe in him. But in the morning, in my own flat, I woke to a different atmosphere; and as I lay in bed and recalled the things he had told me, stripped of the glamour of his earnest slow voice, denuded of the focused, shaded table light, the shadowy atmosphere that wrapped about him and me, and the pleasant bright things, the dessert and glasses and napery of the dinner we had shared, making them for the time a bright little world quite cut off from everyday realities, I saw it all as frankly incredible. "He was mystifying!" I said, and then: "How well he did it!... It isn't quite the thing I should have expected him, of all people, to do well."

Afterwards as I sat up in bed and sipped my morning tea, I found myself trying to account for the flavour of reality that perplexed me in his impossible reminiscences, by supposing they did in some way suggest, present, convey—I hardly know which word to use—experiences it was otherwise impossible to tell.

Well, I don't resort to that explanation now. I have got over my intervening doubts. I believe now, as I believed at the moment of telling, that Wallace did to the very best of his ability strip the truth of his secret for me. But whether he himself saw, or only thought he saw, whether he himself was the possessor of an inestimable privilege or the victim of a fantastic dream, I cannot pretend to guess. Even the facts of his death, which ended my doubts for ever, throw no light on that.

That much the reader must judge for himself.

I forget now what chance comment or criticism of mine moved so reticent a man to confide in me. He was, I think, defending himself against an imputation of slackness and unreliability I had made in relation to a great public movement, in which he had disappointed me. But he plunged suddenly. "I have," he said, "a preoccupation—

"I know," he went on, after a pause, "I have been negligent. The fact is—it isn't a case of ghosts or apparitions—but—it's an odd thing to tell of, Redmond—I am haunted. I am haunted by something—that rather takes the light out of things, that fills me with longings..."

He paused, checked by that English shyness that so often overcomes us when we would speak of moving or grave or beautiful things. "You were at Saint Althelstan's all through," he said, and for a moment that seemed to me quite irrelevant. "Well"—and he paused. Then very haltingly at first, but afterwards more easily, he began to tell of the thing that was hidden in his life, the haunting memory of a beauty and a happiness that filled his heart with insatiable longings, that made all the interests and spectacle of worldly life seem dull and tedious and vain to him.

Now that I have the clue to it, the thing seems written visibly in his face. I have a photograph in which that look of detachment has been caught and intensified. It reminds me of what a woman once said of him—a woman who had loved him greatly. "Suddenly," she said, "the interest goes out of him. He forgets you. He doesn't care a rap for you—under his very nose..."

Yet the interest was not always out of him, and when he was holding his attention to a thing Wallace could contrive to be an extremely successful man. His career, indeed, is set with successes. He left me behind him long ago; he soared up over my head, and cut a figure in the world that I couldn't cut—anyhow. He was still a year short of forty, and they say now that he would have been in office and very probably in the new Cabinet if he had lived. At school he always beat me without effort—as it were by nature. We were at school together at Saint Althelstan's College in West Kensington for almost all our schooltime. He came into the school as my co-equal, but he left far above me, in a blaze of scholarships and brilliant performance. Yet I think I made a fair average running. And it was at school I heard first of the "Door in the Wall"—that I was to hear of a second time only a month before his death.

To him at least the Door in the Wall was a real door, leading through a real wall to immortal realities. Of that I am now quite assured.

And it came into his life quite early, when he was a little fellow between five and six. I remember how, as he sat making his confession to me with a slow gravity, he reasoned and reckoned the date of it. "There was," he said, "a crimson Virginia creeper in it—all one bright uniform crimson, in a clear amber sunshine against a white wall. That came into the impression somehow, though I don't clearly remember how, and there were horse-chestnut leaves upon the clean pavement outside the green door. They were blotched yellow and green, you know, not brown nor dirty, so that they must have been new fallen. I take it that means October. I look out for horse-chestnut leaves every year and I ought to know.

"If I'm right in that, I was about five years and four months old."

He was, he said, rather a precocious little boy—he learned to talk at an abnormally early age, and he was so sane and "old-fashioned," as people say, that he was permitted an amount of initiative that most children scarcely attain by seven or eight. His mother died when he was two, and he was under the less vigilant and authoritative care of a nursery governess. His father was a stern, preoccupied lawyer, who gave him little attention and expected great things of him. For all his brightness he found life grey and dull, I think. And one day he wandered.

He could not recall the particular neglect that enabled him to get away, nor the course he took among the West Kensington roads. All that had faded among the incurable blurs of memory. But the white wall and the green door stood out quite distinctly.

As his memory of that childish experience ran, he did at the very first sight of that door experience a peculiar emotion, an attraction, a desire to get to the door and open it and walk in. And at the same time he had the clearest conviction that either it was unwise or it was wrong of him—he could not tell which—to yield to this attraction. He insisted upon it as a curious thing that he knew from the very beginning—unless memory has played him the queerest trick—that the door was unfastened, and that he could go in as he chose.

I seem to see the figure of that little boy, drawn and repelled. And it was very clear in his mind, too, though why it should be so was never explained, that his father would be very angry if he went in through that door.

Wallace described all these moments of hesitation to me with the utmost particularity. He went right past the door, and then, with his hands in his pockets and making an infantile attempt to whistle, strolled right along beyond the end of the wall. There he recalls a number of mean dirty shops, and particularly that of a plumber and decorator with a dusty disorder of earthenware pipes, sheet lead, ball taps, pattern books of wall paper, and tins of enamel. He stood pretending to examine these things, and *coveting,* passionately desiring, the green door.

Then, he said, he had a gust of emotion. He made a run for it, lest hesitation should grip him again; he went plump with outstretched hand through the green door and let it slam behind him. And so, in a trice, he came into the garden that has haunted all his life.

It was very difficult for Wallace to give me his full sense of that garden into which he came.

There was something in the very air of it that exhilarated, that gave one a sense of lightness and good happening and well-being; there was something in the sight of it that made all its colour clean and perfect and subtly luminous. In the instant of coming into it one was exquisitely glad—as only in rare moments, and when one is young and joyful one can be glad in this world. And everything was beautiful there…

Wallace mused before he went on telling me. "You see," he said, with the doubtful inflection of a man who pauses at incredible things, "there were two great panthers there… Yes, spotted panthers. And I was not afraid. There was a long wide path with marble-edged flower borders on either side, and these two huge velvety beasts were playing there with a ball. One looked up and came towards me, a little curious as it seemed. It came right up to me, rubbed its soft round ear very gently against the small hand I held out, and purred. It was, I tell you, an enchanted garden. I know. And the size? Oh! it stretched far and wide, this way and that. I believe there were hills far away. Heaven knows where West Kensington had suddenly got to. And somehow it was just like coming home.

"You know, in the very moment the door swung to behind me, I forgot the road with its fallen chestnut leaves, its cabs and tradesmen's carts, I forgot the sort of gravitational pull back to the discipline and obedience of home, I forgot all hesitations and fear, forgot discretion, forgot all the intimate realities of this life. I became in a moment a very glad and wonder-happy little boy—in another world. It was a world with a different quality, a warmer, more penetrating and mellower light, with a faint clear gladness in its air, and wisps of sun-touched cloud in the blueness of its sky. And before me ran this long wide path, invitingly, with weedless beds on either side, rich with untended flowers, and these two great panthers. I put my little hands fearlessly on their soft fur, and caressed their round ears and the sensitive corners under their ears, and played with them, and it was as though they welcomed me home. There was a keen sense of home-coming in my mind, and when presently a tall, fair girl appeared in the pathway and came to meet me, smiling, and said, 'Well?' to me, and lifted me and kissed me, and put me down and led me by the hand, there was no amazement, but only an impression of delightful rightness, of being reminded of happy things that had in some strange way been overlooked. There were broad red steps, I remember, that came into view between spikes of delphinium, and up these we went to a great avenue between very old and shady dark trees. All down this avenue, you know, between the red chapped stems, were marble seats of honour and statuary, and very tame and friendly white doves...

"Along this cool avenue my girl-friend led me, looking down—I recall the pleasant lines, the finely modelled chin of her sweet kind face—asking me questions in a soft, agreeable voice, and telling me things, pleasant things I know, though what they were I was never able to recall...Presently a Capuchin monkey, very clean, with a fur of ruddy brown and kindly hazel eyes, came down a tree to us and ran beside me, looking up at me and grinning, and presently leaped to my shoulder. So we two went on our way in great happiness."

He paused.

"Go on," I said.

"I remember little things. We passed an old man musing among laurels, I remember, and a place gay with paroquets, and came through a broad shaded colonnade to a spacious cool palace, full of pleasant fountains, full of beautiful things, full of the quality and promise of heart's desire. And there were many things and many people, some that still seem to stand out clearly and some that are vaguer; but all these people were beautiful and kind. In some way—I don't know how—it was conveyed to me that they all were kind to me, glad to have me there, and filling me with gladness by their gestures, by the touch of their hands, by the welcome and love in their eyes. Yes—"

He mused for a while. "Playmates I found there. That was very much to me, because I was a lonely little boy. They played delightful games in a grass-covered court where there was a sun-dial set about with flowers. And as one played one loved...

"But—it's odd—there's a gap in my memory. I don't remember the games we played. I never remembered. Afterwards, as a child, I spent long hours trying, even with tears, to recall the form of that happiness. I wanted to play it all over again—in my nursery—by myself. No! All I remember is the happiness and two dear playfellows who were most with me... Then presently came a sombre, dark woman, with a grave, pale face and dreamy eyes, a sombre woman, wearing a soft long robe of pale purple, who carried a book, and beckoned and took me aside with her into a gallery above a hall—though my playmates were loth to have me go, and ceased their game and stood watching as I was carried away. 'Come back to us!' they cried. 'Come back to us soon!' I looked up at her face, but she heeded them not at all. Her face was very gentle and grave. She took me to a seat in the gallery, and I stood beside her, ready to look at her book as she opened it upon her knee. The pages fell open. She pointed, and I looked, marvelling, for in the living pages of that book I saw myself; it was a story about myself, and in it were all the things that had happened to me since ever I was born...

"It was wonderful to me, because the pages of that book were not pictures, you understand, but realities."

Wallace paused gravely—looked at me doubtfully.

"Go on," I said. "I understand."

"They were realities—yes, they must have been; people moved and things came and went in them; my dear mother, whom I had near forgotten; then my father, stern and upright, the servants, the nursery, all the familiar things of home. Then the front door and the busy streets, with traffic to and fro. I looked and marvelled, and looked half doubt-fully again into the woman's face and turned the pages over, skipping this and that, to see more of this book and more, and so at last I came to myself hovering and hesitating outside the green door in the long white wall, and felt again the conflict and the fear.

" 'And next?' I cried, and would have turned on, but the cool hand of the grave woman delayed me.

" 'Next?' I insisted, and struggled gently with her hand, pulling up her fingers with all my childish strength, and as she yielded and the page came over she bent down upon me like a shadow and kissed my brow.

"But the page did not show the enchanted garden, nor the panthers, nor the girl who had led me by the hand, nor the playfellows who had been so loth to let me go. It showed a long grey street in West Ken-sington, in that chill hour of afternoon before the lamps are lit; and I was there, a wretched little figure, weeping aloud, for all that I could do to restrain myself, and I was weeping because I could not return to my dear playfellows who had called after me, 'Come back to us! Come back to us soon!' I was there. This was no page in a book, but harsh re-ality; that enchanted place and the restraining hand of the grave mother at whose knee I stood had gone—whither had they gone?"

He halted again, and remained for a time staring into the fire.

"Oh! the woefulness of that return!" he murmured.

"Well?" I said, after a minute or so.

"Poor little wretch I was!—brought back to this grey world again! As I realised the fulness of what had happened to me, I gave way to quite ungovernable grief. And the shame and humiliation of that public weeping and my disgraceful home-coming remain with me still. I see again the benevolent-looking old gentleman in gold spectacles who stopped and spoke to me—prodding me first with his umbrella. 'Poor litle chap,' said he; 'and are you lost then?'—and me a London boy of five and more! And he must needs bring in a kindly young policeman and make a crowd of me, and so march me home. Sobbing, conspicu-ous, and frightened, I came back from the enchanted garden to the steps of my father's house.

"That is as well as I can remember my vision of that garden—the gar-den that haunts me still. Of course, I can convey nothing of that indescribable quality of translucent unreality, that *difference* from the common things of experience that hung about it all; but that—that is what happened. If it was a dream, I am sure it was a day-time and altogether extraordinary dream... H'm!—naturally there followed a terrible questioning, by my aunt, my father, the nurse, the governess—everyone...

"I tried to tell them, and my father gave me my first thrashing for telling lies. When afterwards I tried to tell my aunt, she punished me again for my wicked persistence. Then, as I said, everyone was forbidden to listen to me, to hear a word about it. Even my fairy-tale books were taken away from me for a time—because I was too 'imaginative.' Eh? Yes, they did that! My father belonged to the old school... And my story was driven back upon itself. I whispered it to my pillow—my pillow that was often damp and salt to my whispering lips with childish tears. And I added always to my official and less fervent prayers this one heartfelt request: 'Please God I may dream of the garden. Oh! take me back to my garden!' Take me back to my garden! I dreamt often of the garden. I may have added to it, I may have changed it; I do not know... All this, you understand, is an attempt to reconstruct from fragmentary memories a very early experience. Between that and the other consecutive memories of my boyhood there is a gulf. A time came when it seemed impossible I should ever speak of that wonder glimpse again."

I asked an obvious question.

"No," he said. "I don't remember that I ever attempted to find my way back to the garden in those early years. This seems odd to me now, but I think that very probably a closer watch was kept on my movements after this misadventure to prevent my going astray. No, it wasn't till you knew me that I tried for the garden again. And I believe there was a period—incredible as it seems now—when I forgot the garden altogether—when I was about eight or nine it may have been. Do you remember me as a kid at Saint Althelstan's?"

"Rather!"

"I didn't show any signs, did I, in those days of having a secret dream?"

2

He looked up with a sudden smile.

"Did you ever play North-West Passage with me?... No, of course you didn't come my way!"

"It was the sort of game," he went on, "that every imaginative child plays all day. The idea was the discovery of a North-West Passage to school. The way to school was plain enough; the game consisted in finding some way that wasn't plain, starting off ten minutes early in some almost hopeless direction, and working my way round through unaccustomed streets to my goal. And one day I got entangled among some rather low-class streets on the other side of Campden Hill, and I began to think that for once the game would be against me and that I should get to school late. I tried rather desperately a street that seemed a *cul-de-sac*, and found a passage at the end. I hurried through that with renewed hope. 'I shall do it yet,' I said, and passed a row of frowsy little shops that were inexplicably familiar to me, and behold! there was my long white wall and the green door that led to the enchanted garden!

"The thing whacked upon me suddenly. Then, after all, that garden, that wonderful garden, wasn't a dream!"

He paused.

"I suppose my second experience with the green door marks the world of difference there is between the busy life of a schoolboy and the infinite leisure of a child. Anyhow, this second time I didn't for a moment think of going in straight away. You see—for one thing, my mind was full of the idea of getting to school in time—set on not breaking my record for punctuality. I must surely have felt *some* little desire at least to try the door—yes. I must have felt that... But I seem to remember the attraction of the door mainly as another obstacle to my overmastering determination to get to school. I was immensely interested by this discovery I had made, of course—I went on with my mind full of it—but I went on. It didn't check me. I ran past, tugging out my watch, found I had ten minutes still to spare, and then I was going downhill into familiar surroundings. I got to school, breathless, it is true, and wet with perspiration, but in time. I can remember hanging up my coat and hat... Went right by it and left it behind me. Odd, eh?"

He looked at me thoughtfully. "Of course I didn't know then that it wouldn't always be there. Schoolboys have limited imaginations. I suppose I thought it was an awfully jolly thing to have it there, to know my way back to it; but there was the school tugging at me. I expect I was a good deal distraught and inattentive that morning, recalling what I could of the beautiful strange people I should presently see again.

Oddly enough I had no doubt in my mind that they would be glad to see me...Yes, I must have thought of the garden that morning just as a jolly sort of place to which one might resort in the interludes of a strenuous scholastic career.

"I didn't go that day at all. The next day was a half-holiday, and that may have weighed with me. Perhaps, too, my state of inattention brought down impositions upon me, and docked the margin of time necessary for the *détour*. I don't know. What I do know is that in the meantime the enchanted garden was so much upon my mind that I could not keep it to myself.

"I told—what was his name?—a ferrety-looking youngster we used to call Squiff."

"Young Hopkins," said I.

"Hopkins it was. I did not like telling him. I had a feeling that in some way it was against the rules to tell him, but I did. He was walking part of the way home with me; he was talkative, and if we had not talked about the enchanted garden we should have talked of something else, and it was intolerable to me to think about any other subject. So I blabbed.

"Well, he told my secret. The next day in the play interval, I found myself surrounded by half-a-dozen bigger boys, half-teasing, and wholly curious to hear more of the enchanted garden. There was that big Fawcett—you remember him?—and Carnaby and Morley Reynolds. You weren't there by any chance? No, I think I should have remembered if you were...

"A boy is a creature of odd feelings. I was, I really believe, in spite of my secret self-disgust, a little flattered to have the attention of these big fellows. I remember particularly a moment of pleasure caused by the praise of Crawshaw—you remember Crawshaw major, the son of Crawshaw the composer?—who said it was the best lie he had ever heard. But at the same time there was a really painful undertow of shame at telling what I felt was indeed a sacred secret. That beast Fawcett made a joke about the girl in green—"

Wallace's voice sank with the keen memory of that shame. "I pretended not to hear," he said. "Well, then Carnaby suddenly called me a young liar, and disputed with me when I said the thing was true. I said I knew where to find the green door, could lead them all there in ten minutes. Carnaby became outrageously virtuous, and said I'd have to—and bear out my words or suffer. Did you ever have Carnaby twist your arm? Then perhaps you'll understand how it went with me. I swore my story was true. There was nobody in the school then to save a chap from Carnaby, though Crawshaw put in a word or so. Carnaby had got his game. I grew excited and red-eared, and a little frightened. I behaved altogether like a silly little chap, and the outcome of it all was that instead of starting alone for my enchanted garden, I led the way presently—cheeks flushed, ears hot, eyes smarting, and my soul one burning misery and shame—for a party of six mocking, curious, and threatening schoolfellows.

"We never found the white wall and the green door..."

"You mean—?"

"I mean I couldn't find it. I would have found it if I could.

"And afterwards when I could go alone I couldn't find it. I never found it. I seem now to have been always looking for it through my schoolboy days, but I never came upon it—never."

"Did the fellows—make it disagreeable?"

"Beastly...Carnaby held a council over me for wanton lying. I remember how I sneaked home and upstairs to hide the marks of my blubbering. But when I cried myself to sleep at last it wasn't for Carnaby, but for the garden, for the beautiful afternoon I had hoped for, for the sweet friendly women and the waiting playfellows, and the game I had hoped to learn again, that beautiful forgotten game...

"I believed firmly that if I had not told...I had bad times after that—crying at night and wool-gathering by day. For two terms I slacked and had bad reports. Do you remember? Of course you would! It was *you*—your beating me in mathematics that brought me back to the grind again."

3

For a time my friend stared silently into the red heart of the fire. Then he said: "I never saw it again until I was seventeen.

"It leaped upon me for the third time—as I was driving to Paddington on my way to Oxford and a scholarship. I had just one momentary glimpse. I was leaning over the apron of my hansom smoking a cigarette, and no doubt thinking myself no end of a man of the world, and suddenly there was the door, the wall, the dear sense of unforgettable and still attainable things.

"We clattered by—I too taken by surprise to stop my cab until we were well past and round a corner. Then I had a queer moment, a double and divergent movement of my will: I tapped the little door in the roof of the cab, and brought my arm down to pull out my watch. 'Yes, sir!' said the cabman, smartly. 'Er—well—it's nothing,' I cried. '*My* mistake! We haven't much time! Go on!' and he went on...

"I got my scholarship. And the night after I was told of that I sat over my fire in my little upper room, my study, in my father's house, with his praise—his rare praise—and his sound counsels ringing in my ears, and I smoked my favourite pipe—the formidable bulldog of adolescence—and thought of that door in the long white wall. 'If I had stopped,' I thought, 'I should have missed my scholarship, I should have missed Oxford—muddled all the fine career before me! I begin to see things better!' I fell musing deeply, but I did not doubt then this career of mine was a thing that merited sacrifice.

"Those dear friends and that clear atmosphere seemed very sweet to me, very fine but remote. My grip was fixing now upon the world. I saw another door opening—the door of my career."

He stared again into the fire. Its red light picked out a stubborn strength in his face for just one flickering moment, and then it vanished again.

"Well," he said and sighed, "I have served that career. I have done—much work, much hard work. But I have dreamt of that enchanted garden a thousand dreams, and seen its door, or at least glimpsed its door, four times since then. Yes—four times. For a while this world was so bright and interesting, seemed so full of meaning and opportunity, that the half-effaced charm of the garden was by comparison gentle and remote. Who wants to pat panthers on the way to dinner with pretty women and distinguished men? I came down to London from Oxford, a man of bold promise that I have done something to redeem. Something—and yet there have been disappointments...

"Twice I have been in love—I will not dwell on that—but once, as I went to someone who, I knew, doubted whether I dared to come, I took a short cut at a venture through an unfrequented road near Earl's Court, and so happened on a white wall and a familiar green door. 'Odd!' said I to myself, 'but I thought this place was on Campden Hill. It's the place I never could find somehow—like counting Stonehenge—the place of that queer daydream of mine.' And I went by it intent upon my purpose. It had no appeal to me that afternoon.

"I had just a moment's impulse to try the door, three steps aside were needed at the most—though I was sure enough in my heart that it would open to me—and then I thought that doing so might delay me on the way to that appointment in which my honour was involved. Afterwards I was sorry for my punctuality—I might at least have peeped in and waved a hand to those panthers, but I knew enough by this time not to seek again belatedly that which is not found by seeking. Yes, that time made me very sorry...

"Years of hard work after that, and never a sight of the door. It's only recently it has come back to me. With it there has come a sense as though some thin tarnish had spread itself over my world. I began to think of it as a sorrowful and bitter thing that I should never see that door again. Perhaps I was suffering a little from overwork—perhaps it was what I've heard spoken of as the feeling of forty. I don't know. But certainly the keen brightness that makes effort easy has gone out of things recently, and that just at a time—with all these new political developments—when I ought to be working. Odd, isn't it? But I do begin to find life toilsome, its rewards, as I come near them, cheap. I began a little while ago to want the garden quite badly. Yes—and I've seen it three times."

"The garden?"

"No—the door! And I haven't gone in!"

He leaned over the table to me, with an enormous sorrow in his voice as he spoke. "Thrice I have had my chance—*thrice*! If ever that door offers itself to me again, I swore, I will go in, out of this dust and heat, out of this dry glitter of vanity, out of these toilsome futilities. I will go and never return. This time I will stay...I swore it, and when the time came—*I didn't go.*

"Three times in one year have I passed that door and failed to enter. Three times in the last year.

"The first time was on the night of the snatch division on the Tenants' Redemption Bill, on which the Government was saved by a majority of three. You remember? No one on our side—perhaps very few on the opposite side—expected the end that night. Then the debate collapsed like eggshells. I and Hotchkiss were dining with his cousin at

Brentford; we were both unpaired, and we were called up by telephone, and set off at once in his cousin's motor. We got in barely in time, and on the way we passed my wall and door—livid in the moonlight, blotched with hot yellow as the glare of our lamps lit it, but unmistakable. 'My God!' cried I. 'What?' said Hotchkiss. 'Nothing!' I answered, and the moment passed.

" 'I've made a great sacrifice,' I told the whip as I got in. 'They all have,' he said, and hurried by.

"I do not see how I could have done otherwise then. And the next occasion was as I rushed to my father's bedside to bid that stern old man farewell. Then, too, the claims of life were imperative. But the third time was different; it happened a week ago. It fills me with hot remorse to recall it. I was with Gurker and Ralphs—it's no secret now, you know, that I've had my talk with Gurker. We had been dining at Frobisher's, and the talk had become intimate between us. The question of my place in the reconstructed Ministry lay always just over the boundary of the discussion. Yes—yes. That's all settled. It needn't be talked about yet, but there's no reason to keep a secret from you ... Yes—thanks! thanks! But let me tell you my story.

"Then, on that night things were very much in the air. My position was a very delicate one. I was keenly anxious to get some definite word from Gurker, but was hampered by Ralphs's presence. I was using the best power of my brain to keep that light and careless talk not too obviously directed to the point that concerned me. I had to. Ralphs's behaviour since has more than justified my caution ... Ralphs, I knew, would leave us beyond the Kensington High Street, and then I could surprise Gurker by a sudden frankness. One has sometimes to resort to these little devices ... And then it was that in the margin of my field of vision I became aware once more of the white wall, the green door before us down the road.

"We passed it talking. I passed it. I can still see the shadow of Gurker's marked profile, his opera hat tilted forward over his prominent nose, the many folds of his neck wrap going before my shadow and Ralphs's as we sauntered past.

"I passed within twenty inches of the door. 'If I say good-night to them, and go in,' I asked myself, 'what will happen?' And I was all a-tingle for that word with Gurker.

"I could not answer that question in the tangle of my other problems. 'They will think me mad,' I thought. 'And suppose I vanish now!—Amazing disappearance of a prominent politician!' That weighed with me. A thousand inconceivably petty worldlinesses weighed with me in that crisis."

Then he turned on me with a sorrowful smile, and, speaking slowly, "Here I am!" he said.

"Here I am!" he repeated, "and my chance had gone from me. Three times in one year the door has been offered me—the door that goes into peace, into delight, into a beauty beyond dreaming, a kindness no man on earth can know. And I have rejected it, Redmond, and it has gone—"

"How do you know?"

"I know. I know. I am left now to work it out, to stick to the tasks that held me so strongly when my moments came. You say I have success—this vulgar, tawdry, irksome, envied thing. I have it." He had a walnut in his big hand. "If that was my success," he said, and crushed it, and held it out for me to see.

"Let me tell you something, Redmond. This loss is destroying me. For two months, for ten weeks nearly now, I have done no work at all, except the most necessary and urgent duties. My soul is full of inappeasable regrets. At nights—when it is less likely I shall be recognised—I go out. I wander. Yes. I wonder what people would think of that if they knew. A Cabinet Minister, the responsible head of that most vital of all departments, wandering alone—grieving—sometimes near audibly lamenting—for a door, for a garden!"

4

I can see now his rather pallid face, and the unfamiliar sombre fire that had come into his eyes. I see him very vividly tonight. I sit recalling his words, his tones, and last evening's *Westminster Gazette* still lies on my sofa, containing the notice of his death. At lunch today the club was busy with his death. We talked of nothing else.

They found his body very early yesterday morning in a deep excavation near East Kensington Station. It is one of two shafts that have been made in connection with an extension of the railway southward. It is protected from the intrusion of the public by a hoarding upon the high road, in which a small doorway has been cut for the convenience of some of the workmen who live in that direction. The doorway was left unfastened through a misunderstanding between two gangers, and through it he made his way.

My mind is darkened with questions and riddles.

It would seem he walked all the way from the House that night—he has frequently walked home during the past Session—and so it is I figure his dark form coming along the late and empty streets, wrapped up, intent. And then did the pale electric lights near the station cheat the rough planking into a semblance of white? Did that fatal unfastened door awaken some memory?

Was there, after all, ever any green door in the wall at all?

I do not know. I have told his story as he told it to me. There are times when I believe that Wallace was no more than the victim of the coincidence between a rare but not unprecedented type of hallucination and a careless trap, but that indeed is not my profoundest belief. You may think me superstitious, if you will, and foolish; but, indeed, I am more than half-convinced that he had, in truth, an abnormal gift, and a sense, something—I know not what—that in the guise of wall and door offered him an outlet, a secret and peculiar passage of escape into another and altogether more beautiful world. At any rate, you will say, it betrayed him in the end. But did it betray him? There you touch the inmost mystery of these dreamers, these men of vision and the imagination. We see our world fair and common, the hoarding and the pit. By our daylight standard he walked out of security into darkness, danger, and death.

But did he see like that?

The Presence by the Fire

It never occurred to Reid that his wife lay dying until the very last day of her illness. He was a man of singularly healthy disposition, averse on principle to painful thoughts, and I doubt if in the whole of his married life his mind had dwelt for five minutes together on the possibility of his losing her.

They were both young, and intimate companions—such companions as many desire to be and few become. And perhaps it was her sense of the value of this rare companionship that made her, when first her health declined, run many an avoidable risk rather than leave him to go his way alone.

He was sorry that she was ill, sorry she should suffer, and he missed her, as she lay upstairs, in a thousand ways; but though the doctor was mindful to say all the "preparatory" phrases of his profession, and though her sister spoke, as she conceived, quite plainly, it was as hard for him to understand that this was more than a temporary interruption of their life, as it would have been to believe that the sun would not rise again after tomorrow morning.

The day before she died he was restless, and after wandering about the house and taking a short walk, he occupied himself in planting out her evening primroses—a thing she had made a point of doing now for ten springs in succession. The garden she had always tended, he said, should not seem neglected when she came down again. He had rather his own work got in arrears than that this should happen.

The first realisation, when the doctor, finding all conventional euphemisms useless, told him the fact at last in stark, plain words, stunned him. Even then it is doubtful if he believed. He said not a word in answer, but the colour left his face, and the lines about his mouth hardened. And he walked softly and with white, expressionless features into her room.

He stood at the doorway, and looked for a minute at her thin little features, with the eyes closed and two little lines between the brows, then went and knelt by the bed and looked closely into her face. She did not move until he touched her hair and very softly whispered her name.

Then her eyes opened for a moment, and he saw that she knew him. Her lips moved, and it seemed that she whispered one of those foolish, tender little names that happy married folk delight in inventing for one another, and then she gathered her strength as if with an effort to speak distinctly. He bent mechanically and heard the last syllables of *au revoir*.

For a moment he did not clearly understand what the words were. That was all she said, and as for him, he answered not a word. He put his hand in hers, and she pressed it faintly and then more faintly. He kissed her forehead with dry lips, and the little lines of pain there faded slowly into peace.

For an hour they let him kneel, until the end had come, and all that time he never stirred. Then they had to tap his shoulder to rouse him from his rigour. He got up slowly, bent over her for a moment, looking down into her tranquil face, and then allowed them to lead him away.

That was how Reid parted from his wife, and for days after he behaved as a man who had been suddenly deprived of all initiative. He did not work; he went nowhere outside the house; he ate, drank and slept mechanically; and he did not even seem to suffer actively. For the most part, he sat stupidly at his desk or wandered about the big garden, looking with dull eyes at the little green buds that were now swiftly opening all about him. Not a soul ventured to speak to him of his loss, albeit those who did not know him might have judged his mood one of absolute apathy.

But nearly a week after the funeral the floodgates of his sorrow were opened. Quite suddenly the thing came upon him. Her sister heard him walk into the study and throw himself into a chair. Everything was still for a space, and then he sprang up again and she heard him wailing, "Mary! Mary!" and then he ran, sobbing violently and stumbling, along the passage to his room. It was grotesquely like a little child that had suddenly been hurt.

He locked his door; and her sister, fearing what might happen, went along the passage. She thought of rapping at the door, but on second thoughts she refrained. After listening awhile she went away.

It was long after the first violence of his grief had passed that Reid first spoke of his feelings. He who had been a matter-of-fact materialist was converted, I found, to a belief in immortality by the pitiless logic of her uncompleted life. But I think it was an imperfect, a doubting, belief even at the best. And to strengthen it, perhaps, he began to show a growing interest in the inquiries of those who were sifting whatever evidence there may be of the return of those who are dead.

"For I want my wife now," said he. "I want her in this life. I want her about me—her comfort, her presence. What does it matter that I shall meet her again when I am changed, and she is changed? It was the dear trivialities, the little moments, the touch of her hand, the sound of her voice in the room with me, her distant singing in the garden, and her footfall on the stairs. If I could believe that," he said, "if I could believe—"

And in that spirit it was that he kept to the old home, and would scarcely bear that a thing within or without should be altered in any way. The white curtains that had been there the last autumn hung dirty in the windows, and the little desk that had been her own in the study stood there still, with the pen thrown down as he fancied she had left it.

"Here, if anywhere," he said, "she is at home. Here, if anywhere, her presence lives."

Her sister left him when a housekeeper was obtained, and he went on living there alone, working little and communicating for the most part with these dead memories. After a time he loved nothing so much as to talk to her, and I think in those days that I was of service to him. He would take me about the house, pointing to this trivial thing and that; and telling me some little act of hers that he linked therewith. And he always spoke of her as one who still lived.

"She does" so and so, he would say; "she likes" so and so. We would pace up and down the rich lawn of his house. "My wife is particularly fond of those big white lilies," he would say, "and this year they are finer than ever." So the summer passed and the autumn came.

And one day late in the evening he came to me, walking round the house and tapping at the French window of my study, and as he came in out of the night I noticed how deadly white and sunken his face was and how bright his eyes.

"I have seen her," he said to me, in a low, clear voice. "She has visited me. I knew she was watching me and near me. I have felt her presence for weeks and weeks. And now she has come."

He was intensely excited, and it was some time before I could get any clear story from him.

He had been sitting by the fire in his study, musing, no doubt going over for the hundredth time, day by day and almost hour by hour as he was wont to do, one of the summer holidays they had spent together. He was staring, he said, into the glowing coals, and almost imperceptibly it was that there grew upon him the persuasion that he was not alone. The thought took shape slowly in his mind, but with a strange quality of absolute conviction, that she was sitting in the armchair in front of him, as she had done so often in the old days, and watching him a-dreaming. For a moment he did not dare to look up, lest he should find this a mere delusion.

Then slowly he raised his eyes. He was dimly aware of footsteps advancing along the passage as he did so. A wave of bitter disappointment swept over him as he saw the chair was empty, and this incontinently gave place to a tumult of surprise and joyful emotion. For he saw her—saw her distinctly. She was standing behind the chair, leaning over the back of it, and smiling the tender smile he knew so well. So in her life she had stood many a time and listened to him, smiling gently. The firelight played upon her face.

"I saw her as plainly as I see you," he said. "I saw the smile in her eyes, and my heart leapt out to her."

For a moment he was motionless, entranced, and with an instantaneous appreciation of the transitoriness of this appearance. Then suddenly the door opened, the shadows in the room rushed headlong, and the housemaid came in with his lamp lit and without the shade—a dazzling glare of naked flame. The yellow light splashed over the room and brought out everything clear and vivid.

By mere reflex action he turned his head at the sound of the door-handle, and forthwith turned it back again. But the face he had longed for so patiently had vanished with the shadows before the light. Everything was abruptly plain and material. The girl replenished the fire, moved the armchair on one side, and took away the scuttle lining to refill it with coals. A curious bashfulness made Reid pretend to make notes at his table until these offices were accomplished. Then he looked across the fireplace again, and the room was empty. The sense of her presence, too, had gone. He called upon her name again and again, rubbed his eyes, and tried to force her return by concentrating his mind upon her. But nothing availed. He could see her no more.

He allowed me to cross-examine him in the most detailed way upon this story. His manner was so sane, so convincing, and his honesty so indisputable, that I went to bed that night with my beliefs and disbeliefs greatly shaken. Hitherto I had doubted every ghost story I had heard; but here at last was one of a different quality. Indeed, I went to bed that night an unwilling convert to the belief in the phantasms of those who are dead and all that that belief implies.

My faith in Reid was confirmed by the fact that from late August, when this happened, until December he did not see the apparition again. Had it been an hallucination begotten of his own intense brooding it must inevitably have recurred. But it was presently to be proved beyond all question that the thing he saw was an exterior presence. Night after night he sat in his study, longing for the repetition of that strange experience; and at last, after many nights, he saw her for the second time.

It was earlier in the evening, but with the shorter winter days the room was already dark. Once more he looked into his study fire, and once more that fire glowed redly. Then there came the same sense of her presence, the same hesitation before he raised his eyes. But this time he looked over the chair at once and saw her without any flash of disappointment.

At the instant he felt not the faintest suspicion that his senses deceived him. For a moment he was dumb. He was seized with an intense longing to touch her hand. Then came into his head some half-forgotten story that one must speak first to a spirit. He leant forward.

"Mary!" he said very softly. But she neither moved nor spoke. And then suddenly it seemed that she grew less distinct.

"Mary!" he whispered, with a sudden pang of doubt. Her features grew unfamiliar.

Then suddenly he rose to his feet, and as he did so the making of the illusion was demonstrated. The high light on a vase that had been her cheek moved to the right; the shadow that had been her arm moved to the left.

Few people realise how little we actually see of what is before our eyes: a patch of light, a patch of shadow, and all the rest our memory and our imagination supply. A chance grouping of dim forms in the dusky firelit study had furnished all the suggestion his longing senses had required. His eyes and his heart and the humour of chance had cheated him.

He stood there staring. For a moment the disintegration of the figure filled him with a sense of grotesque horror and dismay. For a moment it seemed beyond the sanity of things. Then, as he realised the deception his senses had contrived, he sat down again, put his elbows on the table and buried his face in his hands.

About ten he came and told me. He told me in a clear hard voice, without a touch of emotion, recording a remarkable fact. "As I told you the other thing, it is only right that I should tell you this," he said.

Then he sat silently for a space. "She will come no more," he said at last. "She will come no more."

And suddenly he rose, and without a greeting, passed out into the night.

PART FIVE

FABLES

INTRODUCTION

To my mind, fable differs from fantasy chiefly by having a didactic aim. Aunt Fantasy tells her tales for their own sake; Uncle Aesop wants us to get the point. (In science fiction, there is a similar difference between stories of other times or planets and the didactic utopia/dystopia.) Fable is often funny or satirical, and uses a pretty broad brush.

These four stories all make their point boldly. "A Vision of Judgment" is an early story, brash and brilliant. H. G. Wells was not what anyone would call a God-fearing man. I think he felt God had a right to ask for respect, but not for fear.

The next two tales, "The Story of the Last Trump" and "The Wild Asses of the Devil" appeared as chapters of a 1915 novel, *Boon*. Wells himself put "Last Trump" into a collection, *The Door in the Wall;* and let us again be grateful to John Hammond for including "Wild Asses" in *The Complete Short Stories of H. G. Wells,* for both pieces stand on their own as inventive and entertaining tales.

"Answer to Prayer" was written much later than all but one of the stories in this book, in 1937, when Wells was seventy-one. It is very short and not sweet.

A Vision of Judgment

1

BRU-A-A-A.

I listened, not understanding.

Wa-ra-ra-ra.

"Good Lord!" said I, still only half-awake. "What an infernal shindy!"

Ra-ra-ra-ra-ra-ra-ra-ra-ra. Ta-ra-rra-ra.

"It's enough," said I, "to wake—" and stopped short. Where was I?

Ta-rra-rara—louder and louder.

"It's either some new invention—"

Toora-toora-toora! Deafening!

"No," said I, speaking loud in order to hear myself. "That's the Last Trump."

Tooo-rraa!

2

The last note jerked me out of my grave like a hooked minnow.

I saw my monument (rather a mean little affair, and I wished I knew who'd done it), and the old elm tree and the sea view vanished like a puff of steam, and then all about me—a multitude no man could number, nations, tongues, kingdoms, people—children of all the ages, in an amphitheatrical space as vast as the sky. And over against us, seated on a throne of dazzling white cloud, the Lord God and all the host of his angels. I recognised Azreal by his darkness and Michael by his sword, and the great angel who had blown the trumpet stood with the trumpet still half-raised.

3

"Prompt," said the little man beside me. "Very prompt. Do you see the angel with the book?"

He was ducking and craning his head about to see over and under and between the souls that crowded round us. "Everybody's here," he said. "Everybody. And now we shall know—

"There's Darwin," he said, going off at a tangent. "*He'll* catch it! And there—you see?—that tall, important-looking man trying to catch the eye of the Lord God, that's the Duke. But there's a lot of people one doesn't know.

"Oh! there's Priggles, the publisher. I have always wondered about printers' overs. Priggles was a clever man ... But we shall know now—even about him.

"I shall hear all that. I shall get most of the fun before ... *My* letter's S."

He drew the air in between his teeth.

"Historical characters, too. See? That's Henry the Eighth. There'll be a good bit of evidence. Oh, damn! He's Tudor."

He lowered his voice. "Notice this chap, just in front of us, all covered with hair. Paleolithic, you know. And there again—"

But I did not heed him, because I was looking at the Lord God.

4

"Is this *all*?" asked the Lord God.

The angel at the book—it was one of countless volumes, like the British Museum Reading-room Catalogue, glanced at us and seemed to count us in the instant.

"That's all," he said, and added: "It was, O God, a very little planet."

The eyes of God surveyed us.

"Let us begin," said the Lord God.

5

The angel opened the book and read a name. It was a name full of A's, and the echoes of it came back out of the uttermost parts of space. I did not catch it clearly, because the little man beside me said, in a sharp jerk, "*What's* that?" It sounded like "Ahab" to me; but it could not have been the Ahab of Scripture.

Instantly a small black figure was lifted up to a puffy cloud at the very feet of God. It was a stiff little figure, dressed in rich outlandish robes and crowned, and it folded its arms and scowled.

"Well?" said God, looking down at him.

We were privileged to hear the reply, and indeed the acoustic properties of the place were marvellous.

"I plead guilty," said the little figure.

"Tell them what you have done," said the Lord God.

"I was a king," said the little figure, "a great king, and I was lustful and proud and cruel. I made wars, I devastated countries, I built palaces, and the mortar was the blood of men. Hear, O God, the witnesses against me, calling to you for vengeance. Hundreds and thousands of witnesses." He waved his hands towards us. "And worse! I took a prophet—one of your prophets—"

"One of my prophets," said the Lord God.

"And because he would not bow to me, I tortured him for four days and nights, and in the end he died. I did more, O God, I blasphemed. I robbed you of your honours—"

"Robbed me of my honours," said the Lord God.

"I caused myself to be worshipped in your stead. No evil was there but I practised it; no cruelty wherewith I did not stain my soul. And at last you smote me, O God!"

God raised his eyebrows slightly.

"And I was slain in battle. And so I stand before you, meet for your nethermost Hell! Out of your greatness daring no lies, daring no pleas, but telling the truth of my iniquities before all mankind."

He ceased. His face I saw distinctly, and it seemed to me white and terrible and proud and strangely noble. I thought of Milton's Satan.

"Most of that is from the Obelisk," said the Recording Angel, finger on page.

"It is," said the Tyrannous Man, with a faint touch of surprise.

Then suddenly God bent forward and took this man in his hand, and held him up on his palm as if to see him better. He was just a little dark stroke in the middle of God's palm.

"*Did* he do all this?" said the Lord God.

The Recording Angel flattened his book with his hand.

"In a way," said the Recording Angel, carelessly.

Now when I looked again at the little man his face had changed in a very curious manner. He was looking at the Recording Angel with a strange apprehension in his eyes, and one hand fluttered to his mouth. Just the movement of a muscle or so, and all that dignity of defiance was gone.

"Read," said the Lord God.

And the angel read, explaining very carefully and fully all the wickedness of the Wicked Man. It was quite an intellectual treat.—A little "daring" in places, I thought, but of course Heaven has its privileges...

6

Everybody was laughing. Even the prophet of the Lord whom the Wicked Man had tortured had a smile on his face. The Wicked Man was really such a preposterous little fellow.

"And then," read the Recording Angel, with a smile that set us all agog, "one day, when he was a little irascible from over-eating, he—"

"Oh, not *that*," cried the Wicked Man, nobody knew of *that*.

"It didn't happen," screamed the Wicked Man. "I was bad—I was really bad. Frequently bad, but there was nothing so silly—so absolutely silly—"

The angel went on reading.

"O God!" cried the Wicked Man. "Don't let them know that! I'll repent! I'll apologise..."

The Wicked Man on God's hand began to dance and weep. Suddenly shame overcame him. He made a wild rush to jump off the ball of God's little finger, but God stopped him by a dexterous turn of the wrist. Then he made a rush for the gap between hand and thumb, but the thumb closed. And all the while the angel went on reading—reading. The Wicked Man rushed to and fro across God's palm, and then suddenly turned about and fled up the sleeve of God.

I expected God would turn him out, but the mercy of God is infinite.

The Recording Angel paused.

"Eh?" said the Recording Angel.

"Next," said God, and before the Recording Angel could call upon the name a hairy creature in filthy rags stood upon God's palm.

7

"Has God got Hell up his sleeve then?" said the little man beside him.

"Is there a Hell?" I asked.

"If you notice," he said—he peered between the feet of the great angels—"there's no particular indication of the Celestial City."

"'Ssh!" said a little woman near us, scowling. "Hear this blessed Saint!"

8

"He was Lord of the Earth, but I was the prophet of the God of Heaven," cried the Saint, "and all the people marvelled at the sign. For I, O God, knew of the glories of thy Paradise. No pain, no hardship, gashing with knives, splinters thrust under my nails, stripes of flesh flayed off, all for the glory and honour of God."

God smiled.

"And at last I went, I in my rags and sores, smelling of my holy discomforts—"

Gabriel laughed abruptly.

"And lay outside his gates, as a sign, as a wonder—"

"As a perfect nuisance," said the Recording Angel, and began to read, heedless of the fact that the Saint was still speaking of the gloriously unpleasant things he had done that Paradise might be his.

And behold, in that book the record of the Saint also was a revelation, a marvel.

It seemed not ten seconds before the Saint also was rushing to and fro over the great palm of God. Not ten seconds! And at last he also shrieked beneath that pitiless and cynical exposition, and fled also, even as the Wicked Man had fled, into the shadow of the sleeve. And it was permitted us to see into the shadow of the sleeve. And the two sat side by side, stark of all delusions, in the shadow of the robe of God's charity, like brothers.

And thither also I fled in my turn.

9

"And now," said God, as he shook us out of his sleeve upon the planet he had given us to live upon, the planet that whirled about green Sirius for a sun, "now that you understand me and each other a little better, ... try again."

Then he and his great angels turned themselves about and suddenly had vanished.

The Throne had vanished.

All about me was a beautiful land, more beautiful than any I had ever seen before—waste, austere, and wonderful; and all about me were the enlightened souls of men in new clean bodies...

THE STORY OF THE LAST TRUMP

1

The story of the Last Trump begins in Heaven and it ends in all sorts of places round about the world...

Heaven, you must know, is a kindly place, and the blessed ones do not go on for ever singing Alleluia, whatever you may have been told. For they too are finite creatures, and must be fed with their eternity in little bits, as one feeds a chick or a child. So that there are mornings and changes and freshness, there is time to condition their lives. And the children are still children, gravely eager about their playing and ready always for new things; just children they are, but blessèd as you see them in the pictures beneath the careless feet of the Lord God. And one of these blessèd children routing about in an attic—for Heaven is, of course, full of the most heavenly attics, seeing that it has children—came upon a number of instruments stored away, and laid its little chubby hands upon them...

Now indeed I cannot tell what these instruments were, for to do so would be to invade mysteries... But one I may tell of, and that was a great brazen trumpet which the Lord God had made when He made the world—for the Lord God finishes all His jobs—to blow when the time for our Judgement came round. And He had made it and left it; there it was, and everything was settled exactly as the Doctrine of Predestination declares. And this blessèd child conceived one of those unaccountable passions of childhood for its smoothness and brassiness, and he played with it and tried to blow it, and trailed it about with him out of the attic into the gay and golden streets, and, after many fitful wanderings, to those celestial battlements of crystal of which you have doubtless read. And there the blessèd child fell to counting the stars, and forgot all about the Trumpet beside him until a flourish of his elbow sent it over...

Down fell the trump, spinning as it fell, and for a day or so, which seemed but moments in Heaven, the blessèd child watched its fall until it was a glittering little speck of brightness...

When it looked a second time the trump was gone...

I do not know what happened to that child when at last it was time for Judgement Day and that shining trumpet was missed. I know that Judgement Day is long overpassed, because of the wickedness of the world; I think perhaps it was in AD 1000 when the expected Day should have dawned that never came, but no other heavenly particulars do I know at all, because now my scene changes to the narrow ways of this Earth...

And the Prologue in Heaven ends.

2

And now the scene is a dingy little shop in Caledonian Market, where things of an incredible worthlessness lie in wait for such as seek after an impossible cheapness. In the window, as though it had always been there and never anywhere else, lies a long, battered discoloured trumpet of brass that no prospective purchaser has ever been able to sound. In it mice shelter, and dust and fluff have gathered after the fashion of this world. The keeper of the shop is a very old man, and he bought the shop long ago, but already this trumpet was there; he has no idea whence it came, nor its country of origin, nor anything about it. But once in a moment of enterprise that led to nothing he decided to call it an Ancient Ceremonial Shawm, though he ought to have known that whatever a shawm may be the last thing it was likely to be is a trumpet, seeing that they are always mentioned together. And above it hung concertinas and melodeons and cornets and tin whistles and mouth-organs and all that rubbish of musical instruments which delight the hearts of the poor. Until one day two blackened young men from the big motor works in the Pansophist Road stood outside the window and argued.

They argued about these instruments in stock and how you made these instruments sound, because they were fond of argument, and one asserted and the other denied that he could make every instrument in the place sound a note. And the argument rose high, and led to a bet.

"Supposing, of course, that the instrument is in order," said Hoskin, who was betting he could.

"That's understood," said Briggs.

And then they called as witnesses certain other young and black and greasy men in the same employment, and after much argument and discussion that lasted through the afternoon, they went in to the little old dealer about teatime, just as he was putting a blear-eyed, stinking paraffin-lamp to throw an unfavourable light upon his always very unattractive window. And after great difficulty they arranged that for the sum of one shilling, paid in advance, Hoskin should have a try at every instrument in the shop that Briggs chose to indicate.

And the trial began.

The third instrument that was pitched upon by Briggs for the trial was the strange trumpet that lay at the bottom of the window, the trumpet that you, who have read the Introduction, know was the trumpet for the Last Trump. And Hoskin tried and tried again, and then, blowing desperately, hurt his ears. But he could get no sound from the trumpet. Then he examined the trumpet more carefully and discovered the mice and fluff and other things in it, and demanded that it should be cleaned; and the old dealer, nothing loth, knowing they were used to automobile-horns and such-like instruments, agreed to let them clean it on condition that they left it shiny. So the young men, after making a suitable deposit (which, as you shall hear, was presently confiscated), went off with the trumpet, proposing to clean it next day at the works and polish it with the peculiarly excellent brass polish employed upon the honk-honk horns of the firm. And this they did, and Hoskin tried again.

But he tried in vain. Whereupon there arose a great argument about the trumpet, whether it was in order or not, whether it was possible for any one to sound it. For if not, then clearly it was outside the condition of the bet.

Others among the young men tried it, including two who played wind instruments in a band and were musically knowing men. After their own failure they were strongly on the side of Hoskin and strongly against Briggs, and most of the other young men were of the same opinion.

"Not a bit of it," said Briggs, who was a man of resource. "*I*'ll show you that it can be sounded."

And taking the instrument in his hand, he went towards a peculiarly powerful foot blow-pipe that stood at the far end of the toolshed. "Good old Briggs!" said one of the other young men, and opinion veered about.

Briggs removed the blow-pipe from its bellows and tube, and then adjusted the tube very carefully to the mouthpiece of the trumpet. Then with great deliberation he produced a piece of bees-waxed string from a number of other strange and filthy contents in his pocket and tied the tube to the mouthpiece. And then he began to work the treadle of the bellows.

"Good old Briggs!" said the one who had previously admired him.

And then something incomprehensible happened.

It was a flash. Whatever else it was, it was a flash. And a sound that seemed to coincide exactly with the flash.

Afterwards the young men agreed to it that the trumpet blew to bits. It blew to bits and vanished, and they were all flung upon their faces—not backward, be it noted, but on their faces—and Briggs was stunned and scared. The toolshed windows were broken and the various apparatus and cars around were much displaced, and *no traces of the trumpet were ever discovered.*

That last particular puzzled and perplexed poor Briggs very much. It puzzled and perplexed him the more because he had had an impression, so extraordinary, so incredible, that he was never able to describe it to any other living person. But his impression was this: that the flash that came with the sound came, not from the trumpet but to it, that it smote down to it and took it, and that its shape was in the exact likeness of a hand and arm of fire.

3

And that was not all, that was not the only strange thing about the disappearance of that battered trumpet. There was something else, even more difficult to describe, an effect as though for one instant something opened ...

The young men who worked with Hoskin and Briggs had that clearness of mind which comes of dealing with machinery, and they all felt this indescribable something else, as if for an instant the world wasn't the world, but something lit and wonderful, larger—

This is what one of them said of it.

"I felt," he said, "just for a minute—as though I was blown to Kingdom Come."

"It is just how it took me," said another. " 'Lord,' I says, 'here's Judgement Day!' and then there I was sprawling among the files..."

But none of the others felt that they could say anything more definite than that.

4

Moreover, there was a storm. All over the world there was a storm that puzzled meteorology, a moment's gale that left the atmosphere in a state of wild swaygog, rains, tornadoes, depressions, irregularities for weeks. News came of it from all the quarters of the earth.

All over China, for example, the land of cherished graves, there was a duststorm, dust leaped into the air. A kind of earthquake shook Europe—an earthquake that seemed to have at heart the peculiar interests of Mr. Algernon Ashton; everywhere it cracked mausoleums and shivered the pavements of cathedrals, swished the flower-beds of cemeteries, and tossed tombstones aside. A crematorium in Texas blew up. The sea was greatly agitated, and the beautiful harbour of Sydney, in Australia, was seen to be littered with sharks floating upside down in manifest distress...

And all about the world a sound was heard like the sound of a trumpet instantly cut short.

5

But this much is only the superficial dressing of the story. The reality is something different. It is this: that in an instant, and for an instant, the dead lived, and all that are alive in the world did for a moment see the Lord God and all His powers, His hosts of angels, and all His array looking down upon them. They saw Him as one sees by a flash of lightning in the darkness, and then instantly the world was opaque again, limited, petty, habitual. That is the tremendous reality of this story. Such glimpses have happened in individual cases before. The Lives of the saints abound in them. Such a glimpse it was that came to Devindranath Tagore upon the burning ghat at Benares. But this was not an individual but a world experience; the flash came to every one. Not always was it quite the same, and thereby the doubter found his denials, when presently a sort of discussion broke out in the obscurer Press. For this one testified that it seemed that "One stood very near to me," and another saw "all the hosts of heaven flame up towards the Throne."

And there were others who had a vision of brooding watchers, and others who imagined great sentinels before a veiled figure, and some one who felt nothing more divine than a sensation of happiness and freedom such as one gets from a sudden burst of sunshine in the spring...So that one is forced to believe that something more than wonderfully wonderful, something altogether strange, was seen, and that all these various things that people thought they saw were only interpretations drawn from their experiences and their imaginations. It was a light, it was beauty, it was high and solemn, it made this world seem a flimsy transparency.

Then it had vanished...

And people were left with the question of what they had seen, and just how much it mattered.

6

A little old lady sat by the fire in a small sitting-room in West Kensington. Her cat was in her lap, her spectacles were on her nose; she was reading the morning's paper, and beside her, on a little occasional table, was her tea and a buttered muffin. She had finished the crimes and she was reading about the Royal Family. When she had read all there was to read about the Royal Family, she put down the paper, deposited the cat on the hearthrug, and turned to her tea. She had poured out her first cup and she had just taken up a quadrant of muffin when the trump and the flash came. Through its instant duration she remained motionless with the quadrant of muffin poised half-way to her mouth. Then very slowly she put the morsel down.

"Now what was that?" she said.

She surveyed the cat, but the cat was quite calm. Then she looked very, very hard at her lamp. It was a patent safety lamp, and had always behaved very well. Then she stared at the window, but the curtains were drawn and everything was in order.

"One might think I was going to be ill," she said, and resumed her toast.

7

Not far away from this old lady, not more than three-quarters of a mile at most, sat Mr. Parchester in his luxurious study, writing a perfectly beautiful, sustaining sermon about the Need of Faith in God. He was a handsome, earnest, modern preacher, he was rector of one of our big West End churches, and he had amassed a large, fashionable congregation. Every Sunday, and at convenient intervals during the week, he fought against Modern Materialism, Scientific Education, Excessive Puritanism, Pragmatism, Doubt, Levity, Selfish Individualism, Further Relaxation of the Divorce Laws, all the Evils of Our Time—and anything else that was unpopular. He believed quite simply, he said, in all the old, simple, kindly things. He had the face of a saint, but he had rendered this generally acceptable by growing side whiskers. And nothing could tame the beauty of his voice.

He was an enormous asset in the spiritual life of the metropolis—to give it no harsher name—and his fluent periods had restored faith and courage to many a poor soul hovering on the brink of the dark river of thought...

And just as beautiful Christian maidens played a wonderful part in the last days of Pompeii, in winning proud Roman hearts to a hated and despised faith, so Mr. Parchester's naturally graceful gestures, and his simple, melodious, trumpet voice won back scores of our half-pagan rich women to church attendance and the social work of which his church was the centre...

And now by the light of an exquisitely shaded electric lamp he was writing this sermon of quiet, confident belief (with occasional hard smacks, perfect stingers in fact, at current unbelief and rival leaders of opinion) in the simple, divine faith of our fathers...

When there came this truncated trump and this vision...

8

Of all the innumerable multitudes who for the infinitesimal fraction of a second had this glimpse of the Divinity, none were so blankly and profoundly astonished as Mr. Parchester. For—it may be because of his subtly spiritual nature—he *saw*, and seeing believed. He dropped his pen and let it roll across his manuscript, he sat stunned, every drop of blood fled from his face and his lips and his eyes dilated.

While he had just been writing and arguing about God, there *was* God!

The curtain had been snatched back for an instant; it had fallen again; but his mind had taken a photographic impression of everything that he had seen—the grave presences, the hierarchy, the effulgence, the vast concourse, the terrible, gentle eyes. He felt it, as though the vision still continued, behind the bookcases, behind the pictured wall and the curtained window: *even now there was judgement!*

For quite a long time he sat, incapable of more than apprehending this supreme realisation. His hands were held out limply upon the desk before him. And then very slowly his staring eyes came back to immediate things, and fell upon the scattered manuscript on which he had been engaged. He read an unfinished sentence and slowly recovered its intention. As he did so, a picture of his congregation came to him as he saw it from the pulpit during his evening sermon, as he had intended to see it on the Sunday evening that was at hand, with Lady Rupert in her sitting and Lady Blex in hers and Mrs. Munbridge, the rich and in her Jewish way very attractive Mrs. Munbridge, running them close in her adoration, and each with one or two friends they had brought to adore him, and behind them the Hexhams and the Wassinghams and behind them others and others and others, ranks and ranks of people, and the galleries on either side packed with worshippers of a less dominant class, and the great organ and his magnificent choir waiting to support him and supplement him, and the great altar to the left of him, and the beautiful new Lady Chapel, done by Roger Fry and Wyndham Lewis and all the latest people in Art, to the right. He thought of the listening multitude, seen through the haze of the thousand electric candles, and how he had planned the paragraphs of his discourse so that the notes of his beautiful voice should float slowly down, like golden leaves in autumn, into the smooth tarn of their silence, word by word, phrase by phrase, until he came to—

"Now to God the Father, God the Son—"

And all the time he knew that Lady Blex would watch his face and Mrs. Munbridge, leaning those graceful shoulders of hers a little forward, would watch his face ...

Many people would watch his face.

All sorts of people would come to Mr. Parchester's services at times. Once it was said Mr. Balfour had come. Just to hear him. After his sermons, the strangest people would come and make confessions in the beautifully furnished reception-room beyond the vestry. All sorts of people. Once or twice he had asked people to come and listen to him; and one of them had been a very beautiful woman. And often he had dreamt of the people who might come; prominent people, influential people, remarkable people. But never before had it occurred to Mr. Parchester that, a little hidden from the rest of the congregation, behind the thin veil of this material world, there was another auditorium. And that God also, God also, watched his face.

And watched him through and through.

Terror seized upon Mr. Parchester.

He stood up, as though Divinity had come into the room before him. He was trembling. He felt smitten and about to be smitten.

He perceived that it was hopeless to try and hide what he had written, what he had thought, the unclean egotism he had become.

"I did not know," he said at last.

The click of the door behind him warned him that he was not alone. He turned and saw Miss Skelton, his typist, for it was her time to come for his manuscript and copy it out in the specially legible type he used. For a moment he stared at her strangely.

She looked at him with those deep, adoring eyes of hers. "Am I too soon, sir?" she asked in her slow, unhappy voice, and seemed prepared for a noiseless departure.

He did not answer immediately. Then he said: "Miss Skelton, the Judgement of God is close at hand!"

And seeing she stood perplexed, he said—

"Miss Skelton, how can you expect me to go on acting and mouthing this Tosh when the Sword of Truth hangs over us?"

Something in her face made him ask a question.

"Did *you* see anything?" he asked.

"I thought it was because I was rubbing my eyes."

"Then indeed there is a God! And he is watching us now. And all this about us, this sinful room, this foolish costume, this preposterous life of blasphemous pretension—!"

He stopped short, with a kind of horror on his face.

With a hopeless gesture he rushed by her. He appeared wild-eyed upon the landing before his man-servant, who was carrying a scuttle of coal upstairs.

"Brompton," he said, "what are you doing?"

"Coal, sir."

"Put it down, man!" he said. "Are you not an immortal soul? God is here! As close as my hand! Repent! Turn to Him! The Kingdom of Heaven is at hand!"

9

Now if you are a policeman perplexed by a sudden and unaccountable collision between a taxicab and an electric standard, complicated by a blinding flash and a sound like an abbreviated trump from an automobile horn, you do not want to be bothered by a hatless clerical gentleman suddenly rushing out of a handsome private house and telling you that "the Kingdom of Heaven is at hand!" You are respectful to him because it is the duty of a policeman to be respectful to Gentlemen, but you say to him, "Sorry I can't attend to that now, sir. One thing at a time. I've got this little accident to see to." And if he persists in dancing round the gathering crowd and coming at you again, you say: "I'm afraid I must ask you just to get away from here, sir. You aren't being a 'elp, sir." And if, on the other hand, you are a well-trained clerical gentleman, who knows his way about in the world, you do not go on pestering a policeman on duty after he has said that, even although you think God is looking at you and Judgement is close at hand. You turn away and go on, a little damped, looking for some one else more likely to pay attention to your tremendous tidings.

And so it happened to the Reverend Mr. Parchester.

He experienced a curious little recession of confidence. He went on past quite a number of people without saying anything further, and the next person he accosted was a flower-woman sitting by her basket at the corner of Chexington Square. She was unable to stop him at once when he began to talk to her because she was tying up a big bundle of white chrysanthemums and had an end of string behind her teeth. And her daughter who stood beside her was the sort of girl who wouldn't say "Boo!" to a goose.

"Do you know, my good woman," said Mr. Parchester, "that while we poor creatures of earth go about our poor business here, while we sin and blunder and follow every sort of base end, close to us, above us, around us, watching us, judging us, are God and His holy angels? I have had a vision, and I am not the only one. I have *seen*. We are *in* the Kingdom of Heaven now and here, and Judgement is all about us now! Have you seen nothing? No light? No sound? No warning?"

By this time the old flower-seller had finished her bunch of flowers and could speak. "I saw it," she said. "And Mary—she saw it."

"Well?" said Mr. Parchester.

"But, Lord! It don't *mean* nothing!" said the old flower-seller.

10

At that a kind of chill fell upon Mr. Parchester. He went on across Chexington Square by his own inertia.

He was still about as sure that he had seen God as he had been in his study, but now he was no longer sure that the world would believe that he had. He felt perhaps that this idea of rushing out to tell people was precipitate and inadvisable. After all, a priest in the Church of England is only one unit in a great machine; and in a world-wide spiritual crisis it should be the task of that great machine to act as one resolute body. This isolated crying aloud in the street was unworthy of a consecrated priest. It was a dissenting kind of thing to do. A vulgar individualistic screaming. He thought suddenly that he would go and tell his Bishop, the great Bishop Wampach. He called a taxicab, and within half an hour he was in the presence of his commanding officer. It was an extraordinarily difficult and painful interview...

You see, Mr. Parchester believed. The Bishop impressed him as being quite angrily resolved not to believe. And for the first time in his career Mr. Parchester realised just how much jealous hostility a beautiful, fluent, and popular preacher may arouse in the minds of the hierarchy. It wasn't, he felt, a conversation. It was like flinging oneself into the paddock of a bull that has been anxious to gore one.

"Inevitably," said the Bishop, "this theatricalism, this star-turn business, with its extreme spiritual excitements, its exaggerated soul crisis and all the rest of it, leads to such a breakdown as afflicts you. Inevitably. You were at least wise to come to me. I can see you are only in the beginning of your trouble, that already in your mind fresh hallucinations are gathering to overwhelm you, voices, special charges and missions, strange revelations... I wish I had the power to suspend you right away, to send you into retreat..."

Mr. Parchester made a violent effort to control himself. "But I tell you," he said, "that I saw God!" He added, as if to reassure himself: "More plainly, more certainly, than I see you."

"Of course," said the Bishop, "this is how strange new sects come into existence; this is how false prophets spring out of the bosom of the Church. Loose-minded, excitable men of your stamp—"

Mr. Parchester, to his own astonishment, burst into tears. "But I tell you," he wept, "He is here. I have seen. I know."

"Don't talk such nonsense!" said the Bishop. "There is no one here but you and I!"

Mr. Parchester expostulated. "But," he protested, "He is omnipresent."

The Bishop controlled an expression of impatience. "It is characteristic of your condition," he said, "that you are unable to distinguish between a matter of fact and a spiritual truth... Now listen to me. If you value your sanity and public decency and the discipline of the Church, go right home from here and go to bed. Send for Broadhays, who will prescribe a safe sedative. And read something calming and graceful and purifying. For my own part, I should be disposed to recommend the 'Life of Saint Francis of Assisi'..."

11

Unhappily Mr. Parchester did not go home. He went out from the Bishop's residence stunned and amazed, and suddenly upon his desolation came the thought of Mrs. Munbridge...

She would understand...

He was shown up to her own little sitting-room. She had already gone up to her room to dress, but when she heard that he had called, and wanted very greatly to see her, she slipped on a loose, beautiful tea-gown *négligé* thing, and hurried to him. He tried to tell her everything, but she only kept saying "There! there!" She was sure he wanted a cup of tea, he looked so pale and exhausted. She rang to have the tea equipage brought back; she put the dear saint in an armchair by the fire; she put cushions about him, and ministered to him. And when she began partially to comprehend what he had experienced, she suddenly realised that she too had experienced it. That vision had been a brain-wave between their two linked and sympathetic brains. And that thought glowed in her as she brewed his tea with her own hands. He had been weeping! How tenderly he felt all these things! He was more sensitive than a woman. What madness to have expected understanding from a Bishop! But that was just like his unworldliness. He was not fit to take care of himself. A wave of tenderness carried her away. "Here is your tea!" she said, bending over him, and fully conscious of her fragrant warmth and sweetness, and suddenly she could never afterwards explain why she was so, she was moved to kiss him on his brow...

How indescribable is the comfort of a true-hearted womanly friend! The safety of it! The consolation...!

About half-past seven that evening Mr. Parchester returned to his own home, and Brompton admitted him. Brompton was relieved to find his employer looking quite restored and ordinary again. "Brompton," said Mr. Parchester, "I will not have the usual dinner tonight. Just a single mutton cutlet and one of those quarter-bottles of Perrier Jouet on a tray in my study. I shall have to finish my sermon tonight."

(And he had promised Mrs. Munbridge he would preach that sermon specially for her.)

12

And as it was with Mr. Parchester and Brompton and Mrs. Munbridge, and the taxi-driver and the policeman and the little old lady and the automobile mechanics and Mr. Parchester's secretary and the Bishop, so it was with all the rest of the world. If a thing is sufficiently strange and great no one will perceive it. Men will go on in their own ways though one rose from the dead to tell them that the Kingdom of Heaven was at hand, though the Kingdom itself and all its glory became visible, blinding their eyes. They and their ways are one. Men will go on in their ways as rabbits will go on feeding in their hutches within a hundred yards of a battery of artillery. For rabbits are rabbits, and made to eat and breed, and men are human beings and creatures of habit and custom and prejudice; and what has made them, what will judge them, what will destroy them—they may turn their eyes to it at times as the rabbits will glance at the concussion of the guns, but it will never draw them away from eating their lettuce and sniffing after their does...

THE WILD ASSES OF THE DEVIL

1

There was once an Author who pursued fame and prosperity in a pleasant villa on the south coast of England. He wrote stories of an acceptable nature and rejoiced in a growing public esteem, carefully offending no one and seeking only to please. He had married under circumstances of qualified and tolerable romance a lady who wrote occasional but otherwise regular verse, he was the father of a little daughter, whose reported sayings added much to his popularity, and some of the very best people in the land asked him to dinner. He was a deputy-lieutenant and a friend of the Prime Minister, a literary knighthood was no remote possibility for him, and even the Nobel Prize, given a sufficient longevity, was not altogether beyond his hopes. And this amount of prosperity had not betrayed him into any un-English pride. He remembered that manliness and simplicity which are expected from authors. He smoked pipes and not the excellent cigars he could have afforded. He kept his hair cut and never posed. He did not hold himself aloof from people of the inferior and less successful classes. He habitually travelled third class in order to study the characters he put into his delightful novels; he went for long walks and sat in inns, accosting people; he drew out his gardener. And though he worked steadily, he did not give up the care of his body, which threatened a certain plumpness and what is more to the point, a localised plumpness, not generally spread over the system but exaggerating the anterior equator. This expansion was his only care. He thought about fitness and played tennis, and every day, wet or fine, he went for at least an hour's walk...

Yet this man, so representative of Edwardian literature—for it is in the reign of good King Edward the story begins—in spite of his enviable achievements and prospects, was doomed to the most exhausting and dubious adventures before his life came to its unhonoured end...

Because I have not told you everything about him. Sometimes—in the morning sometimes—he would be irritable and have quarrels with his shaving things, and there were extraordinary moods when it would seem to him that living quite beautifully in a pleasant villa and being well-off and famous, and writing books that were always good-humoured and grammatical and a little distinguished in an inoffensive way, was about as boring and intolerable a life as any creature with a soul to be damned could possibly pursue. Which shows only that God in putting him together had not forgotten that viscus the liver which is usual on such occasions...

The winter at the seaside is less agreeable and more bracing than the summer, and there were days when this Author had almost to force himself through the wholesome, necessary routines of his life, when the south-west wind savaged his villa and roared in the chimneys and slapped its windows with gustful of rain and promised to wet that Author thoroughly and exasperatingly down his neck and round his wrists and ankles directly he put his nose outside his door. And the grey waves he saw from his window came rolling inshore under the hurrying grey rain-bursts, line after line, to smash along the undercliff into vast, feathering fountains of foam and sud and send a salt-tasting spin-drift into his eyes. But manfully he would put on his puttees and his waterproof cape and his biggest brierwood pipe, and out he would go into the whurry-balloo of it all, knowing that so he would be all the brighter for his nice story-writing after tea.

On such a day he went out. He went out very resolutely along the seaside gardens of gravel and tamarisk and privet, resolved to oblige himself to go right past the harbour and up to the top of the east cliff before ever he turned his face back to the comforts of fire and wife and tea and buttered toast...

And somewhere, perhaps half a mile away from home, he became aware of a queer character trying to keep abreast of him.

His impression was of a very miserable black man in the greasy, blue-black garments of a stoker, a lascar probably from a steamship in the harbour, and going with a sort of lame hobble.

As he passed this individual the Author had a transitory thought of how much Authors don't know in the world, how much, for instance, this shivering, cringing body might be hiding within itself, of inestimable value as "local colour" if only one could get hold of it for "putting into" one's large acceptable novels. Why doesn't one sometimes tap these sources? Kipling, for example, used to do so, with most successful results...And then the Author became aware that this enigma was hurrying to overtake him. He slackened his pace...

The creature wasn't asking for a light; it was begging for a box of matches. And what was odd, in quite good English.

The Author surveyed the beggar and slapped his pockets. Never had he seen so miserable a face. It was by no means a prepossessing face, with its aquiline nose, its sloping brows, its dark, deep, bloodshot eyes much too close together, its V-shaped, dishonest mouth and drenched chin-tuft. And yet it was attractively animal and pitiful. The idea flashed suddenly into the Author's head: "Why not, instead of going on, thinking emptily, through this beastly weather—why not take this man back home now, to the warm, dry study, and give him a hot drink and something to smoke, and *draw him out?*"

Get something technical and first-hand that would rather score off Kipling.

"It's damnably cold!" he shouted, in a sort of hearty, forecastle voice.

"It's worse than that," said the strange stoker.

"It's a hell of a day!" said the Author, more forcible than ever.

"Don't remind me of hell," said the stoker, in a voice of inappeasable regret.

The Author slapped his pockets again. "You've got an infernal cold. Look here, my man—confound it! would you like a hot grog...?"

2

The scene shifts to the Author's study—a blazing coal fire, the stoker sitting dripping and steaming before it, with his feet inside the fender, while the Author fusses about the room, directing the preparation of hot drinks. The Author is acutely aware not only of the stoker but of himself. The stoker has probably never been in the home of an Author before; he is probably awestricken at the array of books, at the comfort, convenience, and efficiency of the home, at the pleasant personality entertaining him . . . Meanwhile the Author does not forget that the stoker is material, is "copy," is being watched, *observed*. So he poses and watches, until presently he forgets to pose in his astonishment at the thing he is observing. Because this stoker is rummier than a stoker ought to be—

He does not simply accept a hot drink; he informs his host just how hot the drink must be to satisfy him.

"Isn't there something you could put in it—something called red pepper? I've tasted that once or twice. It's good. If you could put in a bit of red pepper."

"If you can stand that sort of thing?"

"And if there isn't much water, can't you set light to the stuff? Or let me drink it boiling, out of a pannikin or something? Pepper and all."

Wonderful fellows, these stokers! The Author went to the bell and asked for red pepper.

And then as he came back to the fire he saw something that he instantly dismissed as an optical illusion, as a mirage effect of the clouds of steam his guest was disengaging. The stoker was sitting, all crouched up, as close over the fire as he could contrive; and he was holding his black hands, not to the fire but *in* the fire, holding them pressed flat against two red, glowing masses of coal . . . He glanced over his shoulder at the Author with a guilty start, and then instantly the Author perceived that the hands were five or six inches away from the coal.

Then came smoking. The Author produced one of his big cigars— for although a conscientious pipe-smoker himself he gave people cigars; and then, again struck by something odd, he went off into a corner of the room where a little oval mirror gave him a means of watching the stoker undetected. And this is what he saw.

He saw the stoker, after a furtive glance at him, deliberately turn the cigar round, place the lighted end in his mouth, inhale strongly, and blow a torrent of sparks and smoke out of his nose. His firelit face as he did this expressed a diabolical relief. Then very hastily he reversed the cigar again, and turned round to look at the Author. The Author turned slowly towards him.

"You like that cigar?" he asked, after one of those mutual pauses that break down a sentence.

"It's admirable."

"Why do you smoke it the other way round?"

The stoker perceived he was caught. "It's a stokehole trick," he said. "Do you mind if I do it? I didn't think you saw."

"Pray smoke just as you like," said the Author, and advanced to watch the operation.

It was exactly like the fire-eater at the village fair. The man stuck the burning cigar into his mouth and blew sparks out of his nostrils. "Ah!" he said, with a note of genuine satisfaction. And then, with the cigar still burning in the corner of his mouth, he turned to the fire and *began to rearrange the burning coals with his hands* so as to pile up a great glowing mass. He picked up flaming and white-hot lumps as one might pick up lumps of sugar. The Author watched him, dumbfounded.

"I say!" he cried. "You stokers get a bit tough."

The stoker dropped the glowing piece of coal in his hand. "I forgot," he said, and sat back a little.

"Isn't that a bit—*extra?*" asked the Author, regarding him. "Isn't that some sort of trick?"

"We get so tough down there," said the stoker, and paused discreetly as the servant came in with the red pepper.

"Now you can drink," said the Author, and set himself to mix a drink of a pungency that he would have considered murderous ten minutes before. When he had done, the stoker reached over and added more red pepper.

"I don't quite see how it is your hand doesn't burn," said the Author as the stoker drank. The stoker shook his head over the uptilted glass.

"Incombustible," he said, putting it down. "Could I have just a tiny drop more? Just brandy and pepper, if you *don't* mind. Set alight. I don't care for water except when it's super-heated steam."

And as the Author poured out another stiff glass of this incandescent brew, the stoker put up his hand and scratched the matted black hair over his temple. Then instantly he desisted and sat looking wickedly at the Author, while the Author stared at him aghast. For at the corner of his square, high, narrow forehead, revealed for an instant by the thrusting back of the hair, a curious stumpy excrescence had been visible; and the top of his ear—he had a pointed top to his ear!

"A-a-a-a-h!" said the Author, with dilated eyes.

"A-a-a-a-h!" said the stoker, in hopeless distress.

"But you aren't—"

"I know—I know I'm not. I know ... I'm a devil. A poor, lost, home-less devil."

And suddenly, with a gesture of indescribable despair, the apparent stoker buried his face in his hands and burst into tears.

"Only man who's ever been decently kind to me," he sobbed. "And now—you'll chuck me out again into the beastly wet and cold ... Beautiful fire ... Nice drink ... Almost home-like ... Just to tor-ment me ... Boo-ooh!"

And let it be recorded to the credit of our little Author, that he did overcome his momentary horror, that he did go quickly round the table, and that he patted that dirty stoker's shoulder.

"There!" he said. "There! Don't mind my rudeness. Have another nice drink. Have a hell of a drink. I won't turn you out if you're un-happy—on a day like this. Have just a mouthful of pepper, man, and pull yourself together."

And suddenly the poor devil caught hold of his arm. "Nobody good to me," he sobbed. "Nobody good to me." And his tears ran down over the Author's plump little hand—scalding tears.

3

All really wonderful things happen rather suddenly and without any great emphasis upon their wonderfulness, and this was no exception to the general rule. This Author went on comforting his devil as though this was nothing more than a chance encounter with an unhappy child, and the devil let his grief and discomfort have vent in a manner that seemed at the time as natural as anything could be. He was clearly a devil of feeble character and uncertain purpose, much broken down by harshness and cruelty, and it throws a curious light upon the gen-eral state of misconception with regard to matters diabolical that it came as a quite pitiful discovery to our Author that a devil could be unhappy and heart-broken. For a long time his most earnest and per-sistent questioning could gather nothing except that his guest was an exile from a land of great warmth and considerable entertainment, and it was only after considerable further applications of brandy and pepper that the sobbing confidences of the poor creature grew into the form of a coherent and understandable narrative.

And then it became apparent that this person was one of the very lowest types of infernal denizen, and that his role in the dark realms of Dis had been that of watcher and minder of a herd of sinister beings hitherto unknown to our Author, the Devil's Wild Asses, which pastured in a stretch of meadows near the Styx. They were, he gathered, unruly, dangerous, and enterprising beasts, amenable only to a certain formula of expletives, which instantly reduced them to obedience. These expletives the stoker-devil would not repeat; to do so except when actually addressing one of the Wild Asses would, he explained, involve torments of the most terrible description. The bare thought of them gave him a shivering fit. But he gave the Author to understand that to crack these curses as one drove the Wild Asses to and from their grazing on the Elysian fields was a by no means disagreeable amusement. The ass-herds would try who could crack the loudest until the welkin rang.

And speaking of these things, the poor creature gave a picture of diabolical life that impressed the Author as by no means unpleasant for any one with a suitable constitution. It was like the Idylls of Theocritus done in fire; the devils drove their charges along burning lanes and sat gossiping in hedges of flames, rejoicing in the warm dry breezes (which it seems are rendered peculiarly bracing by the faint flavour of brimstone in the air), and watching the harpies and furies and witches circling in the perpetual afterglow of that inferior sky. And ever and again there would be holidays, and one would take one's lunch and wander over the sulphur craters picking flowers of sulphur or fishing for the souls of usurers and publishers and house-agents and land-agents in the lakes of boiling pitch. It was good sport, for the usurers and publishers and house-agents and land-agents were always eager to be caught; they crowded round the hooks and fought violently for the bait, and protested vehemently and entertainingly against the Rules and Regulations that compelled their instant return to the lake of fire.

And sometimes when he was on holiday this particular devil would go through the saltpetre dunes, where the witches' brooms grow and the blasted heath is in flower, to the landing-place of the ferry whence the Great Road runs through the shops and banks of the Via Dolorosa to the New Judgement Hall, and watch the crowds of damned arriving by the steam ferry-boats of the Consolidated Charon Company. This steamboat-gazing seems about as popular down there as it is at Folkestone. Almost every day notable people arrive, and, as the devils are very well informed about terrestrial affairs—for of course all the earthly newspapers go straight to hell—whatever else could one expect?—they get ovations of an almost undergraduate intensity. At times you can hear their cheering or booing, as the case may be, right away on the pastures where the Wild Asses feed. And that had been this particular devil's undoing.

He had always been interested in the career of the Rt. Hon. W. E. Gladstone...

He was minding the Wild Asses. He knew the risks. He knew the penalties. But when he heard the vast uproar, when he heard the eager voices in the lane of fire saying, "It's Gladstone at last!" when he saw how quietly and unsuspiciously the Wild Asses cropped their pasture, the temptation was too much. He slipped away. He saw the great Englishman landed after a slight struggle. He joined in the outcry of "Speech! Speech!" He heard the first delicious promise of a Home Rule movement which should break the last feeble links of Celestial Control...

And meanwhile the Wild Asses escaped—according to the rules and the prophecies...

4

The little Author sat and listened to this tale of a wonder that never for a moment struck him as incredible. And outside his rain-lashed window the strung-out fishing smacks pitched and rolled on their way home to Folkestone harbour...

The Wild Asses escaped.

They got away to the world. And his superior officers took the poor herdsman and tried him and bullied him and passed this judgement upon him: that he must go to the earth and find the Wild Asses, and say to them that certain string of oaths that otherwise must never be repeated, and so control them and bring them back to hell. That—or else one pinch of salt on their tails. It did not matter which. One by one he must bring them back, driving them by spell and curse to the cattle-boat of the ferry. And until he had caught and brought them all back he might never return again to the warmth and comfort of his accustomed life. That was his sentence and punishment. And they put him into a shrapnel shell and fired him out among the stars, and when he had a little recovered he pulled himself together and made his way to the world.

But he never found his Wild Asses and after a little time he gave up trying.

He gave up trying because the Wild Asses, once they had got out of control, developed the most amazing gifts. They could, for instance, disguise themselves with any sort of human shape, and the only way in which they differed then from a normal human being was—according to the printed paper of instructions that had been given to their custodian when he was fired out—that "their general conduct remains that of a Wild Ass of the Devil."

"And what interpretation can we put upon *that*?" he asked the listening Author.

And there was one night in the year—Walpurgis Night—when the Wild Asses became visibly great black wild asses and kicked up their hind legs and brayed. They had to. "But then, of course," said the devil, "they would take care to shut themselves up somewhere when they felt that coming on."

Like most weak characters, the stoker devil was intensely egotistical. He was anxious to dwell upon his own miseries and discomforts and difficulties and the general injustice of his treatment, and he was careless and casually indicative about the peculiarities of the Wild Asses, the matter which most excited and interested the Author. He bored on with his doleful story, and the Author had to interrupt with questions again and again in order to get any clear idea of the situation.

The devil's main excuse for his nervelessness was his profound ignorance of human nature. "So far as I can see," he said, "they might all be Wild Asses. I tried it once—"

"Tried what?"

"The formula. You know."

"Yes?"

"On a man named Sir Edward Carson."

"Well?"

"Ugh!" said the devil.

"Punishment?"

"Don't speak of it. He was just a professional lawyer-politician who had lost his sense of values...How was *I* to know?...But our people certainly know how to hurt..."

After that it would seem this poor devil desisted absolutely from any attempt to recover his lost charges. He just tried to live for the moment and make his earthly existence as tolerable as possible. It was clear he hated the world. He found it cold, wet, draughty... "I can't understand why everybody insists upon living outside of it," he said. "If you went inside—"

He sought warmth and dryness. For a time he found a kind of contentment in charge of the upcast furnace of a mine, and then he was superseded by an electric-fan. While in this position he read a vivid account of the intense heat in the Red Sea, and he was struck by the idea that if he could get a job as stoker upon an Indian liner he might snatch some days of real happiness during that portion of the voyage. For some time his natural ineptitude prevented his realising this project, but at last, after some bitter experiences of homelessness during a London December, he had been able to ship on an Indiaward boat— only to get stranded in Folkestone in consequence of a propeller breakdown. And so here he was!

He paused.

"But about these Wild Asses?" said the Author.

The mournful, dark eyes looked at him hopelessly.

"Mightn't they do a lot of mischief?" asked the Author.

"They'll do no end of mischief," said the despondent devil.

"Ultimately you'll catch it for that?"

"Ugh!" said the stoker, trying not to think of it.

5

Now the spirit of romantic adventure slumbers in the most unexpected places, and I have already told you of our plump Author's discontents. He had been like a smouldering bomb for some years. Now, he burst out. He suddenly became excited, energetic, stimulating, uplifting.

He stood over the drooping devil.

"But my dear chap!" he said. "You must pull yourself together. You must do better than this. These confounded brutes may be doing all sorts of mischief. While you—shirk..."

And so on. Real ginger.

"If I had some one to go with me. Some one who knew his way about."

The Author took whisky in the excitement of the moment. He began to move very rapidly about his room and make short, sharp gestures. You know how this sort of emotion wells up at times. "We must work from some central place," said the Author. "To begin with, London perhaps."

It was not two hours later that they started, this Author and this devil he had taken to himself, upon a mission. They went out in overcoats and warm underclothing—the Author gave the devil a thorough outfit, a double lot of Jaeger's extra thick—and they were resolved to find the Wild Asses of the Devil and send them back to hell, or at least the Author was, in the shortest possible time. In the picture you will see him with a field-glass slung under his arm, the better to watch suspected cases; in his pocket, wrapped in oiled paper, is a lot of salt to use if by chance he finds a Wild Ass when the devil and his string of oaths is not at hand. So he started. And when he had caught and done for the Wild Asses, then the Author supposed that he would come back to his nice little villa and his nice little wife, and to his little daughter who said the amusing things, and to his popularity, his large gilt-edged popularity, and—except for an added prestige—be just exactly the man he had always been. Little knowing that whosoever takes unto himself a devil and goes out upon a quest, goes out upon a quest from which there is no returning—

Nevermore.

Answer to Prayer

The Archbishop was perplexed by his own state of mind. Maybe the shadow of age was falling upon him, he thought, maybe he had been overworking, maybe the situation had been too complex for him and he was feeling the reality of a failure without seeing it plainly as a definable fact. But his nerve, which had never failed him hitherto, was failing him now. In small things as in important matters he no longer showed the quick decisiveness that had hitherto been the envy of his fellow-ecclesiastics and the admiration of his friends. He doubted now before he went upstairs or downstairs, with a curious feeling that he might find something unexpected on the landing. He hesitated before he rang a bell, with a vague uncertainty of who or what might appear. Before he took up the letters his secretary had opened for him he had a faint twinge of apprehension.

Had he after all done something wrong or acted in a mistaken spirit?

People who had always been nice to him showed a certain coolness, people from whom he would have least expected it. His secretaries, he knew, were keeping back "open letters" and grossly abusive comments. The reassurances and encouragements that flowed in to him were anything but reassuring, because their volume and their tone reflected what was hidden from him on the other side. Had he, at the end of his long, tortuous and hitherto quite dignified career, made a howler?

There was no one on earth to whom he could confide his trouble. He had always been a man who kept his own counsel. But now, if only he could find understanding, sympathy, endorsement! If he could really put things as he saw them, if he could simplify the whole confused affair down to essentials and make his stand plain and clear.

Prayer?

If anyone else had come to him in this sort of quandary, he would have told him at once to pray. If it was a woman he would have patted the shoulder gently, as an elderly man may do, and he would have said very softly in that rich kind voice of his, "Try Prayer, my dear. Try Prayer."

Physician heal thyself. Why not try prayer?

He stood hesitatingly between his apartments and his little private oratory. He stood in what was his habitual children's-service attitude with his hands together in front of him, his head a little on one side and something faintly bland and whimsical about him. It came to him that he himself had not made a personal and particular appeal to God for many years. It had seemed unnecessary. It had indeed been unnecessary. He had of course said his prayers with the utmost regularity, not only in the presence of others, but, being essentially an honest man, even when he was alone. He had never cheated about prayer. He had felt it was a purifying and beneficial process, no more to be missed than cleaning his teeth, but his sense of a definite hearer, listening at the other end of the telephone, so to speak, behind the veil, had always been a faint one. The reception away there was in the Absolute, in Eternity, beyond the stars. Which indeed left the church conveniently free to take an unembarrassed course of action...

But in this particular tangle, the Archbishop wanted something more definite. If for once, he did not trouble about style and manner...

If he put the case simply, quite simply, just as he saw it, and remained very still on his knees, wouldn't he presently find this neuralgic fretting of his mind abating, and that assurance, that clear self-assurance that had hitherto been his strength, returning to him? He must not be in the least oily—they had actually been calling him oily—he must be perfectly direct and simple and fearless. He must pray straightforwardly to the silence as one mind to another.

It was a little like the practice of some Dissenters and Quakers, but maybe it would be none the less effective on that account.

Yes, he would pray.

Slowly he sank to his knees and put his hands together. He was touched by a sort of childish trustfulness in his own attitude. "Oh God," he began, and paused.

He paused, and a sense of awful imminence, a monstrous awe, gripped him. And then he heard a voice.

It was not a harsh voice, but it was a clear strong voice. There was nothing about it still or small. It was neither friendly nor hostile; it was brisk.

"Yes," said the voice. *"What is it?"*

They found His Grace in the morning. He had slipped off the steps on which he had been kneeling and lay, sprawling on the crimson carpet. Plainly his death had been instantaneous.

But instead of the serenity, the almost fatuous serenity, that was his habitual expression, his countenance, by some strange freak of nature, displayed an extremity of terror and dismay.

PART SIX

PSYCHO-SOCIAL
SCIENCE FICTION

INTRODUCTION

I don't like to describe these stories with such a fancy polysyllabic label, but I don't know how else to highlight the amazing variety and originality of Wells's genre writing. Invasions from Mars, time machines, voyages to the moon, invisible men, visions of war and cataclysm and of brave new worlds, all these are his well-known legacy to us. These last two stories enrich that legacy with a different wealth.

In "The Queer Story of Brownlow's Newspaper," which was written in 1932, Wells meets the challenge of living through times of immense and rapid social and cultural change by exaggerating it—imagining a leap forty years into the future, and a tantalizing glimpse of that future.

Now, science fiction is always doing this, and always falling flat on its face, too. Science fiction that has "passed its date" should be unreadable, an object of pity and derision—how *could* they have thought the Cold War would go on forever? how *could* they have thought spaceship crews would all be white, male, and English-speaking? and so on. But the odd thing is, if a story has intelligence and passion, it can pass its date, have all its predictions belied, and yet lose nothing in interest. Orwell's *Nineteen Eighty-Four* is a case in point that almost settles the issue by itself. The fact is, "the future" in science fiction is always more or less a metaphor for the writer's present. What is fascinating now in a story like "Brownlow's Newspaper" is the interplay between Wells's present, which is our long past—Wells's ingeniously imagined future, which is our more recent past—and our present, which we perceive, for a moment, as amazingly contingent....

Moreover, the story has a delectable end-twist.

As for "The Country of the Blind," I incline to think this is the best of all Wells's short stories. I call it science fiction but it could be called fable or fantasy or, best of all, simply fiction. The theme of seeing, of vision, which runs so strong through this whole book, here again is the keynote. Wells published it first in 1904, and again in 1913; he reprinted it with a radically changed ending in 1939. The text given here, for most of the story, is that of the revision. As Wells said, "The two versions open with practically identical incidents, which I have never wished to alter; they run parallel until the distant mountain masses crack." Both endings are given here, the older one first, then the revision; for though the revision is more powerful, the original remains valid, and the difference is both interesting and moving.

Omitting sentences that would give away the story, this is what Wells himself said, in his introduction to the 1939 edition, about why he rewrote it:

> It has been changed because there has been a change in the atmosphere of life about us. In 1904 the stress is upon the spiritual isolation of those who see more keenly than their fellows and the tragedy of their incommunicable appreciation of life ... In the later story vision becomes something altogether more tragic; it is no longer a story of disregarded loveliness and release; the visionary sees destruction sweeping down upon the whole blind world he has come to endure and even to love; he sees it plain, and he can do nothing to save it from its fate.

It is no wonder that between 1904 and 1939 the outlook of this visionary writer became more tragic. It is no wonder that in the year 1939, on the eve of Hitler's war, Wells felt that to see destruction coming, to speak of it, to cry out warnings, might be as vain as trying to stop an avalanche with words. A hard lesson for an old man who had tried all his life to show people the danger of blind unreason, the worlds of promise and beauty they might see if they'd only open the eyes of their intelligence and their imagination.

The Queer Story of Brownlow's Newspaper

1

I call this a Queer Story because it is a story without an explanation. When I first heard it, in scraps, from Brownlow I found it queer and incredible. But—it refuses to remain incredible. After resisting and then questioning and scrutinising and falling back before the evidence, after rejecting all his evidence as an elaborate mystification and refusing to hear any more about it, and then being drawn to reconsider it by an irresistible curiosity and so going through it all again, I have been forced to the conclusion that Brownlow, so far as he can tell the truth, has been telling the truth. But it remains queer truth, queer and exciting to the imagination. The more credible his story becomes the queerer it is. It troubles my mind. I am fevered by it, infected not with germs but with notes of interrogation and unsatisfied curiosity.

Brownlow, is, I admit, a cheerful spirit. I have known him tell lies. But I have never known him do anything so elaborate and sustained as this affair, if it is a mystification, would have to be. He is incapable of anything so elaborate and sustained. He is too lazy and easy-going for anything of the sort. And he would have laughed. At some stage he would have laughed and given the whole thing away. He has nothing to gain by keeping it up. His honour is not in the case either way. And after all there is his bit of newspaper in evidence—and the scrap of an addressed wrapper...

348 · *Psycho-Social Science Fiction*

I realise it will damage this story for many readers that it opens with Brownlow in a state very definitely on the gayer side of sobriety. He was not in a mood for cool and calculated observation, much less for accurate record. He was seeing things in an exhilarated manner. He was disposed to see them and greet them cheerfully and let them slip by out of attention. The limitations of time and space lay lightly upon him. It was after midnight. He had been dining with friends.

I have inquired what friends—and satisfied myself upon one or two obvious possibilities of that dinner party. They were, he said to me, "just friends. They hadn't anything to do with it." I don't usually push past an assurance of this sort, but I made an exception in this case. I watched my man and took a chance of repeating the question. There was nothing out of the ordinary about that dinner party, unless it was the fact that it was an unusually good dinner party. The host was Red-path Baynes, the solicitor, and the dinner was in his house in St. John's Wood. Gifford, of the *Evening Telegraph,* whom I know slightly, was, I found, present, and from him I got all I wanted to know. There was much bright and discursive talk and Brownlow had been inspired to give an imitation of his aunt, Lady Clitherholme, reproving an incon-siderate plumber during some re-building operations at Clitherholme. This early memory had been received with considerable merriment—he was always very good about his aunt, Lady Clitherholme—and Brownlow had departed obviously elated by this little social success and the general geniality of the occasion. Had they talked, I asked, about the Future, or Einstein, or J. W. Dunne, or any such high and se-rious topic at that party? They had not. Had they discussed the mod-ern newspaper? No. There had been nobody whom one could call a practical joker at this party, and Brownlow had gone off alone in a taxi. That is what I was most desirous of knowing. He had been duly deliv-ered by his taxi at the main entrance to Sussex Court.

Nothing untoward is to be recorded of his journey in the lift to the fifth floor of Sussex Court. The liftman on duty noted nothing excep-tional. I asked if Brownlow said, "Good-night." The liftman does not remember. "Usually he says Night O," reflected the liftman—mani-festly doing his best and with nothing particular to recall. And there the fruits of my inquiries about the condition of Brownlow on this particular evening conclude. The rest of the story comes directly from him. My investigations arrive only at this: he was certainly not drunk.

But he was lifted a little out of our normal harsh and grinding contact with the immediate realities of existence. Life was glowing softly and warmly in him, and the unexpected could happen brightly, easily, and acceptably.

He went down the long passage with its red carpet, its clear light, and its occasional oaken doors, each with its artistic brass number. I have been down that passage with him on several occasions. It was his custom to enliven that corridor by raising his hat gravely as he passed each entrance, saluting his unknown and invisible neighbours, addressing them softly but distinctly by playful if sometimes slightly indecorous names of his own devising, expressing good wishes or paying them little compliments.

He came at last to his own door, number 49, and let himself in without serious difficulty. He switched on his hall light. Scattered on the polished oak floor and invading his Chinese carpet were a number of letters and circulars, the evening's mail. His parlourmaid-housekeeper, who slept in a room in another part of the building, had been taking her evening out, or these letters would have been gathered up and put on the desk in his bureau. As it was, they lay on the floor. He closed his door behind him or it closed of its own accord; he took off his coat and wrap, placed his hat on the head of the Greek charioteer whose bust adorns his hall, and set himself to pick up his letters.

This also he succeeded in doing without misadventure. He was a little annoyed to miss the *Evening Standard*. It is his custom, he says, to subscribe for the afternoon edition of the *Star* to read at tea-time and also for the final edition of the *Evening Standard* to turn over the last thing at night, if only on account of Low's cartoon. He gathered up all these envelopes and packets and took them with him into his little sitting-room. There he turned on the electric heater, mixed himself a weak whisky-and-soda, went to his bedroom to put on soft slippers and replace his smoking jacket by a frogged jacket of llama wool, returned to his sitting-room, lit a cigarette, and sat down in his armchair by the reading lamp to examine his correspondence. He recalls all these details very exactly. They were routines he had repeated scores of times.

Brownlow's is not a preoccupied mind; it goes out to things. He is one of those buoyant extroverts who open and read all their letters and circulars whenever they can get hold of them. In the daytime his secretary intercepts and deals with most of them, but at night he escapes from her control and does what he pleases, that is to say, he opens everything.

He ripped up various envelopes. There was a formal acknowledgement of a business letter he had dictated the day before, there was a letter from his solicitor asking for some details about a settlement he was making, there was an offer from some unknown gentleman with an aristocratic name to lend him money on his note of hand alone, and there was a notice about a proposed new wing to his club. "Same old stuff," he sighed. "Same old stuff. What bores they all are!" He was always hoping, like every man who is proceeding across the plains of middle age, that his correspondence would contain agreeable surprises—and it never did. Then, as he put it to me, *inter alia,* he picked up the remarkable newspaper.

2

It was different in appearance from an ordinary newspaper, but not so different as not to be recognisable as a newspaper, and he was surprised, he says, not to have observed it before. It was enclosed in a wrapper of pale green, but it was unstamped; apparently it had been delivered not by the postman, but by some other hand. (This wrapper still exists; I have seen it.) He had already torn it off before he noted that he was not the addressee.

For a moment or so he remained looking at this address, which struck him as just a little odd. It was printed in rather unusual type: "Evan O'Hara, Mr., Sussex Court 49."

"Wrong name," said Mr. Brownlow; "right address. Rummy. Sussex Court 49 . . . 'Spose he's got *my Evening Standard* . . . 'Change no robbery."

He put the torn wrapper with his unanswered letters and opened out the newspaper.

The title of the paper was printed in large slightly ornamental black-green letters that might have come from a kindred fount to that responsible for the address. But, as he read it, it was the *Evening Standard!* Or, at least, it was the "Even Standrd." "Silly," said Brownlow. "It's some damn Irish paper. Can't spell—anything—these Irish . . ."

He had, I think, a passing idea, suggested perhaps by the green wrapper and the green ink, that it was a lottery stunt from Dublin.

Still, if there was anything to read he meant to read it. He surveyed the front page. Across this ran a streamer headline: "WILTON BORING REACHES SEVEN MILES: SUCCES ASSURED."

"No," said Brownlow. "It must be oil…Illiterate lot these oil chaps—leave out the 's' in 'success.' "

He held the paper down on his knee for a moment, reinforced himself by a drink, took and lit a second cigarette, and then leant back in his chair to take a dispassionate view of any oil-share pushing that might be afoot.

But it wasn't an affair of oil. It was, it began to dawn upon him, something stranger than oil. He found himself surveying a real evening newspaper, which was dealing, so far as he could see at the first onset, with the affairs of another world.

He had for a moment a feeling as though he and his armchair and his little sitting-room were afloat in a vast space and then it all seemed to become firm and solid again.

This thing in his hands was plainly and indisputably a printed newspaper. It was a little odd in its letterpress, and it didn't feel or rustle like ordinary paper, but newspaper it was. It was printed in either three or four columns—for the life of him he cannot remember which—and there were column headlines under the page streamer. It had a sort of art-nouveau affair at the bottom of one column that might be an advertisement (it showed a woman in an impossibly big hat), and in the upper left-hand corner was an unmistakable weather chart of Western Europe, with *coloured* isobars, or isotherms, or whatever they are, and the inscription: "Tomorrow's Weather."

And then he remarked the date. The date was November 10th, 1971!

"Steady on," said Brownlow. "Damitall! Steady on."

He held the paper sideways, and then straight again. The date remained November 10th, 1971.

He got up in a state of immense perplexity and put the paper down. For a moment he felt a little afraid of it. He rubbed his forehead. "Haven't been doing a Rip Van Winkle, by any chance, Brownlow, my boy?" he said. He picked up the paper again, walked out into his hall and looked at himself in the hall mirror. He was reassured to see no signs of advancing age, but the expression of mingled consternation and amazement upon his flushed face struck him suddenly as being undignified and unwarrantable. He laughed at himself, but not uncontrollably. Then he stared blankly at that familiar countenance. "I must be half-way *tordu*," he said, that being his habitual facetious translation of "screwed." On the console table was a little respectable-looking adjustable calendar bearing witness that the date was November 10th, 1931.

"D'you see?" he said, shaking the queer newspaper at it reproachfully. "I ought to have spotted you for a hoax ten minutes ago. 'Moosing trick, to say the least of it. I suppose they've made Low editor for a night, and he's had this idea. Eh?"

He felt he had been taken in, but that the joke was a good one. And, with quite unusual anticipations of entertainment, he returned to his armchair. A good idea it was, a paper forty years ahead. Good fun if it was well done. For a time nothing but the sounds of a newspaper being turned over and Brownlow's breathing can have broken the silence of the flat.

3

Regarded as an imaginative creation, he found the thing almost too well done. Every time he turned a page he expected the sheet to break out into laughter and give the whole thing away. But it did nothing of the kind. From being a mere quip, it became an immense and amusing, if perhaps a little over-elaborate lark. And then, as a lark, it passed from stage to stage of incredibility until, as any thing but the thing it professed to be, it was incredible altogether. It must have cost far more than an ordinary number. All sorts of colours were used, and suddenly he came upon illustrations that went beyond amazement; they were in the colours of reality. Never in all his life had he seen such colour printing—and the buildings and scenery and costumes in the pictures were strange. Strange and yet credible. They were colour photographs of actuality forty years from now. He could not believe anything else of them. Doubt could not exist in their presence.

His mind had swung back, away from the stunt-number idea altogether. This paper in his hand would not simply be costly beyond dreaming to produce. At any price it could not be produced. All this present world could not produce such an object as this paper he held in his hand. He was quite capable of realising that.

He sat turning the sheet over and—quite mechanically—drinking whisky. His sceptical faculties were largely in suspense; the barriers of criticism were down. His mind could now accept the idea that he was reading a newspaper of forty years ahead without any further protest.

It had been addressed to Mr. Evan O'Hara, and it had come to him. Well and good. This Evan O'Hara evidently knew how to get ahead of things...

I doubt if at that time Brownlow found anything very wonderful in the situation.

Yet it was, it continues to be, a very wonderful situation. The wonder of it mounts to my head as I write. Only gradually have I been able to build up this picture of Brownlow turning over that miraculous sheet, so that I can believe it myself. And you will understand how, as the thing flickered between credibility and incredibility in my mind, I asked him, partly to justify or confute what he told me, and partly to satisfy a vast expanding and, at last, devouring curiosity: "What was there in it? What did it have to say?" At the same time, I found myself trying to catch him out in his story, and also asking him for every particular he could give me.

What was there in it? In other words, What will the world be doing forty years from now? That was the stupendous scale of the vision, of which Brownlow was afforded a glimpse. The world forty years from now! I lie awake at nights thinking of all that paper might have revealed to us. Much it did reveal, but there is hardly a thing it reveals that does not change at once into a constellation of riddles. When first he told me about the thing I was—it is, I admit, an enormous pity— intensely sceptical. I asked him questions in what people call a "nasty" manner. I was ready—as my manner made plain to him—to jump down his throat with "But that's preposterous!" at the very first slip. And I had an engagement that carried me off at the end of half an hour. But the thing had already got hold of my imagination, and I rang up Brownlow before tea-time, and was biting at this "queer story" of his again. That afternoon he was sulking because of my morning's disbelief, and he told me very little. "I was drunk and dreaming, I suppose," he said. "I'm beginning to doubt it all myself." In the night it occurred to me for the first time that, if he was not allowed to tell and put on record what he had seen, he might become both confused and sceptical about it himself. Fancies might mix up with it. He might hedge and alter to get it more credible. Next day, therefore, I lunched and spent the afternoon with him, and arranged to go down into Surrey for the weekend. I managed to dispel his huffiness with me. My growing keenness restored his. There we set ourselves in earnest, first of all to recover everything he could remember about his newspaper and then to form some coherent idea of the world about which it was telling.

It is perhaps a little banal to say we were not trained men for the job. For who could be considered trained for such a job as we were attempting? What facts was he to pick out as important and how were they to be arranged? We wanted to know everything we could about 1971; and the little facts and the big facts crowded in on one another and offended against each other.

The streamer headline across the page about that seven-mile Wilton boring, is, to my mind, one of the most significant items in the story. About that we are fairly clear. It referred, says Brownlow, to a series of attempts to tap the supply of heat beneath the surface of the earth. I asked various questions. "It was *explained*, y'know," said Brownlow, and smiled and held out a hand with twiddling fingers. "It was explained all right. Old system, they said, was to go down from a few hundred feet to a mile or so and bring up coal and burn it. Go down a bit deeper, and there's no need to bring up and burn anything. Just get heat itself straight away. Comes up of its own accord—under its own steam. See? Simple.

"They were making a big fuss about it," he added. "It wasn't only the streamer headline; there was a leading article in big type. What was it headed? Ah! 'The Age of Combustion Has Ended!'"

Now that is plainly a very big event for mankind, caught in mid-happening, November 10th, 1971. And the way in which Brownlow describes it as being handled, shows clearly a world much more preoccupied by economic essentials than the world of today, and dealing with them on a larger scale and in a bolder spirit.

That excitement about tapping the central reservoirs of heat, Brownlow was very definite, was not the only symptom of an increase in practical economic interest and intelligence. There was much more space given to scientific work and to inventions than is given in any contemporary paper. There were diagrams and mathematical symbols, he says, but he did not look into them very closely because he could not get the hang of them. "*Frightfully* highbrow, some of it," he said.

A more intelligent world for our grandchildren evidently, and also, as the pictures testified, a healthier and happier world.

"The fashions kept you looking," said Brownlow, going off at a tangent, "all coloured up as they were."

"Were they elaborate?" I asked.

"Anything *but*," he said.

His description of these costumes is vague. The people depicted in the social illustrations and in the advertisements seemed to have reduced body clothing—I mean things like vests, pants, socks and so forth—to a minimum. Breast and chest went bare. There seem to have been tremendously exaggerated wristlets, mostly on the left arm and going as far up as the elbow, provided with gadgets which served the purpose of pockets. Most of these armlets seem to have been very decorative, almost like little shields. And then, usually, there was an immense hat, often rolled up and carried in the hand, and long cloaks of the loveliest colours and evidently also of the most beautiful soft material, which either trailed from a sort of gorget or were gathered up and wrapped about the naked body, or were belted up and thrown over the shoulders.

There were a number of pictures of crowds from various parts of the world. "The people looked fine," said Brownlow. "Prosperous, you know, and upstanding. Some of the women—just lovely."

My mind went off to India. What was happening in India?

Brownlow could not remember anything very much about India. "Ankor," said Brownlow. "That's not India, is it?" There had been some sort of Carnival going on amidst "perfectly lovely" buildings in the sunshine of Ankor.

The people there were brownish people but they were dressed very much like the people in other parts of the world.

I found the politician stirring in me. Was there really nothing about India? Was he sure of that? There was certainly nothing that had left any impression in Brownlow's mind. And Soviet Russia? "Not as Soviet Russia," said Brownlow. All that trouble had ceased to be a matter of daily interest. "And how was France getting on with Germany?" Brownlow could not recall a mention of either of these two great powers. Nor of the British Empire as such, nor of the USA. There was no mention of any interchanges, communications, ambassadors, conferences, competitions, comparisons, stresses, in which these governments figured, so far as he could remember. He racked his brains. I thought perhaps all that had been going on so entirely like it goes on today—and has been going on for the last hundred years—that he had run his eyes over the passages in question and that they had left no distinctive impression on his mind. But he is positive that it was not like that. "All that stuff was washed out," he said. He is unshaken in his assertion that there were no elections in progress, no notice of Parliament or politicians, no mention of Geneva or anything about armaments or war. All those main interests of a contemporary journal seem to have been among the "washed out" stuff. It isn't that Brownlow didn't notice them very much; he is positive they were not there.

Now to me this is a very wonderful thing indeed. It means, I take it, that in only forty years from now the great game of sovereign states will be over. It looks also as if the parliamentary game will be over, and as if some quite new method of handling human affairs will have been adopted. Not a word of patriotism or nationalism; not a word of party, not an allusion. But in only forty years! While half the human beings already alive in the world will still be living! You cannot believe it for a moment. Nor could I, if it wasn't for two little torn scraps of paper. These, as I will make clear, leave me in a state of—how can I put it?—incredulous belief.

4

After all, in 1831 very few people thought of railway or steamship travel, and in 1871 you could already go round the world in eighty days by steam, and send a telegram in a few minutes to nearly every part of the earth. Who would have thought of that in 1831? Revolutions in human life, when they begin to come, can come very fast. Our ideas and methods change faster than we know.

But just forty years!

It was not only that there was this absence of national politics from that evening paper, but there was something else still more fundamental. Business, we both think, finance that is, was not in evidence, at least upon anything like contemporary lines. We are not quite sure of that, but that is our impression. There was no list of Stock Exchange prices, for example, no City page, and nothing in its place. I have suggested already that Brownlow just turned that page over, and that it was sufficiently like what it is today that he passed and forgot it. I have put that suggestion to him. But he is quite sure that that was not the case. Like most of us nowadays, he is watching a number of his investments rather nervously, and he is convinced he looked for the City article.

November 10th, 1971, may have been Monday—there seems to have been some readjustment of the months and the days of the week; that is a detail into which I will not enter now—but that will not account for the absence of any City news at all. That also, it seems, will be washed out forty years from now.

Is there some tremendous revolutionary smash-up ahead, then? Which will put an end to investment and speculation? Is the world going Bolshevik? In the paper, anyhow, there was no sign of, or reference to, anything of that kind. Yet against this idea of some stupendous economic revolution we have the fact that here forty years ahead is a familiar London evening paper still tumbling into a private individual's letter-box in the most uninterrupted manner. Not much suggestion of a social smash-up there. Much stronger is the effect of immense changes which have come about bit by bit, day by day, and hour by hour, without any sign of revolutionary jolt, as morning or springtime comes to the world.

These futile speculations are irresistible. The reader must forgive me them. Let me return to our story.

There had been a picture of a landslide near Ventimiglia and one of some new chemical works at Salzburg, and there had been a picture of fighting going on near Irkutsk. (Of that picture, as I will tell presently, a fading scrap survives.) "Now that was called—" Brownlow made an effort, and snapped his fingers triumphantly. "—'Round-up of Brigands by Federal Police.' "

"*What* Federal Police?" I asked.

"There you have me," said Brownlow. "The fellows on both sides looked mostly Chinese, but there were one or two taller fellows, who might have been Americans or British or Scandinavians.

"What filled a lot of the paper," said Brownlow, suddenly, "was gorillas. There was no end of a fuss about gorillas. Not so much as about that boring, but still a lot of fuss. Photographs. A map. A special article and some paragraphs."

The paper, had, in fact, announced the death of the last gorilla. Considerable resentment was displayed at the tragedy that had happened in the African gorilla reserve. The gorilla population of the

world had been dwindling for many years. In 1931 it had been esti-
mated at nine hundred. When the Federal Board took over it had
shrunken to three hundred.

"*What* Federal Board?" I asked.

Brownlow knew no more than I did. When he read the phrase, it
had seemed all right somehow. Apparently this Board had had too
much to do all at once, and insufficient resources. I had the impression
at first that it must be some sort of conservation board, improvised
under panic conditions, to save the rare creatures of the world threatened with extinction. The gorillas had not been sufficiently observed
and guarded, and they had been swept out of existence suddenly by a
new and malignant form of influenza. The thing had happened practically before it was remarked. The paper was clamouring for inquiry
and drastic changes of reorganisation.

This Federal Board, whatever it might be, seemed to be something
of very considerable importance in the year 1971. Its name turned up
again in an article on afforestation. This interested Brownlow considerably because he has large holdings in lumber companies. This Federal Board was apparently not only responsible for the maladies of
wild gorillas but also for the plantation of trees in—just note these
names!—Canada, New York State, Siberia, Algiers, and the East Coast
of England, and it was arraigned for various negligences in combating
insect pests and various fungoid plant diseases. It jumped all our contemporary boundaries in the most astounding way. Its range was
world-wide. "In spite of the recent additional restrictions put upon the
use of big timber in building and furnishing, there is a plain possibility
of a shortage of shelter timber and of rainfall in nearly all the threatened regions for 1985 onwards. Admittedly the Federal Board has
come late to its task, from the beginning its work has been urgency
work; but in view of the lucid report prepared by the James Commis-
sion, there is little or no excuse for the inaggressiveness and overconfi-
dence it has displayed."

I am able to quote this particular article because as a matter of fact
it lies before me as I write. It is indeed, as I will explain, all that remains of this remarkable newspaper. The rest has been destroyed and
all we can ever know of it now is through Brownlow's sound but not
absolutely trustworthy memory.

5

My mind, as the days pass, hangs on to that Federal Board. Does that phrase mean, as just possibly it may mean, a world federation, a scientific control of all human life only forty years from now? I find that idea—staggering. I have always believed that the world was destined to unify—"Parliament of Mankind and Confederation of the World," as Tennyson put it—but I have always supposed that the process would take centuries. But then my time sense is poor. My disposition has always been to underestimate the pace of change. I wrote in 1900 that there would be aeroplanes "in fifty years' time." And the confounded things were buzzing about everywhere and carrying passengers before 1920.

Let me tell very briefly of the rest of that evening paper. There seemed to be a lot of sport and fashion; much about something called "Spectacle"—with pictures—a lot of illustrated criticism of decorative art and particularly of architecture. The architecture in the pictures he saw was "towering—kind of magnificent. Great blocks of building. New York, but more so and all run together"…Unfortunately he cannot sketch. There were sections devoted to something he couldn't understand, but which he thinks was some sort of "radio programme stuff."

All that suggests a sort of advanced human life very much like the life we lead today, possibly rather brighter and better.

But here is something—different.

"The birth-rate," said Brownlow, searching his mind, "was seven in the thousand."

I exclaimed. The lowest birth-rates in Europe now are sixteen or more per thousand. The Russian birth-rate is forty per thousand, and falling slowly.

"It was seven," said Brownlow. "Exactly seven. I noticed it. In a paragraph."

But what birth-rate, I asked. The British? The European?

"It said the birth-rate," said Brownlow. "Just that."

That I think is the most tantalising item in all this strange glimpse of the world of our grandchildren. A birth-rate of seven in the thousand does not mean a fixed world population; it means a population that is being reduced at a very rapid rate—unless the death-rate has gone still lower. Quite possibly people will not be dying so much then but living very much longer. On that Brownlow could throw no light. The people in the pictures did not look to him an "old lot." There were plenty of children and young or young-looking people about.

"But Brownlow," I said, "wasn't there any crime?"

"Rather," said Brownlow. "They had a big poisoning case on, but it was jolly hard to follow. You know how it is with these crimes. Unless you've read about it from the beginning, it's hard to get the hang of the situation. No newspaper has found out that for every crime it ought to give a summary up-to-date every day—and forty years ahead, they hadn't. Or they aren't going to. Whichever way you like to put it.

"There were several crimes and what newspaper men call stories," he resumed; "personal stories. What struck me about it was that they seemed to be more sympathetic than our reporters, more concerned with the motives and less with just finding someone out. What you might call psychological—so to speak."

"Was there anything much about books?" I asked him.

"I don't remember anything about books," he said ...

And that is all. Except for a few trifling details such as a possible thirteenth month inserted in the year, that is all. It is intolerably tanta- lising. That is the substance of Brownlow's account of his newspaper. He read it—as one might read any newspaper. He was just in that state of alcoholic comfort when nothing is incredible and so nothing is re- ally wonderful. He knew he was reading an evening newspaper of forty years ahead and he sat in front of his fire, and smoked and sipped his drink and was no more perturbed than he would have been if he had been reading an imaginative book about the future.

Suddenly his little brass clock pinged two.

He got up and yawned. He put that astounding, that miraculous newspaper down as he was wont to put any old newspaper down; he carried off his correspondence to the desk in his bureau, and with the swift laziness of a very tired man he dropped his clothes about his room anyhow and went to bed.

But somewhen in the night he woke up feeling thirsty and grey- minded. He lay awake and it came to him that something very strange had occurred to him. His mind went back to the idea that he had been taken in by a very ingenious fabrication. He got up for a drink of Vichy water and a liver tabloid, he put his head in cold water and found himself sitting on his bed towelling his hair and doubting whether he had really seen those photographs in the very colours of reality itself, or whether he had imagined them. Also running through his mind was the thought that the approach of a world timber famine for 1985 was something likely to affect his investments and particularly a trust he was setting up on behalf of an infant in whom he was interested. It might be wise, he thought, to put more into timber.

He went back down the corridor to his sitting-room. He sat there in his dressing-gown, turning over the marvellous sheets. There it was in his hands complete in every page, not a corner torn. Some sort of autohypnosis, he thought, might be at work, but certainly the pictures seemed as real as looking out of a window. After he had stared at them some time he went back to the timber paragraph. He felt he must keep that. I don't know if you will understand how his mind worked—for my own part I can see at once how perfectly irrational and entirely natural it was—but he took this marvellous paper, creased the page in question, tore off this particular article and left the rest. He returned very drowsily to his bedroom, put the scrap of paper on his dressing-table, got into bed and dropped off to sleep at once.

6

When he awoke it was nine o'clock; his morning tea was untasted by his bedside and the room was full of sunshine. His parlourmaid-housekeeper had just re-entered the room.

"You were sleeping so peacefully," she said; "I couldn't bear to wake you. Shall I get you a fresh cup of tea?"

Brownlow did not answer. He was trying to think of something strange that had happened.

She repeated her question.

"No. I'll come and have breakfast in my dressing-gown before my bath," he said, and she went out of the room.

Then he saw the scrap of paper.

In a moment he was running down the corridor to the sitting-room. "I left a newspaper," he said. "I left a newspaper."

She came in response to the commotion he made.

"A newspaper?" she said. "It's been gone this two hours, down the chute, with the dust and things."

Brownlow had a moment of extreme consternation.

He invoked his God. "I wanted it *kept!*" he shouted. "I wanted it *kept.*"

"But how was *I* to know you wanted it kept?"

"But didn't you notice it was a very extraordinary-looking news-paper?"

"I've got none too much time to dust out this flat to be looking at newspapers," she said. "I thought I saw some coloured photographs of bathing ladies and chorus girls in it, but that's no concern of mine. It didn't seem a proper newspaper to me. How was I to know you'd be wanting to look at them again this morning?"

"I must get that newspaper back," said Brownlow. "It's—it's vitally important... If all Sussex Court has to be held up I want that news-paper back."

"I've never known a thing come up that chute again," said his housekeeper, "that's once gone down it. But I'll telephone down, sir, and see what can be done. Most of that stuff goes right into the hot-water furnace, they say..."

It does. The newspaper had gone.

Brownlow came near raving. By a vast effort of self-control he sat down and consumed his cooling breakfast. He kept on saying, "Oh, my God!" as he did so. In the midst of it he got up to recover the scrap of paper from his bedroom, and then found the wrapper addressed to Evan O'Hara among the overnight letters on his bureau. That seemed an almost maddening confirmation. The thing *had* happened.

Presently after he had breakfasted, he rang me up to aid his baffled mind.

I found him at his bureau with the two bits of paper before him. He did not speak. He made a solemn gesture.

"What is it?" I asked, standing before him.

"Tell me," he said. "Tell me. What are these objects? It's serious. Either—" He left the sentence unfinished.

I picked up the torn wrapper first and felt its texture. "Evan O'Hara, Mr.," I read.

"Yes. Sussex Court, 49. Eh?"

"Right," I agreed and stared at him.

"*That's* not hallucination, eh?"

I shook my head.

"And now this?" His hand trembled as he held out the cutting. I took it.

"Odd," I said. I stared at the black-green ink, the unfamiliar type, the little novelties in spelling. Then I turned the thing over. On the back was a piece of one of the illustrations; it was, I suppose, about a quarter of the photograph of that "Round-up of Brigands by Federal Police" I have already mentioned.

When I saw it that morning it had not even begun to fade. It represented a mass of broken masonry in a sandy waste with bare-looking mountains in the distance. The cold, clear atmosphere, the glare of a cloudless afternoon were rendered perfectly. In the foreground were four masked men in a brown service uniform intent on working some little machine on wheels with a tube and a nozzle projecting a jet that went out to the left, where the fragment was torn off. I cannot imagine what the jet was doing. Brownlow says he thinks they were gassing some men in a hut. Never have I seen such realistic colour printing.

"What on earth is this?" I asked.

"It's *that*," said Brownlow. "I'm not mad, am I? It's really *that*."

"But what the devil is it?"

"It's a piece of newspaper for November 10th, 1971."

"You had better explain," I said, and sat down, with the scrap of paper in my hand, to hear his story. And, with as much elimination of questions and digressions and repetitions as possible, that is the story I have written here.

I said at the beginning that it was a queer story and queer to my mind it remains, fantastically queer. I return to it at intervals, and it refuses to settle down in my mind as anything but an incongruity with all my experience and beliefs. If it were not for the two little bits of paper, one might dispose of it quite easily. One might say that Brownlow had had a vision, a dream of unparalleled vividness and consistency. Or that he had been hoaxed and his head turned by some elaborate mystification. Or, again, one might suppose he had really seen into the future with a sort of exaggeration of those previsions cited by Mr. J. W. Dunne in his remarkable "Experiment with Time." But nothing Mr. Dunne has to advance can account for an actual evening paper being slapped through a letter-slit forty years in advance of its date.

The wrapper has not altered in the least since I first saw it. But the scrap of paper with the article about afforestation is dissolving into a fine powder and the fragment of picture at the back of it is fading out; most of the colour has gone and the outlines have lost their sharpness. Some of the powder I have taken to my friend Ryder at the Royal College, whose work in micro-chemistry is so well known. He says the stuff is not paper at all, properly speaking. It is mostly aluminium fortified by admixture with some artificial resinous substance.

7

Though I offer no explanation whatever of this affair I think I will venture on one little prophesy. I have an obstinate persuasion that on November 10th, 1971, the name of the tenant of 49, Sussex Court, will be Mr. Evan O'Hara. (There is no tenant of that name now in Sussex Court and I find no evidence in the Telephone Directory, or the London Directory, that such a person exists anywhere in London.) And on that particular evening forty years ahead, he will not get his usual copy of the *Even Standrd:* instead he will get a copy of the *Evening Standard* of 1931. I have an incurable fancy that this will be so.

There I may be right or wrong, but that Brownlow really got and for two remarkable hours, read, a real newspaper forty years ahead of time I am as convinced as I am convinced that my own name is Hubert G. Wells. Can I say anything stronger than that?

The Country of the Blind

Three hundred miles and more from Chimborazo, one hundred from the snows of Cotopaxi, in the wildest wastes of Ecuador's Andes, where the frost-and-sun-rotted rocks rise in vast pinnacles and cliffs above the snow, there was once a mysterious mountain valley, called the Country of the Blind. It was a legendary land, and until quite recently people doubted if it was anything more than a legend. Long years ago, ran the story, that valley lay so far open to the world that men, daring the incessant avalanches, might clamber at last through frightful gorges and over an icy pass into its equable meadows; and thither indeed men went and settled, a family or so of Peruvian half-breeds fleeing from the lust and tyranny of an evil Spanish ruler. Then came the stupendous outbreak of Mindobamba, when it was night in Quito for seventeen days, and the water was boiling at Yaguachi and all the fish floating dying even as far as Guayaquil; everywhere along the Pacific slopes there were landslips and swift thawings and sudden floods, and one whole side of the old Arauca crest slipped and came down in thunder, and cut off this Country of the Blind, as it seemed, for ever from the exploring feet of men.

But, said the story, one of these early settlers had chanced to be on the hither side of the gorge when the world had so terribly shaken itself, and perforce he had to forget his wife and his child and all the friends and possessions he declared he had left up there, and begin life again in the lower world.

He had a special reason to account for his return from that fastness, into which he had first been carried lashed to a llama, beside a vast bale of gear, when he was a child. The valley, he said, had in it all that the heart of man could desire—sweet water, pasture, an even climate, slopes of rich brown soil with tangles of a shrub that bore an excellent fruit, and on one side great hanging pine forests that held the avalanches high. Far overhead, a semi-circle of ice-capped precipices of grey-green rock brooded over that glowing garden; but the glacier stream flowed away by the farther slopes and only very rarely did an ice-fall reach the lower levels. In this valley it neither rained nor snowed, but the abundant springs gave a rich green pasture, that patient irrigation was spreading over all the valley space. The surplus water gathered at last in a little lake beneath the cirque and vanished with a roar into an unfathomable cavern. The settlers, he said, were doing very well indeed there. Their beasts did well and multiplied, and only one thing marred their happiness. Yet it was enough to mar it greatly; some sinister quality hidden in that sweet and bracing air. A strange disease had come upon them, and had made all the children born to them there—and indeed several older children also—blind. So that the whole valley seemed likely to become a valley of blind men.

It was, he said, to seek some charm or antidote against this plague of blindness that with infinite fatigue, danger and difficulty he had returned down the gorge. In those days, in such cases, men did not think of germs and infections but of sins; and it seemed to him that the reason of this affliction must lie in the negligence of these priestless immigrants to set up a shrine so soon as they entered the valley. He wanted a shrine—a handsome, cheap, effectual shrine—to be set up in the valley; he wanted relics and suchlike potent things of faith, blessed objects and mysterious medals and prayers. In his wallet he had a bar of native silver for which he would not account; he insisted there was none in the valley, with something of the insistence of an inexpert liar. The settlers had all clubbed their money and ornaments together, having little need for such treasure up there, he said, to buy them holy help against their ill. I figure this young mountaineer, sunburnt, gaunt and anxious, hat-brim clutched feverishly, a man all unused to the ways of the lower world, telling this story to some keen-eyed, attentive priest before the great convulsion; I can picture him presently seeking to return with pious and infallible remedies against that trouble, and the infinite dismay with which he must have faced the tumbled and still monstrously crumbling vastness where the gorge had once come out. But the rest of his tale of mischances is lost to me, save that I know he died of punishment in the mines. His offence I do not know.

But the idea of a valley of blind folk had just that appeal to the imagination that a legend requires if it is to live. It stimulates fantasy. It invents its own detail.

And recently this story has been most remarkably confirmed. We know now the whole history of this Country of the Blind from that beginning to its recent and tragic end.

We know now that amidst the little population of that now isolated and forgotten valley the contagion ran its course. Even the older children became groping and purblind, the young saw but dimly, and the children that were born to them never saw at all. But life was very easy in that snow-rimmed basin, lost to all the world, with neither thorns nor briers, with food upon the bushes in its season, with no evil insects nor any beasts save the gentle breed of llamas they had lugged and thrust and followed up the beds of the shrunken rivers in the gorges by which they had come. The first generation had become purblind so gradually that they scarcely noted their loss. They guided the sightless youngsters who followed them hither and thither until they knew the whole valley marvellously, and when at last sight died out altogether among them the race lived on. They had even time to adapt themselves to the blind control of fire, which they made carefully in stoves of stone. They were a simple strain of people at the first, unlettered, only slightly touched with Spanish civilisation, but with something of a tradition of the arts of old Peru and its lost philosophy. Generation followed generation. They forgot many things; they devised many things. Their tradition of the greater world they came from became mythical in colour and uncertain. In all things save sight they were strong and able; and presently the chances of birth and heredity produced one who had an original mind and who could talk and persuade among them, and then afterwards another. These two passed, leaving their effects, and the little community grew in numbers and understanding, and met and settled all the social and economic problems that arose, sensibly and peaceably. There came a time when a child was born who was fifteen generations from that ancestor who went out of the valley with a bar of silver to seek God's aid, and who never returned. Then it chanced that a man came into this community from the outer world and troubled their minds very greatly. He lived with them for many months, and escaped very narrowly from their final disaster.

He was a mountaineer from the country near Quito, a man who had been down to the sea and had seen the world, and he was taken on by a party of Englishmen under Sir Charles Pointer, who had come out of Ecuador to climb mountains, to replace one of their three Swiss guides who had fallen ill. He climbed here and he climbed there, and then came the attempt on Parascotopetl, the "rotten" mountain, the Matterhorn of the Andes, in which he was lost to the outer world so that he was given up for dead.

Everyone who knew anything of mountaincraft had warned the little expedition against the treachery of the rocks in this range, but apparently it was not a rock-fall that caught this man Nunez but an exceptional snow-cornice. The party had worked its difficult and almost vertical way up to the very foot of the last and greatest precipice, and had already built itself a night shelter upon a little shelf of rock amidst the snow, when the accident occurred. Suddenly they found that Nunez had disappeared, without a sound. They shouted, and there was no reply; they shouted and whistled, they made a cramped search for him, but their range of movement was very limited. There was no moon, and their electric torches had only a limited range.

As the morning broke they saw the traces of his fall. It seems impossible he could have uttered a cry. The depths had snatched him down. He had slipped eastward towards the unknown side of the mountain; far below he had struck a steep slope of snow, and ploughed his way down it in the midst of a snow avalanche. His track went straight to the edge of a frightful precipice, and beyond that everything was hidden. Far, far below, and hazy with distance, they could see trees rising out of a narrow, shut-in valley—the lost Country of the Blind. But they did not know it was the lost Country of the Blind, nor distinguish it in any way from any other narrow streak of sheltered upland valley. Unnerved by this disaster, they abandoned their attempt in the afternoon, and Pointer, who was financing the attempt, was called away to urgent private business before he could make another attack.

To this day Parascotopetl lists an unconquered crest, and Pointer's shelter crumbles unvisited amidst the snows.

And this man who fell survived.

At the end of the slope he fell a thousand feet, and came down in the midst of a cloud of snow upon a snow slope even steeper than the one above. Down this he was whirled, stunned and insensible, but miraculously without a bone broken in his body; and then the gradients diminished, and at last rolled out and lay still, buried amidst a softening heap of the white masses that had accompanied him and saved him. He came to himself with a dim fancy that he was ill in bed; then realised his position, worked himself loose and, after a rest or so, out until he saw the stars. He rested flat upon his chest for a space, wondering where he was and what had happened to him. He explored his limbs, they ached exceedingly but they were unbroken. He discovered that several of his buttons were gone and his coat turned over his head. His knife had gone from his pocket and his hat was lost, though he had tied it under his chin. His face was grazed; he was scratched and contused all over. He recalled that he had been looking for loose stones to raise his piece of the shelter wall. His ice-axe had disappeared.

He looked up to see, exaggerated by the ghastly light of the rising moon, the tremendous flight he had taken. For a while he lay, gazing blankly at that vast pale cliff towering above, rising moment by moment out of a subsiding tide of darkness. Since the light struck it first above it seemed to be streaming upward out of nothing. Its phantasmal mysterious beauty held him for a space, and then he was seized with a paroxysm of sobbing laughter...

After a great interval of time he became aware that he was near the lower edge of the snow. Below, down what was now a moonlit and practicable slope, he saw the dark and broken appearance of rock-strewn turf. He struggled to his feet, aching in every limb, got down painfully from the heaped loose snow about him, went downward until he was on the turf, and there dropped rather than lay beside a boulder, drank deep from the flask in his inner pocket, and instantly fell asleep...

He was awakened by the singing of birds in trees far below.

He sat up stiffly and perceived he was on a little alp at the foot of a great precipice, grooved by the gulley down which he and his snow had come. Over against him another wall of jagged rock reared itself against the sky. The gorge between these precipices ran east and west and was full of the morning sunlight, which lit to the westward the mass of fallen mountain that had blocked the way to the world. Below him it seemed there was a precipice equally steep, but beyond the snow in the gulley he found a chimney dripping with snow-water down which a desperate man might venture. He found it easier than it looked, and came at last to another desolate alp, and then after a rock climb of no particular difficulty to a steep slope of trees. He took his bearings and turned his face eastward, for he saw it opened out above upon green meadows, among which he now glimpsed quite distinctly a cluster of stone huts of unfamiliar fashion. At times his progress was like clambering along the face of a wall, and after a time the rays of the rising sun were intercepted by a vast bastion, the voices of the singing birds died away, and the air grew cold and dark about him. But the distant valley with its houses seemed all the brighter for that. He presently came to talus, and among the rocks he noted—for he was an observant man—an unfamiliar fern that seemed to clutch out of the crevices with intense green hands. He picked a frond or so and gnawed its stalk and found it helpful. There were bushes but the fruit had not formed upon them.

About midday he emerged from the shadow of the great bluff into the sunlight again. And now he was only a few hundred yards from the valley meadows. He was weary and very stiff; he sat down in the shadow of a rock, filled up his nearly empty flask with water from a spring, drank it down, and rested for a time before he went on towards the houses.

They were very strange to his eyes, and indeed the whole aspect of that valley became, as he regarded it, queerer and more unfamiliar. The greater part of its surface was lush green meadow, starred with many beautiful flowers, irrigated with extraordinary care, and bearing evidence of systematic cropping piece by piece. High up and ringing the valley about was a wall, and what appeared to be a circumferential water-channel, which received the runlets from the snows above and from which little trickles of water had been led to feed the meadows. On the higher slopes above this wall, flocks of llamas cropped the scanty herbage amidst the tangled shrubs. Sheds, apparently shelters or feeding-places for the llamas, stood against the boundary wall here and there. The irrigation streams ran together into a main channel down the centre of the valley, that debouched into a little lake below a semi-circle of precipices, and this central canal was enclosed on either side by a wall breast-high. This wall gave a singularly urban quality to this secluded place, a quality that was greatly enhanced by the fact that a number of paths paved with green, grey, black and white stones, and each with a curious little kerb at the side, ran hither and thither in an orderly manner. The houses of the central village were quite unlike the casual and higgledy-piggledy agglomeration of the mountain villages he knew; they stood in a continuous row on either side of a central street of astonishing cleanness; here and there their parti-coloured façade was pierced by a door, and not a solitary window broke their even frontage. They were parti-coloured with extraordinary irregularity; smeared with a sort of plaster that was sometimes grey, sometimes drab, sometimes slate-coloured or dark-brown; and it was the sight of this wild plastering that first brought the word "blind" into the thoughts of the explorer. "The good man who did that," he thought, "must have been as blind as a bat."

He descended a steep place and so came to the wall and channel that ran about the valley, near where the latter spouted out its surplus contents into the lake. He could see now a number of men and women resting on piled heaps of grass, as if taking a siesta; in the remoter part of the meadow, and nearer the village a number of recumbent children; and then nearer at hand three men carrying pails on yokes along a little path that ran from the encircling wall towards the houses. These latter were clad in garments of llama cloth and boots and belts of leather, and they wore caps of cloth with back and ear flaps. They followed one another in single file, walking slowly and yawning as they walked, like men who have been up all night. There was something so reassuringly prosperous and respectable in their bearing that after a moment's hesitation Nunez stood forward as conspicuously as possible upon his rock, and gave vent to a mighty shout that evoked a thousand echoes round and about the valley.

The three men stopped and moved their heads as if they were looking about them. They turned their face this way and that, and Nunez gesticulated with freedom. But they did not appear to see him for all his gestures, and after a time, directing themselves towards the mountain far away to the right, they shouted as if in answer. Nunez bawled again and then once more, and as he gestured ineffectually the word "blind" came once more to the front of his thoughts. "The fools must be blind," he said.

When at last, after much shouting and irritation, Nunez crossed the stream by a little bridge, came through a gate in the wall, and approached them, he realised that they were indeed blind. He knew already that this was the Country of the Blind of which the legends told. Conviction had sprung upon him, and a sense of great and rather enviable adventure. The three stood side by side, not looking at him, but with their ears directed towards him, judging him by his unfamiliar steps. They stood close together like men a little afraid, and he could see their eyelids closed and shrunken, as if the very balls beneath had shrunk away. There was an expression near awe on their faces.

"A man," one said, in hardly recognisable Spanish—"a man it is—a man or a beast that walks like a man—coming down from the rocks."

But Nunez advanced with the confident steps of a youth who enters upon life. All the old stories of the lost valley and the Country of the Blind had come back to his mind, and through his thoughts ran this old proverb, as if it were a refrain—

> In the Country of the Blind the One-eyed Man is King.
> In the Country of the Blind the One-eyed Man is King.

And very civilly he gave them greeting. He talked to them and used his eyes.

"Where does he come from, brother Pedro?" asked one.

"Down out of the rocks."

"Over the mountains I come," said Nunez, "out of the country beyond there—where men can see. From near Bogota, where there are a hundred thousands of people, and where the city passes out of sight."

"Sight?" muttered Pedro. "Sight?"

"He comes," said the second blind man, "out of the rocks."

The cloth of their coats Nunez saw was curiously fashioned, each with a different sort of stitching.

They startled him by a simultaneous movement towards him, each with a hand outstretched. He stepped back from the advance of these spread fingers.

"Come hither," said the third blind man, following his motion and clutching him neatly.

And they held Nunez and felt him over, saying no word further until they had done so.

"Carefully," he cried, when a finger was poked in his eye, and he realised that they thought that organ, with its fluttering lids, a queer thing in him. They felt over it again.

"A strange creature, Correa," said the one called Pedro. "Feel the coarseness of his hair. Like a llama's hair."

"Rough he is as the rocks that begot him," said Correa, investigating Nunez's unshaven chin with a soft and slightly moist hand. "Perhaps he will grow finer." Nunez struggled a little under their examination, but they gripped him firm.

"Carefully," he said again.

"He speaks," said the third man. "Certainly he is a man."

"Ugh!" said Pedro, at the roughness of his coat.

"And you have come into the world?" asked Pedro.

"*Out* of the world. Over mountains and glaciers; right over above there, half-way to the sun. Out of the great big world that goes down from here, twelve days' journey to the sea."

They scarcely seemed to heed him. "The fathers have told us men may be made by the forces of Nature," said Correa. "It is the warmth of things and moisture, and rottenness—rottenness."

"Let us lead him to the elders," said Pedro.

"Shout first," said Correa, "lest the children be afraid. This is a marvellous occasion."

So they shouted, and Pedro went first and took Nunez by the hand to lead him to the houses.

He drew his hand away. "I can see," he said.

"See?" said Correa.

"Yes, see," said Nunez, turning towards him, and stumbled against Pedro's pail.

"His senses are still imperfect," said the third blind man. "He stumbles, and talks unmeaning words. Lead him by the hand."

"As you will," said Nunez, and was led along smiling.

It seemed they knew nothing of sight.

Well, all in good time, he would teach them.

He heard people shouting, and saw a number of figures gathered together in the middle roadway of the village.

He found it taxed his nerve and patience more than he had anticipated, that first encounter with the population of the Country of the Blind. The place seemed larger as he drew near to it, and the smeared plasterings queerer, and a crowd of children and men and women (the women and girls he was pleased to note, had some of them quite sweet faces, for all that their eyes were shut and sunken) came about him, and mobbed him, holding on to him, touching him with soft, sensitive hands, smelling at him, and listening for every word he spoke. Some of the maidens and children, however, kept aloof as if afraid, and indeed his voice seemed coarse and rude beside their softer notes. His three guides kept close to him with an effect of proprietorship, and said again and again, "A wild man out of the rocks."

"Bogota," he said. "Bogota. Over the mountain crests."

"A wild man—using wild words," said Pedro. "Did you hear that—*Bogota?* His mind is hardly formed yet. He has only the beginnings of speech."

A little boy nipped his hand. "Bogota!" he said mockingly.

"Ay! A city to your village. I come from the great world—where men have eyes and see."

"His name's Bogota," they said.

"He stumbled," said Correa, "stumbled twice as we came hither."

"Bring him to the elders."

And they thrust him suddenly through a doorway into a room as black as pitch, save at the end there faintly glowed a fire. The crowd closed in behind him and shut out all but the faintest glimmer of day, and before he could arrest himself he had fallen headlong over the feet of a seated man. His arm, outflung, struck the face of someone else as he went down; he felt the soft impact of features and heard a cry of anger, and for a moment he struggled against a number of hands that clutched him. It was a one-sided fight. An inkling of the situation came to him, and he lay quiet.

"I fell down," he said; "I couldn't see in this pitchy darkness. Who could?"

There was a pause as if the unseen persons about him tried to understand his words. Then the voice of Correa said: "He is but newly formed. He stumbles as he walks and mingles words that mean nothing with his speech."

Others also said things about him that he heard or understood imperfectly.

"May I sit up?" he asked, in a pause. "I will not struggle against you again."

They consulted and let him rise.

The voice of an older man began to question him, and Nunez found himself trying to explain the great world out of which he had fallen, and the sky and mountains and sight and suchlike marvels, to these elders who sat in darkness in the Country of the Blind. And they would believe and understand nothing whatever he told them, a thing quite outside his expectation. They would not even understand many of his words. For fourteen generations these people had been blind and cut off from all the seeing world; the names for all the things of sight had faded and changed; the story of the outer world was faded and changed to a child's story; and they had ceased to concern themselves with anything beyond the rocky slopes above their circling wall. Blind men of genius had arisen among them and questioned the shreds of belief and tradition they had brought with them from their seeing days, and had dismissed all these things as idle fancies, and replaced them with new and saner explanations. Much of their imagination had shrivelled with their eyes, and they had made for themselves new imaginations with their ever more sensitive ears and finger-tips. Slowly Nunez realised this; that his expectation of wonder and reverence at his origin and his gifts was not to be borne out; and after his poor attempt to explain sight to them had been set aside as the confused version of a new-made being describing the marvels of his incoherent sensations, he subsided, a little dashed, into listening to their instruction.

The eldest of the blind men explained to him life and philosophy and religion, how that the world (meaning their valley) had been first an empty hollow in the rocks and then had come, first, inanimate things without the gift of touch, from these grass and bushes and after that llamas and a few other creatures that had little sense, and then men, and at last angels, whom one could hear singing and making fluttering sounds, but whom none could touch at all, which puzzled Nunez greatly until he thought of the birds.

The elder went on to tell Nunez how "by the Wisdom above us" time had been divided into the warm and the cold, which are the blind equivalents of day and night, and how it was good to sleep in the warm, and work during the cold, so that now, but for his advent, the whole town of the blind would have been asleep. He said Nunez must have been specially created to learn and serve the wisdom they had acquired, and for all his mental incoherency and stumbling behaviour he must have courage, and do his best to learn; and at that all the people in the doorway murmured encouragingly. He said the night—for the blind call their day night—was now far gone, and it behoved everyone to go back to sleep. He asked Nunez if he knew how to sleep and Nunez said he did, but that before sleep he wanted food.

They brought him food, llama's milk in a bowl, and rough salted bread, and led him into a lonely place to eat out of their hearing, and afterwards to slumber, until the chill of the mountain evening roused them to begin their day again. But Nunez slumbered not at all.

Instead, he sat up in the place where they had left him, resting his limbs and turning the unanticipated circumstances of his arrival over and over in his mind.

Every now and then he laughed, sometimes with amusement and sometimes with indignation.

"Unformed mind!" he said. "Got no senses yet! They little know they've been insulting their heaven-sent king and master. I see I must bring them to reason. Let me think—let me think."

He was still thinking when the sun set.

Nunez had an eye for all beautiful things, and it seemed to him that the glow upon the snowfields and glaciers that rose about the valley on every side was the most beautiful thing he had ever seen. His eyes went from that inaccessible glory to the village and irrigated fields, fast sinking into the twilight, and suddenly a wave of emotion took him, and he thanked God from the bottom of his heart that the power of sight had been given him.

He heard a voice calling to him from out of the house of the elders.

"Ya ho there, Bogota! Come hither!"

At that he stood up smiling. He would show these people once and for all what sight would do for a man. They would seek him but not find him.

"You move not, Bogota," said the voice.

He laughed noiselessly, and made two stealthy steps aside from the path.

"Trample not on the grass, Bogota; that is not allowed."

Nunez had scarcely heard the sound he made himself. He stopped amazed.

The owner of the voice came running up the piebald path towards him.

He stepped back into the pathway. "Here I am," he said.

"Why did you not come when I called you?" said the blind man. "Must you be led like a child? Cannot you hear the path as you walk?"

Nunez laughed. "I can see it," he said.

"There is no such word as *see*," said the blind man after a pause. "Cease this folly and follow the sound of my feet."

Nunez followed, a little annoyed.

"My time will come," he said.

"You'll learn," the blind man answered. "There is much to learn in the world."

"Has no one told you, 'In the Country of the Blind the One-eyed Man is King'?"

"What is blind?" asked the blind man carelessly over his shoulder.

Four days passed, and the fifth found the King of the Blind still incognito, as a clumsy and useless stranger among his subjects.

It was, he found, much more difficult to proclaim himself than he had supposed, and in the meantime, while he meditated his *coup d'état*, he did what he was told and learned the manners and customs of the Country of the Blind. He found working and going about at night a particularly irksome thing, and he decided that that should be the first thing he would change in his little kingdom.

They led a simple, laborious life, these people, with all the elements of virtue and happiness, as these things can be understood by men. They toiled, but not oppressively; they had food and clothing sufficient for their needs; they had days and seasons of rest; they made much of music and singing, and there was love among them, and little children.

It was marvellous with what confidence and precision they went about their ordered world. Everything, you see, had been made to fit their needs; each of the radiating paths of the valley area had a constant angle to the others, and was distinguished by a special notch upon its kerbing; all obstacles and irregularities of path and meadow had long since been cleared away; all their methods and procedure arose naturally from their special needs. Their senses had become marvellously acute; they could hear and judge the slightest gesture of a man a dozen paces away—could hear the very beating of his heart. Intonation had long replaced expression with them, and touches gesture, and their work with hoe and spade and fork was as free and confident as garden work can be. Their sense of smell was extraordinarily fine; they could distinguish individual differences as readily as a dog can, and they went about the tending of the llamas, who lived among the rocks above and came to the wall for food and shelter, with ease and confidence. It was only when at last Nunez sought to assert himself that he found how easy and confident their movements could be.

He rebelled only after he had tried persuasion.

At first on several occasions he sought to tell them of sight. "Look you here, you people," he said. "There are things you do not understand in me."

Once or twice one or two of them attended to him; they sat with faces downcast and ears turned intelligently towards him though with a faintly ironical smile on their lips, while he did his best to tell them what it was to see. Among his hearers was a girl, with eyes less red and sunken than the others, so that one could almost fancy she was hiding eyes, and she especially he hoped to persuade.

He spoke of the beauties of sight, of watching the mountains, of the sky and the sunrise, and they heard him with amused incredulity that presently became condemnatory. They told him that there were indeed no mountains at all, but that the end of the rocks where the llamas grazed was indeed the end of the world; the rocks became steeper and steeper, became pillars and thence sprang a cavernous roof of the universe, from which the dew and avalanches fell; and when he maintained stoutly the world had neither end nor roof such as they supposed, they were shocked and they said his thoughts were wicked. So far as he could describe sky and clouds and stars to them, his world seemed to them a hideous void, a terrible blankness in the place of the smooth roof to things in which they believed—it was an article of faith with them that above the rocks the cavern roof was exquisitely smooth to the touch. They called it the Wisdom Above.

He saw that in some manner he shocked them by his talk of clouds and stars, and so he gave up that aspect of the matter altogether, and tried to show them the practical value of sight. One morning he saw Pedro in the path called Seventeen and coming towards the central houses, but still too far off for hearing or scent, and he told them as much. "In a little while," he prophesied, "Pedro will be here." An old man remarked that Pedro had no business on Path Seventeen, and then, as if in confirmation, that individual as he drew near turned and went transversely into Path Ten, and so back with nimble paces to the outer wall. They mocked Nunez when Pedro did not arrive, and afterwards, when he asked Pedro questions to clear his character, Pedro denied and outfaced him, and was afterwards hostile to him.

Then he induced them to let him go a long way up the sloping meadows towards the wall with one complacent individual, and to him he promised to describe all that happened among the houses. He noted certain comings and goings, but the things that really seemed to signify to these people happened inside of or behind the windowless houses—the only thing they took note of to test him by—and of these he could see or tell nothing; and it was after the failure of that attempt, and the ridicule they could not repress, that he resorted to force. He thought of seizing a spade and suddenly smiting one or two of them to earth, and so in fair combat showing the advantage of eyes. He went so far with that resolution as to seize his spade, and then he discovered a new thing about himself, and that was that it was impossible for him to hit a blind man in cold blood.

He hesitated and found them all aware that he had snatched up the spade. They stood alert, with their heads on one side, and bent ears towards him for what he would do next.

"Put that spade down," said one, and he felt a sort of helpless horror. He came near obedience.

Then he thrust one backwards against a house wall, and fled past him and out of the village.

He went athwart one of their meadows, leaving a track of trampled grass behind his feet, and presently sat down by the side of one of their ways. He felt something of the buoyancy that comes to all men in the beginning of a fight, but more perplexity. He began to realise that you cannot even fight happily with creatures that stand upon a different mental basis to yourself. Far away he saw a number of men carrying spades and sticks come out of the street of houses, and advance in a spreading line along the several paths towards him. They advanced slowly, speaking frequently to one another, and ever and again the whole cordon would halt and sniff the air and listen.

The first time they did this Nunez laughed. But afterwards he did not laugh.

One struck his trail in the meadow grass, and came stooping and feeling his way along it.

For five minutes he watched the slow extension of the cordon, and then his vague disposition to do something forthwith became frantic. He stood up, went a pace or so towards the circumferential wall, turned, and went back a little way. There they all stood in a crescent, still and listening.

He also stood still, gripping his spade very tightly in both hands. Should he charge them?

The pulse in his ears rang into the rhythm of "In the Country of the Blind the One-eyed Man is King!"

Should he charge them?

He looked back at the high and unclimbable wall behind—unclimbable because of its smooth plastering, but withal pierced by many little doors, and at the approaching line of seekers. Behind these, others were now coming out of the street of houses.

Should he charge them?

"Bogota!" called one. "Bogota! where are you?"

He gripped his spade still tighter and advanced down the meadows towards the place of habitations, and directly he moved they converged upon him. "I'll hit them if they touch me," he swore; "by Heaven I will. I'll hit." He called aloud, "Look here, I'm going to do what I like in this valley. Do you hear? I'm going to do what I like and go where I like!"

They were moving in upon him quickly, groping, yet moving rapidly. It was like playing blind man's buff, with everyone blindfolded except one. "Get hold of him!" cried one. He found himself in the arc of a loose curve of pursuers. He felt suddenly he must be active and resolute.

"You don't understand," he cried in a voice that was meant to be great and resolute, and which broke. "You are blind, and I can see. Leave me alone!"

"Bogota! Put down that spade, and come off the grass!"

The last order, grotesque in its urban familiarity, produced a gust of anger.

"I'll hurt you," he said, sobbing with emotion. "By Heaven, I'll hurt you. Leave me alone!"

He began to run, not knowing clearly where to run. He ran from the nearest blind man, because it was a horror to hit him. He stopped, and made a dash to escape from their closing ranks. He made for where a gap was wide, and the men on either side, with a quick perception of the approach of his paces, rushed in on one another. He sprang forward, and then saw he must be caught, and swish! the spade had struck. He felt the soft thud of hand and arm, and the man was down with a yell of pain, and he was through.

Through! And then he was close to the street of houses again, and blind men, whirling spades and stakes, were running with a sort of reasoned swiftness hither and thither.

He heard steps behind him just in time, and found a tall man rushing forward and swiping at the sound of him. He lost his nerve, hurled his spade a yard wide at his antagonist, and whirled about and fled, fairly yelling as he dodged another.

He was panic-stricken. He ran furiously to and fro, dodging when there was no need to dodge, and in his anxiety to see on every side of him at once, stumbling. For a moment he was down and they heard his fall. Far away in the circumferential wall a little doorway looked like Heaven, and he set off in a wild rush for it. He did not even look round at his pursuers until it was gained, and he had stumbled across the bridge, clambered a little way among the rocks, to the surprise and dismay of a young llama, who went leaping out of sight, and lay down sobbing for breath.

And so his *coup d'état* came to an end.

He stayed outside the wall of the Valley of the Blind for two nights and days without food or shelter, and meditated upon the unexpected. There were bushes, but the food on them was not ripe and hard and bitter. It weakened him to eat it. It lowered his courage. During these prowlings he repeated very frequently and always with a profounder note of derision that exploded proverb: "In the Country of the Blind the One-eyed Man is King." He thought chiefly of ways of fighting and conquering these people, and it grew clear that for him no practicable way was possible. He had no weapons, and now it would be hard to get one.

The canker of civilisation had got to him even in Bogota, and he could not find it in himself to go down and assassinate a blind man. Of course, if he did that, he might then dictate terms on the threat of assassinating them all. If he could get near enough to them, that is. And—sooner or later he must sleep . . . !

He tried also to find food among the pine trees, to be comfortable under pine boughs while the frost fell at night and—with less confidence—to catch a llama by artifice in order to try to kill it—perhaps by hammering it with a stone—and so finally, perhaps, to eat some of it. But the llamas had their doubts of him and regarded him with distrustful brown eyes, and spat when he drew near. Fear came on him the second day, an intense fatigue, and fits of shivering. Finally he crawled down to the wall of the Country of the Blind and tried to make terms. He crawled along by the stream shouting, until two blind men came out to the gate and talked to him.

"I was mad," he said. "But I was only newly made."

They said that was better.

He told them he was wiser now, and that he repented of all he had done.

Then he wept without intention, for he was very weak and ill, and they took that as a favourable sign.

They asked him if he still thought he could *"see."*

"No," he said, "that was folly. The word means nothing—less than nothing!"

They asked him what was overhead.

"About ten times the height of a man there is a roof above the world—of rock and wisdom and very, very smooth..."

He burst again into hysterical tears. "Before you ask me any more, give me some food or I shall die."

He expected dire punishments, but these blind people showed themselves capable of great toleration. They regarded his rebellion as but one more proof of his general idiocy and inferiority; and after they had whipped him they appointed him to do the simplest and heaviest work they had for anyone to do, and he, seeing no other way of living, did submissively what he was told.

He was ill for some days and they nursed him kindly. That refined his submission. But they insisted on his lying in the dark, and that was a great misery. And the chief elders came and talked to him of the wicked levity of his mind, and reproved him so impressively for his doubts about the lid of rock that covered their cosmic casserole that he almost doubted whether indeed he was not the victim of hallucination in not seeing it overhead.

So Nunez humbled himself and became a common citizen of the Country of the Blind, and these people ceased to be a generalised people and became individualities and familiar to him, while the world beyond the mountains became more and more remote and unreal.

There was Yacob, his master, a kindly man when not annoyed; there was Pedro, Yacob's nephew; and there was Medina-saroté, who was the youngest daughter of Yacob. She was little esteemed in the world of the blind, because she had a clear-cut face, and lacked the satisfying, glossy smoothness that is the blind man's ideal of feminine beauty; but Nunez thought her beautiful at first, and presently the most beautiful thing in the whole creation. Her closed eyelids were not sunken and red after the common way of the valley, but lay as though they might open again at any moment; and she had eyelashes, which were considered a grave disfigurement. And her voice was strong, and did not satisfy the acute hearing of the valley swains. So that she had no lover.

There came a time when Nunez thought that, could he win her, he would be resigned to live in the valley for all the rest of his days.

He watched her; he sought opportunities of doing her little services, and presently he found that she observed him. Once at a rest-day gathering they sat side by side in the dim starlight, and the music was sweet. His hand came upon hers and he dared to clasp it. Then very tenderly she returned his pressure. And one day, as they were at their meal in the darkness, he felt her hand very softly seeking him, and as it chanced the fire leapt then and he saw the tenderness of her face.

He sought to speak to her.

He went to her one day when she was sitting in the summer moonlight spinning. The light made her a thing of silver and mystery. He sat down at her feet and told her he loved her, and told her how beautiful she seemed to him. He had a lover's voice, he spoke with a tender reverence that came near to awe, and she had never before been touched by adoration. She made him no definite answer, but it was clear his words pleased her.

After that he talked to her whenever he could take an opportunity. The valley became the world for him, and the world beyond the mountains where men worked and went about in sunlight seemed no more than a fairy tale he would some day pour into her ears. Very tentatively and timidly he spoke to her of sight.

At first this sight seemed to her the most poetical of fancies, and she listened to his description of the stars and the mountains and her own sweet white-lit beauty as though it was a guilty indulgence. She did not believe, she could only half understand, but she was mysteriously delighted, and it seemed to him that she completely understood.

His love lost its awe and took courage. Presently he was for demanding her of Yacob and the elders in marriage, but she became fearful and delayed. And it was one of her sisters who first told Yacob that Medina-saroté and Nunez were in love.

From the first there was very great opposition to the marriage of Nunez and Medina-saroté; not so much because they valued her as because they held him as a being apart, an idiot, incompetent thing, below the permissible level of a man. Her sisters opposed it bitterly as bringing discredit on them all; and old Yacob, though he had formed a sort of liking for his clumsy, obedient serf, shook his head and said the thing could not be. The young men were all angry at the thought of corrupting the race, and one went so far as to revile and strike Nunez. He struck back. Then for the first time he found an advantage in seeing, even by twilight, and after that fight no one was disposed to lift a hand against him. But they still found his marriage impossible.

Old Yacob had a tenderness for his last little daughter, and was grieved to have her weep upon his shoulder.

"You see, my dear, he's an idiot! He has delusions; he can't do anything right."

"I know," wept Medina-saroté. "But he's better than he was. He's getting better. And he's strong, dear father, and kind—stronger and kinder than any other man in the world. And he loves me—and, father, I love him."

Old Yacob was greatly distressed to find her inconsolable, and, besides—what made it more distressing—he liked Nunez for many things. So he went and sat in the windowless council-chamber with the other elders, observing the trend of their talk, and said, at the proper time, "He's better than he was. Very likely, some day, we shall find him as sane as ourselves."

Then afterwards one of the elders, who thought deeply, had an idea. He was the great doctor among these people, their medicine man, and he had a very philosophical and inventive mind, and the idea of curing Nunez of his peculiarities appealed to him. One day when Yacob was present he turned to the topic of Nunez.

"I have examined Bogota," he said, "and the case is clearer to me. I think very probably he might be cured."

"That is what I have always hoped," said old Yacob.

"His brain is affected," said the blind doctor.

The elders murmured assent.

"Now, *what* affects it?"

"Ah!" said old Yacob.

"This," said the doctor, answering his own question. "Those queer things that are called the eyes, and which exist to make an agreeable soft depression in the face, are diseased, in the case of Bogota, in such a way as to affect his brain. They are greatly distended, he has eye-lashes, and his eyelids move, and consequently his brain is in a state of constant irritation and distraction."

"Yes?" said old Yacob. "Yes?"

"And I think I may say with reasonable certainty that, in order to cure him completely, all that we need to do is a simple and easy surgical operation—namely, to remove those irritating bodies."

"And then he will be sane?"

"Then he will be perfectly sane, and a quite admirable citizen."

"Thank Heaven for the Wisdom beneath it!" said old Yacob, and went forth at once to tell Nunez of his happy hopes.

But Nunez's manner of receiving the good news struck him as being cold and disappointing.

"One might think," he said, "from the tone you take, that you did not care for my daughter."

It was Medina-saroté who persuaded Nunez to face the blind surgeons.

"*You* do not want me," he said, "to lose my gift of sight?"

She shook her head.

"My world is sight."

Her head dropped lower.

"There are the beautiful things, the beautiful little things—the flowers, the lichens among the rocks, the lightness and visible softness on a piece of fur, the far sky with its drifting down of clouds, the sunsets and the stars. And there is *you*. For you alone it is good to have sight, to see your sweet, serene face, your kindly lips, your dear, dear, beautiful hands folded together . . . It is these eyes of mine you won, these eyes that hold me to you, that these idiots seek. Instead, I must touch you, hear you, and never see you again. I must come under that roof of rock and stone and darkness, that horrible roof under which your imagination stoops . . . No, you would not have me do that?"

She shuddered to hear him speak of the Wisdom Above in such terms. Her hands went to her ears.

A disagreeable doubt had arisen in him. He stopped, and left the thing a question.

"I wish," she said, "sometimes—" She paused.

"Yes?" said he, a little apprehensively.

"I wish sometimes—you would not talk like that."

"Like what?"

"It's your imagination. I love much of it, but not when you speak of the Wisdom Above. When you talked of those flowers and stars it was different. But now—"

He felt cold. *"Now?"* he said faintly.

She sat quite still.

"You mean—you think—I should be better, better perhaps—"

He was realising things very swiftly. He felt anger, indeed, anger at the dull course of fate, but also sympathy for her lack of understanding—a sympathy near akin to pity.

"Dear," he said, and he could see by her whiteness how intensely her spirit pressed against the things she could not say. He put his arms about her, and kissed her ear, and they sat for a time in silence.

"If I were to consent to this?" he whispered at last, in a voice that was very gentle.

She flung her arms about him weeping wildly. "Oh, if you would," she sobbed, "if only you would!"

"And you have no doubt?"

"Dear heart!" she answered, and pressed his hands with all her strength.

"They will hurt you but little," she said; "and you would be going through this pain—you are going through it, dear lover, for *me* ... Dear; if a woman's heart and life can do it, I will repay you. My dearest one, my dearest with that rough, gentle voice, I will repay."

"So be it," he said.

And in silence he turned away from her. For the time he could sit by her no longer.

She could hear his slow retreating footsteps, and something in the rhythm of them threw her into a passion of weeping ...

He meant to go to a lonely place where the meadows were beautiful with white narcissus, but as he went he lifted up his eyes and saw the morning, the morning like an angel in golden armour, marching down the steeps...

It seemed to him that before this splendour he, and this blind world in the valley, and his love, and all, were no better than the darkness of an anthill.

He did not turn aside to the narcissus fields as he had meant to do. Instead he went on, and passed through the wall of the circumference and out upon the rocks, and his eyes were always upon the sunlit ice and snow above.

He saw their infinite beauty, and his imagination soared over them to the things he would see no more.

He thought of that great free visible world he was to renounce for ever; the world that was his own, and beyond these encircling mountains; and he had a vision of those further slopes, distance beyond distance, with Bogota, a place of multitudinous stirring beauty, a glory by day, a luminous mystery by night, a place of palaces and fountains and statues and white houses, lying beautifully in the middle distance. He thought how for a day or so one might come down through passes, drawing ever nearer and nearer to its busy streets and ways. He thought of the river journey to follow, from great Bogota to the still vaster world beyond, through towns and villages, forest and desert places, the rushing river day by day, until its banks receded and the big steamers came splashing by, and one had reached the sea—the limitless sea, with its thousand islands, its thousands of islands, and its ships seen dimly far away in their incessant journeyings round and about the greater world. And there, unpent by mountains, one saw the sky—the sky, not such a disc as one saw it here, but a great arch of immeasurable blue, the blue of deeps in which the circling stars were floating.

———

What follows is the original ending to "The Country of the Blind," published in the April 1904 edition of SM.

———

His eyes scrutinised the great curtain of the mountains with a keener inquiry.

For example, if one went so, up that gulley and to that chimney there, then one might come out high among those stunted pines that ran round in a sort of shelf and rose still higher and higher as it passed above the gorge. And then? That talus might be managed. Thence perhaps a climb might be found to take him up to the precipice that came below the snow; and if that chimney failed, then another farther to the east might serve his purpose better. And then? Then one would be out upon the amber-lit snow there, and half-way up to the crest of those beautiful desolations.

———

He glanced back at the village, then turned right round and regarded it steadfastly.

He thought of Medina-saroté, and she had become small and re-mote.

He turned again towards the mountain wall, down which the day had come to him.

Then very circumspectly he began to climb.

———

When sunset came he was no longer climbing, but he was far and high. He had been higher, but he was still very high. His clothes were torn, his limbs were blood-stained, he was bruised in many places, but he lay as if he were at his ease, and there was a smile on his face.

From where he rested the valley seemed as if it were in a pit and nearly a mile below. Already it was dim with haze and shadow, though the mountain summits around him were things of light and fire. The mountain summits around him were things of light and fire, and the little details of the rocks near at hand were drenched with subtle beauty—a vein of green mineral piercing the grey, the flash of crystal faces here and there, a minute, minutely beautiful orange lichen close beside his face. There were deep mysterious shadows in the gorge, blue deepening into purple, and purple into a luminous darkness, and overhead was the illimitable vastness of the sky. But he heeded these things no longer, but lay quite inactive there, smiling as if he were sat-isfied merely to have escaped from the valley of the Blind in which he had thought to be King.

The glow of the sunset passed, and the night came, and still he lay peacefully contented under the cold stars.

———

The following is Wells's revised ending to the story, rewritten and published in 1939.

His eyes scrutinised the imprisoning mountains with a keener inquiry.

It occurred to him that for many days now he had not looked at the cliffs and snow-slopes and gulleys by which he had slid and fallen and clambered down into the valley. He looked now; he looked but he could not find. Something had happened. Something had occurred to change and obliterate the familiar landmarks of his descent. He could not believe it; he rubbed his eyes and looked again. Perhaps he was forgetting. Some fresh fall of snow might have altered the lines and shapes of the exposed surfaces.

In another place too there had been slopes that he had studied very intently. For at times the thought of escape had been very urgent with him. Had they too changed? Had his memory begun to play tricks with him? In one place high up, five hundred feet or so, he had marked a great vein of green crystal that made a sort of slanting way upward—but alas! died out to nothing. One might clamber to it, but above that there seemed no hope. That was still as it had been. But elsewhere?

Suddenly he stood up with a faint cry of horror in his throat.

"No!" he whispered crouching slightly. "No. It was there before!"

But he knew it had not been there before.

It was a long narrow scar of newly exposed rock running obliquely across the face of the precipice at its vastest. Above it and below it was weathered rock. He still struggled against that conviction. But there it was plain and undeniable and *raw.* There could be little doubt of the significance of that fresh scar. An enormous mass of that stupendous mountain wall had slipped. It had shifted a few feet forward and it was being held up for a time, by some inequality of the sustaining rocks. Maybe that would hold it now, but of the shift there was no doubt whatever. Could it settle down again in its new position? He could not tell. He scanned the distant surfaces. Above he saw little white threads of water from the snow-fields pouring into this new-made crack. Below, water was already spouting freshly at a dozen points from the lower edge of the loosened mass. And then he saw that other, lesser fissures had also appeared in the mountain wall.

The more he studied that vast rock face the more he realised the possible urgency of its menace. If this movement continued the valley was doomed. He forgot his personal distress in a huge solicitude for this little community of which he had become a citizen. What ought these people to do? What could they do? Abandon their threatened houses? Make new ones on the slopes behind him? And how could he induce them to do it?

Suppose that lap of rock upon which the mass now rested *gave*!

The mountain would fall—he traced the possible fall with his extended hands—so and so and so. It would fall into and beyond the lake. It would bury the lower houses. It might bury the whole village. It might spell destruction for every living thing in the valley. Something they ought to do. Prepare refuges? Organise a possible evacuation? Set him to watch the mountains day by day? But how to make them understand?

If he went down now, very simply, very meekly, without excitement, speaking in low tones and abasing himself before them. If he said: "I am a foolish creature. I am a disgusting creature. I am unfit to touch the hem of the garment of the very least of your wise men. But for once, I pray you, believe in my vision! Believe in my vision! Sometimes such an idiot as I can *see*. Let me have some more tests about this seeing. Because indeed, indeed, I know of a great danger and I can help you to sustain it..."

But how could he convince them? What proofs could he give them? After his earlier failures. Suppose he went down now, with his warning fresh in his mind. Suppose he *insisted*.

"Vision. Sight." The mere words would be an outrage to them. They might not let him speak at all. And even then if he was permitted to speak, already it might be too late. At the best it would only set them discussing his case afresh. Almost certainly he would anger them, for how could he tell his tale and not question the Wisdom Above. They might take him and end the recurrent nuisance of him by putting out his eyes forthwith, and the only result of his intervention would be that he would be nursing his bloody eye sockets when the disaster fell. The mountain might hold for weeks and months yet, but again it might not wait at all. Even now it might be creeping. Even now the heat of the day must be expanding those sullen vast masses, thawing the night ice that held them together. Even now the trickling snow-water was lubricating the widening fissures.

Suddenly he saw, he saw plainly, a new crack leap across a shining green mass, and then across the valley came the sound of it like the shot of a gun that starts a race. The mass was moving *now*! There was no more time to waste. No more time for pleas and plans.

"Stop!" he cried. "Stop!" and put out his hands as if to thrust back that slow deliberate catastrophe. It is preposterous but he believes he said, "Wait one minute!"

He ran headlong to the little bridge and the gate and rushed down towards the houses, waving his arms and shouting. "The mountain is falling," he screamed. "The whole mountain is falling upon you all. Medina-saroté! Medina-saroté!"

He clattered to the house of old Yacob and burst in upon the sleepers. He shook them and shouted at them, going from one to the other.

"He's gone mad again," they cried aghast at him and even Medina-saroté cowered away from his excitement.

"Come," he said. "Come. Even now it is falling. The mountain is falling." And he seized her wrist in a grip of steel. "Come!" he cried so masterfully that in terror she obeyed him.

But outside the house there was a crowd that his shouts and noise had awakened, and a score of men had run out already and assembled outside the house and stood in his way.

"Let me pass," he cried. "Let me pass. And come with me—up the further slopes there before it is too late."

"This is too much. This is the last blasphemy," shrieked one of the elders. "Seize him. Hold him!"

"I tell you the mountain is falling. It is coming down upon you even now as you hold me here."

"The Wisdom Above us that loves and protects us *cannot* fall."

"Listen. That rumbling?"

"There has been rumbling like that before. The Wisdom is warning us. It is because of your blasphemies."

"And the ground rocking?"

"Brothers cast him out! Cast him out of the valley. We have been foolish to harbour him so long. His sin is more than our Providence can endure."

"But I tell you the rocks are falling. The whole mountain is coming down. Listen and you can hear the crashing and the rending of them."

He was aware of a loud hoarse voice intoning through the uproar and drowning his own. "The Wisdom Above loves us. It protects us from all harm. No evil can touch us while the Wisdom is over us. Cast him forth! Cast him forth. Let him take our sins upon him and go!"

"Out you go, Bogota," cried a chorus of voices. "Out you go."

"Medina-saroté! Come with me. Come out of this place!"

Pedro threw protective arms about his cousin.

"Medina-saroté!" cried Nunez. "Medina-saroté!"

They pushed him, struggling fiercely, up the path towards the boundaries. They showed all the cruelty now of frightened men. For the gathering noise of the advancing rocks dismayed them all. They wanted to out-do each other in repudiating him. They beat at his face with their fists and kicked his shins and ankles and feet. One or two jabbed at him with knives. He could not see Medina-saroté any longer and he could not see the shifting cliffs because of the blows and because of the blood that poured from a cut in his forehead, but the voices about him seemed to fade as the rumbling clatter of falling fragments wove together and rose into a thunderous roar. He shouted weeping for Medina-saroté to escape as they drove him before them.

They thrust him through a little door and flung him out on to a stony slope with a deliberate violence that sent a flock of llamas helter-skelter. He lay like a cast clout. "And there you stay—and starve," said one. "You and your—*seeing*."

He lifted his head for a last reply.

"I tell you. You will be dead before I am."

"You *fool*!" said the one he had fought, and came back to kick him again and again. "Will you never learn reason?" But he turned hastily to join his fellows when Nunez struggled clumsily to his feet.

He stood swaying like a drunken man.

He had no strength in his limbs. He did his best to wipe the blood from his eyes. He looked at the impending mountain-fall, he looked for the high rocky ledge he had noted that morning and then he turned a despairful face to the encircling doom of the valley. But he did not attempt to climb any further away.

"What's the good of going alone?" he said. "Even if I could, I shall only starve up there."

And then suddenly he saw Medina-saroté seeking him. She emerged from the little door and she was calling his name. In some manner she had contrived to slip away and come to search for him. "Bogota my darling!" she cried. "What have they done to you? Oh *what* have they *done* to you?"

He staggered to meet her, calling her name over and over again.

In another moment her hands were upon his face and she was wiping away the blood and searching softly and skilfully for his cuts and bruises.

"You must stay here now," she panted. "You must stay here for a time. Until you repent. Until you learn to repent. Why did you behave so madly? Why did you say those horrible blasphemies? You don't know you say them, but how are they to tell that? If you come back now they will certainly kill you. I will bring you food. Stay here."

"Neither of us can stay here. *Look*!"

She drew the air in sharply between her teeth at that horrible word "look" which showed that his madness was still upon him.

"There! That thunder!"

"What is it?"

"A stream of rocks are pouring down by the meadows and it is only the beginning of them. *Look* at them. Listen anyhow to the drumming and beating of them! What do you think those sounds mean? *That* and that! Stones! They are bouncing and dancing across the lower meadows by the lake and the waters of the lake are brimming over and rising up to the further houses. Come my darling. Come! Do not question, but come!"

She stood hesitating for a moment. There was a frightful menace now in the storm of sounds that filled the air. Then she crept into his arms. "I am afraid," she said.

He drew her to him and with a renewal of strength began to climb, guiding her feet. His blood smeared her face and there was no time to remedy that. At first she dragged upon him and then, perceiving the strain she caused, she helped and supported him. She was sobbing but also she obeyed.

He concentrated himself now upon reaching that distant shelf, but presently he had to halt for breath, and then only was he free to look back across the valley.

He saw that the foot of the cliff was sliding now down into the lake, scooping its waters before it towards the remoter houses, and that the cascade of rocks was now swifter and greater. They drove over the ground in leaps and bounds with a frightful suggestion in their movements as though they were hunting victims. They were smashing down trees and bushes and demolishing walls and buildings, and still the main bulk of the creeping mountain, deprived now of its supports, had to gather momentum and fall. It was breaking up as it came down. And now little figures appeared from the houses and ran hither and thither...

For the first time Nunez was glad that Medina-saroté was blind.

"Climb! my darling," he said. "Climb!"

"I do not understand."

"Climb!"

A rush of terrified llamas came crowding up past them.

"It is so steep, so steep here. Why are these creatures coming with us?"

"Because they understand. Because they know we are with them. Push through them. Climb."

With an effect of extreme deliberation that mountain-side hung over the doomed valley. For some tense instants Nunez did not hear a sound. His whole being was concentrated in his eyes. Then came the fall and then a stunning concussion that struck his chest a giant's blow. Medina-saroté was flung against the rocks and clung to them with clawing hands. Nunez had an instant's impression of a sea of rocks and earth and fragments of paths and walls and houses, pouring in a swift flood towards him. A spray of wind-driven water bedewed him; they were pelted with mud and broken rock fragments, the wave of debris surged and receded a little and abruptly came still, and then colossal pillars of mist and dust rose up solemnly and deliberately and mounted towering overhead and unfolded and rolled together about them until they were in an impenetrable stinging fog. Silence fell again upon the world and the Valley of the Blind was hidden from him for evermore.

Pallid to the centres of their souls, these two survivors climbed slowly to the crystalline ridge and crouched upon it.

And when some hour or so later that swirling veil of mist and dust had grown thinner and they could venture to move and plan what they would do, Nunez saw through a rent in it far away across a wilderness of tumbled broken rock and in a V-shaped cleft of the broken mountains, the green rolling masses of the foothills, and far beyond them one shining glimpse of the ocean.

Two days later he and Medina-saroté were found by two hunters who had come to explore the scene of this disaster. They were trying to clamber down to the outer world and they were on the verge of exhaustion. They had lived upon water, fern roots and a few berries. They collapsed completely when the hunters hailed them.

They lived to tell their tale, and to settle in Quito among Nunez's people. There he is still living. He is a prosperous tradesman and plainly a very honest man. She is a sweet and gentle lady, her basket-work and her embroidery are marvellous, though of course she makes no use of colour, and she speaks Spanish with an old-fashioned accent very pleasant to the ear.

Greatly daring, I think, they have had four children and they are as stout and sturdy as their father and they can see.

He will talk about his experience when the mood is on him but she says very little. One day however when she was sitting with my wife while Nunez and I were away, she talked a little of her childhood in the valley and of the simple faith and happiness of her upbringing. She spoke of it with manifest regret. It had been a life of gentle routines, free from all complications.

It was plain she loved her children and it was plain she found them and much of the comings and goings about her difficult to understand. She had never been able to love and protect them as she had once loved and protected Nunez.

My wife ventured on a question she had long wanted to ask. "You have never consulted oculists," she began.

"Never," said Medina-saroté. "I have never wanted to *see*."

"But colour—and form and distance!"

"I have no use for your colours and your stars," said Medina-saroté. "I do not want to lose my faith in the Wisdom Above."

"But after all that has happened! Don't you want to see Nunez; see what he is like?"

"But I know what he is like and seeing him might put us apart. He would not be so near to me. The loveliness of *your* world is a compli-cated and fearful loveliness and mine is simple and near. I had rather Nunez saw for me—because he knows nothing of fear."

"But the *beauty*!" cried my wife.

"It may be beautiful," said Medina-saroté, "but it must be very terrible to *see*."

ABOUT THE AUTHOR

HERBERT GEORGE WELLS—novelist, social critic, and visionary futurist who became one of the most prolific and widely read writers of his generation—was born in the London suburb of Bromley, Kent, on September 21, 1866. He came from a lower-middle-class background and grew up in circumstances of genteel poverty that would not have seemed out of place in a novel by Dickens. His father was at various times a gardener, professional cricket player, and shopkeeper; his mother was a housekeeper and former lady's maid. The youngster, nicknamed Bertie, became an avid reader at the age of seven while lying bedridden with a broken leg.

Although he left school to become a draper's apprentice at fourteen, Wells later won a scholarship to the Normal School of Science in South Kensington. There he studied zoology under T. H. Huxley, a noted disciple of Darwin who instilled in Wells a belief in social as well as biological evolution. Wells's first prophetic work, "A Tale of the Twentieth Century," was published in 1887 in the *Science Schools Journal*. Upon graduation from the University of London in 1890 he was a tutor until chronic ill health made him decide to make a serious attempt at being a writer. He brought out *A Text-Book of Biology* (1893) and began contributing articles and fiction to magazines such as the *Pall Mall Gazette*. Impoverished and unhappily married, Wells eloped with Amy Catherine ("Jane") Robbins, a former student of his, whom he later married and by whom he had two sons.

The serialization of *The Time Machine* in 1895 made Wells famous overnight. A string of other scientific romances—including *The Island of Dr. Moreau* (1896), *The Invisible Man* (1897), *The War of the Worlds* (1898), *When the Sleeper Wakes* (1899), and *The First Men in the Moon* (1901)—consolidated his reputation.

A socialist who believed in the perfectibility of mankind, Wells focused on utopian social and political themes in works of nonfiction beginning with *Anticipations* (1901), *The Discovery of the Future* (1902),

Mankind in the Making (1903), *A Modern Utopia* (1905), and *The Future in America* (1906). Wells joined the Fabian Society in 1903 but left after fighting an unsuccessful war of wit and rhetoric over its policies with George Bernard Shaw.

Tired of being labeled "the English Jules Verne," Wells wrote two popular comic novels featuring resilient Cockney heroes who triumph over adversity, *Kipps* (1905) and *The History of Mr. Polly* (1910). The latter underscored one of his most basic themes: "If the world does not please you, *you can change it.*" A liaison with the young Fabian Amber Reeves inspired the novel *Ann Veronica* (1909) and produced a daughter, Anna Jane. Also published in 1909 was *Tono-Bungay*, a panoramic if scathing view of Edwardian England that many regard as his greatest novel.

Wells's later fiction became increasingly autobiographical. *The New Machiavelli* (1911) and the best-selling *Mr. Bristling Sees It Through* (1916) were the most notable. Others, such as *Marriage* (1912), prompted a young journalist named Rebecca West to dismiss him as the "old maid among novelists." Yet the two conducted a ten-year love affair and had a son, Anthony West. Wells continued to produce compelling prognostications. Despite having dubbed World War I "the war that will end war," he wrote *The World Set Free* (1914), a speculative history of the future that predicted the coming age of nuclear warfare.

In 1920 *The Outline of History*, an encyclopedic work written to further the cause of world peace, brought Wells to the height of his fame. An international best-seller, the book included this memorable saying: "Human history becomes more and more a race between education and catastrophe." The same year he traveled to Russia to meet Lenin and reported on the new Communist regime in *Russia in the Shadows* (1920).

In 1923 Wells ended his relationship with Rebecca West and later moved to the south of France with his new mistress, political exile Odette Keun. There he wrote *The World of William Clissold* (1926), his most ambitious novel of the period. Upon returning to London in 1930 Wells brought out *The Science of Life* (1930) and *The Work, Wealth and Happiness of Mankind* (1932), two companion volumes to *The Outline of History*.

With the rise of fascism Wells became less optimistic about the future, and in *The Shape of Things to Come* (1933) he accurately predicted a second world war that would begin in 1939. However, he journeyed to the United States and Russia in 1934, attempting to promote global peace. Back in England he published his memoirs, the masterful two-volume *Experiment in Autobiography* (1934), and worked with Alexander Korda on a film version of *The Shape of Things to Come*. Though happily involved with Moura Budberg, the Russian spy who was his last companion, Wells remained fatalistic about mankind. The advent of World War II only heightened the author's despondency as he lived to see many of his dire predictions come true. "Reality has taken a leaf from my book and set itself to supersede me," he bitterly observed. A final work, *Mind at the End of Its Tether* (1945), bleakly foretold the destruction of civilization.

H. G. Wells died suddenly and peacefully on August 13, 1946, just a few weeks before turning eighty, at his home in Hanover Terrace, London. Three days later his body was cremated and the ashes scattered over the English Channel near the Isle of Wight. A third volume of autobiography, *H. G. Wells in Love*, appeared posthumously in 1984.

A Note on the Type

The principal text of this Modern Library edition
was set in a digitized version of Janson, a typeface that
dates from about 1690 and was cut by Nicholas Kis,
a Hungarian working in Amsterdam. The original matrices have
survived and are held by the Stempel foundry in Germany.
Hermann Zapf redesigned some of the weights and sizes for
Stempel, basing his revisions on the original design.